Blood OF THE Moon

Blood OF THE Moon

S D SIMPER

Blood of the Moon

Copyright © 2019 Endless Night Publications

Cover art by Jade Mere

Cover design and interior by Jerah Moss

Map by Mariah Simper

ISBN (Paperback): 978-1-7324611-6-1

Visit the author at www.sdsimper.com

Facebook: sdsimper
Twitter: @sdsimper
Instagram: sdsimper

For Kristen,

My dearest friend; my beloved wife

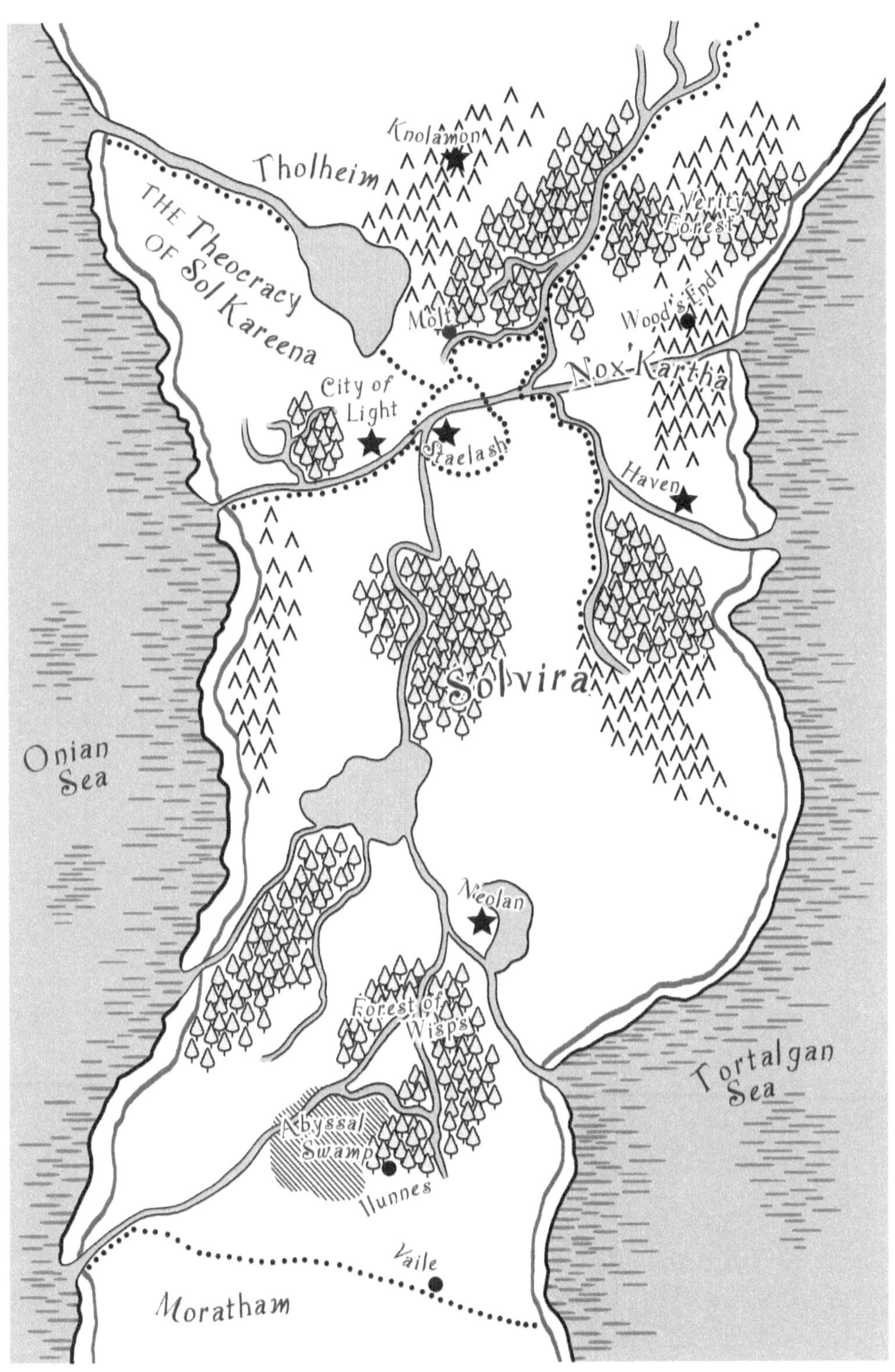

Tholheim
Knolamon
THE Theocracy OF Sol Kareena
Verity Forest
Molt
Wood's End
City of Light
Nox-Kartha
Staelash
Haven
Onian Sea
Solvira
Neolan
Forest of Wisps
Tortalgan Sea
Abyssal Swamp
Ilunnes
Vaile
Moratham

Names

THE ROYAL COUNCIL OF STAELASH

Marielle Vors – Mair-ee-el Vohrs

Etolié – Eh-toh-lee-ey

Thalmus – Thah-muhs

Flowridia – Floh-rid-ee-uh

Sora Fireborn – Sohr-ruh Fire-bohrn

Zorlaeus – Zor-ley-uhs

FOREIGN DIGNITARIES

Alauriel Solviraes – Ah-law-ree-ehl Sohl-veer-es

Casvir – Kas-**veer**

Murishani – Mer-eh-shah-nee

Xoran – Zoh-ran

Lunestra – Loon-es-truh

OTHER PLAYERS

Demitri – Dih-**mee**-tree

Ayla Darkleaf – Ai-luh Dahrk-leef

Khastra – Kas-truh

Odessa – Oh-**des**-uh

Soliel – Suh-**lil**

Mereen – Mer-**een**

Zoldar—**Zohl**-dar

VARIOUS GODS, ANGELIC AND DEMONIC

Sol Kareena – Sohl Kuh-**ree**-nuh

Eionei – **Eye**-uhn-eye

Alystra – Ah-**lees**-truh

Staella – **Stey**-luh

Neoma – Ney-**oh**-muh

Ilune – Eye-**loon**

Izthuni – Iz-**thoo**-nee

Ku'Shya – Koo-**shy**-uh

Onias – Uhn-**eye**-uhs

Kingdoms did not fall in flame or to the sword. They fell to pestilence, to disease, to corruption from within, the usurping of power. Ravage the body, and the body would heal. But cut off the head, and all would fall.

Khastra had seen it hundreds of times, the rise and fall of empires. She knew the intricacies of warfare like the flow of her weapon, felt it in her blood. Thus, she saw the writing on the walls, the unspoken reality of her kingdom's plots.

Kingdoms fell, and Khastra accepted that like she had learned to accept all things. Change was a cycle, and Nox'Kartha's rise to supremacy was inevitable, just as it was inevitable that it would someday fall. Truthfully, excitement welled in her gut at the oncoming conflict, the opportunity to embrace her birthright, to once again live up to her name as *Bringer of War*.

People would die. She would bathe in their blood. Within her, the monster laughed with glee.

Yet, an unspoken truth plaguing her heart drove her to step into Casvir's office, a map in her hands. She knocked, as was polite, and waited for the curt reply of, "Enter."

Imperator Casvir sat hunched over his desk, quill in hand, and spared Khastra a glance before returning his attention to the documents before him. Khastra would never admit aloud that his straightforward approach to life was refreshing. "Imperator, we need to speak."

Casvir set his quill aside and turned to her, saying nothing but that was true to form. He gave her the respect of his time; Khastra accepted nothing less.

"At our last meeting, you presented the outline of your plans and asked me to work on details." She unraveled the map in her hand and spread it out on Casvir's desk. "The

Theocracy falls first, for they would join in any conflict," she said, her finger tracing the lengthy borders, "but no one will join them for fear of unbalancing the delicate peace we hold. Shock and awe—scare the rest into submission."

Casvir glanced between she and the paper, waiting to hear something new. Khastra, unfortunately, had little to add . . . only a concern to voice.

"From there, the conflict goes north to Tholheim. They are stubborn, but their military is primitive. I hold to my opinion that Solvira should be usurped by insidious means—war would be suicide, but their leadership is fallible. The empress is wise, but she is young and capable of being manipulated. However, in all of this, there is no mention of Staelash." Khastra looked up to Casvir, scrutinizing his stoic countenance. "What of Staelash, Imperator?"

"Are you sentimental?"

"No," Khastra replied, and it was no lie. "Their goals are admirable but short-sighted. They were doomed the moment they faced a new generation of leadership. I saw this from the start. But I cannot help but notice a pattern in the treatment of their founders—the truth of Clarence's assassination is suspected among the council, and my own convenient demise, while not your doing, did work well to your cause. What of Etolié?"

Casvir replied, "Whatever must be done."

Khastra shook her head. "She is brash at times, but she will not fall to manipulation. Marielle is weak and corruptible, and while Sora is loyal, it is to Sol Kareena—not to Staelash. They will be yours with no bloodshed, but what of Etolié?"

"As I said–"

"*Imperator—!*" Khastra shut her mouth, seizing control of her tongue. Her blood pulsed; the Bringer of War so often fought to escape. But weakness would not be tolerated, not by herself or by Casvir. "Forgive me. I forget my place."

Wordlessly, lest she reveal her hand, Khastra rolled up the map, and when she gripped the doorknob to leave, Casvir said, "General Khastra, should you do it yourself, it would guarantee it be painless."

The doorknob crumpled like paper in her grasp. "I respectfully decline," she muttered, and saw herself out.

The worth of her presence far outweighed a gilded doorknob—Khastra knew this to a numerical value. She would be left alone for her slight.

"General Khastra? A moment, if you would."

Khastra saw Murishani draped casually against the wall, grinning like a viper. She crossed her arms, purposefully flexing, knowing full well the threat of her form. "Viceroy?"

Never come to them, she knew. Let them grovel. Murishani approached, hands outstretched in a false show of comradery. He smelled of pretentious perfumes and the barest traces of magic, but not of fear. "Casvir is boorish in his methods, I know, and stubborn to a fault. His plan is decided, infallible in his own mind, and this . . . irks you."

Khastra had built decades-old walls around her core of self-control, and though Casvir's words had stripped them of layers, they held. Murishani's gentle jab cracked the very foundation.

"If I thought I held a hope to sway him, I would try, but you and I both have our hands tied. He will not be convinced, but . . ." The benevolence of his mask faded, revealing a smile as wicked as his soul. "You and I both know you have cards you've yet to play. One in particular, and you keep her very close to your heart."

Again, with his placid words, poisoning her resolve by degrees. She knew his kind. Her grip on her arms tightened, for he had revealed a card in his own metaphorical hand, a weakness she could not purge.

A weakness her mechanical heart ached to contemplate. "Cease your rambling. Tell me what you want."

"I have a proposal, one to work in everyone's favor—yours and mine *and* Casvir's. Will you listen?"

She hated him down to his slimy core. But cracks spread across the walls of her control, revealing soft light reminiscent of ethereal wings.

"Tell me."

Murishani beckoned her to follow.

Chapter 1

Faced with the sea, Flowridia was nearly blinded by the sun's reflection off the waves. Salty air whipped at her face, her auburn hair sticky from the elements as she gazed out over the ocean. All of it lay secure in a single, impossibly thick braid, lest it irrevocably tangle. Trousers felt strange, the rough cloth confining around her thighs, but Casvir had insisted on them for this particular adventure.

For days, she had spent most of her time standing upon the deck of the ship, enthralled by the sight of the sun on the sparkling waves. The warm, ochre tones of her skin had darkened beneath its light, bringing with it a faint splatter of freckles. Sailors moved about, largely ignoring her as they maintained the ship.

There, at the helm, Imperator Casvir shone as a beacon of menace in his black armor. In his hands, he held an artifact of depthless power—a black, crackling orb. But though he cast a daunting aura, his frightening, demonic physique no longer filled her with fear. Behind his horns and claws was civility, and though he held the strength to smash through the mast of the ship, she loved him as a mentor. Perhaps even a friend.

The expansive sea spread in all directions, and Flowridia found the sun upon the sparkling waves as magical a sight as she'd ever seen.

Retching from beside her interrupted the serenity. Demitri's head leaned over the ship as he vomited the contents of his stomach—it had become a daily thing. *Wolves weren't meant for this.*

She soothed his fur as he continued vomiting. "It won't be forever."

As distracted as she was, she didn't notice Casvir's approach—not until his shadow loomed above her. "We have arrived."

Demitri snorted beside her. *I don't like this. Not one bit.*

"I'll be fine, my dearest Demitri," Flowridia said. She wrapped her arms around his neck and kissed his cheek. "But you'll be much safer up here than down there."

A De'Sindai woman had accompanied him, a witch perhaps twice Flowridia's age. She glanced nervously between Flowridia and Casvir. "The spell is ready," she said stiffly. Like Zorlaeus, she flinched at Casvir's every movement, ready to spring into a bow at any moment.

Casvir looked to Flowridia. "Are you prepared?"

Flowridia nodded and kissed Demitri one last time. "Stay dry. I'll return with an orb."

His tongue lashed gently across her cheek. She cringed at the scent of vomit but suspected he hadn't meant to be rude. *I won't sleep until you're back. That's a threat.*

"I believe you." She turned to Casvir. "Let's go." From her bag, she pulled out a pair of goggles, designed specifically to protect her eyes from the salt and the murky ocean environment. She secured them on her face.

When offered a pair of boots by Casvir, she looked at them oddly, noting the metal at the bottom, almost like a horseshoe. "You will only sink so far on your own," Casvir said as she thrust her feet inside, and when she tried to walk, it felt like trekking through a bog.

The witch pulled a small stick out of her satchel and crushed it between her hands. Blue mist swirled around her fingers. She blew with the gentleness one might blow a kiss, and the mist settled around Flowridia. "Breathe deeply," the witch said, "then jump into the ocean."

Flowridia obeyed, a sharp sting lacerating her throat as she did. She coughed, gripping at her neck, but when she tried to breathe again, she felt nothing but a burning sensation. Casvir's clawed hand pushed her towards the waves. "The price for breathing water is that you cannot breathe air. Go."

When she panicked, he shoved her; she toppled overboard.

The icy waves shocked her body. She sank deep, weighted down by her clothing and hair and metal boots, but when she might've panicked, she stole a breath.

All was well.

Bubbles blocked her vision. Something sharp grabbed her waist. Casvir's entire hand clutched at her core, dragging her down as he, weighed down by his armor, sank to the bottom of the sea.

"You can speak freely," she heard him say, and when she looked over, she saw he had no difficulty breathing.

It had never occurred to her that Casvir didn't need to breathe.

She reached up to touch her neck and felt deep cuts along the tender skin. "This isn't permanent, right?" Deeper and deeper they sank; the ocean darkened.

"No," Casvir said, his voice clear despite the ocean depths. "You should have nearly a day's worth of transformation. Plenty of time to reach our destination."

Tiny silver fish darted past them, and Flowridia moved to cover her long braid for fear of them getting caught. Their feet touched solid ground—sand and rock and unstable terrain. She took tentative steps around the treacherous seafloor, the metal-plated boots doing well to keep her from floating away.

"Research has told me," Casvir continued, "that there was once a great underwater city called Stelune. The merfolk who lived there were a rich and prosperous people, protected by a great dragon."

A shark swam past, not twenty feet away, but Flowridia realized undersea creatures held the same fear of Casvir as those on land. Plants appeared as they walked, vibrant and colorful, the coral blossoming in various shades of pink and orange.

"But the dragon was defeated," Casvir continued, "by a great monster. The creature that slew the dragon slaughtered the people in its charge."

"That's awful." Flowridia's small hands gripped at Casvir's forearm, perfectly happy to let him drag her forward. "So, we'll be fighting whatever slew the dragon and stole the orb," Flowridia speculated, her heart beating fast at even the thought.

"It would seem so."

The ground ceased to be at a decline, and Casvir continued trudging forward. Ruins, massive and made of stone, appeared. Enormous structures, cracked and covered in aquatic plants, dotted the scenery, rich in detail and form. Remains of an entire civilization did not disappear easily, and Flowridia saw unnatural pockets of light—perhaps some sort of residual magic.

Unnerved at the scenery, she noticed something odd. Though she was long used to creatures fleeing at Casvir's approach, this was something else entirely. There simply was nothing—no fish, crabs, nothing. Colorful plants dared to live on, but no animals met her view. "And you know we're close?"

"The black orb resonates," he said simply. "It hums. We are very close."

A cloud of black suddenly billowed toward them. Casvir pulled Flowridia into his armored chest. "Do not breathe," he said, and then they were consumed.

Never in her life had such crippling darkness blinded her. She hid her face in his side, feet weighted against the ocean floor. A voice, a deep, earth-shaking rumble, met her ears and vibrated through her bones. "Little mortals. I have no time for little mortals."

Flowridia kept her breath in her chest but dared to look out. Consuming black still covered the area.

"I sense power. What have you brought with you?"

Finally, the cloud dissipated. Casvir's calm whisper met her ears. "You can breathe now," he said calmly. Flowridia looked out again and gasped when she saw what looming monstrosity stood before them. Tentacles, hundreds of feet long each, floated leisurely against the undersea current. Round pustules lined their undersides, enormous suckers larger than Casvir. But the shadowed, deep green creature those tentacles were attached to stared from a distance with a single, illuminate yellow eye. "This noble leviathan has asked you a question, Lady Flowridia," Casvir continued, loud enough so the monster could hear them.

Flowridia had been sung to sleep with songs of leviathans, the monstrous spawn of a mortals and the demon god, Onias. They appeared as gargantuan squids capable of crushing and devouring ships. But they were residents of Sha'Demoni, or so she'd heard.

A faint light—an unmistakable blue—caught her attention. But she maintained eye contact and smiled politely. "I am Lady Flowridia–" She hesitated but managed to cover it with a bow. Would titles impress an undersea behemoth? It couldn't hurt to try. "I am Lady Flowridia, Grand Diplomat of Staelash. With me is Imperator Casvir,

First and Last of his Name, Tyrant of Nox'Kartha and Marshall of the Deathless Army."

"What use have I for mortal titles?" the leviathan replied. "You did not answer my question."

Flowridia took a stabilizing breath, masking it under what she prayed was boundless civility. "What you sense, perhaps, is a companion to your blue orb. I seek these orbs and use them to find others."

"So you would steal from me?"

"Certainly not," Flowridia, knowing it was a blatant lie. "But I would strike an agreement with you."

A single black tentacle slowly snaked towards them. "But you have no intention of leaving without it."

From her peripheral vision, Flowridia saw it slowly twist around the back of them. She kept her gaze forward. "Consider what Nox'Kartha can do for you–"

The tentacle shot back in, Casvir in its grasp. A purple glow appeared from his hands, but before he could swing his summoned weapon, he disappeared behind the leviathan's enormous, beak-like mouth.

"No!" she cried, but she bit back the rest, her hands covering her mouth lest she sob. She could not have grabbed him—no chance to have saved him.

Casvir had simply gone.

"You're a pretty picture," the leviathan bellowed. She suddenly felt another tentacle wrap itself around her waist, nearly engulfing her entire being in its bulk. "Let me look at you more closely."

Her breath failed her as the tentacle reeled her in toward the monster, bubbles trailing behind. Close now, Flowridia could see the sleek scales protecting the beast, the ferocious beak capable of consuming her whole. It held her up to its eye, an eye that easily could have ensnared three or more of her in its diameter.

She shoved aside all thoughts of Casvir and simply kept her gaze at the black center of the eye. Shock stilled her sorrow, though her eyes threatened to seep tears—instead, she knew only survival. "What is your name?" she asked, hoping her voice did not shake.

Beside her, another tentacle stopped within a foot of her, flaunting a small blue orb stuck in its sucker. "I am Yu'Khrall. Why do you seek my orb?"

One last effort to secure her release, she decided, and then she'd return with all the terror an army of the dead could bring. Nox'Kartha would wish to avenge their imperator. "Do you know the stories of the Old Gods, Yu'Khrall? The God of Order has returned and is set on restoring the world to what it used to be. He will separate the planes, destroying Celestière and Sha'Demoni and causing irreparable damage to this one. He seeks the orbs. Give it to us, and we will protect it."

Deciphering emotions from a leviathan proved an impossible task. All she could see was that enormous, unblinking eye.

She waited, tense as the leviathan seemed to consider her words. "I have no interest in the affairs of mortals and forgotten Gods," Yu'Khrall said, each word near deafening. "If he comes, I will slay him as I slew your imperator."

Flowridia didn't doubt this beast would make a formidable foe for Soliel, but he had slain a dragon more ancient than Yu'Khrall—and with three orbs, Flowridia wondered if any force on earth could stop him.

Now was not the time to consider defeat. Casvir had led her this far, and she would complete it on her own.

Flowridia let her thoughts mellow, even as she felt the pressure on her body increase from the leviathan's grasp. Months of practice slowed her heartbeat, for necromancy rose from pain—rather, to set aside that pain and grasp onto the void of nothing within.

A crackling, purple aura seeped from her pores. Strength surged into her being, quickly overwhelming her. Yu'Khrall's life force proved to be too much, threatening to split her in two.

Yu'Khrall released her. Sinking now, Flowridia saw the purple mist swirling from burns in the leviathan's tentacle. Thick green liquid seeped from the maimed flesh. The tentacle shot back toward its master, the force sending Flowridia tumbling farther away.

Though her stomach churned, she finally touched the ground. As the leviathan cried out in agony, Flowridia's gaze landed on the orb. With all her strength, she lifted her weighted feet, finding the boots cumbersome. Biting back panicked curses, she forced them off her feet, swearing she tore her skin with it, and flailed her arms about, slowly propelling toward the ensnared artifact. Flowridia had never learned to swim. Every awkward motion rose from both pure instinct and the realization that grabbing the orb might be her only hope for survival.

When the leviathan's tentacle darted away, with it dashed her hopes.

Another painful cry suddenly ripped from Yu'Khrall's being. He began contorting, then violently flailing, and Flowridia swam away for fear of being crushed. His tentacles beat upon his own body as he released a deafening screech.

His eye split down the middle, a distinct purple glow cutting straight down. Casvir burst through the center of the eye in a grotesque fog of sticky, green ichor and dropped straight down from the weight of his armor. Upon hitting the ground, he slashed his summoned sword at the leviathan's body, dismembering tentacles that wriggled even after being severed.

One of those tentacles held the orb. The awkward waving of her arms slowly moved her forward. With as much speed as she could muster—it wasn't much—Flowridia floundered toward the gently falling limb, ignoring the agonized roar of the beast and shoving away the relief she felt at Casvir's return. Closer, closer, the orb glowed bright as she approached, still suctioned to the brutalized tentacle.

She touched the orb.

At the moment of contact, Flowridia felt her senses expand. The water did nothing to obscure her sight; she saw, with absolute clarity, the scene before her—Casvir's fury as he swung his mystical, summoned sword, the individual scales lining the leviathan's body, each seeping wound lacerating the beast's flesh. With effort, she managed to peel the suctioned tentacle from the orb as she sank to the floor. Her feet touched the ground, and she ran towards the scene with the same speed and control she would on land.

Fascinating.

Black and purple lightning suddenly danced across Casvir's skin. Flowridia saw him pluck his own orb from his armor as he surged up to touch the maimed beast. The leviathan flailed, shriveling at the contact, horrible pustules bursting beneath its skin as it withered under Casvir's touch.

Flowridia focused on her new power and felt an unbearable chill surge from within her. An icy sheen appeared on the creature's flailing body—which quickly stilled.

A blackened, emaciated, frozen corpse settled upon the ocean floor.

The purple aura around Casvir faded. He looked to Flowridia with interest, a grin pulling at his lips when he saw the orb in her hand. "It seems your gills no longer suit you."

"Casvir, I–" Ignoring his words, Flowridia studied him with concern. "You're alive. You're all right?"

"I might have emerged sooner, but listening to you attempt to subdue the creature was intriguing. I wished to see if you would succeed." He raised an eyebrow, glancing between the orb and her face. "An interesting tactic, to reason with an ancient monster."

Flowridia frowned. "What choice did I have?"

"I did not say it was wrong. With the dragon, you succeeded. You did what you deemed best, and it failed. But you showed no weakness. In diplomatic situations, whatever else you do, to appear weak is to appear a fool."

"Casvir, I appreciate your advice," Flowridia said, but exhaustion, both physical and emotional, weighed her down, even with the surge of power from the orb. Tears threatened to overtake her, and she set her sights to the floor. "But I thought you were dead."

"And you did not let that stop you. Excellent work."

Flowridia stepped forward, eyes squeezing shut to fight tears. What impulse drove her actions, she could not quite say—love? Concern? Fear? But she set her head against his black, weighted armor, as affectionate a gesture as she dared.

She could feel Casvir's eyes on her. "You are victorious. Crying is foolish–"

"Oh, shut up!" Emboldened by her rage, she wrapped her arms around his armored form—as far as she could reach—and held him as she fought the urge to sob. The orb still rested in her hand, but she barely felt it. She found she didn't care much for it, not when Casvir might have died.

But Casvir was here. The clawed hand settling against her back confirmed that.

Down in the recesses of her library, Etolié drank to drown the fire of her rage.

Which was a really fucking stupid plan, given that alcohol was hardly flame resistant.

"Zoldar, you're a damned coward!" she cried out into what she knew wasn't a void, because that cursed bug was hiding somewhere. She saw a flash of emerald green up in the rafters, but Etolié was too tired to fly after him. "I swear if you don't get your skittering ass down here this *instant*, I'll–"

Scuffling from the door stole her words. Etolié took a drink from her flask before barreling forward. "Zoldar–"

Empress Alauriel Solviraes rounded the corner, and Etolié stopped dead in her tracks. "Oh. Well, fuck me, I guess."

"It's nice to see you too, Etolié," Lara said, and when she smiled, Etolié didn't see a grown woman with a crown and an empire. She saw a little toddler gleefully embracing her any time she visited. "Not meshing well with your bookkeeper?"

"I love Zoldar, and I would die for him." Etolié took another sip and offered the flask forward—Lara, of course, accepted. "Unless he dies by my hands first."

Lara, Empress of Solvira and likely an alcoholic, took several gulps from the bottomless flask before responding. "And what did our Skalmite friend do this time?"

"He's a passive aggressive little shit, is what he is. Dropped bacon at my feet and said he wouldn't work until I ate it."

"I'd say he's doing his job perfectly well, then."

Etolié frowned and plucked her flask back from Lara out of spite. "I thought you were busy investigating our orb-stealing friend."

"I came because I became privy to the guest list for Marielle's wedding," Lara continued, clutching her hands behind her back—her default pose when stressed. "Nox'Kartha has invited the Theocracy of Sol Kareena, and I cannot say I approve."

"Take it up with the viceroy. I haven't lifted a finger for this endeavor and thank Alystra's Fine Ass for that."

Lara shook her head. "No, the deed is done, and we cannot uninvite them. But I wanted to know what measures have been taken to prevent any friction."

"Lara, when I say Viceroy Murishani said he would take care of everything, according to the inspirationally long list of things to not worry about he sent, he meant it. I need only provide space."

Lara nodded, lips pursed and quickly losing color. They'd match her eyes in general pale-ness at this rate, though that was hardly a failing. Quite the opposite—Lara's silver eyes were both reminiscent of her heritage and a token of unparalleled beauty. "Etolié, to be perfectly honest, this entire event has my stomach in knots, and I am sorely tempted to put a stop to it, diplomacy be damned. The costs threaten to outweigh what we would gain, if insults are passed between the Theocracy and Nox'Kartha."

"You'd be facing Marielle's wrath, but I'd be relieved."

"Etolié, I need your promise of support, to take watch with me and stand as a barrier between the two countries if needs be. I won't stop the wedding, but I will need help in navigating these waters."

Etolié took a sip, then tossed the flask aside, letting it fall back into the pocket dimension from which it came. "Of course I'll help."

"Can you, though?"

Etolié frowned, debating whether or not to be offended. "You know that I-"

"Have been absolutely falling apart."

The statement lingered. Etolié felt a rise of some uncomfortable thing in her throat, the thing she couldn't name, but whatever it was it made her blood boil and her stomach want to vomit. "I'm fine," she said curtly, but Lara, damn her, knew better. She looked away, uncomfortable beneath the empress' scrutinizing gaze.

"I had hoped with Khastra's apparent return that you would be able to pick yourself back up, but it's been months since your visit to Nox'Kartha, and you're still in shambles."

Etolié smacked her lips, the popping sound not serving its purpose of distracting from the point. "Rude."

"I need you to be at your best, but to be perfectly honest, you look three degrees away from death and it worries me more than even this political cesspool we'll be dipping into."

Etolié wrapped her arms around her body, as though it would hide her bony frame. Whatever illusions she cast to hide her frailty, it seemed Lara knew her better. "I think you're conveniently overlooking all the work I've accomplished in my apparent depression—like my research into the Old Gods, or my seventeen dissertations to the Theocracy on why the orb is safer with Solvira, or the restructuring of taxes that even Thalmus had to begrudgingly agree was brilliant, and–"

"Etolié . . ." Lara smiled, but it held no joy. "Perhaps you should take a few days for yourself," she continued, gentler than before. "The guests will be here in a week. Take some time away. When's the last time you visited home? Celestière would do you well."

Etolié shook her head, the notion making her head swim.

"Then at least talk to someone. Eionei, perhaps?"

"Grandpa would only worry."

"I'm worried, Etolié."

"Then let's reduce the collateral damage, eh?"

Lara stepped forward; Etolié stared at the ground. "I don't ask this as your empress, but as the girl you helped to raise—Etolié, what's going on?"

"I don't know."

There was no lie in the words. Etolié hurt like a held breath, one she couldn't release no matter how hard she tried.

Lara approached, shorter than Etolié by far though she held herself like the monarch she was. In an unregal gesture, she pulled Etolié into a hug, no doubt feeling her ribs. Etolié resisted the urge to cringe, because touch itched like a gods-damned mosquito, but she loved Lara enough to swallow it.

"You can always talk to me." Lara released her, but her touch lingered, prickling at Etolié's sensitive skin.

"Can we talk about literally anything else but this, please?"

Lara nodded. "Perhaps we can coax Zoldar down from the rafters." She looked up, and when Etolié followed her gaze, she saw the barest hints of movement. A flash of emerald, but nothing more.

Between herself and Zoldar, Etolié couldn't say who the bigger drama queen was.

Flowridia's talents lay in coaxing plants to grow and occasionally controlling dead things—water was something very different.

How strange it was, to sit beneath the pond's surface in absolute serenity, feeling the gentle pull and tug of the water at her beckoning. So different than the divinity she wielded at her fingertips, and nothing like the void it took to summon death. The orb glowed in her hands, casting her face and the earthen slopes in vibrant hues of blue and white. How beautiful it was, and as Flowridia cupped it in her hands, she felt the depthless well of power.

With more study, it might be a formidable weapon. For now, it was the most practical orb she had discovered, by far. In peaceful motions, as simple as walking, Flowridia floated to the surface of the pond, letting the water cushion her back. Her hair billowed around her, a pillow upon her watery bed. Listening to the whistling birds, the rustling trees, she forgot the whole world.

Demitri's voice whispered in her head. *Someone's coming. Smells dead.*

That description hardly narrowed it down in the city of the dead, but Flowridia looked up and saw a familiar face stepping down the garden path. Surprised, she floated to the water's edge, and as she left the pond's embrace, the water fell from her clothing and body in a large puddle.

If anything, the orb's capacity to dry her hair made it her favorite. "Khastra!"

The dead half-demon never moved idly, instead surveying every path like a battlefield—the peaceful Nox'Karthan garden included. As she approached, their size difference became starkly apparent, given that Flowridia's head reached her diaphragm if she stood straight. With sweeping, elegant horns and hooves, Khastra was in no way human, though her half-elven features showed in her delicate cheekbones and pointed ears. But the silver tattoos etched into her blue, muscled skin were likely an anomaly no matter where she went. Khastra was the most unique person Flowridia had ever met.

The undead general looked at the orb in Flowridia's hands as she stopped. "It is true, then. You and Imperator Casvir were successful."

Flowridia offered the orb up, unsurprised when Khastra merely stared. "I don't know that anyone could have gotten it without his help."

"Staelash will be pleased."

The reminder of home brought an unpleasant sinking in her stomach. "Only a day more, and we'll know for certain."

Tomorrow, the Nox'Karthan caravan would arrive in Staelash for Queen Marielle's wedding. Tomorrow, Flowridia and Casvir would join them at the gates. She would return to her chosen family with honor, successful in her quest. With the orb, Etolié and Empress Alauriel would have a chance to find the rest—before the God of Order could claim them for himself.

Empress Alauriel... the mere name caused Flowridia's blood to run cold.

"I must admit, I am not yet sure if I will go."

Flowridia frowned. "Why?"

"I never cared much for Marielle," Khastra replied, and her sharp, glowing eyes gazed upon the garden landscape, studying the beloved plot of land Flowridia had been all but gifted. "She was charming as a child, but she returned from finishing school as a woman I found annoying. I have no purpose being at her wedding."

"It's not about her—it's about visiting... everyone else." Flowridia had very nearly said a rather damning name and hoped Khastra thought nothing of it. "All of Staelash loved you."

"All the more reason to let my memory there rest in peace."

Khastra's new position had been publically announced some two months ago, once the mechanical heart in her chest had proven its worth. Beneath the woven shirt she wore, Flowridia could just see the unnatural protrusion of metal.

"I won't tell you what to do," Flowridia said softly, her friendship with the half-demon still tentative at best, "but I know Etolié would miss you."

The reveal of Khastra's amorous affection toward her Celestial friend to Flowridia had been accidental, but not surprising. The half-demon's countenance revealed nothing of her feelings, aside from the faint and broken smile tugging at her lip. "I have heard nothing from her in months. Not since her visit. Etolié has to move forward with her life, as do I."

Their reunion had been touching, but still stained with the pain of their inevitable parting. Etolié's affection for

Khastra was merely friendly, but Flowridia recalled her final words.

Etolié had been remiss to leave, not-so-subtly coaxing Flowridia to convince her to set up at a tavern in the city. *"Etolié, your home needs you much more than I do."*

She wasn't subtle at all, that eccentric Celestial. She had glanced behind Flowridia's head, hesitation in her eyes. *"It doesn't feel much like home anymore."*

"Tiny one," Khastra continued, interrupting Flowridia's thoughts, "I believe I told you once that there is no greater burden than a secret. My feelings for Etolié are heavy as of late. It is best I stay away. Allow me to be selfish." Her smile held all the weight of the years she carried. "But I did not come here to burden you with my troubles. I wished to congratulate you. You shall be returning home in victory."

Flowridia wished it were so, but a damning truth perpetually whispered in her ear—that her quest would only just begin.

Absently, she touched her sternum, where a secret lay secure and safe. "Thank you," she said softly, wishing she could feel joy in her triumph.

With nothing else to say, they bid each other farewell. Alone again, Flowridia reached into her bodice and withdrew Ayla's ear. Water did not harm it, she had learned. It remained a shriveled, hardened shell, containing the very essence of the woman she loved.

Flowridia slipped the orb into her pocket, wondering if Soliel would dare to stalk her here. Doubtful—even with his victory over the imperator, to attack him in his own home was another matter entirely.

Though, with three orbs . . .

Flowridia stepped deeper into the garden proper, Demitri at her side. "The sooner we get this orb to Staelash, the better."

Won't you need it?

She looked at him oddly. "For what?"

To bring back Lady Ayla? You'll need all the help you can get.

"I don't know that a single orb would do any good against . . ." She trailed off, for she dared not say the name. Everything had ears here.

Fire and water. Water beats fire. Lara has the Silver Fire. You have the orb.

"I don't think that's how the Silver Fire works, Demitri."

She'd done little study in her final few months here, frightened beyond measure of her task. The Silver Fire was a magic she did not understand, though she knew a few things—that it was the capacity to absorb pure magical energy; that it cut through the planes with the ease of a knife. She'd experienced that once, when Empress Alauriel had plucked Flowridia and her party from afar and saved their lives from Soliel.

That same empress was the last heir of the bloodline, her father having been murdered by the God of Order. That same empress, the one who ruled her country with benevolence and wisdom, who had shown Flowridia nothing but kindness, and who held all the power in the world in the veins beneath her skin, was the one she must kill.

The Shadow God had spoken, and Flowridia knew her quest—that to bring back Ayla Darkleaf would require the blood of the moon.

In the dark recesses of her mind, she still heard the vampire's screams as she'd burned from within. Flowridia touched upon a floral bush, letting a healing spell filter through her fingers, watching as it grew vibrant before her very eyes.

By every god—she'd rather face Soliel than the silver-eyed empress.

Discomfort welled in her gut, but she willed it away, replaced it with nothing, with a familiar void she'd come to crave. When purple smoke swirled from her fingers, she touched that same flower, the one she had healed, watched it desiccate and die in her hand. Its energy filled Flowridia, slight as it was, and when she breathed out again, counterfeit life filled the withered plant.

It bloomed once more, vibrant and bright, more perfect than before. In death, it would remain so forever.

Without the dark orb, fueling undeath into plants required a focus that strained even she, though with months of practice it had become simple enough, at least in small amounts. To recreate her attack on the God of Order might be years off.

And she wondered, in her bitter heart, what Staelash would think of her new talent.

Whenever Etolié entered the Temple of Eionei, the room always respectfully cleared.

It was little more than an upscale tavern, really, but that was Eionei's way, his rejection of finery for the sake of inclusion and partying something she could respect. All taverns were considered temples to the Drinking God, but this one held an actual altar to his glory. A statue of the deity, bearing a perfect likeness—Etolié had made certain of that—stood before a dish wherein supplicants could spill a drop or a full drink as an offering. By late into the night, it always bore an abominable amalgamation of different drinks which mysteriously disappeared by morning. Some called it a miracle—Etolié called it a bribed employee paid for both secrecy and the duty of emptying it every night into the garden out back.

The garden inexplicably flourished—that was the real miracle.

Etolié spilled a portion of her flask into the chest-height dish and awaited real magic.

The liquid in the dish sparkled and churned, frothing in ways an offering of wine simply didn't, then began spewing like a fountain, though no mess was made. Instead, the flowing liquid formed the likeness of a man bearing the visage of the statue behind him.

Eionei stood taller than Etolié, and his wings bore a fractal quality, shifting in and out of view as they moved, reforming translucent and wine-stained. Though he bore the texture of maroon liquid—not *unlike* blood, but Etolié refused to barrel down that path of thought—every feature was sharp and distinct, from his chiseled cheeks to his lithe physique and his intelligent, witty eyes.

Grandpa smiled. "What's the latest, Starshine?"

This had been one of the only ways she'd communicated with Eionei in over thirty years, his true coloring slowly becoming a distant memory. "I need your help. The wedding party arrives tomorrow, and I need your promise of endless booze."

"Endless booze?"

"To keep the peace. Extra strong; help them pass out sooner than later. They'll be sleepy before any of the parties can turn into dick-waving contests."

Eionei's laughter brought fond memories of childhood—some of the only ones she had. "I like your style. But will it really make a difference when half your guest list will be demons and undead? Sometimes both at once?"

"I figure Murishani will provide the unholy shit." One did not simply forget the poison a certain vampire bitch had offered. "De'Sindai can get wasted like any of the rest of us. So let's keep them and the Theocracy from fighting. I figure Sol Kareena would approve."

"She would, so I'll do it."

"Didn't know you were her bitch."

Eionei laughed, and Etolié joined him, loving the grounding sound. "I've been her bitch for ten thousand years, Starshine."

"I thought that was Alystra."

"Half that time, and she's *my* bitch."

Good ol' grandpa. "You're a dick, you know that, right?"

Eionei nodded solemnly. "It's served me well so far." Etolié had a retort on her tongue, something about whether or not he had the balls to say that to the bitch's face or if she'd tear them off, but Eionei kept talking. "Will Nox'Kartha's Imperator be there?"

"The fuck if I know. Likely, but he wasn't at the coronation—the asshole knows how to deliver an insult." Not that she blamed him, given the absolute uselessness of the event. "The viceroy will be, though. He's heading the affair."

"What about their general?"

Hm. Subtle, that one. "I don't know. We haven't spoken since I visited." Because, you know, Khastra hadn't contacted her at all. It's not like she didn't have access to the literal other half of Etolié's mirror or anything.

"Oh. Sorry to hear that."

He said it with a pleasant, otherwise innocuous grin, and Etolié felt her own twitch. "No. You're not."

They just sort of smiled at the other for a moment, both of their mouths spread a little bit too wide, but Etolié wasn't gonna start this fight again.

Eionei was kind enough to end the stand-off. "Booze for the wedding. Got it."

"You're a hero."

"Best of luck."

Eionei's form bubbled as it collapsed back into the dish, sloshing about the edges but never spilling out. Etolié saw herself out.

Winter had come, the chill pleasant against her skin as she made her way through town. The tavern wasn't far from the manor, so she didn't bother to mask her appearance; she was Magister Etolié for all the populace to see. She waved at a gaggle of half-giant children playing in the snow, constructing a snowman taller than herself. She smiled at their ensuing giggles.

There was joy in her golden shackles. Staelash was a burden, but a rewarding one, though in the past six months it had grown heavier.

Lara had proposed she visit home.

Etolié stopped her footsteps and looked to the sky, knowing full well that Celestière wasn't up there but a parallel world all around them; still, traditionally mortals sent their prayers to the beyond high above. She shut her eyes, recalling Vanir Sol and its splendid, illuminate streets, the eternal night of her mother's home, the faded edges and fog and the corpse on the floor—

Her stomach sickened; Etolié shoved those memories back inside the metaphorical box. Still, she rubbed her hands together, desperate to banish the sensation of blood on her skin.

"Breathe, Etolié . . . Breathe with me."

Callused hands cupped her face, catching her tears. Etolié managed shaky breaths, following the cadence of Khastra's own.

"There is no secret you hold that would ruin my love for you. Now, start from the beginning . . ."

Etolié arrived at the manor, nodding politely to the guards at the gate, but strode around to the back. In the final days before Nox'Kartha would arrive, she'd spent more time than she'd admit to anyone in Flowers' garden.

The world was quiet there, for though the plants had slowly diminished over time without their protégé keeper, the wards woven into the earth remained strong. Etolié reached the sanctuary, idly traversing the frost-bitten path. She breathed the clean air, peace descending upon her as her mind quieted.

The garden was still lovely. Less grand, but perhaps that was merely winter's doing. Etolié passed familiar bushes and trees, kicking at leaves scattered along the path.

As she walked, she came across a little tree, one she'd given no mind to before, save once.

Nearly a year ago, when Flowers was a new face in the manor, a storm had come to her garden, wrecking the few months of growth. She'd helped Flowers clear out the damage, picked up fallen branches, even scooped out puddles of water drowning the daffodils.

One tree, scarcely two feet high, had bent at the middle, nearly torn by the winds.

"You might as well dig it up, Flowers. This little guy won't grow."

But Flowers, silly thing, had resolved to save the plant. She staked a large slab of wood beside it, then tied it and the little fucker with twine. *"It isn't ruined. It just needs some stability."*

The tree nearly reached Etolié's head, now, healed by Flowers' magic and her practicality.

"What happens if you remove the stake?"

"Depends on whether or not the tree has taken proper root."

Etolié laid on the ground in a clearing, flask in hand, the yellowed grass at her back cool on her bare skin.

She took a long drink, quietly simmering at Eionei. He was up to the same bullshit as always, but that was nothing compared to the raging boil she felt toward a particular half-demon bitch who'd waited months to finally come clean about not, you know, *being fucking dead,* and only because of the coaxing of their mutual flowery friend.

She remembered her visit to Nox'Kartha, remembered the joy and relief in Khastra's presence . . . but it wasn't her demon. It was a secretive bitch with Khastra's face who smiled and waved away all her questions.

"So tell me about that neat tick-tock heart of yours–"

"In cohorts with the imperator now, huh? How's that going?"

"Show me around the castle! Do they have other undead like you?"

Etolié felt tears and blamed them on the booze. She swallowed them, just as she swallowed from her precious flask, and hoped Khastra hated herself as much as Etolié hated her right now.

Footsteps drew her attention. She glanced down the path, only to match eyes with a startled Zorlaeus.

"Magister Etolié," the De'Sindai said, straightening his stance. "M-My apologies. I didn't think anyone would be here."

"Do you usually come here?" Etolié sat up, brushing frosty flecks of ice from her silver hair.

Zorlaeus fidgeted as he always did, his fingers twitching against his pant leg. Nervous little fucker, that one. "It's quiet here. I'm anticipating chaos and wanted to take a moment to breathe." He offered a nervous chuckle, then stepped away. "I should go. I shouldn't be here anyway."

"Listen, Lae Lae, knowing Flowers, she's thrilled someone came here to enjoy her garden," she said, but noticed the faltering in the man's smile. "Sorry—not Lae Lae. I'm a pet name sort of girl, but you don't seem to like that one much."

Zorlaeus shyly shook his head. "Reminds me of, uh . . . Nothing. Never mind."

"Pale and fanged and thankfully dead?"

"I did hate it when Ayla used it. It's not quite the whole story, though."

Zorlaeus was looking increasingly like a nervous rodent, so Etolié opted to not follow that rabbit hole. "But you're not thrilled about this wedding business either?"

"I'm not looking forward to the festivities, but I'm overjoyed to be marrying Marielle," he replied, noticeably wistful as he smiled. Etolié had always found him endearing, in the same way mortals gushed over puppies. She looked at him a second longer than normal and realized who he reminded her of, wondering how she'd never noticed before.

"I hope this isn't weird to say, but you are so much like Clarence. Which is a compliment—I miss him more than I generally admit."

She truly did. A year ago, his life had been cut short by a knife wound through the back in the middle of the night—and she'd lost one of the first true friends she'd ever had.

"Well," Zorlaeus said thoughtfully, "people are generally attracted to those who subconsciously remind them of their parents, so I don't see the issue with it."

Etolié couldn't suppress her scoff. "I don't think that's true. Between you and me, I don't especially want to relive my parents."

"I've also heard they can veer toward the absolute opposite," Zorlaeus added, an apology in those puppy eyes.

"But, if you don't mind me saying it, given that you've said before you aren't attracted to anyone, you might simply be a statistical outlier."

Zorlaeus had just used the term 'statistical outlier' in a proper context, and Etolié decided then and there that she liked him. "True," she replied, making sure to exaggerate her non-offense for the anxiety-ridden boy's sake. "I don't quite understand the appeal of sexy-times."

"Which isn't to say," Zorlaeus continued, apparently having switched into science brain—a state of mind Etolié could relate to, "that people who don't experience sexual attraction can't enjoy sex as a physical release or as a way to bond with someone they love, given that romantic attraction can exist in its own sphere–"

"You sound like you recited that from a book," Etolié said, resisting the urge to say her real feelings, which veered closer to 'sounds fake but all right.'

Zorlaeus' blush on his maroon skin stained his cheeks like fine wine. "It's entirely possible. I've read quite a bit about this."

"Well, not to piss on the scientific method, but I'm willing to call any experimentation on my end over and done. I've had sex, and it's terrible. In sex's defense, I was generally more focused on murder than pleasure, but I'm still glad those days are far behind me."

Zorlaeus looked mighty concerned at that, and Etolié remembered then that over-sharing was generally frowned upon in polite society, honest or not. "There's a very nice bench farther in; join me. We'll discuss my unsavory murder days."

To her surprise, Zorlaeus accepted, his smile relaxed for the first time.

Chapter 2

The next morning, in the dark recesses of Ayla's old bedroom, Flowridia placed what few belongings she would need into a bag, all under the judgmental gaze of her familiar.

You're not actually going to wear the green one.

Flowridia picked up the lacy ensemble, remiss to admit that it revealed more cleavage than she would ever wear outside the bedroom. Staring into Demitri's golden eyes, she folded it and placed it in the bag. "You never know," she said, knowing full well she spoke only because of spite. "Perhaps Etolié will borrow it."

Etolié doesn't wear clothes, dummy.

Flowridia stuck her tongue out at her rude boy.

Sequestered in a sack beside her bracelet of maldectine waited the blue orb—muted in its presence, lest it be discovered. In theory, as long as she didn't use it, it would be safe from Soliel.

It would be safer in Solvira, or Staelash—wherever it ended up. Yet she hesitated, unsure of what to make of the clenching in her gut.

Demitri had said she might need it. She shook her head and placed the small sack in her bag, deeming it a problem for the future.

At her feet, Ana sniffed her legs, or at least mimed the act, given she was a skeleton and could not actually sniff. Flowridia bent down to offer a hand, allowing the undead fox to nuzzle it. "You'll like Staelash," Flowridia said brightly, but then her optimism withered. "I only hope they like you."

She resumed her packing, pausing only when the ear slipped out from her bodice.

She removed it from her neck, wondering what the better part would be—to leave it here and miss its comfort, or bring it at the risk of Staelash finding it on her person.

It would hardly endear her to anyone, for them to know she loved Ayla still.

A knock echoed across Ayla's door. Flowridia stuffed the ear back down her dress. "Come in," she said, and Casvir himself entered.

The faint light from the globes cast his skin in luminous hues of blue—much livelier that the sickened, drowned grey his skin generally adopted. His armor shifted as he stepped inside. "Are you ready?"

The rest of Nox'Kartha, those who would be attending the wedding at least, had already left. But she and Casvir needn't walk. "I am."

"Shall we–"

Another knock surprised them both. Flowridia opened the door.

There stood Khastra, forced stoicism on her countenance and a bag swung over her shoulder. "Forgive me. I have changed my mind, Imperator. I would like to attend, if you would allow me to come with you and the tiny one."

Casvir gave a mere nod of acknowledgement.

Flowridia beamed. "What changed your mind?" she dared to ask.

"I should see my friends," she said cryptically, but Flowridia understood.

Casvir ripped his claw through the air. Vertigo struck, nauseating her as a tear appeared in space, widening to accommodate their sizes. Casvir stepped through.

Flowridia grabbed Ana and her own bag, watching as Demitri went through with Khastra. She spared a final glance to Ayla's bedroom, praying all would be kept safe until her return.

Within her bodice, the ear remained. She supposed her choice had been made.

She slipped her hand inside her bag and gripped the bracelet of maldectine, silencing its power before she stepped through—lest its magical nullifying abilities ruin the portal. She stepped through. Her stomach flipped as she floated through space, weightless for a heartbeat before her feet touched grass.

They appeared in the midst of a splendid cacophony. Dancers adjusted their costumes, entire orchestras rehearsed their tunes, and chaos abounded as people—mostly De'Sindai—ran about. It stretched as far as her small stature could see. Flowridia held Ana close to her chest and stepped into Casvir's shadow, knowing she might never find him if she lost sight. Demitri stood close, watching the scene with intrigue.

She released the maldectine, the orb's power subduing once more. "All this for a foreign wedding?" she yelled, though her voice barely carried.

"Zorlaeus was one of Murishani's favorites before I claimed him." His lips barely moved, yet she heard his voice clearly. "More importantly, Murishani will take any excuse to plan an event."

A voice suddenly boomed through the crowd. "Friends, I do believe it is time to begin." High above, a cloud rose, and draped upon it was a decadently dressed individual, one with flowing, golden hair. He was beautiful, perfectly chiseled, his eyes gleaming with life.

Two eyes. Apparently the one Kah'Sheen had stabbed had healed. Pity.

Murishani laughed, musical and pleasant. "Khastra! Wonderful to see you. I have a surprise for you—something to accommodate your size."

A servant, at those words, gestured for Khastra to follow. She disappeared among the throng of De'Sindai.

"Just as we rehearsed—into formation!"

Immediately, the crowd scattered, and Casvir gripped Flowridia's shoulder. He pulled her into his side just as she might have been trampled by a man balancing a lit torch on his nose. "You and I shall be near the back," Casvir said. "It is safer there."

"Casvir, don't be such a bore!" Flowridia glanced up and saw Murishani staring directly at them from his perch. "I've a special place in the center for you." He pointed, raising an expectant eyebrow.

Casvir sneered, purposefully avoiding eye contact with the Viceroy. "You will ride by my side, on Demitri." As he spoke, he moved to mount an armored, skeletal beast. He painted such a picture in his full armor, his magnificent horns adding to his substantial height. Silhouetted by the sun, he cast an ominous shadow, a subtle menace amidst an otherwise amiable crowd.

Flowridia nodded, eyes wide as she watched the chaos swirl into something precise. Demitri bent his front legs, allowing Flowridia to sit side-saddle atop his back. She realized, as Demitri stood, that she nearly matched Casvir in height. She gripped his fur and leaned forward to whisper in his ear. "I think you'll impress everyone with your growth spurt."

I'd better. You think this was easy?

She giggled and returned her attention to Casvir, each imprinted detail of his blackened armor burned into her memory. "Are you going to wear your armor for the entire wedding?"

"Why would I not?"

"It looks so cumbersome. "Does it get heavy?"

"No," he said simply.

Demitri's enormous feet padded along behind Casvir's horse. Amidst performers and dancers, acrobats and fire-eaters, a plethora of guards interspersed themselves among the Nox'Karthan citizens. A circle of them stood near the back, the space in the center just large enough for a giant wolf and an armored horse. Flowridia took her place beside Casvir, and as she stared forward, high atop Demitri, she realized she could just see the towers of her kingdom appearing in the distance.

The parade began moving.

By Alystra's Supple Ass—Murishani knew how to stage a parade.

Etolié sat on the manor's roof, perched above a balcony, her translucent wings listlessly floating behind her. The parade had burst through the gates like a shattered dam, flooding the city in Nox'Karthan revelers.

And, well, joy too, Etolié supposed. She stole a sip of her flask, willing her annoyance to settle. She searched the crowd for familiar faces. One in particular. Her gut clenched at the thought of the half-demon-who-would-not-be-named, but her mind was a nervous buzz.

Music played, steadily increasing in volume as the parade wound through the streets. In the distance, she saw dancers twirling in time, watched acrobats enthrall the masses with their tricks. Gold littered the streets—party favors, she supposed, those pompous assholes—and she saw it glittering in the hands of children and adults alike.

Radiant above all was Murishani, unmistakable atop a carriage gleaming from literal gold plating, mingling with the crowd and smiling with easy charm. He kissed their hands and tossed out trinkets like seeds to a crowd of pigeons.

Etolié took a long sip of her flask, then suddenly smelled something . . . oddly familiar and gut-churningly sweet. Not a scent to fear, no—it was the smell of peaceful nights, when the monster was docile and Etolié knew her momma was safe instead of—

Breathe . . . Just breathe.

But though Etolié's stomach suddenly knotted, her curiosity remained the stronger force.

She scooted herself toward the edge of the roof where a small stream of smoke wafted up from the balcony. Peering down, she saw Sora casually puffing little circles into the air. If Etolié stared carefully at her impressive mane of rope-like hair—stark blonde despite her amber skin, which Etolié had never bothered to ask about—she could see a little bird happily snoozing on her head.

"Why are you–"

Sora gasped, visibly startled, which was odd given the half-elf was notorious for having the reflexes of a fucking lion. "Etolié! I didn't see you there."

"This isn't my normal perch, but it's doing its job. I'll float down once Flowers reaches the front." Speaking of, Etolié glanced up, just able to spot a gigantic wolf in the distance. She spread her wings wide, hoping they were shiny enough to attract attention; when she waved, the girl atop the wolf waved back.

"I'm nervous," Sora admitted, the pipe in her mouth muffling her words. "You seem to be too."

"True." Etolié stole another swig of her flask, savoring the burning ale and the muted sensation it brought. "But I drink my weight to stay functional in mortal society." When Sora furrowed her brow, Etolié realized they hadn't had this talk yet. "The curse of my lineage—it's pretty damn difficult for me to actually get drunk, though not impossible. But the curse of just being me is that the world screams in my ear like a bitch I can't break up with. Booze keeps it at least a little quieter."

When Sora took another puff on that pipe of hers, Etolié raised an eyebrow. "But this is just another day for me. You're taking the prize, smoking that shit. Chaos' Spore, right? I'm fairly confident this is illegal in Zauleen."

Sora's smile was uncharacteristically nervous for the former stablemaster. "Most people here don't know what this is."

"The dick momma should have sucked instead of fucked basically wore that shit like perfume. I know a few things. You diluted it with something else, something sage-y, by the smell of it, which is for the best considering we're supposed to be on our best behavior in front of the scary undead kingdom." Etolié reached down. "Share, and I'll keep your secret."

Sora's grin was more amused than relieved. She offered the pipe up, and Etolié sat back, lounging on the roof as she breathed in the sweet, noxious vapors.

Immediately, she felt her agitated nerves begin to mute. "By Ku'Shya's Loose Cunt, you're a fucking hero." Rather than transcend to any so-called higher planes, Etolié offered the pipe back down, already less anxious. "Where do you even find this shit on this continent?"

"I grew it. No one's using the garden right now."

Etolié raised an eyebrow. "Are you implying that you grew mushrooms in our resident Flowers' garden?"

"I think I collected them all, but . . ." Sora took a puff, apparently unwilling to answer the rest.

Etolié chuckled. "Don't come say hi until you smell less blasted."

"I wasn't going to come down at all until you made me."

In the few months since Sora had accepted her promotion to 'third in the kingdom that's supposed to be an oligarchy, *Marielle,*' she'd done a damn fine job of following in an unmentionable half-demon's footsteps by saying absolutely nothing in meetings and agreeing with everything Etolié said—which she was grateful for. "Stay out of trouble. I'll see you tomorrow at the meet-and-greet."

Etolié shot up into the air, her wings little more than pure light, but truthfully, so was she. Though she descended slowly, she narrowly avoided ripping herself open on the corner of the roof—perhaps the Spore had been a mistake—

but managed to land on her feet beside Thalmus, who smiled only because Flowers actively approached.

He'd gone greyer in the last six months; Etolié suspected he worried more than he showed, that gods-damned mom of a man.

Shadowed by the imperator, Flowers dismounted Demitri—who was *holy shit levels of huge*—and ran up the steps, followed closely by the aforementioned huge wolf.

Marielle stole her first, and Etolié suppressed a grin as poor Flowers tried to not get lost in that impressive cleavage. From her pouch peeked that strange little fox thing, which Etolié still wasn't entirely convinced wasn't just a wind-up toy.

When Demitri approached, her heart soared, gleefully bombarded by a mound of coarse fur. "I missed you, you good boy."

Flowers, freed from her prison, looked prepared to speak, but Thalmus stole her then—for the best.

Etolié was well aware of Thalmus' real feelings regarding her drunk-ass self, but they'd shared quiet glances affirming their common goal of keeping that flower girl safe—he as a stable, fatherly figure, and she as a drunk aunt of sorts.

Etolié released Demitri at Casvir's approach. Even in the shadow of the manor, the world darkened around him. His stone stare studied them all, lingering a moment on Thalmus as his eyes glanced to the enormous hand engulfing Flowers' shoulder.

Their ensuing stare-down, brief as it was, held more tension than Alystra and Eionei on a good day.

But when he met her own gaze, he stared a bit longer, and Etolié hoped he didn't see past her literal illusion of elegance, given she hadn't washed her hair in six days. In times of stress, basic hygiene was often forgotten. His stare was alarming in ways far different than most men—he gave no care to beauty, or so she'd heard. He looked more like he plotted her death.

Funny. She preferred that.

But then he looked down at Marielle, impartial and polite. He nodded. "Queen Marielle."

Etolié could feel the fiery annoyance radiating from Marielle and frankly found it gratifying. "Imperator Casvir," the queen said, standing tall.

Zorlaeus visibly shriveled and dropped to one knee. Casvir barely mumbled, "Zorlaeus," and returned his stare to herself. "Magister Etolié," he said, nodding in deference. "It is refreshing to be in the presence of true power."

From anyone else, she'd call it blatant flattery. Casvir was far too deliberate a bastard, in his speech and actions both. "It's a pleasure to be hosting you and yours in our kingdom, Imperator Casvir," she said, her grin as sincere as she could manage.

She spared a glance for the continuing parade, uncertainty welling in her stomach as she sought a familiar face—and quietly cursed herself for it. She stole Flowers into an embrace, her touch less itchy than most—she gave nice hugs, all right? Oddly tight for someone of her size—and said, before she could swallow back the sour taste of the words, "Where's General Beefcake?"

Flowers pulled back, those large eyes as lovely as ever. "She's farther back in the parade."

So Khastra was here.

Like a sunrise over the mountaintops, Viceroy Murishani burst onto the scene. He stood atop a decadent throne, supported by four shirtless, well-built De'Sindai men, and beamed to those in attendance. "Oh, what fun that was." He laughed, joyous and boisterous, before descending from the throne, bits of swirling clouds cushioning his feet like steps.

Etolié fought to keep her mouth shut at the outlandish display. From his luscious clothing to those bright green eyes, practically glowing as he smiled, this man bore the stench of absolute insanity.

"Queen Marielle, it is a joy to finally meet you!" He ran forward, taking both of her hands into his, and kissed both her cheeks. "What a wonderful kingdom you have! And such a marvelous home. I look forward to your hospitality more than I can express." Sincerity dripped from every word. His eyes fell upon Zorlaeus, who still trembled on one knee, and laughed. He offered a hand and kissed Zorlaeus' as he rose. "And Zorlaeus, he who breaks my heart! You'll be leaving us for good this time, I suppose." He placed a dramatic hand on his chest but beamed nonetheless. "This shall be the send-off you deserve."

Marielle beamed. "It's wonderful to meet you too, Viceroy Murishani."

"Oh, titles are so pretentious," Murishani said, scoffing. "Marielle, I have so much to discuss with you, but first..." His eyes traveled to Etolié, and he grinned with obvious interest. She smiled back, resisting the urge to cringe. "I should be bowing to you, Daughter of Staella." And he did, crossing his arm over his chest and bowing deep. "To stand in your presence is an honor. Your courageous exploits against slavery are the stuff of legend."

Etolié accepted his hand when offered, fighting a grimace when he kissed her knuckle. "You are too kind, Viceroy."

He looked up to Thalmus, and Etolié, as much as she didn't care for him, nearly stepped between them, prepared to prevent a fight. "Sir Thalmus, is it? Goodness, your hair is gorgeous." With a dramatic flourish, his hand gestured down the braid flowing down Thalmus' back. "An honor to make your acquaintance. I'm told you are a working man, and a skilled one. Is it true you make weapons from glass?"

Thalmus hesitated, tentatively accepting Murishani's offered hand with the one not clinging to Flowers' shoulder. "It is."

"Fascinating. I would love nothing more than to view a sampling of your wares."

His eyes fell upon Flowridia only a moment, but he turned aside. Weird, but fine in Etolié's book. Instead, he directed his attention to Zorlaeus and Marielle. "Dear Zorlaeus, if I might, I'd love to have a moment alone with your intended. Nothing untoward; there is so much to discuss!" He took Marielle's hand and led her away, a whirlwind personified.

The parade continued in the foreground, and from the throng came a glittering rainbow of grandeur and ... *fuck*.

Well, atop what appeared to be an undead elephant, General Beefcake wore glittering, gem-encrusted armor and a grin much happier than Etolié would've cared to see.

Her gut clenched. Fury rose from the depths of who the fuck knew where and she said, "Nice horse," as the half-demon approached. "Weirdest thing I've ever seen you ride."

Khastra smiled, perhaps more radiantly than Murishani, blinding to Etolié who could see nothing else. "Not the strangest creature I have mounted, but certainly a treat." Etolié expected a hug; not a surge of anger when Khastra slighted her by having the audacity to greet other people. "It is wonderful to see all of–"

"Well, damn, you blunt-eared whore. A few months in Nox'Kartha, and look at you cutting loose."

Khastra didn't laugh, which made the ensuing silence that much more awkward. Worse, her smile faded, but Etolié stood her ground—until Flowers stammered, "P-Plenty of things to bone in the city of the dead."

The uncomfortable silence shattered at that absolute abomination of a jest. Khastra's smile returned to her eyes, and, even weirder, Casvir slowly reached up to cover his own flickering grin.

Etolié was then *ignored* as Khastra looked to Thalmus instead. "I presume Etolié told you."

"She did."

His curt response was unsurprising, but it certainly illustrated their many *many* disagreements. Etolié recalled when she'd told the council the news of Khastra's continued existence. He'd said nothing at all. His face had spoken louder than words.

Perhaps noting his stark disapproval, Khastra instead turned to Flowers. "Murishani has already stolen Marielle, yes?"

Etolié couldn't stand to look at her. "Zorlaeus, kindly escort Imperator Casvir to his room." She spared a glance for the half-demon and her stupid, infectious grin. "Your old room awaits, Khastra."

She stole Flowers' arm and took her away. Demitri followed, though he had to squeeze to fit through the doorway of the manor.

The door shut. Flowers frowned, shooting glances back to Demitri. "Casvir will wonder where I've–"

"By Eionei's Asshole—can you even believe her audacity?!" she spat, imagining Khastra's outline through the door. "Bitch just slides on in here like she never fucking left."

"Do you mean Khastra . . ?"

"Who else? Fuck it—let's not talk about it." Etolié shoved said half-demon bitch out of her mind, ignoring the clenching in her ribcage. Etolié kinda hoped it was a heart attack. At least if she died she'd be free of this wedding bullshit. "Flowers, you have to meet Zoldar."

"Who?"

She breathed out her anger, feeling at least ninety percent better after admitting to herself Khastra was definitely being the bitch here and not her. "My new assistant. You'll love him."

Etolié wove them down the familiar maze of hallways, forgetting a moment that Flowers had lived here and knew her way around. She cracked a grin when Demitri struggled through the doorway. "Guess we'll have to expand it. You're only gonna get bigger."

Flowers, the silly thing, giggled at whatever Demitri said, or whatever she imagined he said—Etolié hadn't figured that one out yet. "He appreciates your faith in him."

Etolié glanced around the shelves, and cried, "Zoldar!"

"When will the rest of the guests be coming?"

"Tomorrow night. Zoldar!"

"Will the empress be among them?"

Etolié whipped around to face her at that. "Yes, in fact. Didn't know you cared."

"I can only assume you told her about Soliel and the dragon. There's something I need to . . ."

Flowers' words faded. The shock on her preciously young face told Etolié all she needed to know. When she turned around, a familiar Skalmite approached from behind a shelf, green and lanky with his insect-like physique, his crystalline eyes utterly foreign. Around his rail-thin neck hung a rough chunk of maldectine. "Flowers, meet Zoldar. He took your old job."

Flowers approached Zoldar, smiling as she cautiously held out a hand. "My name is Flowridia. Perhaps we met at the cave."

Zoldar ignored the offered hand, instead looking to Etolié and emphatically waving his arms across his torso, and then Flowers'. She listened to his clicking, managing to decipher enough. "He remembers your injury. He–" The oversized bug spat on the floor, and Etolié sneered at the rude bookkeeper. "He's the one who patched you up."

Light filled Flowridia's eyes, and when she took a step forward, she suddenly stopped herself and placed her hands on her heart. "Would it be rude to hug him as a thank you?"

Etolié looked to Zoldar and mimed a hug, as well as offering a series of clicking patterns she had come to understand as meaning, *"please,"* in Skalmite. Zoldar mimed in return, and when Etolié nodded, he wrapped his spindly arms around Flowridia, who offered her own warm embrace.

Cute. "We're not entirely certain what his name is, but when I asked, the name 'Zoldar' was the closest my mere Celestial ears could interpret from his speech patterns. He likes it, though. He's doing well here in the underground, though he avoids the skylight. Generally, he's nocturnal, but he wanted to be awake to meet you."

Flowridia's smile looked ready to split her face in two. "I'm truly touched, Zoldar."

He didn't understand, but with care he reached out to pat her head, then he climbed up the shelves in his insect way and returned to work.

"He lives in a void of magic—the crystal around his neck is always activated."

"I suspected. I could feel it."

"Lara was concerned about my well-being," Etolié said, staring wistfully up at the Skalmite she would never admit to adoring, "and sent a spy. He clicks in my ear when I don't eat. In other news, I can't say, 'hello,' in Skalmite, but I do know how to say, 'eat some fucking breakfast, you skinny whore.'" Etolié grinned at her own jest as she stepped farther into the library, but realized Flowers . . . didn't.

"Speaking of calling people 'whores,'" Flowers said, and already Etolié shied from her tone, "you were rude."

Bold of her. Uncharacteristically bold. Perhaps Casvir had been good for the shrinking violet. "Don't know what you're talking about–"

"Are you angry with Khastra?"

It wasn't Etolié's fault none of them understood humor. "It was a joke, Flowers. I say shit like that to her all the time."

"Not like that, no."

Who was this child? Etolié frowned at Flowers, recognizing her face but not this sudden combative streak. "Well, I-"

"Etolié, listen," Flowers implored. "She's only here because of you."

Oh, was she now? "Seems like the two of you have gotten mighty close, if she's confiding in you," Etolié said, and somehow the statement irked her. She crossed her arms, defensive in ways that only pissed her off more because she didn't *understand*—

"We're better friends than before, but not as good as you and her. In my six months in Nox'Kartha, you're the only one she's asked about."

Oh, was she? Etolié managed to bite her tongue.

"For my own peace of mind, will you please talk to her?"

"Everything is fine, Flowers." It was, because Etolié willed it to be.

The ensuing silence was unbearably loud to Etolié's drunken mind, and she took another sip, refusing to think that, perhaps, the world wasn't the problem, but she herself.

Flowers' bag glowed when she opened it, and what she withdrew nearly caused Etolié to spit out her booze. "Flowers, you—!"

She held an orb. Etolié stared first at the radiant blue and white artifact, then at Flowers, noting her darling, triumphant grin. "We found it less than a week ago. Had to kill a leviathan."

"I need this story." Summoning an illusionary handkerchief to protect her from the splitting headache that came from touching these bastards, she plucked the orb from Flowers' hands.

"Will you come with me to the kitchen?" Flowers asked, a familiar sweetness in her smile—there was the girl Etolié knew. "I haven't baked anything since I left."

"First, we take care of this thing." On a forgotten shelf, covered in dust she refused to let Zoldar clear, sat a gem-encrusted box, one that had once held a counterpart to the orb in her hand. She blew a short breath, coughing at the swirls of dust, and opened it with care. The orb fit perfectly within the velvet-lined box. "Let's go."

The kitchens were as she remembered, and Flowridia felt a bit of peace fall upon her, seeing the familiar cupboards and shelves. Home felt different in ineffable ways, but the ingredients were where she'd left them. She spoke of her adventure, filling in details she hadn't the last time she and Etolié had spoken.

"The Coming Dawn was *who?!*"

Flowridia laughed at Etolié's bafflement. "The Coming Dawn is Khastra's sister. Well, half-sister. Apparently her youngest. She was odd, but once we were past her trying to kidnap me, she was really very nice. Her name is Kah'Sheen."

She elected to not mention that Kah'Sheen had saved her from Murishani. The viceroy's true character wasn't something Etolié needed to worry about.

Yet.

"Hm." Etolié's perturb was palpable. Flowridia tried to not stare as the Celestial said, "Well, I never knew that."

"Perhaps it never came up."

"In twenty-three years of running this place? Not once?"

Flowridia steeled her annoyance—Etolié's decorum would end with her being smacked at this rate. "Then perhaps you should discuss it with Khastra, if you're this offended."

"I'm not."

And then Etolié had changed the subject.

The muffins, once done, were assembled prettily onto a porcelain plate. She plucked one from the top and offered it to Demitri, who easily ate the entire pastry in one bite. "I'm glad you still like my baking."

But what if you made a giant muffin?

"I think what you want is a cake."

A muffin cake.

The words brought a blush and a smile. "Might as well pass out the rest."

Etolié followed her outside, heading out the back door with Ana and Demitri in tow. Flowridia was surprised to find a riotous bit of organized chaos. Behind the manor, hundreds of Nox'Karthans ran about, carrying supplies and painting lines upon the grassy area. Various beams were being measured and erected, and at the center Flowridia saw an enormous one lying on the grass, perhaps twice the size of the manor.

Taller than the surrounding foreigners, Thalmus stood with his back to her, watching the busy scene. Flowridia ran forward, dodging builders and managing to keep her muffins level. "Thalmus!" she said, smiling as he turned. "What's going on?"

"Apparently, this will be the tent housing the wedding," Thalmus said, and the warmth in his smile when she offered him the plate of muffins radiated. How she had missed that kindness and comfort, she mused, touched when his enormous fingers took a single muffin into their grasp.

He could have eaten it in one bite. But he took the tiniest nibble, savoring each crumb. Flowridia beamed. "And you're supervising?"

"At Marielle's request, yes."

When Demitri affectionately sniffed Thalmus' arm, the half-giant offered a hand. "His growth spurt is impressive."

"Isn't it?" Flowridia knelt down to lift Ana into her arms. "Did you see my fox? She's as little as Demitri used to be."

With visible apprehension, Thalmus glanced at the skeletal fox, who wagged her tail at the attention. "I did see it, yes."

"Her," Flowridia clarified. "Her name is Ana."

Thalmus nodded slowly, directing his attention back to the flurry of workers. Flowridia shuffled in front of him, standing on her toes to try and steal his attention. "Thalmus–"

"Flowra . . ." He shut his eyes, and each passing second grew longer than the previous.

Long ago, Flowridia had felt the sting of loved ones staring like they'd never known her, of lifelong friends turning their backs when they'd known her truth. She had been fifteen, and far too young to lose a family.

She still remembered their hateful cries: *"Witch!"*

Flowridia waited, realizing he held her hope to a needle that might burst all she had worked for.

"Any sign of Marielle?"

Praise Etolié and her ability to cause a slightly less awkward mood.

Thalmus merely shook his head as he opened his eyes.

"Too bad. Perhaps we'll find her somewhere else," she said as she grabbed Flowridia's arm. She dragged her away, back inside and into the hallway. "You all right, Flowers?"

"I'm fine, Etolié."

"I sensed a mood."

"Whatever it is he has to say," Flowridia said, swallowing the sudden emotion in her throat, "I don't know if I'm ready to hear it."

When she tried to take a step forward, Etolié blocked her, eyes soft. "It's not what you do; it's what you do with it. You're one in a million, Flowers, no matter what he thinks."

"Let's keep moving, please," she whispered, and she moved down the hallway and to the stairs. "I didn't know we were looking for Marielle."

"We weren't, but it seemed like a believable excuse. I think she's upstairs."

On the second floor, they passed Flowridia's old bedroom. Later, perhaps, she would explore, but for now she felt determined to keep her emotions in check. All the memories her bedroom held might be overwhelming.

They turned a corner, expecting to find more rooms, but the duo stopped in their tracks at what madness they nearly ran into. An enormous arch, golden and gleaming, stood in place of what had been a guest wing, and from within some sort of pocket dimension roared with life. Flowridia and Etolié both peered forward, taken aback at the ostentatious visual, but more so at what waited inside. De'Sindai servants hurried about, and one met them at the entrance. A bit bedraggled and likely drunk, the man smiled languidly. "Can I help you?"

Etolié, expression utterly serious, slowly pulled a flask from her pocket and took several long, deep gulps. Flowridia tilted her head, staring past him. "What is this?"

"Viceroy Murishani doesn't go anywhere without packing a tent. A home away from home, you might say."

Actual stone connected the various entryways and rooms within, and a fountain at the center—a stone depiction of Murishani—spewed what appeared to be a sparkling red wine from his mouth. "Is Marielle here?" Flowridia tentatively asked.

The man nodded. "Just a moment." He disappeared within the array of people and rooms.

Flowridia looked to Etolié. "This is what he takes camping."

"We're considered camping."

"Flowridia! Etolié!" They saw Marielle, side by side with Murishani, both of them beaming as they approached. "There's a tailor here who has promised the dress of my dreams! And a jeweler to decorate it. This place is spectacular!"

The lengths to which Murishani went to avoid making eye contact with her were truly impressive. His eyes darted from Marielle to Etolié, even to the muffins on the plate, but Flowridia genuinely couldn't say he even stole a glance for her fingertip. "I'm sure it's something," Flowridia said, peering inside the archway. It expanded in every direction. Looking back, the hallway of the castle remained, but the bright lights and bustling dimensional space were a sight.

Marielle took a muffin and turned it over in her hands before taking a bite. Flowridia stared at Murishani, offering the plate and grinning when he stared off to the side. She stepped forward, holding the plate under his nose, vindictively amused at his antics. "Muffin?"

Murishani, staring out just beyond Marielle, covered the half of his face pointed at Flowridia with his hand. "Marielle," he cooed, "would you mind delivering a message for me? To Lady Flowridia? Remind her that if I even so much as look at the sweet thing that Casvir has sworn to rip my head from my neck and feed me to the streetsweepers."

"Why . . ?" Etolié said, and Flowridia cringed, preparing a lie to get out of this conversation without sparking an international incident.

"I truly don't know!" he said, placing a rather pathetic hand on his heart. "All I ever wanted was to make sweet Flowra feel at home, but it seems Casvir misjudged my intentions, that brute. He's very possessive of her, you know."

Etolié nodded pleasantly. "We've noticed," she said, just as politely, and Flowridia wondered how difficult it would be to deliver poisoned muffins to the viceroy.

"Such a pity, to be a vivacious flirt! It's simply second nature, you see, even when I don't mean it. My intentions were noble, but we were both burned in the end, mutually deprived of friendship."

"Murishani–" Flowridia stopped when the Viceroy pointed his finger at Marielle. Rolling her eyes, Flowridia said, "Marielle, would you please ask Viceroy Murishani if he would like a muffin?"

Marielle stared expectantly at Murishani, but when he didn't answer, she furrowed her eyebrows and spoke. "Flowridia wants to know if you'd like a muffin."

Murishani smiled brightly from behind his covered face. "I would be absolutely delighted! Tell Lady Flowridia I would love nothing more than to bury my face in her offered muffin." From behind his fingers, Flowridia saw the lecherous smirk twisting his lip. He stared at her from the corner of his eyes, coy and teasing.

Hesitation laced Marielle's tongue. "Um, Flowridia, Murishani says–"

"I heard." Grimacing, Flowridia offered the plate forward. Murishani made no move to accept it. Instead, Marielle took one from the plate and placed it into Murishani's hand.

"Do either of you," Flowridia asked, lowering the plate, "know where Casvir is?"

Marielle gestured with her head. "Next door."

Next to the enormous archway, a smaller, non-magical door met her view. With Etolié flanking her, Flowridia knocked.

A pause, and then an, *"Enter."* Flowridia pushed the door open and found Casvir seated in a sparse guest room. What few supplies he had brought lay untouched beside his bed. But piles of paper neatly covered the desk he sat at, organized chaos at its finest.

"Lady Flowridia," he said politely. "Magister Etolié."

"A pleasure to see you again," Etolié said, and Flowridia realized that Ana rested in her arms. "Flowers speaks highly of you."

Casvir returned his attention to Flowridia. "Can I help you?"

"Why are you doing paperwork?" she asked, a bit of laughter in her tone.

"There is little else for me to be doing."

Flowridia approached him and offered him the plate. "What you don't know about me is that I bake."

"I do know you bake," Casvir said, utter indifference coloring his face as he studied the plate of baked goods. He reached out and accepted one, placing it at the corner of his desk. "Anything else?"

"How did you know I bake?"

"When I learned of Ayla's pursuit of you, I questioned her on your day to day activities to be certain she posed no danger. She mentioned baking as a pastime of yours."

To mention Ayla's name brought sorrow, but Flowridia hid it behind a curt nod. "Murishani brought quite the tent. I don't know how I'll get through this wedding without brushing up against him."

"You may interact with him," Casvir said smoothly, returning his attention to his paperwork. "But given his recent behaviors, I do not trust him."

Beside her, Etolié whispered, "What recent behaviors?"

Flowridia cringed. "Ask me later." She set another muffin beside the untouched one at the desk and said farewell.

As she and Etolié trekked down the hallway, the Celestial spoke up. "He's opaque, that one."

Flowridia shook her head. "Normally he's perfectly transparent."

"What recent behaviors, Flowers?"

"Murishani and I . . ." She shook her head. "He doesn't like me." Ignoring Etolié's frown, she continued forward.

"You can always tell me–"

"It's–" Flowridia stopped, hands clenching the plate at the memory of dread. She remembered fear. She remembered her utter helplessness, knowing if Kah'Sheen had not appeared, she might have perished . . . or succumbed. "I'd rather not say it. But what matters is that Casvir wanted to protect me from the darker aspects of his kingdom. Murishani manipulated me into seeking it out for myself."

Etolié followed; Flowridia refused to look at her. "You have me awfully worried–"

"None of it affects you or Staelash. Please, let it go."

When she did finally face Etolié, the Celestial stared at her as though they'd never met.

Flowridia hit a growth spurt once as a child, wherein she shot up and slimmed like the weed she apparently was and had to receive an entirely new set of clothing at the orphanage. Her dresses had hung in awkward ways—too tight and too loose all at once, unable to reach her ankles.

Staelash, she realized, fit her like her old dresses. She had grown in odd, inexpressible ways.

"Who else can we deliver muffins to?" Flowridia asked, breaking the uncomfortable silence.

"We can try and hunt down Sora if you really want. She watched the parade from a perch—namely, the balcony. I don't know how involved with the festivities she'll be."

Sora couldn't hide forever. Flowridia wasn't sure what she would say to the half-elf—hopefully nothing at all.

But they passed Khastra's old room, right as the half-demon exited. As gracefully as she could, Flowridia offered the plate to the undead general. "Muffin?"

Khastra shook her head. "Your baking is delightful, but I cannot enjoy it as fully as I could in life. I will pass." Her smile faltered when she glanced at Etolié. "Give Etolié my share."

"What, still worried about my skinny little ass?"

Etolié's palpable ire curdled Flowridia's blood, but Khastra replied with a frank, "I am."

Etolié said nothing, instead opting to sneer. Khastra gave a polite nod before stepping away.

When Khastra's hooved footsteps stopped reverberating across the walls, Flowridia turned a steely glare to her Celestial friend. "Etolié, what's going on?"

"I don't know what you're—"

"You have been rude to her from the moment she's arrived." Flowridia recalled their tearful reunion months ago, Etolié's shambled form, but watching her now . . . it was as though they hardly knew the other.

Etolié's lip trembled, and Flowridia realized she'd struck a nerve. "Truthfully, I don't know, but I definitely don't want to talk about this here."

Flowridia grabbed her arm and escorted her down the hallway, refusing to speak until the door to her own bedroom shut behind her. "You aren't being yourself, Etolié."

Flowridia set the plate of muffins onto the mirrored vanity. The shift of power was jarring, but she shoved the thought away. Whatever her own cognitive dissonance, she loved Etolié still.

"Ever since my visit to Nox'Kartha," Etolié said stiffly, "I've been furious. And I don't know why."

"Furious at Khastra?"

"Maybe? I don't understand it, Flowers. I was overwhelmed to know she was alive, and now I can't stand to look at her."

Condemning words. Flowridia frowned. "Why are you angry with her?"

Etolié crossed her thin arms, and Flowridia wondered if she still maintained an illusion on her appearance. She wondered if Etolié were well at all. "Why didn't she tell me she was alive?" Etolié whispered, her red-rimmed eyes shedding no tears. "You knew. Most of Nox'Kartha knew. But not me, and I'm the only person in the world she even likes. Or not, given she wouldn't tell me when I asked her to her face."

Etolié spoke out of bitterness. Flowridia's hands turned nearly white as she clenched her fists, debating whether to respect Khastra's wishes. "She had her reasons, and it isn't my place to say anything."

"You always did keep a thousand secrets, Flowers." Etolié shrugged and lowered her stare to the floor. "It never bothered me. But I won't lie and say it doesn't feel a little bit personal this time."

"Please, Etolié–"

"Does she not trust me?" Etolié implored, suddenly facing her again. "Or is she throwing away everything about her past life?"

"Neither of those," Flowridia replied, yet she knew both statements were, in their own ways, entirely true.

"Then, Flowers–" Etolié's voice caught. Her fingers dug into her arms. With her jaw stiffened, she whispered, "I've barely slept since I came to visit you, and I don't know why. And believe me, I fucking hate not knowing why. I'm supposed to eat, but I *can't–*" Etolié's fingers dug deep, and Flowridia worried she would draw blood. "I don't know what the fuck is wrong with me. I generally make sure I'm too busy to figure it out. But, Flowers–" Her stance relaxed all at once, head falling slack. "I shouldn't be unloading this on you. I'm supposed to be the adult."

"You've never been an adult, Etolié." Flowridia said it with kindness and hoped Etolié received it as such.

But the Celestial gave no reaction except her words. "If I asked her, would she tell me?"

"No," Flowridia said, knowing full well it was true. Internally, she contemplated the cost of her next words: to break Khastra's trust, but for the chance to save her friendship with Etolié. "And if I tell you, will you apologize?"

Etolié nodded, finally meeting her gaze.

Flowridia was fond of Khastra, but she knew Etolié loved her more than anyone. She braced herself and said, "Did Khastra explain her biology to you?"

"She has a clockwork heart and a few other tricks."

"She was an unprecedented experiment," Flowridia explained, forcing her emotions to steady at the memory. "The clockwork heart was the fifth attempt at a heart transplant, the other four of which were biological. She was conscious for all of it, because as an undead, there wasn't another option."

Etolié's expression steadily filled with realization, her lavender eyes growing wide.

"And in light of the unspeakable torture," Flowridia whispered, "she didn't want you to know, because she feared what your reaction would be. She never told me; Murishani showed me. I saw–" Her voice caught. Her fists clenched. Etolié's face didn't change. "First I watched her heart fail, and the agony it brought. But Murishani showed me the aftermath. It was, as I said, unspeakable. Khastra wanted to protect you from the truth and didn't want to give you false hope if she died her permanent death after all." Hesitation stopped her tongue, but the final phrase slipped out. "She certainly begged for it."

Etolié's eyes glistened, but tears did not fall. She stared in silence, visibly contemplating Flowridia's words.

"But she knew she was doing you wrong," Flowridia whispered. "She . . . She cares about you, Etolié. More than anyone else, I think."

She knew, but it was not her place to say. She wondered what Etolié's reaction would be, to know that Khastra loved her so.

Etolié gave a sharp nod. "I need to think," she said, and she saw herself out.

Flowridia hugged Demitri, silent and stable. "Either she's about to rip Casvir's head off, or I've actually managed to save their friendship."

I'm fully in support of that first one.

She gripped his warm fur, forcing herself to laugh. "Never change, dearest Demitri."

She would leave Etolié to Etolié. There was somewhere important she needed to be.

The soothing rustling of wind through shaded bushes and trees bespoke her return to her greatest joy. The plants sang at their reunion, despite winter's chill. The wards had not waned, written into the earth itself, only strengthening with time as the plants grew deeper and taller.

Flowridia passed through the invisible barrier, senses alight, tears welling amidst the joy she felt reunited with her sanctuary.

Ana darted about, but at her word stayed within the barriers. The wards may not have faltered, but the slight imperfections of the plants stood out to her attuned mind. Flowridia brushed her fingers across parched gardenias, their vibrant white having dulled. With a gentle touch, she rubbed her fingers against the petals, silently asking what help she could give.

Healing magic left her hand. The bush absorbed the potent dose, and Flowridia swore it stood physically taller, full of pride and joy. Flowridia kissed the center of a flower and left the bush alone.

Demitri ducked to avoid branches and bushes, sniffing all the while. *Your garden shrunk.*

"I suppose I'll have to make it bigger."

Thalmus had cared for this place in her absence, or so he'd sworn. He had done what he could, she saw. Winter had done what winter would, but the magic in the earth held more influence than even the changing seasons—the plants still flourished, despite the biting cold.

She noticed, then, her dearest creation, the unnamed breeding of moon lilies and gardenias, the ones that had dotted Ayla's hair—wilted and browned. Flowridia fell to her knees, cupping one of the precious buds and kissing the side. "Please live," she pled, feeling how the plant cried for sustenance, for life.

She touched them, and she felt pain. The once vibrant blossoms were far nearer to death than to life.

It wounded her, to lose something so beautiful and rare. The last perfect reminder of Ayla and her memory, and oh, it stung.

Flowridia gripped the branches, purple mist swirling from her hands. She breathed out, and the same deep purple escaped her lips.

When she inhaled, the flowers wilted, leaves and petals withering before her eyes.

Flowridia breathed out again, giving life—or something like it—to the ruined plant. Immediately, the small flowers grew flush and vibrant, turning their petals to the sky.

More beautiful than ever, in death. Fitting, given who they had been bred for. They would live on for eternity, sustained by dark magic.

She clipped one of the gorgeous stems and wove it into her hair, then moved on to inspect the rest.

Etolié stayed underground for an indeterminable amount of time—long enough for the sun to set and the stars to shine. For a moment, her concentration failed, leaving her with the visual reality of her own withering form.

She should be preparing for guests. She should be hostess-ing and entertaining and all those other things she was good at. Instead, collapsed beneath her skylight, Etolié wrapped her thumb and pointer finger around her bony wrist. Stress had taken a toll, one she refused, even now, to confront.

Her favorite lie was to wax poetic on the energy she gained beneath the stars' light, a manifestation of her heritage, but in truth she was a fraud who wanted the world to leave her the hell alone about her stress-eating habits—or lack thereof. Her hands fell back into the nest of scarves and blankets, the illusion returning of Etolié at her finest, the illusion Khastra saw through, again and again.

And Lara, somehow. Etolié hadn't questioned that one yet.

She drank a stomach's worth of ale and wondered when the hell she had lost her mind.

"What the fuck is your obsession with my eating habits, hmm?! Not a fan of my skinny ass? Maybe you should just go to hell and mind your own fucking business!"

But Khastra, who was a gods-damned brick wall, gently knelt before her, ignoring the vitriol Etolié spewed from her makeshift cave of toppled shelves. "You are lovely at any weight," she said gently, perhaps unwilling to startle the feral animal Etolié had become, "but my own peace of mind prefers it be a healthy one." She placed the dinner plate on the ground and slid it forward, just within arm's reach. "I know it is not so simple, but I want you to know, I care for you dearly. I want you safe."

She pulled herself up and knew what she had to do.

Khastra was not in her bedroom. She was not in the kitchen. This meant either Khastra was somewhere in that gaudy tent of Murishani's or perhaps somewhere more sentimental.

Khastra's workspace sat outside the manor, built well before Thalmus decided to outdo her with a kiln. A place for peace, and for her gems, and Etolié had bothered her there a thousand times before. Once upon a time, they had gossiped about council members and foreign dignitaries all through the night.

When Etolié peered through the dusty window, the lamplight spoke true—Khastra sat at her workbench, tidying the space. She wore no armor, simply a shirt and trousers and no shoes, because, well, when you had hooves, shoes seemed like more of a nuisance than anything.

Etolié entered without knocking. "I thought I'd find you here, ya big lug."

Khastra smiled, somehow brighter than the lamp and the moon outside both. "Good to see you, Etolié."

"What are you doing?" she asked, but in her gut, she knew. Khastra's gems were covered in dust but steadily being collected by the half-demon herself.

"Cleaning," she replied, affirming Etolié's suspicions. "I have no need for this place. Now you can use it for whatever my replacement wishes."

She said it with no ire, only frankness. But Etolié shook her head. "No one could replace you."

Gods, that was sweet. Perhaps she was more drunk than she'd thought.

"Listen," Etolié continued, shaking her head at her own sentiments, "I'm here because Flowers seems to think I offended you this morning, and I told her she was crazy, so . . ."

Khastra set down the pouches and gems she'd collected. With a resigned sigh, she said, "You did offend me."

"I've called you worse–"

"But never out of anger."

So it *was* palpable. Etolié leaned back against the door, wishing she could phase through it and die from the sheer amount of boundless shame filling her. "Oh."

It was all she could manage.

Khastra resumed her work in silence. Her hands were large and yet lithe in impossible ways, nimble after a thousand years of experience. More. And it blew Etolié's young mind. Despite the animal instinct to run away, she took a small step forward. "I'm sorry," she whispered, unsure of what else to add.

Khastra smiled, but there was nothing joyful about it. "So am I."

In the silence, they met each other's gaze, and Etolié saw a great chasm between them.

"Flowers–" Etolié choked, but by Morathma's Whore Mother *she would not cry.* "Flowers told me why you didn't tell me you were alive. She told me what they'd been doing to you. Don't be angry; I guilted her. And now I feel like the biggest ass in the realms for being so bitter that you didn't tell me you were alive because systematic torture seems like a pretty fucking valid reason even if I could have had no way of knowing—My *point,*" she said, finally taking a breath, "is that I'm sorry." Etolié shut her eyes, cursing the sudden rise of tears, willing them away. "I hate feelings. But I hurt. I don't know if I've breathed in six months. Even with you alive, I'm struggling to catch it."

She dared to look up and saw Khastra staring, saw her hesitating in her seat, her glowing eyes luminous among the candle-lit features of her elegant face. Gods, she was gorgeous in her otherworldly way. Perhaps Etolié had simply been used to it before.

"I never wanted to hurt you," Khastra whispered, her lips pulled into a perfect line. "I wanted to protect you, and I see now I made a mistake. What do you need from me? If you need me to leave you alone–"

"No!" Etolié said, surprised at her own sharpness. "That was never on the table, demon-spawn–" She stopped, recalling suddenly that pet names were suspect. "I-I mean, you beautiful, blue Bringer of . . ." Etolié trailed off when Khastra chuckled. The melodious noise settled her nerves, because truthfully, she constantly sought the sound. "I think we need time to remember how to be friends. I want to try."

Khastra smiled, and Etolié could have cried for relief. "I would be happy to try." From a bag hung on the chair, Khastra withdrew a small pouch and offered it forward. "I did not know if you would accept this before."

Etolié had been drowned in gifts over the years, castoffs the half-demon had deemed 'practice' or 'not flawless enough for Solvira' but Etolié had deemed her full of shit because everything Khastra crafted was perfect.

From the pouch, Etolié withdrew an odd metal ring, one with intricate loops and shifting parts and a rainbow of gems to decorate the sides. "Not that it isn't pretty, but what the hell?"

Khastra's laughter brought joy. "It is an elven design. The ring comes apart, like a puzzle, if you are clever. Something to help you focus at your meetings."

Etolié slipped it on her finger, already spinning the miniscule gears. "Damn, that's neat." She grinned, and Khastra beamed to match.

They chatted all through the night, illuminated by the lamp. Although Etolié still felt claws around her lungs, the tentative illusion of normalcy was comforting.

Khastra was safe and constant.

In the evening, when Flowridia finally returned to her bedroom, she took a moment to actually *look.*

Dust and disuse should have covered the furniture and bed, but the fresh sheets were neatly folded, the surfaces clean. Demitri's sniffing became the only sound as he crept through the small bedroom. *I remember this being bigger.*

"You were hardly as tall as my thigh when we left." To emphasize, she flattened her hand against her leg and slowly brought it up above her head, until she could pat Demitri on his ear. "If you think you'd be more comfortable outside, I can set something up."

I would be more comfortable keeping you safe.

Flowridia stood on her toes to kiss his nose, meeting him when bent his neck down so she could reach. Glancing around, she saw her beloved chess set, the cracked wardrobe, and upon the windowsill . . . twelve roses in a vase, wilted and dried, yet as precious as gold.

She swallowed the rise of feeling in her throat, instead kneeling beside her discarded bag. She pulled out her nightclothes, quickly changing into the soft fabric.

Once in bed, Flowridia stared silently at the ceiling. Demitri snoozed on the floor, but his gentle breathing did nothing to soothe her. She clung to Ana, the affectionate little skeleton content in her arms.

The reality of her quest and intentions slowly settled like a shadow over her heart.

If she rolled over, she might see Ayla, silent as a shadow as she placed a rose on her table. If she shut her eyes, she might feel cold hands run against her skin. The window stood open; Flowridia longed to see that lithe silhouette, illuminated by moonlight.

Try as she might, though she had embraced her dreams, the nightly presence of her love, they were elusive and frustrating more often than not, leaving her frozen half to death with the memory of a ghostly touch on her lips.

Loneliness seeped into her heart. "Demitri," she whispered, and in the faint light she saw a golden eye open. She sat up. "Would you like to try sleeping in my bed?" Desperation bled into her words, and though she cringed, to deny it would mean to lie.

Demitri stood and placed his head on the side of her bed, illustrating to both the problem of his size. *What's wrong?*

Flowridia's hands came to rest in her lap. "You're wonderful company, but . . ." She shut her eyes. "It's difficult to be here. More than I could have imagined."

A large paw settled on her leg. *You miss Ayla.*

"So much, yes. But it's more than that." She thought of Thalmus and his silent dismissal; she thought of Etolié and her blind trust. "You've grown too big for this room, Demitri. And I think I may have too."

Do you think you might stay in Nox'Kartha?

"I don't belong here," she whispered, and she let her head fall into her hands. "In Nox'Kartha, I would be able to fully grasp my talents. But that still isn't what I want." Her entire body grew lax as she released a defeated sigh. "I have no goals, save Ayla's return."

The bed creaked as Demitri's paw pushed against it. Another paw appeared next to the first, and suddenly a mass of dire wolf hoisted itself onto the bed. Flowridia grabbed Ana and rolled over to make room, even as the wood groaned and sagged. He curled up beside her, as well as he could. *Once she's back, you can decide where to go.*

"I certainly can't bring her here." She pressed her body against his warm, thick musculature. "But I don't think I can bring her to Nox'Kartha either–"

With a crack, the bed collapsed. The center hit the floor with a splintered crack. Yelping, Flowridia clung to Demitri. Her eyes snapped open. "Are you all right?" The mattress remained intact, but it dipped.

Perfectly fine. He stood, Flowridia moving with him. Beside her, Ana shook, bones clattering as she righted herself. *But it seems I'm too big for the bed.*

Flowridia quirked a smile, despite her racing heart. "Now you're too big?"

I'm offended at your wording. Too big for the bed, yes. Not too big. Never too big.

"Let's find somewhere else to sleep, then."

I will accept the floor, wherever that may be.

The library seemed the best option, but Etolié was more emotionally draining than she could handle. Truthfully, she could go to any available guest bed, though she sincerely doubted whether any remained unoccupied.

Save one. And it might be the one place in the manor where she felt truly safe. "Would you be angry if I asked to sleep in Casvir's room?"

She didn't have to see his sneer to hear it. *I'll join you tonight. I may find somewhere else if this continues.*

"I'm sure we could find you somewhere." When she opened the door, Ana skittered out, nearly bumping into the far wall before veering dangerously and arcing to reappear at Flowridia's feet.

As she took steps down the hall, she cringed at the thought of Casvir's judgment. Would he think her codependent? Unable to spent a night away from familiarity?

Yet, had he ever judged her before? If she kept quiet, she would be met with indifference, and indifference still meant sleep.

Passing the enormous golden arch of Murishani's tent brought some amusement, but she continued on without investigating. At Casvir's door, she knocked quietly before peeking her head inside.

Casvir sat, as expected, at his desk. His eyes narrowed when he looked up, though not from any apparent anger. "Good evening, Flowridia," he said, a question in his tone.

She opened the door further, revealing her bedclothes and Demitri's disapproving stare. Ana skittered around her feet. "This won't help the rumors," Flowridia said curtly, matching his eyes without fear, "but I know you won't be using that bed. Can I sleep in here?"

"Yes."

Wordlessly, she went to the untouched bed, helping Ana leap up beside her. Demitri curled on the floor, and she gave him an affectionate pat on the head before lying down and pulling Ana into her arms. Once settled, only her head peeked out from the blankets. "Demitri broke my bed," she whispered, and she smiled at Casvir's quick scoff of a laugh.

The light dimmed. Finding comfort in Casvir's familiar presence, she drifted into a light sleep.

# Chapter 3

In the early morning, Flowridia stood before an armored, demonic attacker.

Once, on a day that lived in vibrant, gory detail behind her eyelids, Flowridia had lost a precious gift to the God of Order's power—a spear of infinite worth, hand-carved by a man she adored.

She missed it. Instead, she sparred with a discarded spear from the Staelashian armory.

Casvir was relentless, despite the frosty, biting chill. "Back in your stance."

Any hope Flowridia held of impressing anyone with her spear had long ago escaped, like the strands springing from the unruly tail of hair behind her head. Now, she hoped only to survive—

Pain suddenly radiated from her calf. Her grip on her spear tightened as she stumbled.

"You still put too much weight on your right side," Casvir said, and then he lunged. He came at half speed, if not slower. She knew this. Casvir's size did nothing to hinder his speed. Still, she barely managed to parry. She lunged in return, and he swatted her again. Same side; same calf. Brilliant red blossomed along the tender skin.

Cold stunted her motions. Sunlight barely glinted across the landscape. "You have a talent for making me regret every decision I've ever made," she whined, and another whack against her leg caused her to yelp.

Casvir stopped, passively studying her trembling figure. "Should we be done for the morning?"

She managed to nod, putting her weight against her spear. With her eyes shut, she released a breath, and with it came the steady release of healing magic, immediately soothing her brutalized calf.

Her eyes shot open when a weight landed on her head. Casvir's hand lightly ruffled her sweat-soaked hair, a bemused expression on his features. "If you were as useless with magic as you were with weapons, I would not have taken an interest in fostering your talents," he said softly. Glancing above her head, he continued. "You are being watched."

She followed his gaze; at the sidelines, Thalmus watched, too far away for her to see what sort of expression rested on his face. "Thank you," she said, smiling briefly at Casvir. She nervously walked toward her audience, using the spear to support her tired body.

As she approached, she saw a worried smile spread across Thalmus' face. "You look like you took a beating to your leg."

"I already healed it. I'm simply exhausted. And sweaty."

With some hesitation, he looked back to Casvir. Flowridia followed his gaze and saw that the imperator had begun practicing his own stances, his movements perfect, fluid, precise. "Where is Demitri this morning?"

"Still asleep, silly thing. I told him to keep watch of . . ." She let the words trail off, hiding the rest behind a forced smile. To mention Ana would be too much.

If he noticed the slip, Thalmus hid it well. "I've missed your company," he said kindly, placing a hand on her shoulder. "Will you come eat breakfast with me?"

Flowridia leaned into the touch, realizing how desperately she craved affirmation of his affection. She nodded and followed by his side, letting her arm rise to settle at the small of his back. "How was the sunrise this morning?" she asked sincerely.

"Perfect," he replied. "But marred by Murishani's tents."

Flowridia followed the half-giant's gaze and saw an enormous, decorated tent obscuring the horizon. "Is it permanent?"

"I don't know. I told Marielle to ask more questions, but she seems to trust Murishani."

"That's a mistake," Flowridia mused, and Thalmus nodded in response.

De'Sindai servants bustled about at the early hour, carrying a legion of trays to an array of tables, no doubt preparing breakfast for the Nox'Karthan guests and residents of Staelash. But Thalmus led her to the manor, for which Flowridia was grateful. They walked the familiar path to the kitchen. "I know little about him, but he seems to know an awful lot about us."

"He's under threat of death to never speak to me," Flowridia admitted. "Casvir doesn't trust him."

"Something he and I might agree on."

Thalmus said nothing else, not until they reached the private kitchen. Flowridia instinctively moved about to prepare food, but Thalmus shook his head. He gestured to the table, where she saw a small cake.

Astonished at the sight, she placed the spear against the table and joined Thalmus when he sat. "What is this?"

"The joy of your return has been lost by the celebrations. I wanted to make sure you knew you weren't forgotten." His smile was unbearably kind, the aging lines of his weathered face deeper than they were in her memory. He was far from elderly, but hints of silver streaked his onyx hair, braided and falling to his belt.

As she cut herself a slice, she watched his gaze flicker to the spear. Guilt filled her, knowing what he must have thought. "I need to confess something," she said as she placed her piece upon her plate. "Your spear . . . It was ruined when Casvir and I confronted the God of Order in Verity Forest." She still recalled the charred remains she had been handed, remembered her tears when she'd run her hand across the delicate remains of the carvings. "I'm sorry."

"Did it help you?"

No, but she couldn't admit that. It had been strapped to the horses, useless as the battle had waged. "It saved my life," she lied, the words as easy as the smile on her face.

"Then it served its purpose." His expression held nothing but sincerity; relief washed over her like a cold bath. She took a bite of the cake, the taste sweet but not too much so—as she preferred. "I can't say I was pleased to watch you fight Imperator Casvir," Thalmus continued. "He clearly thinks very highly of you. High enough to expect you to parry within six months of learning how to even hold a spear."

"Less than that," Flowridia admitted, but she stiffened nonetheless. "He's more patient than you think."

"Would he come to your defense the way you come to his?"

"If I deserved it, yes."

Thalmus said nothing, only cut a slice for himself. But his bristling mood was palpable.

"Thalmus," she began, more aggressive than she felt, "what are you thinking?"

His attention remained on the cake. "You would prefer to not know."

"I think you're trying to protect me," Flowridia said, the biting words escaping before she could stop them. "Though I think I already know what you're protecting me from. Say it, please."

He placed the slice on his plate, miniscule crumbs collecting beneath it. "I remember the first time I saw you," he said, something wistful in his countenance. "I've never forgotten the image of that little girl dressed in rags, who cradled a wolf pup like he was her only lifeline. But even though you were afraid, I saw light. I saw a little girl who had been through hell and still managed to see hope. I found that inspiring. *You* inspired me."

It wasn't the speech she expected. She watched, searching for any explanation in his tired features.

"You are older than I think, and it's my fault for holding that against you. I am younger than I feel. But it doesn't change that I despise how he watches you, how he's changed you."

There could be only one 'he.'

"I hated Ayla because she hurt you," Thalmus continued, the soft rumbling of his voice juxtaposing the anger in his words, "but at least, in her twisted mind, she wanted you as you were. I hate him because he's molded you into something else–" Thalmus' fist clenched, then. His voice shook, and Flowridia shied at his efforts to steady it. "Necromancy is evil, Flowra, and despite whatever words he's twisted to convince you otherwise, Imperator Casvir is evil–"

"You don't know him," Flowridia said, angry tears welling in her eyes.

"*Everyone* knows him. Study his history, Flowra. The kingdoms he's leveled and the monarchs he's burned to instill fear into his citizens are documented in every history book, and the magic he utilizes spits in the face of everything good and right in the world. For him to take you, someone gentle and good, and twist you into a pawn–"

"That's not what happened!" Flowridia steadied her tears, swallowing back the horrid lump in her throat. "I'm good at necromancy—better than good. In six months, I've accomplished what takes most years to achieve. And I've used it for *good*, Thalmus. I've saved lives. I fought off the God of Order. Skeletons raised from the dead are one thing, but imagine if I could restore life entirely. It's within my grasp. Why should I not pursue it?"

"What's the cost? Is it damnation to yourself and those you claim to save?"

"Do you understand what I'm doing? Yes, it's a responsibility, but I can handle it. You know I'm capable."

But Thalmus shook his head, his mouth trembling as he fought to control his voice. "When you left here, you were gentle. You were meek. What happened to my little flower girl?"

"She grew up," Flowridia whispered, the words lacerating her heart. She stood from her seat. "Thank you for the cake. But I think I need to be alone for a while."

Thalmus followed and reached toward her. "Flowra–"

"You're not my father, Thalmus," Flowridia said, her words trembling, eyes misting. "I think sometimes you forget that."

Visibly crestfallen, Thalmus let his hand drop. Flowridia slammed the door behind her.

In the late morning, guests began arriving. Etolié hadn't slept, but that was nothing new. Instead, she'd spoken to Khastra until the sun had risen, finding it a much better use of her time, anyway.

"Time to smile and wave," she mumbled to the only sane person in the room.

Beside her, standing as straight as a rod while her hands fidgeted behind her back, Sora Fireborn gave a quick nod. The long ropes of her stark blonde hair were neatly plaited into an impressively massive bun atop her head. The half-elf wore a tabard bearing Sol Kareena's sigil, but beneath it were breeches and a pressed tunic more suited to her outdoor tastes. Upon her shoulder, the little bird looked as uncomfortable as she did. "And hide our knives behind our backs, yes?"

Etolié grinned, her oft-quoted advice apparently well-received. The guards moved to open the doors to the small throne room, and she slipped a flask into the half-elf's twitching hand.

Sora turned away from the guests, indulgently gulping the offered liquid courage. "Bless you," she said, handing it back. "I'll be smoking a pipe after all this. Feel free to join me."

The mass of people entered, and Etolié's gut squirmed.

Marielle practically glowed as she stood before her throne, graciously accepting gifts from the endless line of well-wishers. Zorlaeus looked faint, but he did manage to smile. Meanwhile, Etolié and Sora greeted them after, thanking them for coming, asking about their children, complimenting their shoes, and so on . . .

Mostly Solviran nobles, but Nox'Kartha had invited nearly everyone in the realms, it seemed. The princess from Tholheim gifted a pair of ornate shoes, crafted from gold and spider silk—over which Marielle positively gushed, as she should because they were pretty fucking neat—and even the Iron Elves, some of the most standoffish people in the realms, sent an ambassador and a gold-plated firearm.

Most exchanged pleasantries, and Etolié responded to them all:

"All the way from Zauleen? It's a delight to have you join us."

"Why, yes, my hair is naturally silver. No illusions here."

"My mother is doing well. I took a trip to see her not a week ago—she's absolutely delighted by this union, of course!"

Sora side-eyed her for that last one. "Did you really visit Celestière last week?"

Subduing her momentary panic at being caught in a blatant lie, Etolié shook her head, grinning pleasantly to an approaching Tholheimr noble. "No," she said behind smiling teeth, "but sometimes I lie about shit mom says."

"Why?"

Nosey Sora, asking more questions. "People thought my momma was dead for a thousand years. I'm doing what I can to dispel that."

No, she hadn't visited home in a long time.

Gold and clothing and inventions, invitations, promises of land—all of it piled behind the meager Staelashian throne. When the Theocracy of Sol Kareena stepped through the doors, Etolié was surprised to see both the Archbishop and High Priestess Lunestra—with the orb on its staff, no less—and hoped, however irrationally, that might be their gift.

Alas, they gave a priceless pendant instead. "Always an honor to meet with you, Magister Etolié," Archbishop Xoran said. Etolié knew a dismissal when she heard it and smiled nonetheless. Perhaps she'd annoyed him, constantly peppering him with queries about the orb.

Seventeen dissertations didn't generally endear you to a person.

But to Sora, he added, "You are welcome in our fair kingdom anytime. I would love nothing more than to meet with the champion of the goddess herself."

Etolié swore Sora blushed, but to her credit, she kept it together. "When the excitement from the wedding has died down, I will certainly make it a priority to visit."

Lunestra gave similar well-wishes as her brother, half-dismissing Etolié but greeting Sora as an old friend. The two women bore hair of similar styles and texture, and Etolié wondered if Sora's human progenitor were also from the City of Light. "The children of the cathedral still speak of you and your resurrection."

Cute, thought Etolié. When they'd left, she whispered, "I'm sending you to negotiate next time."

"I'd be terrible, and you know it."

Etolié shrugged and shook the hand of some nice duke from Solvira.

Nox'Kartha was not the last in line, but they were certainly a few hours in. Etolié wanted a glass of water and perhaps a hot bath, but there came Murishani and Casvir . . . and Flowers?

And Khastra.

Imperator Casvir said nothing during Murishani's flowery speech about love and beauty and whatever other bullshit his mouth spewed. Khastra had never liked him during her time as general in Staelash, and while the half-demon was a far more judgmental bitch than Etolié would ever tell anyone, her opinions were never grounded in pettiness.

So when Murishani greeted her with advances far too flirtatious to be sincere—*"Your beauty out-matches the stars themselves, Magister Etolié!"*—she let him kiss her hand and swallowed the weird pit in her stomach that formed any time her beauty was acknowledged.

She nearly missed Flowers' speech and gift—a crown of flowers she claimed would never die, that predictable little sap—but shook her hand nonetheless. "Didn't know you were sniffing around with Nox'Kartha, now," Etolié said, cringing at how petulant she sounded.

But Flowers' response was sincere. "I've been listed as a guest and will be seated with them. I'll play the part."

The kid had learned.

When Flowers stepped away, she hesitated in front of Sora, and Etolié could have cut the tension with a knife and used the pieces to stab it again. "Sora, I . . ." She offered a hand, visibly mulling over what to say.

But Sora picked up the phrase as she accepted her hand. "Bygones are just that." She smiled at Demitri and the little skeletal fox peeking out from Flowers' bag. "You're different."

"I am," Flowers affirmed, and Etolié could have told you that, but she got the impression something monumental was happening, and so she withheld her snark.

Casvir gave a nod to both of them—which Etolié, of course, dramatically returned, much too distracted by the sight of Marielle weeping in Khastra's embrace to be offended at the dismissal.

"You must never die again, you hear?" she cried, and Etolié rolled her eyes, annoyance prickling at her skin. The embrace had gone overlong.

"Doing my best," Khastra said simply, and when Marielle pulled away, she politely patted the queen's head.

Etolié quickly offered a hand. "You waited hours with *that* crowd?" she whispered, tilting her head toward the Nox'Karthan rulers, plus Flowers. "By Eionei's Asshole, you're more patient than me."

"Tiny one and I discussed tactics for her to practice with her spear." Khastra's hand was warm, but Etolié's blood chilled. "The time passed quickly enough."

"Oh, well," Etolié said, pulling her hand back. "Of course. Talk with your best friend Flowers over there. Makes sense."

And there it was again, that horrible choking sensation in her stomach.

Khastra smiled, but it lacked the general sincerity of her other smiles. Etolié clenched her fists as Khastra faced Sora—because, well, there Etolié went being a bitch again.

Sora's countenance held warmth, and somehow that surprised Etolié. "Sol Kareena has not forgotten your sacrifice. Her people are indebted to you."

Khastra's smile showed the laughter lines at her eyes. Etolié might have returned the gesture, but it was for Sora and not for her. "It was as glorious a death as I could have hoped for."

When Khastra shook her hand, Sora said, "It's so wonderful to see you again."

Diplomacy at its finest. When Khastra left, Etolié whispered, "Does Sol Kareena truly think well of Khastra? I know Khastra died to protect her people, but she's not really keen on the whole . . . undead thing."

"Sol Kareena condemns those who practice necromancy, but not those subjected to it. Khastra can't help what she is, only what she does with her free will."

"I wish Eionei thought the same," Etolié replied, and immediately regretted it because she'd buried those feelings pretty fucking deep.

Sora side-eyed her for that. "Eionei doesn't have a stance on necromancy, I thought."

They paused to shake hands with a baron in the Nox'Karthan outskirts, smiling and complimenting his wig, then Etolié whispered, "When they're mindless undead, he doesn't care, but he views necromancy as a form of slavery, if their mind is intact." She looked to Khastra, watched her laugh at whatever charming statement her flowery ward said, as the stark reality of her friend's new life settled in her mind. "And I suppose I feel the same."

Etolié complimented some De'Sindai noble—she had forgotten to pay attention—then added, "But grandpa doesn't have many nice things to say about demons, and Khastra's demon enough. He's made his opinion on our friendship well known. Many times."

"Sol Kareena accepts all, including demons themselves, if they'll accept her," Sora replied, following

Etolié's line of sight. "With respect to Eionei, I can't say I agree with his stance."

Etolié returned her attention to the guests, forcing her smile as usual.

Finally, and thank every god for it, Empress Alauriel appeared, along with a portion of her royal court. She stood with a man Etolié knew well—the magister of the court, Reginal, an ancient man who dressed with all the colorful insanity of an eccentric, Celestial sorcerer—and a woman Etolié knew in passing—the slightly less ancient High Priestess Jules, envoy to Sol Kareena, as well as a few other Solviran lords and ladies Etolié couldn't say she was familiar with.

After Lara greeted the queen, Etolié hugged her baby empress, propriety be damned. "Gods, I'm not drunk enough," she whispered.

"Neither am I," Lara whispered back. "Has Khastra arrived?"

They'd not seen each other since Khastra's untimely death, Etolié realized. "She's somewhere with Nox'Kartha. Look for Flowers."

Lara's hands quite suddenly began sweating. "I'd forgotten she would be here, too."

Etolié chose to withhold any and all comments on the matter, given that she and the empress had already had a few too many conversations on this cesspool of emotion. "Come find me in the library after this," she said simply.

She shook hands with Reginal, accepted his embrace when he offered one even though she forcibly fought to not stiffen. She liked the man; he just . . . itched. "What, no General Irons?"

Reginal shook his head. "He didn't care for the guest list."

Pretentious, stuffy paladins.

"Have you met my husband, Eirlyn?"

Etolié hadn't, and she politely shook his hand. Though he bore the same dark coloring as his spouse, Eirlyn's manner of dress was significantly more subdued.

Jules embraced her next, the Celestial woman beautiful in her matronly age. "Etolié, you look well. Lara has been worried sick about you."

Great. People talked. "Nothing worrying here."

The line didn't end until well after lunch, and Etolié's sobriety headache pounded. The last guest left; Etolié plopped down on the floor and immediately began drinking.

Sora sat beside her. "And we get to do it all again tonight, at the ball."

Etolié kept drinking.

Murishani reappeared, buzzing about like a particularly annoying bee before whisking Marielle away, prattling on about flowers and shoes. Zorlaeus' sigh as he watched them go was a little bit pathetic.

"Join me outside?" Sora said, and Etolié tossed her flask back into its pocket.

She was supposed to meet Lara, but what was five minutes? "For a little while." As she sat up, her moral center began tingling. "Lae . . . *us*. Zorlaeus, hi." The groom-to-be perked up. "Sora and I are gonna go outside and smoke contraband. Want to join?"

"Sure?"

The trio ended up at the side of the manor, largely hidden from spectators and guests. A pipe passed between them, one carved from burnt wood and etched with elven characters. It wasn't Spore this time, but something woodsy and pleasant.

"I hate people," she said simply.

Zorlaeus was no stranger to pipes, to Etolié's surprise. The boy smoked like it was second nature. "I don't disagree."

"I generally like them," Sora replied, occasionally pressing closer to the wall to avoid being spotted. She'd stop caring for her reputation soon enough, Etolié figured. "But I can't say I like these ones."

Etolié chuckled darkly. "You were never this friendly when you worked for Meira, no offense."

"Crippling self-confidence issues will do that. But now I can't hide in her shadow."

At least she was honest. "I respect that, though my confidence is obviously through the roof."

"Well, being half of something makes you a pariah of both," Sora said, then she offered the pipe again, the saccharine smoke wafting in a steady stream. "Though it seems you didn't have that problem."

"Angels have their issues, but racism toward little Celestials isn't one of them."

Sora glanced to Zorlaeus, offering him the pipe. "What about you . . . Lae Lae?"

"Don't call him that," Etolié said.

"Sorry. My question stands."

"My father was a former slave, rescued by one of Etolié's parties," he said, and Etolié felt mighty self-conscious at that, blushing unbidden. "But I grew up in Nox'Kartha, so I can't say I've personally experienced racism." He handed the pipe to Etolié, who savored the sweet smell.

"My extended relatives were mostly assholes," Sora replied, "but my parents were always kind to me. My father was my biggest supporter."

"Cute," Etolié said, her bitterness quite apparent, "but can't relate. The botched abortion known as my father wasn't exactly an inspiration when it came to parental things." When they said nothing, Etolié spared them a glance, realizing her companions stared in abject horror. "What?"

"That was a very aggressive statement," Sora replied, and that's when Etolié realized she was being judged.

"Listen. Not all of us had charmed childhoods."

"It can't have been that bad . . ."

Sora's voice trailed off, perhaps in response to what Etolié hoped was a boiling glare. Etolié, who'd been a simmering pot for days, occasionally spewing words she shouldn't, nearly blew her top. She exhaled a steadying breath, her stomach suddenly tight.

"I'm sure your father tried–"

"Sora, I like you, but shut the hell up."

When she offered the pipe, Sora accepted, but Etolié couldn't look at her, instead hearing something contrite in the half-elf's words. "I'm sorry."

"It's fine. He's dead anyway—I made a few extra stab wounds to make sure."

The half-elf, who stood easily at eye level with Etolié, looked like she'd forgotten to breathe. Etolié smiled and winked, the sort that hopefully suggested she was joking, because that was how normal people made friends—by joking about hilarious things like patricide.

Zorlaeus gave the most obvious segue cough Etolié had ever heard. "My parents and I also had a few disagreements over the years," he offered. Etolié was prepared to metaphorically bitch-slap him when he added, "We're civil now, but we've essentially cut ties. They won't be at the wedding."

Though she was curious, to pry would've been rude. Instead, Etolié gave Zorlaeus a conciliatory ruffle on his fluffy maroon hair, mindful of his horns.

"My parents are both dead?" Sora offered, and Etolié felt the icy mood between them fade.

"Who needs parents," Etolié said, and they all nervously laughed, because, well, otherwise they'd be a crying heap.

They said little else, and she left with only a quick farewell.

Lara waited, as expected, in the library.

Solviran royals wore finery cut for angel wings in homage of their grand heritage, and Lara's was the grandest of all. From her gold-laden pauldrons to the draped fabric revealing the bare skin of her back, she was an empress in appearance, yet her stance betrayed her nerves. When she peered behind her shoulder at Etolié's approach, the gentle turn of her lip revealed a frown.

She shook her head, her braided hair twisting with it. "I am a fool, Etolié. I'm a coward and a fool."

"You're the empress of the fucking world—you can be anything you want to be." Etolié smiled and hoped it was reassuring. She offered a flask, but Lara waved it away. "Talk to her. She'll be at the ball tonight, and if you ask me nicely, I'll pull her out of Casvir's shadow so she's easy prey."

"She's practically a child."

"Not even," Etolié replied, harsher than she meant. But she'd heard this all before, and Lara would say anything she could to talk herself out of this. "Not in age, or experience. Talk to her."

"And then she'll think I'm a fool as well."

"No, she'll think you're the slightly intoxicated Empress of Solvira—forgive me, but I know you."

Lara looked near tears, so Etolié beckoned for her to follow, to be seated in the nest of scarves beneath the skylight. When Lara sat, Etolié began pushing and piling the blankets around her. "Be cozy. This is a safe space." A watery sheen filled Lara's silver eyes. "What's this actually about?"

Silly Etolié, asking questions she already knew the answer to. Lara knew as well. "Nothing we haven't talked about before." She shut her eyes. "I have a duty to my people, Etolié. As the last of my line, I *must* bear a child—"

"Lara . . ." Etolié knelt beside her, remembering all those months ago after Marielle's ball, the tearful confession and her own words of comfort: *"Yes, she is of age, no, you aren't broken, your father would not have hated you, no . . ."*

Alauriel Solviraes, bereaved and having only just lost her father not days earlier, was not in an emotional state to face a crisis of sexuality. Etolié had told her such.

"She'll still be here, and if not her then someone else . . ."

And then, of course, a certain vampire bitch had mucked a few things up.

"I like men, Etolié. I've been with men, and I've fallen for men. Someday I shall marry, and it shall be to—"

"Lara, first of all, you're the gods-damned empress of the world. You can do anything you want. You can pursue a man, you can pursue *her,* or anyone. But don't talk yourself out of this because you're afraid." Then, Etolié lost any and all semblance of pandering. "Second, need I remind you, spawn of the moon and stars, that your entire kingdom exists because my romantic of a mother married Neoma and popped out the half-sister-we-do-not-name?"

"Etolié, it's a story—"

"Excuse you, Alauriel Solviraes, blood of Neoma, but Staella is very much alive and real."

Lara pursed her lips as she glared. "They were gods. For the rest of us, babies don't—"

"My *point,*" Etolié said, "is that there's a pretty strong precedent of lady-loving ladies in your kingdom, so be kind to yourself. They call them 'Daughters of Neoma' for a reason—because your literal ancestor goddess had a reputation."

A reputation for loving women and for being a total bitch, but Etolié wasn't one to focus on details.

Half-buried in blankets, Lara clutched the ones in reach with her small, dainty hands. "I was drawn to her the moment I saw her in the garden," she whispered, and these weren't words Etolié had heard said aloud before, "though I didn't recognize the feeling for what it was. It only continued to grow. It's at least a little bit your fault." Confused, Etolié watched her fight a smile. "I didn't expect to see her naked at the ball."

"She wasn't naked—"

Had the skylight shattered above them, it might have illustrated Etolié's sudden and exquisitely horrible realization. "She borrowed my dress."

"Your dresses aren't real, Etolié."

"So you *do* willfully disbelieve my illusions." Etolié came closer but simultaneously held up a blanket to cover her naughty bits. "You waited twenty-three years to tell me—"

"Etolié, I've been seeing you naked since birth. It isn't weird to me."

"Fuck my life, moonbeam—"

Of course, that was when a knock on the bookshelf signified company.

They both looked up, surprised to see Murishani smiling brightly as he peeked around a shelf. "I do hope I'm not interrupting." He stepped forward, looking around at the hexagonal arrangement of shelves, the treasures hiding in her trove. "This is spectacular," he said, awestruck. "You maintain this?"

Etolié nodded. "I spend all my time here. Work here, sleep here, forget to eat here. This is my life."

"Then I apologize again," Murishani said, chuckling as he placed a hand on his chest. "It's rude to intrude uninvited upon a lady's bedroom."

"People do it all the time."

He swept into a low bow, his robes luxuriously billowing around his figure. "Empress Alauriel, it's always an honor to share your presence. I hope you wouldn't mind if I stole Staelash's Magister?" He looked to Etolié now. "If you could spare a moment, magister, to go over a few last minute logistics of the ball tonight—table arrangements, and such—I don't want to bother our sweet bride-to-be more than I have to."

As Etolié stood up to follow him, she flashed a reassuring smile to Lara. "The worst that can happen is you'll know it's a no," she said, hoping it were cryptic enough for a certain viceroy to mind his own business. "At best, who knows?"

Etolié followed Murishani, bracing herself as he babbled on about decorations and guests and party favors. Back to the real world.

Flowridia avoided the other guests, most especially a certain Theocracy High Priestess she'd been rude to in the woods.

She spent most of the day tending her garden, grateful for the solitude and peace the wards offered amidst the outside cacophony. Rather than exhaust her limited energy for social gatherings by greeting everyone as they came, Flowridia stayed with Demitri and Ana instead.

That evening, she dressed in her old bedroom, one of Ayla's gifted dresses donning her form. Black lace, modest but attractive, and with a neckline that revealed only collar bones, it was a perfect match to the large moon lily in her hair. Flowridia primped and preened in the mirror, ignoring the little fox running at her feet, content to waste as much time as possible. If she arrived late, no one would notice her entrance. She would stand beside Casvir and be ignored all night.

She attended as a guest and had no duty other than to smile and show up.

Demitri watched from behind her shoulder. *You're pretty. Stop worrying.*

"I'm not worrying."

Demitri's tongue suddenly licked a line from her chin to her hair. Flowridia cringed and immediately ran to the ruined bed to wipe it clean with a blanket. *Still pretty.*

"You're so thoughtful," she said, sardonic as she wiped away the sticky kiss. "Are you coming tonight?"

I would get squished and die.

Flowridia raised an eyebrow at that. "Seriously?"

I will use that excuse forever and ever.

"Watch Ana, then. She would actually get squished and die."

You wound me.

Flowridia wondered what she'd done to be cursed with so petulant a familiar. Still, perhaps there was a use for him; from her bodice, she withdrew the ear, the cord it was attached to quite visible. "Will you take care of this for me?"

I have to nanny Ana and Lady Ayla?

He took the chain in his mouth, all the same. "I don't anticipate being out late," she said, and she placed a kiss on his furry cheek.

For all of Ayla's faults, she had delivered on one promise—the dress was easily long enough to hide her bare feet. Comfortable against the carpeted floor, Flowridia quickly descended the stairs and entered the ballroom.

The déjà vu struck her hard, that of the ballroom strung with lights, filled to near capacity with ambassadors and royalty. Most were those of human and angelic descent, but enough of Murishani's De'Sindai were scattered about to cast a presence. Dwarves as well, and even a few elves.

Alone and overwhelmed, Flowridia knew familiar faces had to be among the crowd, but she saw no one. She backed toward a wall, inhaling deep to let her senses prickle out, faintly touching upon any dead energy, any sort of void of life in the room.

She felt undeath radiating from the alcohol, and when she dared dive back into the crowd, Flowridia found Casvir standing by the barrels of ale. To her surprise, his claws wrapped around a large tankard, one he sipped in slow, steady measures. He radiated an aura of disdain, but Flowridia watched a moment as braver fools would come to introduce themselves. Casvir would nod, perhaps mumble a greeting, but his arrogance shone in his sneer. The imperator was below no man and treated all as such.

When she slid up beside him, he nodded in acknowledgement before taking a small sip of whatever liquid swirled in his tankard. "Enjoying the festivity?" he asked.

"Not particularly."

She saw his lip twitch, perhaps in approval.

"Do you need to be drunk to tolerate parties?"

"I have never been drunk."

Flowridia crossed her arms and stared into the crowd, joining Casvir in people-watching. "Then what are you drinking?"

"A specialty of Nox'Kartha, from my personal stores. I believe you were first exposed when Ayla stole the flask from my belt."

She did recall, because any drink strong enough to down Etolié would surely wake even the dead.

"But only enough to remove the stress from social affairs. To over-indulge is weakness."

"Ayla warned me against trying it."

Casvir set his tankard down, staring at Flowridia fully now. "Uncharacteristically wise of her."

In the crowd, Flowridia spotted Etolié's ethereal form, glittering amidst the nobles. Her silver hair, done up in a bun, sparkled in the light as she turned toward Flowridia and waved. To her surprise, the tall Celestial wove through the sea of people, toward her and Casvir.

"Etolié's coming," Flowridia said, and then she realized the Celestial hadn't come alone.

She shouldn't have been surprised, given the motherly role Etolié had played in the empress' life, but Empress Alauriel Solviraes followed, her hair braided back with jewels. Luxurious waves made up her purple dress, the open back held together by decorative, golden chains. Feathered pauldrons covered her shoulders, and a small crown sat perfectly centered upon her head. Every part the empress, and with her soft silver eyes she surveyed the scene and smiled.

Flowridia struggled to smile back. Everything she would say now would be lies and subterfuge.

Etolié offered a curtsy to the imperator but addressed Flowridia. "Have you seen the Solviran envoy?"

Flowridia had not and shook her head.

Unlike the rest of the guests, Lara did not bow to Casvir, but she did nod in deference. "Imperator Casvir, it's always a pleasure when you make a rare appearance."

Casvir bowed.

Flowridia prayed her shock did not appear too brightly on her face, because Casvir went down to one knee and bowed before Empress Alauriel.

Flowridia realized that Etolié had zero reservation about hiding her surprise as she pulled a flask from the air, perhaps not drunk enough to decipher what cryptic message this wrote.

The guests nearest the void that was Casvir and his aura reacted the same—Casvir bowed to no one, yet he had fallen to one knee, managing for even his horns to fall beneath Lara's diminutive stature.

Lara, however, stood tall, the mysteries of politics perhaps not so mysterious to her. Casvir stood and said,

"Empress Alauriel, no one shows you the respect you deserve."

Flowridia's eyes darted between Lara and Casvir, grateful no attention had been drawn to herself.

"Your compliment is well-received," Lara said sincerely. "I wished to thank you for the kindness you've shown my cousin. Your funds pay for a wedding that promises to be breathtaking, and I know she is grateful. She and Zorlaeus are a joyous couple, and while Viceroy Murishani receives the praise, your role cannot be overlooked."

"You are welcome."

Lara smiled, and with a nod she turned to Flowridia. "It's wonderful to see you again, Lady Flowridia."

She did not offer a hand, which was just as well; Flowridia feared that to touch her would mean to transfer the deepest, darkest thoughts in her mind. "Likewise," she said simply, but then realized it was terribly rude to slight someone Imperator Casvir had bowed to.

So Flowridia, panicking, bowed as well. When she looked back up, Lara had gone sheet-white.

Etolié was kind enough to interrupt the awkward exchange. "Drinks are on Eionei," Etolié said, and to Flowridia's horror, she winked at Casvir. "A wedding gift, you might say. But your brews have a reputation for waking the dead—are they enough to down a Solviraes?"

Utterly stoic, Casvir said, "Very little can defeat a Solviraes."

"I think that's a challenge." From the air, Etolié pulled a wineglass and wasted no time in filling it with the noxious Nox'Karthan brew. She handed the glass to Lara. "Sip slowly. I made a mistake once."

At Etolié's urging, Lara was dragged from Flowridia and Casvir's presence. Once gone, Flowridia whispered, "Casvir, you bowed."

"As I said, no one shows her proper respect."

"Casvir, I've never seen you bow, or even thought you capable."

"Empress Alauriel is above my station. Her lands and citizens outnumber mine." He took a sip of his tankard. "The Silver Fire is something I have studied relentlessly. To understand my enemy means to defeat it. Given preparation, her life would be forfeit to my might, but placed across each other in an arena, she might win." Another sip, and Flowridia saw his red eyes practically flash at the prospect of a true challenge. "I would never say that lightly."

Casvir had fallen to the might of the God of Order, who wielded two orbs at the time. "I've done some study as well," she said cryptically. "I know Solviraes blood is powerful."

"She is descended from two Goddesses, and what has resulted is a unique and potent bloodline."

Flowridia stared out at the crowd, daring to search for the soft-eyed empress. "Tell me what you know."

"The Silver Fire is the culmination of the power between the Stars and the Moon, giving the Solviraes the ability to absorb magic and blast it back tenfold. It manifests as a silver flame of pure, potent energy, granting them enormous feats of power, such as the ability to transport themselves and others across the planes. Some say it is the very essence of creation when mastered, but more often pure destruction."

"That's incredible," Flowridia whispered, but Casvir continued.

"To absorb magic is to understand it at a level that I can never fathom. You have finesse, as does she, but she also holds the reserve to wield it in masses that could level a kingdom. Consider that, the next time Etolié drags her around like a pet." He took another drink, and Flowridia wondered if it were capable of emptying. "*No one* shows her the respect she deserves."

Flowridia read magic and plucked on the individual strings threaded through the tapestry of the world. But Lara, it seemed, was capable of grabbing the entire mass and shaping it to her will. This was the woman whose throat she had to slit. "I . . . have somewhere I need to be."

Casvir nodded in acknowledgement.

Flowridia slipped into the crowd, her small stature useful in darting around chatting guests. From far away, she spotted Murishani lounging upon a luxurious couch, draped in men and women.

In the far corner, she saw representatives from the Theocracy sitting apart from the riotous Nox'Karthan attendees. Flowridia kept alert, realizing the archbishop himself might be present, which also meant—

"Flowridia!"

Flowridia turned, horrified to see High Priestess Lunestra rapidly approaching. Too late to run and feign oblivious, Flowridia simply accepted her offered hand. "High Priestess Lunestra?"

Never had she seen Lunestra wear finer robes—literal gold thread embroidered the sigil of Sol Kareena onto her tabard. From the dark hue of her skin to her graying hair, plaited into an ivory crown, she was perfection even in her elderly age. "It's wonderful to see you again," the priestess said, and Flowridia wondered if her sweetness could be genuine. Perhaps, with the woman's half-full wineglass, but sweetness could turn bitter in a turn of phrase.

Flowridia's heart raced as she struggled to respond. She managed a smile, one that grew desperately wide when she realized Sora stood beside her. "Oh, good. A witness." She paused, realizing she'd spoken aloud. "To our friendship," she added. "A witness to our friendship."

Lunestra laughed, and Flowridia had the sinking suspicion in her stomach that there was a cruel game afoot. "Yes, High Priestess Sora, be a witness to our friendship. The more who know, the merrier."

Sora stood stiffly, eyes darting back and forth between the pair. "I didn't realize you two were so close."

"We were able to find out much more about the other in the woods," Lunestra said, either oblivious or purposefully ignoring Flowridia's increasing discomfort. "I had hoped to see her here, safe and sound."

"Who's safe and sound?" Classy as ever, Etolié approached. With her, Lara looked a bit red in the cheeks, eyes unfocused as she swayed, clearly living in her own world. The wineglass filled with Nox'Karthan Ale was half empty. "High Priestess Lunestra, lovely to see you again."

"Likewise," Lunestra replied, but Flowridia sensed an odd tension between the pair. "As I was telling Sora, Flowridia and I met in the woods, a few months back. I was saying I'm happy to see her home safe."

Flowridia's blood pounded in her ears as Etolié responded. "Quite the coincidence, running into the other."

"Not at all. I sought her out." Lunestra smiled at Flowridia, and it was far too knowing, holding the barest hint of a threat. She held her gaze. "I simply wanted her to know that the negotiation is still on the table, should she wish to revisit it."

Flowridia thought of the ear upstairs, grateful she'd thought to leave it with Demitri. "Lunestra, I'm afraid it's already been taken care of. Though, I suppose it's hardly disappointing to say, given the goal was to have it destroyed." She looked to Etolié and Sora, refusing to allow Lunestra's simmering insinuations haunt her. "Lunestra was kind enough to track me down while I was on my adventure with Imperator Casvir, out of fear for my well-being. But she was also quite clear in her kingdom's continued interest in the ear of Ayla Darkleaf. Which has already been taken care of," she repeated, content to mirror Lunestra's deliberate smile.

She found she was entirely capable of doing so, recalling she and Lunestra held a direct blood relationship. Internally, she prayed Lunestra said nothing of offering the orb, lest she be forced to explain to Etolié that she'd turned down the offer of the very artifact her kingdom sought for the sake of something so silly as 'romance.'

"What did ever happen to that?"

Of course Etolié would ask. "Destroyed in Nox'Kartha," Flowridia replied, praying her lie was seamless, "per my request. As I said in the woods—" She looked to Lunestra, studied her polite demeanor. "—she was mine to do with as I wished, and I wished to give her a peaceful end."

Lunestra met her gaze with the slightest of nods, understanding in the gesture, and Flowridia realized better than she ever had the subtle nuances of politics, how a thousand different things could be conveyed in merely a glance.

"Cute," Etolié said, and Flowridia silently thanked every god for the segue. "Flowers, have you seen my favorite beefcake?"

Lunestra grinned at the pet name, clearly not understanding, but Flowridia replied with, "No, I haven't. Though I'd guess with Solvira—there doesn't seem to be a Nox'Karthan table."

Understanding dawned onto Lunestra's elegant features. "I would second what Lady Flowridia said—your friend, yes? I do believe I saw General Khastra conversing with Magister Reginal of Solvira."

Flowridia saw a dare in the high priestess' gaze, but not to her—to Etolié, who had visibly tensed. "Yes, she is my friend. I'm rather fond of her."

"I merely wondered where your loyalties lie. Friendship can be complicated, yes?" Lunestra winked at Flowridia, who suspected she'd stumbled into something well beyond her depth. "Especially so, when they cross political barriers."

Months ago, a rather unfortunate misunderstanding had been had regarding her own apparent 'friendship' with Ayla Darkleaf. "Depends on your definition of friendship," Flowridia said simply. "Though I think making assumptions can be dangerous territory. If you'll kindly excuse me—" She cut herself off, instead darting into the crowd.

A void of people surrounded Thalmus, perhaps because of his palpable discomfort. Flowridia longed to join him, but her heart still lay shattered from his words. His kindness would be an insult.

In the crowd, she could just see Marielle giggling among a crowd of Murishani's people, her blotchy cheeks suggesting she'd already drunk enough for one night. Zorlaeus stood beside her, visibly petrified as he sipped what Flowridia suspected was water.

Flowridia decided not to engage. Instead she heard uproarious laughter from the Solviran corner and spotted Khastra downing the Nox'Karthan Ale.

Slurred words spoke from behind. "Flowridia!"

Flowridia turned, surprised to see Lara behind her. When she swayed, Flowridia set a hand at her waist. "Hello, Empress," Flowridia said, realizing her dress opened deep enough at the back that she touched bare skin, soft and warm. Her hand fit perfectly at the dip of her waist. "Are you enjoying—"

Flowridia stiffened when she felt full lips against her cheek. "I love drinking with friends."

"Are you all right?"

Lara giggled, the glass in her hand swaying dangerously. "You're so pretty." Then, she cupped Flowridia's cheek with her hand, Nox'Karthan Ale strong on her breath as she said, "Is that why Casvir wants to fuck you?"

"Lara, that's not—"

"I'm sorry, I'm sorry . . ." Lara took a final sip from her wineglass, then tossed the partially full glass aside—it sparkled a moment before it vanished. "That was rude of me." She smiled, a girlish giggle on her tongue. "I missed you. How are you?"

"I'm happy to be home." Flowridia caught a glimpse of star-lit hair. "Etolié!"

The Celestial swayed as she appeared beside them.

"Etolié, Lara's delirious. I think it's the Nox'Karthan Ale."

Etolié opened her mouth, then shut it again, and the words from her lips held the barest hint of conspiracy. "Then she should probably get to bed before she embarrasses her kingdom. Would you mind? I have to babysit this party."

Lara giggled as she leaned against Flowridia. "I can," Flowridia said, then she gently took Lara's waist. With care, she took small steps, leading her through the crowd. "Come on, empress."

"You don't have to call me that," Lara mumbled, and her head fell against Flowridia's shoulder.

Fortunately, Lara stood shorter than her, and she could support her well enough. With her hands firmly around the empress' waist, Flowridia led Lara out the door and into the quiet hallway.

Two flights of stairs, down the hall, turn to the right, and there, she knew, were the Solviran guest suites. The stairs would be difficult.

Flowridia leaned down and set one hand at Lara's knees, attempting to scoop her into her arms . . . but nearly dropped her instead. The empress giggled. "Trying to get under my clothes?"

"Lara, wait here. I'll go find Thalmus. He can help you up the stairs."

"Why are we going upstairs?"

"We're taking you to bed."

The ground began glowing. Flowridia barely managed to say, "Lara, what—" before the world shifted. The hallway disappeared, replaced by Lara's guest suite. A large bed rested at the center, lit by stars gleaming through the window. Dizzy, Flowridia fell against the bedpost, steadying herself amidst Lara's continued laughter. "All right," she groaned. "That'll work."

Again, soft lips brushed her cheek. Flowridia pulled back. "You're so sweet," Lara cooed. "Please be sweet to me."

"Will you please lay down, Lara?" Flowridia said, firm in her words. "I'll help you take your shoes off—"

Lara fell onto the bed, dragging Flowridia with her. The empress lay on her back, still laughing to her heavily drunken self and smiling as she blushed. Flowridia sat up, grateful when Lara didn't follow. "Will you stay here if I leave? It's time for you to sleep now."

Lara gave a soft sigh, her eyes fluttering shut. "But I'm always alone."

In slow movements, Flowridia placed her hand on Lara's shoulder, endeared when the intoxicated woman held her hand. "I'll stay until you fall asleep."

In Lara's drunken state, Flowridia couldn't say whether or not the smile gracing her lips was genuine or not. Etolié often said that alcohol caused men's tongues to loosen, yes, but they never spoke lies.

The Solviran Empress had lost her father only seven months prior. Had she anyone else in her pristine palace?

Outside, the moon shone in a familiar grin, one that had haunted her for months. It beamed down upon her, upon Lara who still clung as tight as her drunken self could to Flowridia's hand. Descended of the moon and stars, wielding power unmatched, the Silver Fire gave her an understanding of magic beyond what anyone else could dream to attain, but Flowridia realized in that moment that Lara held a very exploitable weakness.

Casvir had said that on the battlefield, the empress might best him. But alone in bed, Lara held her hand and kissed her cheek.

"Lara?"

A gentle, "Hmm?" left the empress' lips.

Flowridia leaned in close and brushed aside errant strands of brunette hair from Lara's face, fingers trembling at the touch of her soft skin. Lara smiled to blind the moonlight. So easy it would be, to place kisses on her cheeks and those soft, flush lips, to steal her heart and . . .

Flowridia's very soul revolted at the wickedness of it. She pulled away, allowing the intoxicated empress to touch her hand and nothing more. She could not have left if she tried, for how light her head had become.

With evil thoughts prickling at her mind, ones that sickened her to her core, she waited until Lara's breathing grew steady and deep. Flowridia withdrew her hand, grateful when Lara gave no reaction. She stumbled from the room, fearful of the plot echoing in her head.

Down the stairs and through the hallway, Flowridia returned to the ballroom against her better judgment.

The doors opened before she could reach it, and out slinked Murishani, attached at the lips to a young man. Interlaced with his fingers was the hand of a lovely woman, who giggled when Murishani pulled away and placed a kiss on her neck.

His bright eyes matched Flowridia's, and to her surprise, he smiled. "Are you enjoying the party?"

"Well enough—Hold on." she replied, eyes darting between the enamored young man hanging off Murishani's hip, and the woman whose hair he kissed. "You're not supposed to—"

"I'm not talking to you." Murishani continued planting kisses on the breathless, giggling woman. "How is the sweet empress?" he cooed in her ear.

Flowridia frowned, yet dared to play his game. "She had too much to drink. I took her to bed."

"A pity she couldn't stay longer. She's breathtaking, that one. I would have loved to speak with her. But it's kind of you to care for her."

Flowridia simply nodded, faint at the thought.

Murishani seemed to notice. He released his hold on the drunk, amorous couple and stepped forward. "Are you all right?"

"Remember the thing about your head being thrown to—"

"I'm talking to the stars." He stopped exactly ten feet away from her and stared at the ceiling. "It must be difficult for you to be here," Murishani said, and Flowridia heard nothing but sincerity in his soothing voice. "All this effort spent on dear Marielle's happiness and love while you still fight to retrieve yours."

"Insightful," Flowridia said, her tone purposefully biting. "I didn't think the stars were so heartbroken."

"No, but I heard the moon might be."

His words froze something in Flowridia's blood.

He was baiting her. But the mere fact that he was able to meant he knew.

"I hear she's desperately lonely, after the death of her father. Emperor Malakh was one of the only friends and confidants she had. Such an isolated existence in her palace of glass. All the wealth and power in the world . . . but no one to cherish." Murishani gave a 'tsk tsk' noise. "Such a sad tale, that of the moon waiting for someone to light up her life."

Everything inside of her screamed to stop, but she said, "You're telling me nothing I don't already know. What do you want?"

"I want the annoying little mouse in my home to see herself out, but that won't happen until she accomplishes her goals." Now, Murishani did look at her, not wicked but utterly serious. "And if I can help her, don't we all win?"

Poisonous words, and Flowridia wanted nothing to do with them. She stepped away without another word, too sick to return to the ball.

She went, instead, to Casvir's room, head swimming, content to lie down and let sleep soothe her.

But to her surprise, there sat Casvir at his desk, idly humming to himself as he perused his paperwork. He spared her a glance. "Back so soon?"

"I could say the same to you."

"I made an appearance."

She collapsed into bed, shoes and all. "Keep humming. It helps me sleep."

He did.

When Lara left with Flowers, Etolié kinda hoped she just wouldn't see them again. Alternatively, Flowers had an honor code and likely wouldn't take advantage of a drunk empress.

She stood alone in the crowd, sipping her drink, mulling over Lunestra's words, trying to make sense of the layered questions, and at about the point she might've felt awkward, she heard her name. "Etolié?"

She recognized Sora, but she didn't know the Celestial woman accompanying her. Etolié guessed she was from the Theocracy, given her apparent association with the half-elf and because she hadn't been seen with Solvira. "Etolié, this is Priestess Emilla Redin of the Theocracy of Sol Kareena. She's a close associate of Archbishop Xoran."

The woman had her hair done up in the way elegant women did when they actually knew what the fuck they were doing with a brush, whereas Etolié hadn't brushed her hair today at all and was relying on a series of well-maintained illusions to give off an aura of civility instead of homelessness. When Emilla offered a hand, Etolié accepted, but fought her surprise when the woman lifted it to her lips and placed a light kiss on her knuckles. "I'm absolutely delighted to meet you, Magister Etolié. I'm the one who was graced to receive your sixteen dissertations on why your charming kingdom should take possession of the holy orb."

"Seventeen," Etolié mumbled, but she smiled with all the radiance of a sheep among a pack of wolves, pretending to be one of them.

"To be quite honest, I've been petitioning your cause. I was hoping we might speak more of it; perhaps I could garner more information to sway him—or incentive." When Emilla quirked an eyebrow, Etolié's stomach lurched, but she was fairly confident she kept her head on her shoulders. "Perhaps after the party, we could speak in private."

Sora, innocent little bastard, new to political jargon, kept her pleasant smile, as though a petition had not just been made to warm Etolié's bed.

It was not the first time Etolié had been given the offer of seduction for favors. The first time had been during year one of Staelash, and Khastra had set the precedent of, *"Absolutely not, Etolié."*

"He did say he'd forgive the border dispute, if—"

"We own nothing to Tholheim. We do not need them soft on us. Let me deal with this in my way."

Khastra had sent herself and a number of Solviran troops to carve a literal line in the sand to mark the border, sneering all the while.

Etolié forced a smile because they did need the Theocracy soft on them, because if this woman held the sway she claimed to—

Unmistakable bravado lit the room with laughter. Across the crowd, Etolié saw a half-demon in the throes of riotous revelry. "I have a prior engagement with Solvira this evening, but you're very kind to even think of me. Perhaps we can touch base tomorrow, before the wedding."

"Of course, and my apologies," Emilla replied, her eyes following Etolié's gaze. "I would never wish to come between you and . . . *Solvira.*"

Emilla spoke politics as a second language, her insinuation understood. When the priestess bid her goodnight, Etolié politely accepted her farewell. They parted; she didn't expect for Sora to tug on her arm not three seconds later. "Solvira can wait. She can get us the orb."

"You are welcome to meet with her in private tonight, Sora," Etolié replied, a bit of coldness filling her limbs—the same sort of nerves that always debilitated her when someone saw her as a body to fuck. "But I can't."

Sora clearly didn't understand, but Etolié left her alone to stew anyway.

She wove her way through the crowd toward the magnetic laughter, realizing she had stumbled upon a contest of dangerous prowess.

Khastra sat at one end, several empty tankards of Nox'Karthan Ale spread around her, with Reginal on the other with Eionei's brew. Khastra, being undead and immortal, would surely win any drinking contest—except, well, against Etolié herself, perhaps—but Reginal was old enough to have little to lose.

They had attracted quite the crowd, a large envoy of Solvirans, Staelashians, and even a few Nox'Karthans cheering on the two combatants.

Khastra and Reginal slammed down their tankards in tandem, erupting into riotous laughter. "Seven!"

"Where do I place my bets?" Etolié said as she met Khastra's eye.

Save for the evidence of scarring across Khastra's face, in her street clothes she looked as living as the rest. Well, not quite street clothes—she had cleaned up nicely, her long-sleeved tunic all shiny and embroidered, even with the eerie protrusion of her mechanical heart beneath the fabric.

Khastra grinned. "Speak to Jules. But this will not go on much longer."

Reginal looked near puking, but he smiled right back. "I could best you in life, and I'll best you in death."

They started chugging number eight, and Etolié stood beside Jules, nursing her flask until the high priestess spoke. "I thought Lara was with you."

"The Nox'Karthan Ale defeated her. Flowridia is escorting her to bed."

They lapsed into silence, Etolié's thoughts louder than even the game before them.

She recalled an interaction of years past, of the first she'd ever heard of *those* rumors—"*. . . can't believe he had the gall to insinuate . . .*"

"*But did it keep him away from you?*" Khastra's laugh held *warmth enough to soothe Etolié's irritation. "Let them believe what they will about us. It means nothing.*"

And yet it had meant everything, for who would dare try to steal what belonged to the eldest of Ku'Shya? From her pocket dimension, she withdrew a few coins and placed them in the high priestess' waiting hand. "On Khastra."

Within three more rounds, Reginal vomited into a bucket and Khastra reigned supreme. When the half-demon stood up, she swayed ever so slightly, and Etolié ran to steady her, ignoring that her friend would crush her if she fell.

"Careful," Etolié said, grabbing Khastra's waist, which felt much more like iron than flesh. Death hadn't hindered her physique. Etolié's face fell at about the base of Khastra's sternum, so when the half-demon brought her hand down, it met the small of Etolié's back. "I want to be alive to collect my victory earnings."

Most people had bet on Khastra, so the pool was largely spread out.

"Where is the empress?" Khastra asked, her hooves unsteady as she stepped. "I have not yet seen her."

"Drunk as hell. Flowers took her to bed." Etolié quickly scanned her oversized friend. "Do *you* need to go to bed?"

"This will wear off within a few hours."

"Oh. That's good. Guess you don't need me, then." She winked, but Khastra shook her head, apparently going to call Etolié out on her accidental truth.

"I always need you, Etolié."

Gods, that was sweet. "You're drunk. Have a seat."

Khastra obeyed, settling right where she had just been. She kept her hand on Etolié's waist, and the Celestial leaned into the touch, then plopped onto her lap.

Just like old times. Sincerely so—when the world was too loud and she was too sober, Khastra would shield her in her arms, letting Etolié hide her face, blocking sound with her hand and chest.

For a moment, Etolié contemplated faking the need to do so, but then she spotted a flash of white at the corner of the ballroom. "Oh, that damned orb," Etolié muttered, shaking her head. "One of the Theocracy Priestesses invited me to engage in a 'private conversation' to discuss Staelash's claim to it. Apparently she was a fan of my seventeen dissertations."

Khastra, who wasn't an oblivious idiot, shook her head, her grip on Etolié's waist suddenly steel. "Tactless, to initiate diplomatic discussions at a party."

"Since when did you pay attention in diplomat school?"

Khastra chuckled. "I attended meetings with you for twenty years. I learned from the best."

"A couple thousand years working for Solvira obviously had nothing to do with it." When Khastra continued laughing, Etolié smiled and rested her head against the half-demon's shoulder, avoiding brushing against the mechanical protrusion as she settled contentedly against her chest. Still, her stomach brewed discomfort. "I'm still dwelling on it."

Khastra, who knew her better than she knew herself, held her tenderly, allowing Etolié to hide behind her skin.

"I know you're all happy with your new life," Etolié said, as softly as she could in the noise of the party, "but do you ever miss Staelash?"

"Not particularly."

Rude. "Getting all the glory from Nox'Kartha, then?"

Etolié didn't know what Khastra's expression was, given that her head was tilted to rest on Etolié's. "Their army will be the largest I have ever led. I look forward to that day."

That was ... actually rather suspicious. Etolié's political bullshit senses tickled in her mind. "Well, my drunk companion, when do you think that day will be?"

Khastra's hand appeared at Etolié's chin, gently tilting it to face her. With a tenderness that shook Etolié's very core, Khastra stroked aside her hair.

All the party faded. What remained was Khastra's touch and glowing eyes.

"Nothing to worry about, Etolié. Trust me."

Her hand fell away. The noise of the party returned, as did its guests and the silent whispers of those who thought the same as Priestess Emilla. They sat touching, yet Etolié felt like there were some great canyon between them—the stark chasm dividing the secrets they held and could share.

Again, the true costs of Khastra's death weighed heavily in Etolié's mind. She pulled her flask from the air, unable to tear her gaze away from Khastra's as she took a sip. She offered it forward, and when the half-demon accepted, her stare ripped away, freeing Etolié.

Etolié stood up and accepted the flask when offered. Instead of drinking, she tossed it back into its pocket realm. "I'm obligated to stay until the end of tonight's bit of fun."

"Etolié, when is the last time you slept?"

"Well, not last night because I was talking with you."

Exhaustion weighed on Khastra's eyelids, but Etolié knew she didn't need to sleep. "You have to take care of yourself. I am no longer here to care for you."

Again with the gods-damned choking in her throat. All the bitchiness Etolié had so lovingly tucked away rose to strangle her. "You aren't my mother, Khastra. Not that my actual mother contributed much to the 'keeping me fed and watered' fund—My *point,*" Etolié said, cursing her rambling tongue, "is I'm a big girl who can drink herself to death if she wants to, so fuck off."

Somewhere in Etolié's cold, black heart, she had hoped this might get a rise out of Khastra, but to the detriment of her guilt complex, her dearest half-demon only looked hurt. The gentleness in her tone cut deep. "Etolié–"

"Please, don't," Etolié said, suddenly swallowing tears. "I can't handle you right now." She walked away, willing herself to vanish into the crowd.

Her own words had surprised her, coming from some horrible place within her that was probably in touch with its feelings. Etolié drank, willing all her discomfort away, and opted to make nice instead, flattering nobles the whole night through.

Chapter 5

Flowridia, who slept without the damned ear, dreamt a vision she hadn't seen in months.

"Flower Child, there's nothing more endearing than a man compelled to love you." Mother idly laid the strips of meat upon the cutting board, where they would stay until she hung them to dry. "Well, except the darling look of betrayal when you slit his throat during..." Her voice trailed off, her laughter rising to fill the silence. "Don't be so embarrassed. You'll surely find a young lady to lure in and–"

Banging at the door awoke Flowridia from a fitful sleep.

She sat up from bed, realizing tears had welled in her eyes, just as Casvir went to twist the knob—

And nearly toppled over, bombarded by a frantic wolf bursting through the doorframe. Demitri shot past him to Flowridia's bed. *First you never come back, and now you're crying!*

Clicking on the floor meant Ana had followed. The skeletal fox tried and failed to leap onto the bed—perhaps because of the chained ear wrapped around and through her ribs. Flowridia lifted her up and sought to untangle it, panic filling her. "I'm fine. Just a bad dream. Why does Ana have–"

What if you'd been taken? Or killed? I'd go from intelligent wolf to intelligent orphan—

"Demitri, stop being so dramatic!" Casvir leered behind him, and Flowridia worked to steady her breathing. "I apologize for Demitri's behavior," she finally said.

But Demitri would not be detoured and kept poking at her dress with his nose. *You don't usually cry after nightmares. You just whine.*

"Tell Demitri," Casvir said, a wicked glint in his eye, "that I accept his challenge to spar."

86

Demitri turned at that, releasing a low, emanating growl.

Having finally freed Ana from the macabre accessory, she stuffed it down her bodice, chain and all, then glanced down at her rumpled lace dress and said, "If you'll give me a moment to change, I'll fight on his behalf."

Without waiting for a reply, she pushed Demitri forward and escorted him from the room.

Ana's nails clicked through the hallway, but Demitri stopped, refusing to budge once they'd left Casvir's room. The gold arch of Murishani's 'tent' stood near them. *I wasn't challenging him—*

"You really let Ana walk around with . . . *that?* What if someone had seen?"

No one did. They're all drunk and asleep.

Flowridia glared, but Demitri was apparently immune to her withering stare. "That's not the point." She continued down the hallway, forcing down her fury and her remaining tears. "Now, kindly explain why Ana had the ear?"

She said she wanted to carry it.

"Ana doesn't–"

You always talk for her. Now, it's my turn.

Petulant boy. Flowridia rolled her eyes, then wiped them on her sleeve.

But why were you crying?

"Demitri, it's . . ." Flowridia stopped, her hand rubbing against the long lace sleeve of her gown. She thought of Lara and her slurred words, her penchant for raining drunken kisses, and wondered if perhaps the empress' kindness toward her held more meaning than Flowridia had previously considered. "You know my quest," she whispered. "Last night . . . If I'm truly wicked, she'll never see it coming."

What do you mean?

Her steps continued their shuffling, her tears finally stemming. "What I mean is that if I move forward, my behavior might appall you." The very thought lacerated her heart. "I've never felt so trapped. I love Ayla. I love her with all of my heart. But I can't do what must be done."

Demitri rubbed his head against her, conveying what comfort he could.

Sparring distracted her exhausted mind, though a layer of frost covered the ground, the sun having not quite risen. But the threat of Casvir's weapon held her focus, and by the end she managed to hold a sincere smile.

Once she'd cleaned herself, Flowridia made her way downstairs to the library. The wedding was a few more hours away, but the excitement up above threatened to drive her mad. With Ana prancing around her ankles, she silently opened the door, wondering what drunken state she would find Etolié in.

Layered shelves met her view, blocking the center, where she knew she'd find the usual piles of scarves, a skylight, and hundreds of books.

She hadn't expected to hear voices.

". . . accused her of fucking Imperator Casvir. I remember that much."

Flowridia stopped, holding up a finger to stop Demitri. He loomed like a shadow by the door.

"She's been accused of fucking Casvir by everyone and their wolf at this point," came Etolié's voice. "She won't hold it against you."

"I resent you for letting her take me to bed."

"The worst that could've happened is nothing. The best is all your dreams come true. I don't regret anything."

Flowridia was quite certain she hadn't been meant to hear that. The pit in her stomach expanded, threatening to rise up her throat and choke her.

"It's too soon. The woman she loved died only six months ago."

"Listen. I, for one, sleep better at night knowing that sadistic bitch is dead."

Flowridia felt her raw heart seize at Etolié's words.

"Etolié, it's cruel to speak so ill of the dead," came Lara's indignant voice. "Whatever your opinions on the matter, Flowridia obviously cared for Ayla."

Flowridia peered through the cracks between books and saw Etolié move to sit beside a despondent figure. Lara looked well, given she'd partaken the Nox'Karthan brew, but vulnerability radiated from her slumped figure. Etolié didn't quite touch her, but she did hover like an excitable bee. "How about I talk to Flowers?"

Lara tore her gaze from the ground. "Etolié, no! You don't need to do that."

"Look at you," Etolié said, and Flowridia silently shrunk back, realizing her eavesdropping would lead to trouble. "Empress of the world and insecure about–"

Ana's spine was suddenly beneath her foot; with a yelp Flowridia stepped back and smacked into Etolié's bookcase.

"Flowers? That you?"

Heart racing, Flowridia said, "Hi, Etolié."

Favoring her nearly-punctured foot, Flowridia peered around the corner of the bookcase, feigning surprise at seeing Lara. "Good morning, Lara. How are you feeling?"

"Flowridia!" Lara smiled too wide, a vivid blush coloring her cheeks. She spared a glance for Ana and Demitri. "I feel fine. It's an odd consequence of the Silver Fire, that alcohol burns quickly through my body. My memory is frazzled, but I remember you escorting me back to my bedroom." She stood, stepping forward with noticeable hesitation. "You have my thanks. I let my inhibitions get the better of me, and I apologize for inconveniencing you."

Despite the apology, Lara remained stiff. Flowridia said simply, "You're welcome. It was no trouble."

Visibly bracing herself, Lara's blush darkened. "Did I kiss you?"

Acutely aware of Demitri and Etolié's stares, Flowridia nodded. "A few times, yes."

Lara cringed, smiling apologetically, then turned around to face the skylight instead. "Etolié told me about the orb and the dragon. A tragedy, to lose the last one."

"His name was Valeuron," Flowridia said, saddened at the reminder. "I'd never seen anything so . . . magnificent."

"Perhaps, with your aid, I might commission a portrait of him, to memorialize him for all to see and know. He died defending both you and Casvir, making him a hero of Staelash and Nox'Kartha."

Touched at the thought, Flowridia couldn't help but smile, though it faded when Lara's matched. "Be that as it may, Soliel has three orbs now."

The resignation in Lara's sigh suggested she had contemplated this many times. "Yes, he does. But because of you, we have a fighting chance. Once the wedding has ended, Etolié and I will be studying the blue orb—you are, of course, welcome to join us, assuming you'll be staying."

It was an offer so much as a question. "I have a few matters to take care of before I can leave Nox'Kartha—by my own choice. But I would be honored to help."

Lara smiled, but Flowridia didn't miss Etolié's frown in the background. "Your insight was invaluable in deciphering the God of Order's identity. We'll be blessed to have you. But, tell me more about this interaction with Valeuron—he would have willingly relinquished the orb to you?"

"He would have," Flowridia replied, the magnitude of the gesture having never faded from her memory. "He saw my life just as I saw his; and I saw his death before it occurred, though I didn't understand it. It means he saw mine as well. He saw my whole life."

Soliel, she recalled, had said something similar, yet ominous: *"I know your death . . . today is not that day."*

But she kept that to herself, though it plagued her to consider it.

"It may mean nothing," Lara said, though not unkindly, "except that you prove yourself worthy. I think that's wonderful." Flowridia nodded, though much too self-conscious to necessarily agree.

"I should go," Etolié said suddenly, smoothing what Flowridia knew was an illusionary gown—she was impressed at her commitment to the act. "Marielle requested me at her dress fitting today. Leave it to Murishani to put the fitting and the wedding on the same day. But, uh, you two feel free to keep talking things out."

She grinned as she left, and judging by Lara's wide-eyed confusion, Flowridia suspected a conspiracy.

They were left alone. Silence settled once Etolié shut the door. "I don't know that there's much else to discuss," Flowridia said, watching Lara curiously.

The empress remained composed, yet Flowridia saw cracks within it, subtle hints of nervousness. "I'm terribly embarrassed for last night," she said lightly, her smile apologetic. "I don't normally behave so untoward. I'm sorry if I made you uncomfortable."

"Only as far as my worry," Flowridia said, and it wasn't a lie. "You're very lonely."

In a moment of unexpected vulnerability, Lara blushed, her stare turning to the floor. "I have a few loved ones in Solvira. But since my father's death, it's been a bit cold in my home, I will be honest."

Flowridia hesitated, unsure of what to say. "I'm also an orphan," she eventually said, soft in her reminiscence. "I know what it feels like to lose a family. And I know how dark it feels to be alone in the world.”

When Lara glanced up, Flowridia saw the faint beginnings of light returning to her eyes. “I didn’t know that.”

“I was raised in an orphanage in Ilunnes,” she admitted, though it felt odd to speak it aloud—she had said this to no one, not since Ayla. “I was discovered as a witch at fifteen and would have been killed had I not run away. But I discovered my mother was still alive. I was able to meet her before her death.”

“My mother died in childbirth,” Lara said softly, then shook her head, swallowing what Flowridia feared were tears. “I’m sorry. You hardly know me.”

“I wouldn’t be sad to, though.” At Lara’s faint smile, Flowridia regretted the words, but forced more out, knowing this was the path she must take. “May I hug you?”

When Lara nodded, Flowridia embraced her petite figure, though not so small as Ayla’s and certainly a bit softer. She was warm and soothing to touch, unquestionable life flowing through her veins. Flowridia remembered the sweet smell of her hair from the funeral, finding it just as much so now as Lara clung to her comfort.

When they parted, Lara’s blush had darkened. “I-I should go. Marielle will also be wanting to see me. And I haven’t even had the chance to meet with Khastra yet, if you can believe it. I’m supposed to be supervising this whole affair, and I’m amazed we’ve come this far without an incident.”

Flowridia couldn’t disagree with that. “Good luck. I’ll see you tonight?”

Lara’s shy joy showed in her nod.

Once the empress had gone, Flowridia lingered in the library, her guilt as loud as her thoughts.

“It needs to be bigger,” Marielle said for the umpteenth time, and the pair of De’Sindai women charged with styling her fiery locks looked nervous as they nodded.

Etolié watched them pile curl upon curl—her hair would be taller than Marielle herself at this rate. "Marielle, your hair is beautiful, so will you please chill your perky tits?"

The bride-to-be's jaw dropped. "Etolié, forgive me for wanting to be perfect on *my wedding*. If you're going to be a bitch, leave."

Etolié deserved that, admittedly.

In Marielle's dressing room, decorated with mirrors and at least a thousand floral arrangements, the Celestial stepped around the flock of De'Sindai preening the queen's hair and makeup and said, "I'm sorry. I don't understand all the kerfuffle. And to be honest, I'm not looking forward to making nice with more diplomats." She sighed, the familiar visage behind Marielle's made-up face one she'd known since she was an infant. "But I'm happy you're happy. You deserve to feel like a princess on your wedding day, Queen Marielle."

Marielle beamed, and were she not covered from head to toe in fluffy, stiff curls of fabric, Etolié suspected they might've hugged. She was relieved, because physical affection was weird. But she did care about Marielle, even if her patience ran thin.

A knock sounded at the door, and Lara came to greet her, ever the monarch with her brilliant smile. Etolié might've thought it sincere—and perhaps it was, despite both their misgivings about the wedding itself. Marielle was happy; therein lay the important part, at least on a personal level. Today was for celebration.

Tomorrow was for navigating the inevitable political catastrophe. "I'll leave you two alone," Etolié said to the chattering women.

Once alone, Etolié realized she was ignored among the crowd of servants and guests, all hastily moving toward the enormous tent behind the manor. With a single swipe of her hand, her dress was replaced with the illusion of something spectacular, her hair done up in a curled bun. Truthfully, Etolié hadn't brushed her hair in days.

She had finally bathed, however. If there were no other victories today, she'd take that to the treasury.

She pulled her flask from the air, then said to no one in particular, "I swear on Morathma's Whore Mother—if I'm ever daft enough to get married, it'll be . . ." She continued mumbling as she brought the blessed flask to her lips.

"In a church on a hillside, yes?"

Etolié spat out her booze. Thankfully she didn't spray Murishani, but it seeped through her mouth and nose, forcing her to wipe the alcohol onto her fake dress sleeve. "Good evening," she said between stinging coughs. She sniffed and *oh fuck her life she regretted that.*

Well, with alcohol actively burning her nostrils, at least she'd finally hit rock-bottom. Etolié blinked back tears as Murishani said, "Sorry to startle you." He placed a hand on his heart, his smile reminiscent of a dying calf. "I was on my way to check on the bride."

"Well, she's beautiful." Etolié forced a grin, trying to hide the beer seeping from her nostrils. "Good work."

When Murishani offered a handkerchief, she wasn't too proud to accept it. "Duty calls. I'm off and away!"

He spread his arms rather dramatically as he 'away-ed,' and Etolié wondered just how much was an act and how much of this absolute fop was sincere.

Mentally preparing herself for chaos, Etolié entered the tent.

Judging by her radiating headache, she suspected some sort of extra-dimensional magic had been utilized to make the enormous tent that much larger—chairs were packed not even close to capacity, yet could have seated a small army. The aisle in the center held a carpet of white silk, gently sprinkled with rose petals, and not a single section of the wall was bereft of decoration.

Etolié paced around the gaudy tent, her illusionary dress sparkling as it swished around her legs. Sometimes she forgot it was fake—which was risky, given that sort of thinking sometimes led to it flickering out of existence.

She took a long sip from her flask, watching as guests slowly filtered in. She saw Flowers in the distance, watched her seat herself beside Casvir in the Nox'Karthan sector, and wondered if the prickling feeling of betrayal was real or only in her gut.

Lara had yet to arrive, and so Etolié had nowhere to sit. Well, she had her assigned seat, right up front, but assigned seating was for proletariats—not magisters in their own homes. If she wanted to sit by her little moonbeam, Etolié reserved that right.

She took another drink, but the next guest who entered caused her to choke. As she coughed out the burning liquid, Etolié glanced at the disconcerting stranger idly searching for her seat. By all accounts, the woman was

Khastra—she was blue and tattooed and her biceps were girthy enough to speak for themselves—but her outfit left Etolié's jaw hanging slack.

Perhaps she'd sipped a few sips too many. Etolié teetered down the aisle, and when Khastra met her eye, she said, "What in Onias' Hell are you wearing?"

Khastra wore a *dress,* first of all, and that dress happened to be a rather dark orange and pale yellow, so while her color theory was on point, Etolié had never seen her out of brown or jewel tones or glittering stones. But the dress was sleeveless and somehow accentuated all the best of her musculature, in addition to being cut down to nearly her *navel,* thus showing off the rather fascinating, semi-protruding mechanical masterpiece that was her heart. The fact remained, however, that in over twenty years of knowing Khastra, not once had Etolié given a second thought to the fact that her half-demon friend had breasts.

There they were, peeking out from the fabric, more silver than blue—but paler blue, since Khastra wasn't generally one to let half her tits out to see the sun.

She barely noticed when Khastra frowned, and rather darkly. "I am wearing the height of De'Sindai fashion, *Etolié–*"

"Fuck, that's not . . ." Etolié bit her lip because she just couldn't stop being a bitch apparently. "I'm sorry. I've never seen you wear a dress. You didn't wear a dress to Clarence and Lyra's wedding."

"I was on duty for Clarence and Lyra's wedding."

Khastra still held the tone of 'I'm-definitely-offended-and-rightfully-so,-ma'am,' so Etolié met her gaze, whispered, "You look beautiful," and meant it. "Like a sunset. With the orange and your dark blue . . ." Her voice faded, contrite and embarrassed and a little self-loathing, if she were being honest.

Khastra's offense disappeared, replaced with a genuine smile. "Thank you," she said, the gentleness in her tone utterly jarring—contrary to everything Etolié knew of her favorite beefcake. "You look stunning, Etolié."

"Look at you and your fancy compliments, jerk," Etolié said, grateful when Khastra kept her smile at the jest. "Thanks. Will you sit with me?"

With a glance to the seat obviously assigned to her, given its impressive size, Khastra replied with, "I am to sit with Nox'Kartha."

"Fuck 'em. You can swap with Sora. It'll do her well to acquaint herself with the enemy." She winked and stole Khastra's hand, grateful when she was amiably led through the aisle.

When she looked away from Khastra's elegant face, she saw an ensemble from the Theocracy of Sol Kareena whispering as they stared at her and Khastra's intertwined fingers. Priestess Emilla was among them, her knowing smirk twisting Etolié's stomach.

Etolié released her.

Khastra sat in the comically small seat, one that somehow accommodated six hundred-or-so pounds of muscle, but Etolié was, if she were being honest, extremely hung up on the unexpected cleavage. She didn't mean to stare, but the swirls of silver tattoos peeking from the garment suggested they really did cover *all* of Khastra, which was a thought Etolié had contemplated a time or two, but never in the context of them marking Khastra's naughty bits.

Khastra's hand on her forearm startled Etolié out of her inner monologuing. "You are very quiet."

Etolié met her eye, realizing that she had zoned out while staring at the aforementioned cleavage. "Thinking. Sorry." She looked down to Khastra's arm and stole it, turning it over as she ran a gentle finger along the lines etched into her forearm, marveling at how they shone at her touch—the magic in them, Khastra had once explained, reacted to the magic innate within Etolié.

"They are demonic writings, Etolié. This one is for strength . . . for aim . . . for protection against the undead . . ."

"Why are you stressed?"

Etolié continued the motions, finding the patterns soothing to her addled brain. "I don't know," she whispered.

She refused to think on it, quieting her brain except for the illuminate tattoos. Etolié's finger slowly traced up Khastra's arm, her substantial bicep coming alight as the sigils on her forearm faded. Beautiful, all of them, hues of silver and blue bearing patterns relaxing to Etolié's manic mind.

Something was different, and it was tearing Etolié apart.

The thought jarred her from the repetitive motions. She released Khastra's arm and instead placed her hands in her lap.

She missed the touch. Etolié took Khastra's forearm and wrapped hers around it.

Something was different, as told by this bottomless divide between them. Even touching, they were no longer close enough.

"Khastra!"

Etolié quickly took her arm back, forcing a smile when Lara approached the pair. Khastra immediately rose and embraced the empress, and Etolié felt the void where her touch had once been. "Hello, Lara."

Like Etolié, Khastra had been a sort of kindly, overbearing aunt to Lara, their visits to the screaming toddler princess frequent and, despite the aforementioned screaming, something to cherish. Lara wiped away tears when she pulled away.

Whatever conversation they shared, Etolié didn't listen, instead content to look to the back of the tent. Flowers caught her eye, smiling broadly as she waved.

Etolié could never stay angry with the doe-eyed girl for long. She grinned and might've moved to say hello, but the lights dimmed.

Murishani came to stand at the front of a decorated podium, spouting a practiced speech about love and matrimony and the beautiful union they would soon be blessed to witness, etc, etc. He gushed, and Etolié found his sincerity remarkable.

With Lara at one side and Khastra on the other, Etolié nearly felt whole. She wrapped her arm around the half-demon's bicep, swallowing the sudden rise of panic at the gesture. The normalcy would be short-lived. Lara would return to Solvira, Khastra would be whisked away, and, though seated far behind, Etolié thought of Flowers and suspected she would soon too.

Etolié smiled as Thalmus walked Marielle down the aisle, even teared up when Zorlaeus burst into some rather ugly sobs. Her grip on Khastra's arm tightened as the couple clasped hands, and when Murishani dared to mention Marielle's father, Etolié silently cursed the viceroy's name.

Whatever her happiness at Marielle's joy, the queen played Staelash right into Nox'Kartha's hands, and Etolié was left alone to pry them out.

She'd once had a wonderful life. Clarence's passing had jarred her future forward, but she hadn't felt life slipping away in the moment—it wasn't until Khastra's death that she'd realized the hourglass had finished.

Khastra placed a hand on Etolié's, squeezing to convey what comfort she could.

When the couple kissed, Etolié pulled her arm away and joined in the applause, realizing life would never be the same again.

The wedding party marched themselves away.

The festivities began. Mountains of food were wheeled in on banquet tables, along with barrels of ale and stores of wine—none of which Etolié had been asked to provide.

For risk of offending Eionei, Etolié drank from her own flask tonight, casually standing away from the revelers. Lara stood somewhere within, making nice with politicians, Etolié was sure.

Looking a bit lonely in the corner, Flowers surveyed the scene. Etolié thought to join her, but Khastra came up instead, sipping at the stein in her hand. "Maintaining the peace?" the half-demon said, her smile as wide as the walls of the tent.

"By avoiding the chaos? Absolutely." Etolié took a long drink of her flask, basking in the burning promise of non-sobriety as it gushed down her throat. "I've made nice for too many days in a row now. Marielle can take the lead."

The monarch stood with her new husband, laughing as she greeted well-wishers.

"You have had guests for two days, Etolié."

"Don't call me out like this."

Khastra chuckled, and it felt like the better days of Staelash, when Clarence had completed their unwilling trio and Khastra had been as constant as a shadow.

Etolié swallowed the sudden rise in unpleasant feelings. Weddings were meant for fun, not existential crises.

Instead, she looked back to Marielle and Zorlaeus and couldn't help but smile at their radiant joy. "I've never understood marriage," she said aloud. "They don't have it up in Celestière. Everyone's immortal, so why commit?"

"Nor in Sha'Demoni," Khastra replied, a wistful sort of joy overtaking her features. She was either drunk as hell or merely reminiscent. "I accept that I am odd."

"My mom's a loony too. No shame." Etolié brought her flask up to her lips but dropped it instead, letting it fall into the extra-dimensional space she'd claimed. "Explain it to me, then. Why marriage?"

Khastra's perfect control manifested in her thoughtful actions and words both. Etolié had admired that for all their years together. She grew quiet, her elegant face showing only stoicism. "Living for someone else is, at times, what makes life worth living at all. To care for someone, and to know you are in turn cared for, and to have the hope of building a life together is a beautiful thing." Her full lips pulled into a frown, faint lines marring her smooth skin. "May I burden you with a story? Perhaps it will illustrate my point."

All the party had disappeared. "Always, Beefcake."

"When I was young, but still older than you, I fell into a deep despair. Immortality was a daunting reality I had not accepted, and so I sought to end it. I threw myself off Chaos' Sorrow—the tallest cliff in Zauleen."

In twenty-four years of knowing Khastra, Etolié had never known that.

"I lived. I was discovered by an elven fisherman who took me into his home and tended to me, showed me a tenderness I had never experienced. With him, I felt warmth, and in time, he felt the same. Which isn't to say I had never had conquests in my past, but I had never felt such joy with anyone. We fell in love, and we married. My life held meaning for the first time in centuries.

"He passed too soon, succumbing to illness before he could grow old. I was heartbroken, but I was changed. I understood a fundamental truth about life that Sha'Demoni could not teach me, that life was about balance—conflict brought glory and power, but love brought security and joy. It took a hundred years for me to grieve, but when I met an elven priestess of the Goddess Chaos, although I was surprised to feel my heart yearning for her, I embraced it. We married, and I was blessed to have her grow old at my side. I loved her until she passed in her sleep.

"What I mean to say, Etolié, is life has different meanings for different people. Marriage is about living for someone other than yourself, and it is what I needed in those times of my life."

Etolié thought of nothing, merely listened and perhaps understood. When Khastra paused, she dared to ask, "And you've been married, what, twelve times?"

"Eleven. Seven husbands; four wives. I also did not marry everyone I loved—elven marriages are for status and money and rarely for love. The human woman I married lived only a few precious years, but the child we raised lived on to bring me many years of joy. All my children did, even those who inherited my mother's wickedness. Even those I had to slay." Khastra's smile held the weight of ten thousand years, and never, in all their time together, had Etolié felt so unbearably young. "Eleven different lives, each one a bittersweet delight."

Etolié's gut brewed an anxiety she couldn't name. "Think you'd ever make it twelve?" she teased, and she dared to add a wink.

But Khastra shook her head. "Not in Nox'Kartha. Not with a future as an undead general. My life is over, Etolié. Now, I embrace death as a new adventure."

Etolié didn't think when she reached over to steal Khastra's hand, the one not holding Nox'Karthan Ale. Whatever emotion overwhelmed her—and overwhelm her, it did—it still paled to her need to comfort her demon's cold, metal heart and see her smile.

Something ineffable had twisted their friendship, something Etolié couldn't name. But she interlaced their fingers and shyly met Khastra's gaze. "Khastra–"

A gasp from the audience, stole her attention, and then her own stole Khastra's. With wide eyes, Etolié's jaw dropped at the absolute scandal before them.

In the ensuing bustling of servants, the wheeling out of food and fresh flowers and a gorgeous cake, no one noticed Flowridia weeping in the corner.

Demitri, never one for parties, had elected to stay behind. To spite him, Flowridia wore the green dress, the one that showed too much of her chest and left him with Ana and the ear once more. Now, she wished she'd begged him to come so she could hide behind his fur.

She'd leave soon, but first force a smile, wish Marielle well, then hide in her garden, warded tonight to detour even innocent wandering guests, lest it be a meeting place for drunken festivities.

By every god—the wedding had hurt.

Marielle had earned her joy, had loved Zorlaeus from the start. And Flowridia truly was happy for them. But she remembered a notebook waiting back in Nox'Kartha bearing a name she longed for but had not earned; she remembered the veil serving as a funeral shroud for its maker.

Flowridia wondered what a joy it would be to be here with Ayla, to be aghast at her perturbed snark toward the bride, to share a drink and dance and simply . . . be.

To simply be, instead of heartbroken and sick with the price of her return. In watching Marielle's joy, she'd caught a glimpse of a future she craved above all, to stand across an altar in white and pledge her affection—to be *Flowridia Darkleaf* in more than merely spirit.

Mother would have called her a romantic fool to tie herself to anyone, to stunt her potential, or so she would have called it. But Flowridia had never aspired for power or for a name to inspire fear. A quiet life in the woods—just she, Ayla, and Demitri.

Flowridia forced a smile as she stood against the wall of the tent, surveying the sea of guests. She saw Etolié alone and might've joined her, had Khastra not come to stand beside her. There was Marielle and Zorlaeus, standing beneath a decorated arch, greeting guests as they came. In the distance, Flowridia saw Lara among the Solviran party, casually sipping from a wineglass.

"You're an absolute tragedy to watch."

From the other side of the cake, Flowridia realized Murishani spoke. She peered around, watching him eye the crowd with intrigue. On instinct, she searched for Casvir.

"To know you must damn yourself to save your lover's soul . . . I can't even imagine your grief."

"You aren't supposed to talk to me."

Murishani peered around, forced shock on his composure. "Goodness! I hadn't even noticed you." Then, he returned to his spot, hidden behind the cake. "As I was saying, you and I both know I don't have your best interest at heart." A slight clinking of glass, and Murishani slid a wineglass across the table. "For courage."

Flowridia took the stem, carefully sniffing the liquid. "What is this?"

"Courage, as I said. Nothing more. A bit of wine, and the empress will say anything—I wonder if it'll do the same for you."

Flowridia watched the liquid swirl in the glass, realizing her hand trembled.

"What you want is wicked, Flowridia. Ayla is wicked. And you'll have to be wicked if you want to be worthy of her."

Izthuni had said the same. By every god—she remembered Palace's screams.

"I don't know that I was ever as precocious as you," he mused. "But I do remember my first truly heinous act. I had a younger sister once. A half-sister—can't say I loved her, but I was loyal. When I was thirteen, I learned a group of children had been bullying her. Now, I knew the woods around the city where our mother whored. Well enough to befriend those same children and convince them of a grand treasure waiting inside a cave—a pity, that the treasure was a mother bear. The rest is history." His smile held pure malice, as wicked as his soul. "There is merit in learning to twist words and coerce the sheep around you. Whatever your aspirations, it pays to have people like you."

The red in the glass was as dark as blood. "What are you asking me to do?" Flowridia said, dread filling her stomach.

"There are three driving forces in this world—sex, money, and power. I told you that. Which does Empress Alauriel crave, and how will you exploit it to get what you want?"

Flowridia merely shook her head.

"And so Ayla will have died for nothing."

Fresh tears welled in her eyes.

"No one will do this for you; not if you crave that happy ending. One wicked act, and then your world is restored."

The wineglass fell. It shattered on the ground, nearly splattering Flowridia's dress. When a servant came by with a tray, she stole two more and forced them down. By every god—it *burned,* fouler than even the vile concoctions her mother had brewed in the swamp. Coughing, sputtering, tears stung her eyes as she placed the empty glasses on the table.

"You've given your all for the world, Lady Flowridia. Take one thing for yourself."

She held no certainty as she stumbled forward. Swallowing tears, she wove into the crowd—

Only for the empress herself to stumble back into her. Wine flecked across Lara's dress and chest, shock marring her features. "I am so sorry," Lara said, visibly horrified.

Flowridia shook her head. "I'm fine. But your dress–"

Lara seemed sober enough, though the slight swaying of her stance meant she had consumed something. "No, no— I have spare dresses. This one wasn't comfortable anyway. I can pop out and back in–"

"I can help you if you'd like."

Lara shook her head, a blush coloring her cheeks. "I couldn't ask that of you."

"At the very least, I can help you take it off."

Those silver eyes searched Flowridia's face, perhaps looking for meaning. Gathering her courage, and praying the wine dampened her self-loathing soon, Flowridia stepped forward. With a permissive glance, she gently pressed their lips together.

There she lingered, the shocked crowd lost among the flush movements of Lara's lips. A scandal, to publicly kiss a foreign ruler.

She pulled back, taking in Lara's surprise. The Solviran Empress slowly brought a hand to cover her blushing cheeks. "That was . . ." Her words trailed off as she glanced around at the staring crowd, then set her gaze to the ground. ". . . forward."

A creeping, cold wash of embarrassment filled Flowridia. "Was I mistaken–"

Lara's words came in a flood. "No, not mistaken, but let's take this somewhere private?"

Something earnest waited in those silver eyes. When Lara offered a hand, Flowridia accepted, confused until her stomach suddenly twisted—

They were no longer at the wedding, but in Lara's suite in the manor.

Flowridia's hand fell to the bedpost for stability, head still reeling from the portal magic. "Sorry," came the shy voice before her.

"You did this last night too. I'll be used to it in no time."

Flowridia met her eye and smiled, though her frayed nerves threatened to unravel. Alone, Lara's visage was illuminated by the silver moon beyond, unquestionably lovely—she'd be a liar to deny it.

Flowridia righted herself, then placed a gentle hand at Lara's waist and pressed their lips together once again.

The pleasure of it shocked her—oh, it had been so long since she'd last touched another woman, and the softness of Lara's lips held tenderness and delight. A tentative hand cupped her cheek, the tips of Lara's fingers skimming her hair.

Flowridia directed them to bed, to sit on the mattress as they continued their tentative exploration. Lara's mouth parted; Flowridia deepened the kiss, a gentle moan escaping her partner's throat. Were it not for the warmth, that small mouth could have been . . . someone else.

Her hand brushed the dip of Lara's waist, travelling up her back as she savored the thin fabric and skin beneath it. Lara's own hands stayed shy; Flowridia finally placed the one not at her hair on her ribs, the curve of her breast hardly a breath away.

The invitation wasn't received, apparently. Flowridia let her own hand wander to Lara's stomach, expecting taut skin, surprised to find softness, but when her fingers skimmed the base of Lara's breast, she felt the empress stiffen.

Flowridia pulled back, lips and hands both. "I'm sorry–"

"N-No, I'm sorry," Lara replied, her wary eyes expecting reproach. "You do smell intoxicated, though. A- And I'm . . ."

Flowridia shook her head, then placed a gentle kiss on Lara's cheek. "I'm not drunk *yet*, but I did down two wineglasses for courage."

"Flowridia!" Lara said, but it was much more a laugh.

"So it's inevitable that I'll be drunk," she continued, realizing that her words might've been slurring a bit, "but I am doing this because I want to." She brushed another kiss upon Lara's lips, at the corner of her mouth. "I'd be thrilled to at least kiss you, if you'd be comfortable continuing."

Enthusiasm showed in Lara's nod, even if it happened impossibly fast in Flowridia's oddly shifty vision. She turned into Flowridia's mouth, the gentle motions continuing, and Flowridia felt caught between the innate pleasure of the touch and her own addled thoughts, of a touch that was too warm, sweet moans too high-pitched . . .

Drunkenness, fortunately, damped her arousal. Their lips brushed until Flowridia's sight grew hazy, until Lara helped her lay down. "Do you need me to take you to bed?"

Flowridia thought she answered affirmatively, but the words were lost behind the pounding in her head. Instead, lips met her own once more. "Oh, Ay-Lauriel . . ."

It might have been humorous, but it worked. "I can't carry . . ." The words were lost when Flowridia blinked. She felt hands at her feet, tugging her shoes. ". . . stay here. I don't . . ."

Then, a kiss at her cheek, and a blanket tucked up to her chin. She remembered nothing else.

Flowridia and Lara disappeared from the party in a flash of light. Etolié couldn't say she was sad about a bit of scandal.

"Good for Lara," she mumbled, then she took a sip from her trusted flask. "And thank Alystra's Supple Ass—Flowers picked a good one for once."

Khastra, rather cruelly, began laughing. "I am inclined to agree."

Etolié surveyed the party, filled with an entire legion of diplomats and ambassadors and well-wishers she ought to be making nice to. But the party, while not riotous, was tiresome. She spared a glance for her half-demon friend. "Listen, ya big lug—wanna get smashed in the library? For old time's sake."

Khastra's grin could have blinded the sun, and it relieved Etolié to see. "I would."

With their fingers still intertwined, they wound their way through the partiers, quickly entering the manor and descending the stairs to the underground sanctuary.

There, they spent the night giggling over the ceremony and Murishani's pretentious games. Etolié told the tale of his ridiculous *'away!'* and listened as Khastra told more, of days in Nox'Kartha surrounded by ridiculous nobles.

It felt so wonderful to laugh.

When Etolié was finally drunk enough to sway, Khastra laid her down amidst her sea of scarves. She remembered Khastra saying, "You should sleep."

"I'm on a streak, though."

"I will be much happier if you do."

Etolié, with her clammy, drunken hands, managed to grasp Khastra, who swayed but was not yet smashed. "Stay."

"If it will get you to sleep."

With every blink, her eyelashes grew unbearably heavy, but when Khastra settled beside her and pulled her to her chest, Etolié felt a strange sort of bittersweetness, to know that this moment of normal, of Khastra by her side once more, would end.

In her sleepy haze, she could pretend there was no divide between them. She swallowed the bitterness and savored the touch, unable to contemplate that notion further—she quickly descended into sleep.

Chapter 5

Lara slept, and specks of silver glistened against her skin. The woman radiated energy, and for it to manifest against her skin was only a taste of the power this woman had coursing through her blood.

This powerful, beautiful, lonely woman.

Lara slept, but Flowridia was wide awake, though sunrise had yet to flicker across the horizon. She sat up, careful not to jostle her sleeping companion as the sheets pooled around her torso. Her mouth held stickiness, but her head felt fine, despite her excessive indulgence. She brushed aside Lara's hair, and silver glistened off her fingers, their beauty reflecting only regret. Her face fell into her hands, tears pooling in her eyes.

Lara was beautiful, the very image of royal perfection, a direct descendent of angels. But when Flowridia gazed down at her serene form, all she remembered was her too warm skin, her cautious, gentle touch, those soft silver eyes, the moan that held too high a pitch . . .

Ice seeped into her veins.

She slipped out of the bed, catching a glimpse of her figure in a mirror. With her tear-streaked face and tousled hair, she was the very image of disaster.

Opening the door, she gasped. Demitri stared down at her. *Hope you had a good night.*

"Demitri, please," she whispered, and she gently shut the door behind her. "I have a lot to think about."

In a daze, she went to her old bedroom and stripped off the sensuous green gown, realizing with some disdain that it had been useful after all.

What happened?

Flowridia changed into a plain dress, one of her old ones—simple frock of white and brown, stained at the bottom from garden dirt. She slipped on boots, though her feet protested. "Nothing happened. But . . . Lara happened."

But why?

"I told you," she whispered, voice choking as she forced out the words, "that I would have to become someone wicked to bring Ayla back. B-But, Demitri–" Her voice caught. Flowridia's face fell into her hands. "I can't do it."

She craved the outdoors. There was only one place she felt truly safe.

Partygoers slept like the dead. With a quilt thrown over her shoulders, Flowridia passed a few who had collapsed from drunkenness on couches. Despite her streaking tears, she needed no spells to mask her presence.

Standing in the doorway, she realized a gentle blanket of snow covered the scene. Grateful she had elected to wear shoes, she pulled the blanket tight around her as she stepped outside.

She heard commotion and saw a team of De'Sindai disassembling the gaudy tent—with the wedding over, though there would be some revelry today, she and many other guests would be leaving. Murishani and his team would be gone late that night.

She cringed, wondering if Casvir were even here—he had made it known he wished to leave after the reception, but Flowridia had disappeared.

Perhaps he'd left her to go home with Murishani's team, or to live out her days in Staelash. It would not be out of character.

At the entrance of her garden, Flowridia saw smoke rising from beyond—Thalmus was at work.

Fearful but desperate for comfort, she turned her back to her garden and stepped toward the smoking kiln instead, Demitri in tow.

Thalmus' rough skin seemed equipped for any weather—he wore a simple coat, uncaring of the cold. She knocked on the doorframe of his workshop.

He turned from stoking the fire, a rod of glass in his hand. His smile immediately melted her fears. "Good morning, Flowra. Did you have a nice night?"

Her stomach clenched. "Are you mocking me?"

"No." Genuine confusion furrowed his brow. "I said goodnight to Marielle once the wedding ended. Did something happen?"

Fresh tears welled in her eyes. Flowridia stepped inside the warm building and sat herself on a bench. "I did something very stupid," she confessed, realizing it was Thalmus and only Thalmus she could unburden herself to—here at home, in Staelash, she felt like a child once more. "And if I tell you, you must swear to not hate me."

Thalmus knelt before her, having placed his glass rod aside. He offered a hand; she held it with one of hers.

"I kissed Empress Alauriel. Surely everyone knows. I kissed her at the reception, and then we went to her room and . . ." She dabbed at her eyes with the quilt, trembling from her quiet sobs.

"Why would I hate you for that?" Thalmus asked, and he looked very near smiling. "Flowra, she's a wonderful woman–"

"She is. She's a beautiful person. But now I have to go break her heart because—because–" *Because otherwise I have to kill her,* she couldn't say. A quiet sob escaped her lips. "Thalmus, I know it's terrible to say, but I miss Ayla. Last night was too much." She wept, safe in Thalmus' presence as she burdened him with the memory of a woman he hated. "I'm sorry. I know she was awful, Thalmus. You must think me a fool for missing her."

"We have many disagreements, Flowra," Thalmus whispered, "but I have never thought you a fool. Just because Ayla is dead doesn't mean a piece of her isn't lingering in your heart. You loved her. I never doubted that. Tell Lara what you told me—because you aren't ready. There's no shame in admitting that." Thalmus glanced out the open door, past where Demitri lounged. "The sun is about to rise. Will you join me?"

She let him lead, leaning into his side as the first flickering of sunlight breached the horizon, casting light onto the frozen earth. The snow would melt. The day would come.

And Flowridia . . . would flounder. "Thalmus," she whispered, her cracked resolve threatening to break, "you and I–" She blinked; tears brimmed as she watched the light filter slowly above the trees. "I fear you're doomed to hate me, because of what I'm doing. I didn't choose my talents. I've simply sought to do what good I can with them." She tore her gaze away from the light to Thalmus himself and saw that he looked to her too. "You were the first person I trusted in Staelash," she said softly, lip trembling at the words. "You made me that darling chess set so I would feel welcome and taught me to play when I admitted I'd never heard of it. I'd just lost a family, Thalmus."

It was more than she'd ever admitted to him, but the kindness in his gaze suggested he already knew.

"I'd lost everything and everyone I'd ever loved," she continued, heart breaking at the words. "I'm slowly able to speak of it, but it still hurts to think–"

She remembered, over four years ago, when the stares of people she'd known all her life had looked at her like she were a stranger, the reveal of her magic branding her as a witch.

Then her mother, the one who should have loved her yet had made her life a living hell . . . and who she had killed.

She had lapsed into silence; she only noticed when Thalmus spoke to fill it. "I had a daughter once. Had she lived, she'd be your age."

Flowridia watched as he struggled to speak, heartbreak in his scarred features.

"I will not speak of my history as a slave, but know that I had many children, all of whom were stolen and sold in infancy, save one. Her name was Kedira, and she was kept in the same camp I lived in, perhaps to meet a fate like mine someday. But life wouldn't break her the way it had broken the rest of us. She found beauty in small things, like the rare sprig of plant life in the desert and the sparkling of the sunrise along the sand." He smiled, and it held such sorrow, his reminiscence wrenching to behold. "She tried to convince me that it was not the same sun that rose each morning but a new one ignited by Morathma, and she gave it a different name each day."

Thalmus had never shied from sincerity, and so when he blinked, he made no effort to hide the gentle glistening around his eyes. "Kedira fell ill in her sixth year. She might have recovered; she was on the mend, but my keeper lost his patience on the fifth day of her fever. He threw her into a pit of jackals–" His voice cracked; Flowridia's own heart broke with it. "I watched them tear her apart."

"Oh, Thalmus," she whispered, but there was nothing else to say, nothing she could do to comfort this gentle father who'd lost the world.

The sun cast light upon the glistening streaks on his face. He did not weep, merely shed silent tears. "Every morning since, I've named the sun 'Kedira,'" he whispered, "except for the days when I worry for you and bless it with your name instead."

They watched the sun as it fully burst above the horizon, soon too blinding to stare at. Thalmus remained a silent pillar of heartbreak, stoic and unbending. Flowridia merely took his hand, relieved and pained, his story stinging as deep as her soul.

"I could never hate you," came his whisper, and then he said no more. In silence, they welcomed the sun.

Flowridia gathered her thoughts and courage as she approached the manor, the weight of Thalmus' words slowing her footsteps.

This was the final nail in Ayla's coffin. A body waited in Nox'Kartha, locked away . . . and it might remain so, forever.

Demitri nuzzled her hair. *What are you thinking?*

"We shouldn't speak here," she whispered, any excuse to delay the future cherished. She diverted to the garden, the noise of the world immediately fading away as she stepped past the invisible walls. Flowridia stepped through the peaceful path, grateful for the silence as she gathered her thoughts. "Thalmus gave me the advice of the kind father he is—to tell Lara the truth as far as he knew, which is that my heart isn't ready. It would be the righteous path, in every respect but . . . I don't feel peace." She clenched her fists, quivering as she quelled the virulent storm of feelings. "I have her. The decision was easy until it became real."

Demitri listened, casting no judgement.

"To bring about Ayla's return," she continued, softer now as defeat settled into her soul, "I have to become a person that I'm not—a person I will likely despise. Izthuni said I'd have to destroy everything I am. But I'm not-" Again, she squashed her feelings, her soul heavy with guilt and sorrow. "I would do this and only this—my one wicked act upon this earth and then live a life of peace and joy, or so I hope. I don't know, Demitri. I don't know anything. I need help. I don't have a plan, much less the conviction to murder." She clutched her wrist, nails digging into the tender skin.

Then make a plan.

She turned to her familiar, curiosity piqued.

Make a plan. Follow it. You can turn back at any time.

Flowridia knelt before a path of tulips, somehow flourishing despite the frost. Pure white, for forgiveness, and Flowridia let her magic trace through to the roots, her soul singing as the plants praised her return. "I have a body. I have no blood. I have nowhere to work, nowhere to hide–"

The oddest thing met her sight.

Flowridia rose to her feet, frowning at the interloper. It was unseasonal, for a mushroom to peek its cap out in the winter. They craved warmth and darkness, moist air and rot, and she covered her hand with her skirt as she plucked out the mysterious fungi.

The chill of the morning touched her soul, the dreadful realization that there was an inheritance she had not claimed, a hell she could capture and rule. Mother's home was empty, and Flowridia alone knew how to pass through the ancient wards.

"There is one orb left unclaimed—or so everyone thinks. Casvir has told no one of the black orb, and neither have I. It's a lure . . . but not if it lies hidden behind wards powerful enough to detour even the God of Order. No one would know of it, except for me." She looked to Demitri, dropping the mushroom onto the frosted dirt. "What if I told you my mother had held an orb?"

Did she really?

"No. But you believed it. And Lara would too." By every god—her wicked mind shook her to her soul. "And so I bring her there. I slit her throat over the body–" Mother had given Flowridia a thousand gifts, none of which she'd asked for or wanted. But perhaps her home and sanctuary would be a present from the afterlife. "Demitri, I shouldn't."

Why?

"Your inherent lack of morality is frightening sometimes."

But this is what you want.

Was it?

You don't have to make a decision yet. But it is good to have a plan.

"I suppose you're right," she whispered. "I don't have to make a decision." She swallowed, her next words pained and stilted. "But I should make sure I haven't closed any doors."

The meanings of flowers held powerful symbolism, and as Flowridia moved to collect a bouquet, old lessons drifted through her memory. She cut tulips of every color, for gratitude, for love, and for royalty. Lara, she doubted, would decipher the meaning, but let this all be a warning.

Geranium in the brightest blue for comfort. Flowridia added a few sprigs to the growing bouquet. An odd arrangement, but who would judge but the lonely empress?

Roses, of course, but what color? Bushes and bushes of the thorned flower met her gaze, and she soon settled on yellow. Yellow for friendship. Yellow for young, new love.

The pastel arrangement would make a pretty gift as is, but as she left, a bush of hydrangea pulled her view. They were an odd flower, rarely seen in gift giving. She plucked a few, the brilliant purple adding some vibrancy to her bouquet. Hydrangea for mischief. Purple for heartlessness.

Perhaps most meaningful of all, a single, white daffodil. Rebirth, eternal life ... and unrequited love. In groups, the flower could mean a new beginning. Alone, it meant misfortune.

Let it all be a warning.

Sunrise reflected off the gorgeous bouquet, and Flowridia paused as a thought occurred to her—she sucked the lingering life from the flowers and let the energy settle inside her. She breathed in, intoxicated by their potent energies, then gripped the dried husk and exhaled, filling the bouquet with necromantic energy.

Purple tendrils caressed the dead flowers. Death flowed through it, causing it to twitch and grow, rejuvenated by those unholy energies. What rested in her hand bloomed brilliant and bright, better than before though utterly dead. Large and vivacious, they would make a splendid gift; a gift that would never fade.

Flowridia returned to the entrance of her garden, surprised to see a figure waiting.

Murishani looked downright perturbed, his foot impatiently tapping the stone path. He glanced up at her approach, then smirked and stepped forward—

Only to be visibly repelled. His charmed expression flickered, revealing fury beneath as he stumbled back. "Impressive wards. Are you truly so desperate for alone time that you detour anyone who comes your way?"

"Something like that." The apparent 'reveal' of Murishani's ill intent toward her was hardly surprising. She supposed it was good to have it reaffirmed. She stopped just before the barrier, a literal wall of magic between them. "What do you want?"

"That's a stunning bouquet. For your conquest?"

Flowridia glared, hoping it might cause at least a dent in the viceroy's pleasant airs. If so, it didn't show. "You're awfully proud of yourself."

"I really am."

"It's a gift, to twist people's minds with your silver tongue." Flowridia felt Demitri bristling behind her. "Are you sincere in anything? I'm truly curious."

"I'm sincere in my absolute hatred of you," he said, fondness in his charming smile. "Did my plan work? Will you be crawling back to your whorehouse now?"

The insult meant nothing. It was his tone, the implication of his victory, and Flowridia felt her resolve only harden. "Murishani, to be entirely transparent, the thought of sleeping with Casvir sickens me down to my core, but it would nearly be worth it just to imagine you sulking in the dirt like the worm you are. That's my spite. Fuck off."

Flowridia returned to the garden, ignoring whatever snide remark he made about rib-cracking. He could not follow her here, and she stepped all the way down the path, flowers still in hand. "Demitri, I think I might kill him someday."

It would make Casvir mad, so I like that plan.

"Knowing him, he'd forgive me if I agreed to take Murishani's job." Flowridia shook her head, the thought unpleasant at worst, but 'viceroy' was not a title she wanted.

Just pretend Lara is Murishani when you have to slit her throat.

To hear him say it sickened her. "Not the worst plan, but I still hate it."

Flowridia crept through the underbrush to escape her garden sanctuary, then returned to the manor.

She went to Lara's bedroom, Demitri waiting beside her. When she knocked, a quiet voice told her to enter.

Lara paced, having donned a new dress, her guest room sparse and void of her personal effects. The smile she gave Flowridia held hope. "Good morning! I was hoping you'd come back. I was worried I'd have to leave before I saw you again."

Flowridia stepped fully inside, sheepishly holding the bouquet. "You're leaving?"

"Solvira is large, and its affairs never end. And, with respect to his station, I'd prefer to avoid saying goodbye to Murishani, so we're leaving before his afterparty. Etolié already knows."

For a moment, Flowridia forgot her subterfuge, instead daring to smile and say, "I don't like Murishani either."

"I never said that," Lara replied, offering a teasing wink. "It would be improper if I did."

Flowridia pushed the bouquet into Lara's hands. "I grew these. They're for you."

Lara glanced between the flowers and Flowridia's face before blushing. "Thank you."

"I'm sorry for falling asleep in your bed. I don't normally drink . . . ever."

"But it took two glasses of wine for you to have the courage to kiss me?" Lara's grin held laughter, her silver eyes sparkling. "I'm flattered. And I didn't mind."

"My contract with Imperator Casvir is fulfilled—however, there are a few final things I have to get settled. Our time together will be over soon. When it's done, I'd like to visit. And talk. About this."

Without entirely thinking, Flowridia leaned forward and captured Lara's lips in a kiss.

Lara's lips were full and warm. Kissing Lara held comfort, like walking through a summer rain or reading by a fireplace. Flowridia moved her hand to cup Lara's cheek, stroking the soft skin and reflecting on the smile she felt tug at Lara's lips.

When she pulled back, Lara stared, wide-eyed but smiling. "I-I'm sorry. I'm normally more articulate than this."

"So am I," Flowridia said, the sudden rush of emotion threatening to overwhelm her resolve. "But I'll visit soon. We can . . . practice articulating . . ." She grimaced, but Lara's giggle held a familiar infatuation, her mind recalling a little girl of six months prior.

"I think I'd be happy to articulate with you." Lara's blush betrayed her innuendo, and while Flowridia had certainly considered it, it felt too damning amidst Lara's innocent laughter.

"Goodbye, Lara."

Lara barely had time to give her own farewell before Flowridia bolted, Demitri at her heels.

Lara's lips were full and warm. Peaceful, like a serene lake glittering with silver moonlight. A taste of something beautiful, a future that Flowridia, forever discontent, could never accept.

For what use was warm rain when Flowridia had been drowned in a storm?

Flowridia was almost surprised to find Casvir seated at his desk. "Are we leaving soon?"

He looked up from his endless paperwork. "Assuming you were planning to come with me, yes."

"For a short time." She thought of the bag in her room, already packed. Impressive, how little truly tied her here. "I don't think I can stand to say goodbye. I—"

But there was something she did need to do first. Demitri, wise and belligerent beyond his years, had spoken a fundamental truth.

"As soon as I return, we will need to leave immediately."

Intrigue crossed Casvir's face. "All right."

"Can you wait in my old bedroom?"

He nodded as he packed up his papers.

Flowridia left, guilt swamping her gut. "Demitri, wait with Casvir."

She ran to the stairs, heading down to the library.

Etolié was often sleepless, but Flowridia didn't hear the typical bustling of her drunken friend or the skittering of her Skalmite bookkeeper. Flowridia tip-toed on her boot-clad feet, regretting not removing them once she'd returned indoors.

She peered past the bookshelves, only to meet Khastra's eye.

The half-demon lay in the nest of scarves with Etolié fast asleep in the crook of her shoulder. She held a book in her hand, her other idly stroking the Celestial's hair. With care to not jostle the scarves or the Celestial buried within them, she placed the book aside and put a finger to her lips.

Flowridia saw tenderness in Khastra's touch, a longing in her demeanor that she knew and emphatically understood. "How is she?" Flowridia whispered.

"Finally sleeping. I would not move if Izthuni himself demanded a challenge."

Flowridia knew Khastra wasn't bluffing. Though it was stupid, she came closer, approaching the shelves where Etolié kept her prized trinkets—including one hiding an object of depthless power.

She kept perfect eye contact as she plucked the case from its shelf and moved to walk away.

"Tiny one."

Flowridia kept walking.

"I ask only that you keep the box here."

That was . . . not what she had expected. Curious, Flowridia opened the crafted box, the encrusted maldectine stones glittering in the sunlight cast down from the skylight. Blue light illuminated Flowridia's face, power surging through her veins as she held the orb in her hands.

She placed the box back onto the shelf, leaving nothing suspicious to see. "Will you tell her?"

"If she asks."

Flowridia merely stared at the half-demon, noting the exhaustion in her face. She slowly backed out, keeping watch until Khastra disappeared behind the shelves.

Paranoia fueled her. She ran, orb stashed in her dress. She passed servants and guards, but none tried to stop her. She raced up the stairs, and when she threw open her bedroom door, there stood Demitri, his golden gaze suspicious, and Casvir, Flowridia's own bag in his hand. Ana sat on her bed, the cord of the ear threaded between her ribs as she wagged her tail. "We should go now," she said.

Casvir asked no questions; he ripped his claw through the air, and Flowridia's gut churned as a portal opened.

Despite the urgency, she hesitated, instead detouring to grab the vase of roses on the windowsill.

She muted the maldectine and stepped through the portal.

Etolié awoke to a gentle hand stroking her hair. "You're getting sentimental on me, ya big lug," she mumbled, and Khastra merely smiled.

Yet, there was something sorrowful in it. "Simply savoring our time, Etolié. I will stop if you ask."

Etolié shook her head as she pressed closer to the half-demon's chest, content to quiet the world.

She remembered the time before, where they would sometimes drink to spite their livers and awaken tangled in the others' arms. Etolié had loved it so.

"Do you remember," Etolié muttered, her voice muffled by Khastra's cloth shirt, "in our first year here, when you took me out for my birthday?"

Khastra's chuckle reverberated across Etolié's entire body. "Well enough. Why?"

"It was the first time we both passed out from being drunk as hell. I woke up in your tent, and you were holding me like this."

"You had spent half the night..." Etolié looked up, wondering at Khastra's hesitation, but realized her multi-lingual companion apparently just forgot a word. "...how do you say...*gushing?*"

Etolié laughed. "Gushing?"

"Yes. Gushing. You spent the night telling me how lonely you were in Celestière. That there were no children for you to befriend because there were simply no children. You *gushed* to me about how wonderful it was to have a friend. And I was very amused."

Heat bloomed across Etolié's cheeks. "All right. That's a little pathetic."

"Perhaps, but you have always been honest, at least to me. I appreciate that."

"I just can't believe *that's* what you remember."

Khastra's arms had never been a cage—more like a fortress, wherein Etolié felt safe and quiet.

"And you don't miss Staelash? Even with memories like that?"

"No." But right as Etolié's heart sank, Khastra's lips settled into her silver hair, in a gesture that both warmed her heart and stopped it all at once.

Again. That horrible choking closed her throat.

"But I do miss you, Etolié." Khastra never whispered, never hesitated. But even Etolié felt the humming of something unspoken, words Khastra swallowed back.

Silence settled. Etolié wondered, somewhere in the depths of her self-preservation, if this were a normal thing best friends did, which was alarming only because it wasn't a question she'd ever felt the need to ask before.

"Perhaps . . . you could visit?"

Khastra said nothing, but she felt her shrug.

Etolié stammered, "I-I could visit."

The fortress grew smaller as Khastra's arms drew tighter around her. "I . . ."

Etolié didn't dare to move in the weighted silence, lest she stumble and fall into the great chasm dividing them.

"Perhaps, Etolié."

"I could." Etolié struggled against her bonds, suddenly suffocating in Khastra's arms. Khastra released her, and Etolié nervously clutched the half-demon's hands. "It wouldn't have to be an official visit from Staelash. You can ask Imperator First and Last for a night off. I'll rent us a room at an inn—we'll drink until the sun rises, and just . . . be together."

Khastra remained stoic, and Etolié wondered what the hell she had done to ruin what should have been a perfectly nice cuddling session. "I have a gift for you," Khastra whispered, but it wasn't like before with the ring Etolié still spun around her finger—she . . . wasn't happy. "It is difficult to transport, but I want it to be a surprise. Can I ask you to meet me?"

"Of course."

Khastra's hand cupped her cheek, and again she felt that suffocating agony in her chest. The rough calluses of Khastra's large hands were familiar and comforting, welcomed as her thumb stroked gentle lines along Etolié's face. "Make nice with the party guests," Khastra whispered. "Murishani is throwing a goodbye party before Nox'Kartha leaves tonight."

And so there was a definitive end to Khastra's presence in Staelash.

"But come here, to the library, at noon. Alone."

Etolié reached up to touch Khastra's hand—to keep her there a moment longer. "I will."

Something was different, and Etolié thought, for a moment, that it wasn't only with her. Khastra's smile was so . . . so *sad* as she pulled her hand away. The half-demon sat up, her tousled hair falling from its braid.

"Why does this feel like goodbye?"

Khastra's smile returned to what Etolié knew. "You are imagining things."

"No, I'm not." Fuck, there it was—the suffocation rising in her throat. Perhaps it would finally just choke her and let her rest. Etolié sat up, struggling with the blankets wrapped around her form. "Something's different. Why are you different?"

Hurt settled onto Khastra's face, but Etolié couldn't back down now. To her horror, she was given an answer. "I work for different people, Etolié. I am adapting. I worked for Solvira and played a part very different to what I played in Staelash, and now in Nox'Kartha, I must again be something new. But I am trying to hold onto what I was to you, for a little longer, because . . ." Again, she hesitated, and Etolié wanted to scream. When Khastra brought a hand up to touch her shoulder, it burned. "Because I have always been what you needed me to be, and I would have been content to perish with that as my final duty. Fate said otherwise."

The words brought panic to Etolié's stomach. As she stared at Khastra, the half-demon shook her head to dissuade her fears. "I do not mean we cannot be friends. I only mean that our relationship can only be as friendly as our kingdoms, else we fall into scandal. We live in different worlds and must adapt."

The little cuts in Etolié's heart were like a small child struggling with shears, causing mayhem but never making a clean cut—just a thousand tiny lacerations. She'd bleed to death nonetheless.

But she was right. Things were different, and it was tearing Etolié apart.

"Funny," Etolié spat, "because everything you're saying hinges on the idea that there would ever be friction between our kingdoms." Her eyes studied Khastra, desperately sought for a lie, for an explanation. "Which is odd, because here we are at the end of a wedding promising to seal us in symbolic matrimony. So what would be the issue, Beefcake? What's there to be caught in bed with?"

Khastra said nothing at all. Etolié pulled away, tearing Khastra's touch from her shoulder. It stung like she'd ripped the skin with it.

"Khastra, stop fucking with me. Is there a threat?"

Khastra looked at the ceiling. "No."

"You're a shit liar."

"Perhaps," came the reply, but Etolié couldn't stand to look at her. "A shit liar who would be flayed alive if she spoke the truth."

"Or dead since, you know . . ." Etolié swallowed her wry comment. Steeling her jaw, she stood up before looking back to Khastra, taller by far with the half-demon still buried in blankets.

A voice inside her screamed to *stop,* especially when Khastra looked near tears. Whatever would come to pass was not the half-demon's fault. She was a slave to the imperator; Etolié knew this like an errant grain of sand in her lung.

But, like a properly stubborn idiot, she didn't. "You always did hate Staelash. Will it vindicate you to watch it fall?"

"Staelash's soul was paid for."

Again, she searched Khastra's grit jaw for truth, desperately stared at her glowing eyes—yet she only saw a stranger. "What the fuck does that mean?"

Beside her, Khastra slowly began to stand.

Etolié pushed harder, her wounded heart spitting vitriol. "Nox'Kartha's up to something. You're up to something."

Khastra said nothing, merely straightened her stance.

"You were always a shit politician! Can't hide anything."

Khastra brushed past her.

Etolié's fury rose. She gathered her illusionary skirts and stalked forward, content to bring hell even though every word tore at her skin, leaving her raw and bleeding. She stood before Khastra, daring the half-demon to cross her, but when Khastra merely stopped and would not match her gaze, Etolié's wings spread aloft, visible at her will, and she floated up, their faces level.

Tension rose. Khastra's face remained iron, the subtle etchings on her countenance the only indication of her great age, the laughter lines at her glowing eyes not laughing but familiar and beautiful beyond Etolié's comprehension.

For a moment, she longed to touch them, trace them as she traced the tattoos on her arms. She nearly did, caught in a trance she daren't give a name to. Etolié lifted her hand, forgetting her fury, the compulsion to feel skin beneath her fingers louder than her anger.

But when Khastra stole her hand, stopped it from its course, the spell broke. Etolié wrenched it back. "Get out," she whispered.

Khastra's face revealed nothing except slight glistening rimming her eyes. She gave a curt nod and stepped past Etolié, who still hovered in the air.

Etolié watched her go, watched the sway of her hips and her tail. She thought to scream and wondered if it would do her good. She thought to cry and wondered if Khastra would come to comfort her.

If she fell, would Khastra still save her?

When the door shut, she settled back to the ground, tears welling in her eyes. She released a single, anguished sob but bit back the rest when unmistakable skittering approached from the shelves. Behind her misted vision, Etolié saw Zoldar, his foreign clicks somewhat understandable, even to her distracted brain. "Slow down. Use your arms."

Whatever Zoldar tried to convey, the emphatic little bug clearly had a lot of feelings about. He waved his arms, mimed something about a ball and a girl with a dog—"What's this about the orb and Flowers?"

His clicking grew more frantic, and he gestured for Etolié to follow, escorting her to the shelf of beloved gifts from a certain demon she wasn't currently thinking about. "What are you–"

He grabbed a crystal box and placed it in her hands. Etolié opened it—

There was no orb.

"Zoldar, who did this?"

He mimed hair. Bushy hair. Bushy hair with flowers—

"Gods fucking *damn it,*" she yelled, nearly throwing the box back onto the shelf. She ran from the room, up the stairs, screaming the betrayer's name—*"Flowers!"*

Those she passed looked merely concerned. She glanced about wildly, searching for a wolf, a flowery head, even the imperator since he was her new favorite.

Outside, the wedding tent had been taken away, but an array of tables and finery awaited the party that afternoon. *"Flowers!"*

"Etolié?"

Etolié turned to the new voice. Murishani grinned as he approached. "Have you seen Flowers?"

"She left this morning with the imperator," he replied, absolute innocence on his tongue. "They've returned to Nox'Kartha."

"By Alystra's Tight Ass, I'm gonna . . ." Etolié seethed as she withdrew her mirror from the air, tapping it furiously as it glowed. "Talk to me, damn you."

No one answered.

Etolié slipped the mirror away, forcibly calm as she spoke to Murishani. "I might kill her."

"Something irritating you?"

"Life irritates me," she replied, and then she remembered that Murishani was a foreign ruler and not a punching bag for her moods. "Thank you for your help."

She stalked off to find Lara instead, hoping her party hadn't left yet.

F lowridia stumbled into Casvir's office, relieved beyond measure to have returned.

The thought surprised her. But it was as she'd feared—that home didn't fit, compressing her in ways she had simply outgrown. It broke her heart.

Demitri emerged, and then Casvir, his red eyes surveying his office with some remiss. "I would ask," he said simply, "that you wait until evening to depart. That will give me time to prepare."

"Prepare?"

"If I did not stop you, you would leave immediately."

She would.

"In the meantime, I have a gift."

He left his office; she took the cue to follow, careful to keep the orb secure in the folds of her dress. Despite its worth, the roses held more value to her heart. She held the vase with care.

She was led through the winding, carpeted halls. The familiar pillars of black sand greeted her every twenty feet or so, and it was odd to think that she could feel them now and recognize their dark energy.

"I wished to have it completed before the wedding, but I can at least send it with you."

His words intrigued her, especially when he stopped before Ayla's bedroom and gestured for her to enter.

All was as she'd left it, without even a layer of dust on the furniture. The globes of light held memories of joy, illuminating the desk and the chaise—

And there, on the ornate couch that had become her bed, was a spear of infinite, precious worth.

Flowridia set the vase on the table and took the carved, familiar weapon in her hand. It was as she remembered, decorated with images of flowers, the wood lighter than met the eye. The glass head reflected the minimal light, and Flowridia's eyes brimmed with immediate tears.

Casvir's voice came softly behind her. "It took time to figure out how to properly restore it to its former beauty. My attempts to have it recreated were met with failure; in the end, I found a man with the magic to turn the wheels of time within a small sector. He managed to restore it to what it was before its destruction. Expensive, but the results are perfect."

Flowridia hugged the beloved weapon to her body.

"Such a *breathtaking* piece should not simply be discarded."

She smiled at the familiar jest, looking to him with misted vision. "Thank you," she managed to mouth.

"Rest and recover. Find me in the afternoon."

Casvir left. Flowridia could scarcely fathom the thoughtfulness of his gift and the meaning it held.

A simple gesture, yet it meant the whole world.

He had left her bag on the floor. She knelt and placed the orb within, securing it beside the maldectine bracelet.

Its aura faded.

Lara had already left. Etolié got drunk on the roof instead.

At noon, she went to the library because she was a fucking sucker.

No Khastra; no suspicious gifts. "Beefcake?"

Nothing.

Etolié sat at the edge of her nest, her memory dwelling on that morning—before Etolié's inner bitch had decided to rear up from the depths and ruin her friendship with Khastra for good.

But ... Khastra had forgiven her for probably worse things. Hopefully. Perhaps everything would be fine.

And perhaps everything might have been, except Etolié heard a strange *click* from the door.

And the quietest *thump*.

"Zoldar?" Etolié stood up, but knew the little guy was likely fast asleep. Instead, her nerves oddly frazzled, she crept toward the array of bookshelves, peering between them before inspecting the next.

When she reached the door, she twisted the knob—

The door was locked.

Etolié twisted the lock again, this time with intent on her mind and it opened. Not much aplomb, but as the Savior of Slaves she had a few odd talents she generally forgot to tell people about, such as unlocking things.

But it wouldn't budge. Etolié pushed the door with all her might, but it stayed firmly put. She peeked through the doorframe and saw the barest hints of a gigantic, over-polished purple gemstone.

Then, beyond, Etolié heard screaming.

She gave a final push, heaving herself against the door, but of course it did nothing, and a horrible suspicion in her gut threatened to make her ill. She ran to the center of the library, the screaming faint. Though she loathed to utilize it, there was more than one exit from the library.

Etolié grabbed the heaviest tome she could find—*A History of De'Sindai Expansion*—and held it above her head as her wings burst from her body. She shot up, toward the skylight—

The window shattered. Etolié flew freely.

Amidst Murishani's afterparty, guests from Tholheim and the Theocracy ran about in a panic. What was once joyous had erupted into screams. Frantic party-goers sought to run, and in the riotous crowd, Etolié saw a flash of white light—the orb.

A battalion of Nox'Karthan guards faced a monster— one with a name Etolié knew well.

Soliel.

With his blade of fire, the God of Order swiped through the crowd like shears to paper, leaving a trail of charred bodies and blood. Etolié saw his target—Archbishop Xoran stood with the orb, his envoy ahead as they attempted to rush him away.

Hovering in the air, Etolié began to shine. *All right, grandpa, we're doing this.*

Grandpa, of course, answered the call.

A strange sensation, to feel another entity wear your body like a glove. Tingly, like when you slept on your arm wrong and it felt like pins and needles as the blood rushed back—with a bit of pinching and pulling, Eionei settled into place. *He feels different, Starshine.*

Etolié—Eionei—they dove, rapier in hand, prepared to fight the god wielding three orbs. For fuck's sake—where was Khastra?!

Her headache would split her in two. *What do you mean?*

Eionei responded by landing before the fallen god, sword aloft as he said, *"At least you know a good party when you see one. Shall we? Two on one—"*

They *'oomphed'* as Soliel delivered a swift kick to their stomach. Stars flew across their eyes as what Etolié was fairly confident was an elbow cut across their face. That was, um, new. Disoriented, they staggered back—only a moment, but long enough for the God of Order to leap through the crowd.

Etolié heard screaming. Their vision stopped spinning, and Etolié watched as Soliel *dropped his sword—*

Only to maul through the Theocracy party with his bare hands. Etolié felt their magic, but it did nothing. Instead, she and Eionei burst into the air, in time for Etolié to scream, *"No!"* when Soliel grabbed the archbishop's head—

Soliel's fingers dug into his eyes. Blood poured from his eyelids. Xoran's agonized screams cut off quickly when his entire skull cracked beneath the God of Order's hands. Archbishop Xoran fell to the earth as a bloodied pulp, and Soliel lifted a bloodstained staff, topped with the white orb.

Eionei and Etolié dove toward Soliel, sword aloft, but the God of Order grabbed it as though it were nothing, his eyes oddly glazed as he matched their stare. His face was beautiful, yet wrong, an ambivalence to his gaze that spat in the face of the hateful eyes she knew. Something was off, and Etolié's headache screamed.

The hold on Eionei's sword released. Soliel dodged with no weapon, dancing around Eionei's rapier with a nimbleness his heavy armor shouldn't have allowed. *"Nothing quippy?"* Eionei said, as though they hadn't just watched the brutal assassination of a benevolent ruler. *"No lightning? I recall that being mighty unpleasant last time, but at least—"*

Purple smoke erupted at Soliel's feet. Almost like fire but . . . darker. The entire sky blackened, Etolié realized, but in the split moment of distraction, Soliel burst into dark flame—and disappeared.

They stared at the spot Soliel had once stood, shock stilling Etolié's own actions. *Let me take the lead, Starshine,* Eionei said in her head, and she merely existed in herself as Eionei quelled the masses, his appearance nearly as startling as the God of Order's.

Archbishop Xoran was dead, and Etolié saw the slaughtered party of people around him—a death toll she couldn't yet stomach to count. High Priestess Lunestra wept, her pristine robes now splattered in her brother's blood, and Etolié cried with her, giving silent kudos to Eionei for speaking even as her own glittering tears fell from her eyes.

When Eionei did finally return to Celestière, proclaiming that he would speak to Sol Kareena herself, Etolié alone was left with the cleanup.

Celebration had turned to mourning. It had ended in mere minutes—less, perhaps, the shock as debilitating as the death toll. A somber mood settled as servants went from cleaning platters of food to cleaning bodies.

Twenty-two people. Twenty-two innocent people— guards, servants, and Theocracy envoys—had been slaughtered. Viceroy Murishani gave tearful condolences, offered to fund the funerals, and Etolié couldn't even summon the will to mock him.

Sora joined the cleanup, and Etolié worked beside her as she used her goddess-granted power to heal the wounded, her little bird chirping with each success. She'd never personally witnessed Sora's power—small but unmistakable, and she managed to maintain her calm throughout.

Etolié said little, merely helped soothe the panic. She cleaned until her hands and arms were coated in blood.

It wasn't until sunset that Murishani praised her work and bid her to rest, told her to wash and be at peace but that he would, *"call her in case of the worse . . . assuming things can be worse."*

Etolié washed and wept.

All Flowridia lacked was food.

After bathing, she spent hours sorting through the memories scattered around the room: countless glowing globes stacked with care on an array of shelves, a pile of papers bearing memories more precious than gold, a book with broken binding writing the damning future she craved—*Flowridia Darkleaf,* etched into fine leather—even Ayla's clothing, lovingly hung. Flowridia plucked one—a black dress she thought she knew, its plunging neckline reminiscent of the first time Flowridia saw her—and hugged it to her body, the lingering scent of perfume and blood and the ineffable aura of Ayla soothing to her lonely soul. It was a silly thing to bring along, but pack it she did, folding it and gently placing it at the bottom of her travel bag.

A reminder, if she needed it, of why she willingly marched herself to hell.

The orb sat idly on the chaise beside her bracelet. Within the small aura the bracelet cast, the orb did not glow, muted and hidden within a void of magic. She prayed it would be enough to hide her from Soliel. She'd heard nothing of him since their meeting in Verity Forest.

Behind her eyelids, she still saw Valeuron burning alive, the great dragon who gave his life to save them. It wounded her beyond measure, the lingering mystery of his words still unsettling her soul.

"I have seen your life; I know your death."

She placed them together, the orb and the bracelet, in a pocket of her bag, then piled in a few changes of clothing. When Ana clawed at her leg, she placed the little fox in the bag as well, amused when she peeked out her head but obediently sat. She took her spear in her hands. "Are you ready, Demitri?"

Demitri looked up from his rug, sleep apparent in his glazed eyes. *All my things are packed.*

Flowridia smiled at her sweet familiar's jest, though it held the weight of the journey ahead.

They traversed the winding halls together. Flowridia was grateful the walls were built to accommodate Casvir—Demitri, though he stood taller than she, fit perfectly well. Down the familiar stairs, past gossiping servants, but Flowridia slowed at the throne room, the furious cry of, *"You hole of an ass! You absolute* slut *of a virgin!"* stopping her in her tracks.

She placed her ear against the door.

"... have no right to be angry with me. This kingdom would be facing ruin if not for my actions! Yes, I helped her—you think she can conjure any sort of illusions? I have my ways."

By the Gods—that was Murishani.

And the icy, baritone reply was Casvir. She could hear only pieces of it—"... not your right to interfere ..."

"You would have brought the wrath of Ku'Shya herself upon our kingdom. Your purposeful ignorance of mortal nature would have destroyed everything we worked for! By holding the knife to the Daughter of Stars' throat, you keep Khastra in line. By slitting, there's nothing to stop her from summoning her mother to slaughter you and half the kingdom!"

"She is under my control–"

"Not if Ku'Shya wears her like a meat-puppet! You think she would warn you before she stabbed you in the back? Casvir, she wants one thing in all the world, and if you take it, it will be our ruin."

The ensuing silence was jarring; Demitri's voice, even more so. *I feel like plotting to kill Etolié is a valid reason to hate him.*

She managed to nod.

"Instead," she heard Murishani say, subdued now, "the Theocracy is yours for the taking. Their entire leadership is unsettled, ripe for plucking, and with no white orb, they have nothing to counteract us. Khastra will lead us into victory, and all you mustn't do is kill one measly Celestial cunt. Etolié won't be touched by Nox'Kartha—that's the bargain we made, and for the price of a demi-god's compliance, it's a small one to pay. Everyone wants something, Casvir. Remember that. Exploit that."

She heard footsteps echoing from within. Quickly, she dragged Demitri back, making a show of walking toward the door as it opened, revealing the viceroy himself. "Lady Flowridia! What a delight to see you."

"We aren't supposed to be talking."

"You are so right!" And he brushed past her without another word.

She glared at his back as he left, despite the crippling realization that something terrible had happened, but it had saved her dear friend's life.

The room held sweeping, high walls and a simple iron throne—because the throne of bones had reassembled. There stood the bone dragon, docile as it watched Flowridia enter. Casvir looked almost perturbed as he looked to her. "Did you enjoy eavesdropping?"

She hardly heard it. Her breath failed her when she saw the second dragon.

Burned beyond its mortal beauty, the macabre corpse of Valeuron met her gaze, though nothing intelligent shone in his ancient eyes. His neck held iron stitches, sealing his severed head to his undead form, and his wings—oh, his majestic wings—bore patches of leather, sealing the wounds caused by the burns.

He conveyed no magnificence in death—only fear.

"Despite my best efforts," Casvir said, "I could not grasp Valeuron's soul; he is merely a body."

It sickened Flowridia to see the once-beautiful dragon. Casvir's apparent failure filled her with relief—at least Valeuron would be free of servitude.

"Flowridia?"

They were alone. She could speak her mind. "How could you?" she whispered.

"Such a beast would be a waste to let go. Even without his intelligence, he is still capable of flight. He will be an invaluable asset to my army."

She merely stared, the desecration of this glorious creature horrifying, but nothing she could fix. With a silent apology to Valeuron's spirit, she turned to face Casvir, the stark juxtaposition of his character wounding her, especially as she said, "What happened to Etolié?"

"Nothing. The Daughter of Staella is safe and shall remain so."

"What happened?"

"News will reach you soon, I am sure—but the Archbishop of the Theocracy of Sol Kareena has been murdered by the God of Order. His orb was stolen."

The terrible shock might have overwhelmed her, had she not overheard Murishani tearing into Casvir over incompetence not a minute ago. "What's the unofficial story?"

"Not for your ears."

The darkness in his tone unsettled her—she had taken a step too far. "I see."

It reminded her of an important truth, that Nox'Kartha, for all its splendor, was not her home, merely a place of temporary refuge.

By the throne, Flowridia noticed a small wagon bearing a familiar coffin, a crystal emanating warmth, and a trunk as long as her arms. "You may recall your food storage from our journey together," Casvir said. "This is the same technology, but on a more efficient scale. It is my gift to you, lest you succumb to your mortal limitations of hunger. I have also included a map."

She smiled, touched by the gesture despite her bitterness. "Thank you."

Then, he offered her a letter. "Open this when you take time to rest. Will you need money?"

"No, but thank you," she repeated, and she meant it.

She knew not what he was to her—a mentor, yes, a strange and wicked sort of father, absolutely; perhaps a friend; perhaps not. But he cared for her, in his odd and foreign way, and she wondered if she were the first and only person for whom he held compassion.

She offered a hand, and when he moved to shake it she stepped forward and stole him into an embrace, one he returned. "Where are you going?" he asked.

She pulled away and said, "I can't tell you that."

"Not in detail, but it would be trivial for me to summon a portal to speed along your journey."

It would save her over a month of travel. "The outskirts of Ilunnes—the village where I grew up."

Casvir ripped his claws across the air. A portal appeared. "I have one final question."

She stopped before the portal, staring into the black void of space. "Yes?"

"With the archbishop's passing, you are the true heir to the Theocracy. Will you reveal yourself and take it?"

She considered her future, the many paths laid before her—a kingdom she could rise to claim, a Goddess who still sought her loyalty. Perhaps she could do well. "How soon do you need an answer?"

"Now. You have had long enough."

Truthfully, she had never given it more than a passing thought. She had but one dream, and power held no part in it. "In that case . . . no. Perhaps I am royal in blood, but not in spirit. I do not want it."

She graced him with a smile, one he returned. Then, she stole the handle of the wagon and stepped through the portal, bidding farewell to the kingdom she had come to love.

Her stomach lurched, but she soon landed in a familiar, grassy clearing. Houses beyond glowed in the evening light, but even from a distance, she saw signs of people.

The village of Ilunnes held memories of a lifetime past. Quaint was the kindest thing one could say about it. Yet, to gaze upon it, even from a distance, pulled a tragic sort of longing from her, for familiarity, for a family she had lost.

You grew up here?

Flowridia looked upon the sleepy village, the setting sun casting deep shadows. She knew it all, nostalgia welling the urge to take a walk, to visit the bakery with her favorite strawberry pies, to the orphanage she had lived her whole childhood. "I did."

Smells like shit.

Aghast, she frowned at her rude familiar. "It's the swamp. Now, take that back."

If Casvir did anything good, it was pulling you out of this garbage pile.

"Listen, just because I was run out of town for witchcraft doesn't mean it's all bad."

You mentioned that. I demand this story.

Flowridia rolled her eyes and headed for the woods.

Realistically, she ought to have spent the night in Nox'Kartha, but she was eager to move forward.

Well . . . not quite eager. That wasn't the word to use when plotting regicide.

Let me hold that.

Demitri looked at the wagon. She offered the handle; he took it in his jaw. *See? I can still talk.*

"My dearest Demitri, never change."

She pulled Ana from her bag, delighted as the little fox pranced around her feet. "Stay close," she commanded, grinning as the darling thing ran circles around her.

Once secluded in the trees, her curiosity outweighed the need for speed. Filtered sunlight from the thick trees illuminated the parchment she held in her hand, the letter from Casvir:

Lady Flowridia, First of Her Name, Grand Diplomat of Staelash,

You never fail to surprise me.

I cannot begin to express my pride in your eminent victory. This letter is advice I fervently hope you shall heed.

You are no longer answerable to only yourself. You have Demitri, Ana, and the remnants of Ayla. They look to you for guidance and protection. You are now in the position of a noble. You do not have lands, but you have subjects that listen to you and depend upon you to care for them. You must treat them with fairness and wisdom. Note that I did not say kindness; kindness has no place in the life of those who rule. The late goddesses of Solvira knew that justice and mercy are to be ever balanced; one must not outweigh the other, lest your kingdom topple. Balance should be sought after in all aspects of your life.

Because of your privilege, you are obliged to be better than those of a lesser status. This does not mean to be cruel or arrogant, but to be better. Being noble constrains one to honorable behavior. Never shirk your responsibilities, to those who follow you or to yourself.

The time spent with you has been enjoyable. You are young, and your potential is limitless. Never stop learning. Watching you grow and change over these last few months has been a great pleasure to me and a memory I will treasure. You have been a rare joy to have in my life.

If you desire to return to Nox'Kartha, you will have a place here. You will be remembered as long as I live, and your family and progeny will always be welcome within my walls.

You are counted among my friends, and if you are ever in need of aid, call upon me and I shall answer. Your presence will be sorely missed.

May your foes cower at your passing and tremble at your name,

Imperator Casvir, First and Last of His Name, Tyrant of Nox'Kartha and Marshal of the Deathless Army

What does it say?

She folded the letter, her mind reciting the words. It was so unbearably Casvir and yet not, and it touched her to her core.

She tucked the letter away, the document something to cherish. "It says, that if I falter, there is still a place for me in the world."

The thick cover of trees mimicked the night as they walked. "A long time ago," she began, recalling Demitri's previous question, "I lived in Ilunnes. I was raised in an orphanage for little girls, and I loved them. The Matron, Willa, was strict but never cruel and merely rolled her eyes when I'd disappear to the woods for hours to 'read.'" She smiled at the memory, an odd longing in her heart for the time before her innocence had been shattered by her mother. "In truth, I met with Aura in the woods. She taught me good and beautiful things, magic any priest of Sol Kareena would condone. But it meant nothing in the end." She kept her pace, though her heart remained wounded.

"I pray you never know the pain of having those you love look at you like they never knew you." She saw the faces of her loved ones from long ago, recalled the dreadful day she had been found out as a witch.

"Witches are still feared in the southern parts of Solvira. Sol Kareena has no quarrel with demons, but even I can understand, with Odessa being the plague she was, the fear it would inspire. I was run out of town when I was fifteen. That's when I went to find my mother."

And you never saw them again?

She shook her head. "I lost a family that day, and my mother was hardly fit to fill that void. It wasn't until Etolié found me that I felt truly accepted, but now . . ." She shrugged, her footsteps breaking branches beneath her. "I fear I'll lose them too."

But even if you do, you'll have Lady Ayla.

Flowridia saw her impossible dream before her, the family she sought to build with Ayla. "Say those words anytime I falter, my dearest Demitri."

She told him stories of a lifetime ago, of she and Aura and the time before Odessa.

Chapter 7

The stench only grew. Soon, the ground sloshed at Flowridia's feet, perpetually damp.

A faint, green mist rose to engulf them. Flowridia lifted Ana from her feet, brushed the mud from her skeletal paws, and held her close. "Watch out for bogs."

Sorrowful, drooping trees littered the skyline, blocking the sunrise. Flowridia's very soul reeled at the memories, the stench, the sickening hues of green and yellow.

Are we here?

"We are here," she echoed quietly.

This is much more disgusting than the village.

"I won't argue with that."

The trees grew dense as they walked, eerie signs of life crying out in the distance—birds, insects, perhaps even predators waiting for her to slip.

When mud coated her ankles, she said, "Demitri, could I–"

She shrieked when Demitri's entire front half fell into a puddle. Her familiar flailed, trapped in a bog, but the harder he pulled, the suction only increased. Hopelessly smaller, Flowridia could not save him by strength alone. Magic could not help; she couldn't control water—

Flowridia threw her clothing from her bag as she clawed out the orb. Immediately, nature sang to her, the very condensation in the air hers to bend and weave. When she bid the water eating her Demitri to rise, it ripped out in a torrent, splattering the trees in mud.

Demitri leapt out, having fallen into nothing but a damp hole. He coughed, mud expelling from his lungs. *I hate this. I hate this. I hate this—*

He was cut off by her embrace. Flowridia clung tight, her panicked heart still thumping in her ears. "New plan," she said into his fur. "Can I ride you?"

She repacked her bag while Demitri shook himself free of mud—all over her. She bit back her annoyance, having nearly just lost him, and once her familiar had stopped trembling, he ducked, allowing her to climb atop his back. With Ana secure in her hand, she lifted the orb once more. An impossible plan formed in her head. "Trust me, Demitri. Start walking."

He took the wagon back in his jaw, but as he tugged it along, ice formed beneath his feet, the water freezing at Flowridia's will and melting once they'd passed.

I like this much more.

When she deemed them far enough in, perhaps an hour of travel more, she said, "Demitri, stop a moment. I need to focus. Mother's house is impossible to find unless you know what to look for."

The sky had darkened—not from night, but from the sheer density of the trees above. She slipped Ana back inside her bag and slid from Demitri's back, the damp earth stable and cool as it solidified into smooth icicles. She sat upon a flat disk of ice, content when Demitri's leg touched her back. Not much lived here, but things could have changed. It had been a year.

Flowridia let her senses expand, allowing her innate connection to this place and to the magic residing within it meet. She felt some life ... mostly plants ... but there, not a mile away, waited a beacon of guarded magical energy. Amazing, how such a powerful vessel of magic could be hidden away underneath layers of more magic, but Mother had been thorough. She had terrorized this land for centuries, and not once had she been found; not unless she'd wanted to be and lured them in.

"That's the true beauty of my garden, Flower Child. My wards are as immortal as their roots."

Flowridia opened her eyes. "Come on," she said, as she stood. "It's this way."

She regretted her bare feet, but with the orb she crossed the water without fear, ice solidifying beneath she and Demitri as they stepped. Nothing delicate met her view; she recalled that there were no flowers here. The few in her hair would be dried and treasured.

An unnatural wave of nausea struck her. The first of many wards, but she stepped through and pulled Demitri along. "You may feel some dread. It's all an illusion, dearest Demitri."

You say Aura stalked the border?

Flowridia nodded. "She managed to get past this one. It was the obscuring ones that stopped her. It wasn't until I reached out that she could break through."

She was very committed.

"She loved me."

Flowridia continued forward, letting her power reach out to touch the lingering magical wards. Time had weakened nothing; these had been meant to last for centuries. Thank the gods Odessa had not survived with them.

She stopped. Reaching forward, she felt what could have been mistaken as a physical wall. Slowly, she pressed her hand through, like molten glass without the heat, and followed at the same pace. "It'll let you through. Just focus on me."

Demitri paused like she feared he would, but then he pushed through, and though his movements were strained, he persevered. The edges seemed to tug at his fur, pushing him back, but with a tense growl he emerged.

"Wonderful," Flowridia said, and she turned to kiss his face. "I've been here. I helped install a few of them, so I'll have a much easier time breaking through." Her fingers gripped the fur at his neck as they continued forward.

Another barrier ward met them, and this time Demitri broke through more smoothly. A cottage could be seen in the distance, but Flowridia prevented him from increasing his pace. "Just because you can see it doesn't mean it'll be easier."

Suddenly, from the water's surface, an enormous, mottled, vine-laden creature burst from underneath. With its round body and attached appendages, instinctive fear filled Flowridia's heart, but she knew it was for naught.

Demitri immediately snarled, his pitch matched by the monster, but Flowridia cried, "Stop!" and held out a hand. Demitri continued growling. Flowridia moved toward the creature, hand outstretched, and let her arm pass right through. The illusion vanished, and she breathed a sigh of relief. "They're as real as you believe them to be. The victim dies of fear. It's a simpler enchantment than placing actual monsters and keeping them stagnant until a fight."

Your mother had an intelligent mind.

With one hand still on Demitri, she moved forward. "My mother was a monster. But I did learn a few useful things."

The house came closer, a stone's throw away. Flowridia stopped, letting her senses reach ahead of her. "Demitri?" she whispered, her voice beginning to tremble.

Is something wrong?

"Promise me you'll shut your eyes when we step forward. No matter what you feel. Just keep moving."

She glanced back, and the wolf had obeyed. She led him slowly, resisting the urge to vomit as the final wards pushed against them. Fear struck her. Crippling weakness threatened to end her, but she gripped his fur and pulled him forward, shaking with each step.

There, on the porch, ethereal beings sat by the door. Eyeless, slowly rotting, some of them covered in fungi or hacked to pieces . . . All appeared as they had at their death. Harmless and silent yet cursed to haunt this forsaken place, ghosts watched—every victim Odessa had claimed in her cottage.

Her stomach clenched for the infant boy laying in the windowsill, blood eternally dripping from his abdomen.

They stood as a final warning, forever watching. Demitri's tender heart didn't need to see that.

She grabbed her spear and the warming crystal from the wagon, wrapping it in her skirt to protect herself from the heat. "Leave the wagon. There are steps ahead of you, dearest Demitri. Keep your eyes closed."

The rotting wood—unkempt after Mother's death—creaked under his enormous bulk. The door swung open with ease, and Flowridia led him into the dark, moist room.

"Open your eyes," she soothed once the door clicked shut, and she hugged him close as the shadowed room came into his view. From her skirt, she withdrew the warming crystal, letting its flickering light fill the room.

It was as she remembered—the garden overturned, the kitchen a mess of scattered utensils, blood dried on the floor. Whether it was her mother's or Aura's, she truly didn't know. She moved toward the fireplace by the door and placed the crystal within the enclosure and the spear beside it. The rounded room illuminated, but even with the artificial warmth, Flowridia felt cold. "I think I'll clean up a bit," she managed to say, and she stole a broom from the corner. She began sweeping the rounded front room, dirtied from upturned earth. She'd remove the raised planter boxes later, fix the floors . . .

Demitri began sniffing around the kitchen attached to the front room. Two doors stood off to the side. *What's in here?*

"A bedroom," Flowridia said softly, "in one. The other was her workspace, where she kept her cauldron and all her potions, supplies, ingredients—anything you might need for something nasty."

She swept her substantial pile of dirt toward the door, pushed it open with her foot, and then brushed it all outside. A mess still remained, but at least her feet wouldn't grow dank simply from stepping around. When she leaned the broom against the wall, an amused smile tugged at her lips when she looked to Demitri, who stood much too large to be comfortable in the small cottage. He could squeeze through the front door, but she doubted he could do much more than peek into the others.

Flowridia approached the door farthest from the front and swung it open, a bit of light let in from the crystal. She pulled the orb from her bag, confident the wards could mask it, along with Ana. She set the fox down before letting the glowing artifact light the eerie workshop.

Small and compact, the enormous cauldron took up the majority of the room. Flowridia could have easily curled inside of it with room to spare, though as a child she would have been petrified at the thought. She recalled what horrors she had seen go in . . . and what monstrosities she had seen come out. Surrounding the cauldron, shelves and jars lined the walls, squeezed together but organized according to Odessa's mad mind.

Flowridia placed her bag down and turned her attention to the other door. She opened it, the serene blue light of the orb filling the small bedroom. A cot lay covered in dust, as well as a small wardrobe and a full-length mirror. No windows. Nothing homey, save a small table next to the bed. Flowridia stepped inside, marveling at how not even a spider twitched in the corner. She stared into the dusty mirror, her visage eerie in the blue light.

Something twitched. Flowridia stepped forward, eyes squinting, watching the hazy image move as she moved. But something floated at her neck . . . A carving knife?

Gasping, Flowridia whirled around. At first glance she saw herself, but with a knife sticking from her throat.

The phantasm cackled hysterically.

Flowridia stumbled backward into the mirror, and from the corner of her eye she saw Demitri trying to muscle his way inside. *What's wrong—?*

Demitri's words died in her head as he stared at the laughing figure before them. Flowridia's heart raced, her ragged breathing betraying her terror.

The figure finally quelled her laughter. "Forgive me," she said, waving her hand in dismissal. "Oh, Flower Child, you haven't changed a bit."

Her gut clenched. Flowridia struggled to stand up straight. "M-Mother?"

"In the flesh," Odessa said, and she gave an exaggerated bow. "Or something like that." She appeared as she did in death, a knife embedded in her throat, but her figure was translucent, casting a blue light to rival the orb. She floated slightly, her feet not quite landing on the floor, and Flowridia saw their differences—Mother's luxurious hair that fell in docile waves, the natural paleness of her skin, her sultry figure bearing the curves of childbirth—but oh, their faces were mirrors, spitting images. Flowridia couldn't form a response.

Odessa raised an eyebrow. "Well, what did you expect? Apparently you came all this way to visit. Why so disappointed that I'm here?" The eerie doppelganger grinned at Demitri. "Oh, you got a new one. He's much bigger than your last wolf. What's this one's name, Flower Child?"

"Demitri," Flowridia said, her skin crawling at Odessa's stare.

Demitri, however, simply glared. *I take it you didn't know about her.*

Flowridia shook her head.

"And who is this? A grandchild?" Odessa stooped down and offered a hand to Ana. The tiny fox obliviously continued bouncing around Flowridia's feet. "How fascinating," she cooed, looking back at Flowridia with interest. "Does your potential have no bounds?"

"Mother, how are you here?" Flowridia still felt stiff, and she knew her words were the same.

"Oh, come to the kitchen. Put on a kettle, and I'll pretend I can make you some tea." Odessa's form flew right through Demitri, and he shuddered and snarled. "I've become very good at miming. Not much else to do around here."

Flowridia followed tentatively, watching as the ghostly form floated about the kitchen. "Forgive the mess," Odessa continued. "It's a disadvantage of being incorporeal. I'm effectively useless. But to answer your question, I'm so tied to this house that after you threw your little tantrum . . ." Odessa shrugged. "Well, where else did I have to go?"

"You've been alone all this time?"

"Who would ever visit? My wards will last through eternity, and it looks like I'll be around to see it, too." Odessa floated down beside her, almost affectionate as she smiled kindly. "So. What brings you back to visit your dearest mother?"

Flowridia's eyes narrowed as she went out the front door. She slipped the orb into her bag, the stench of swamp bombarding her senses. "I'm not here to see you. I need to borrow your house."

"And I grant you permission," Odessa said, with a flourishing bow. She lingered at the doorframe, perhaps unable to leave. "Use my supplies as you wish. Clearly, I have no use for them."

At the wagon, Flowridia gently lifted the coffin, careful as she carried it up the stairs. She went to her mother's workshop, squinting in the dim light when Odessa's voice cut through. "There are matches. Up there."

Flowridia glared, but she stood and grabbed the box from the corner and lit the candles lining the room.

"What's in the box?"

Flowridia ignored her. Instead, once she'd illuminated the room in candlelight, she knelt and dug through her bag, withdrawing her bracelet.

She took the maldectine in her hand and thrust it forward, straight inside Odessa's body. Icy cold enveloped her arm, piercing like knives. The witch glanced between her penetrated abdomen and Flowridia's face. "Why?"

"I thought it might get rid of you," Flowridia said, setting the crystal back beside the orb. "It was worth a try."

"Darling, I'll leave you alone if you wish to be left alone." She gave a dramatic sigh as she floated away and disappeared around the open door. "Even though I've been *all alone* for so long."

From her bag, Flowridia withdrew precious cargo—Ayla's dress, a bit muddied but still wearable, still able to be held. She set it aside.

"No? Nothing?" Odessa peeked her head back in. "That would have worked when you were younger." She floated down and knelt beside Flowridia, staring at Ana. "So, tell me about the fox," she said, nudging her. Her elbow went right through Flowridia's side, sending an icy tingle through her. "That's no party trick."

"Ana is my fox," Flowridia said stiffly. "Yes, I raised her. From the dead."

"Necromancy, how cute," Odessa cooed, but her smile held sincerity. "Truly, I'm impressed. Have you ever raised anything else?"

Flowridia nodded as she pulled Ana into her lap and sat against the wall, frowning at Odessa. Demitri watched from the doorframe.

"No need for petulance, sweet Flower Child. I only feel that I've missed so much of your life." Her expression fell. "Will you at least tell me why you're here? Perhaps I can help. I'm useless at most things, but I still have my mind."

Flowridia's stare went briefly to the box, and Odessa turned, curiosity in her gaze. She placed her ethereal hand on top of it, which proceeded to fall through. "You'll have to help me out, sweetheart."

"You asked me if I had ever raised anything else," Flowridia said her glare growing strong again. "I'm going to raise that."

Genuine confusion shone in Odessa's eyes. "If there's something dead in there, it'll take darker magic than even I have on my own to bring it back. How long has it been dead for?"

"Over a millennium, technically."

A wicked grin twisted Odessa's lip. "So this is dark magic. How divine." She chuckled, and Flowridia actively fought a grin—she'd die before she admitted amusement at the jest.

"But I needed somewhere safe to keep it," Flowridia continued, remiss to admit the mood was lighter at the humor. "I thought I could keep her here and perform the ritual once I have what I need."

"What are you missing to bring back this body, Flower Child?" The feigned innocence in Odessa's words drew fresh anger from Flowridia.

"A sacrifice," she said simply, then left the room, back into the warming crystal's light.

Odessa suddenly appeared before her, her expression pleading. "Have I offended you, sweetheart?"

"Mother, stop," Flowridia snapped. "Your false sweetness sickens me. Stop the act." She folded her arms, shifting her weight onto one hip. "What game are you playing?"

Any lingering good humor suddenly melted, and all that remained was cruel insincerity. "Flower Child you may be, but a child you are not." The room darkened as Odessa glared. "Be aware that while you are in my house, I do retain some power, including the power to cast you and yours out. Let your precious corpse rot in the mud for what I care. But I will let you stay, I will let you perform your ritual, and I will even help. You're still my daughter, and I do love you dearly despite what lies you've used to soothe yourself to sleep."

Flowridia's gaze matched that of her mirror, and the very foundation of the house creaked. "What's your price?"

"I need a host," Odessa said, and Flowridia's blood chilled at the word. "Someone near death and up to my standards of beauty. You may perform your sacrifice as you need to, but this is my bargain, and I will not forget. Betray me, and once I find a way to restore my powers on my own, not even death will keep you from me."

A trade. Two deaths instead of one. Alauriel Solviraes and whatever unfortunate soul Flowridia managed to coerce into coming back with her.

Though her mind reeled, she had already committed to one murder. "I agree," Flowridia said, and she extended a hand. Odessa mimed to accept it. "I ask for one addendum; let me perform my ritual first. Once I've succeeded, finding you a host will be a matter of saying who and where."

"And why?" Odessa seethed.

"You told me bedtimes stories of The Endless Night. What if I said she was the one in the coffin?" A smile pulled at Flowridia's lips unbidden at Odessa's intrigue. "Ayla Darkleaf sleeps, but once she's restored, she could whisk herself away and return in minutes with your prize."

"Sweet Flower Child . . ." Conspiracy twisted Odessa's full lips. "Never again will I underestimate you. I agree to your addendum. Raise Ayla Darkleaf and command her to bring my quarry to me."

"I would never dream of commanding her. But she's rather weak to begging."

"I always wondered what monsters your pretty face would lure—seems you've managed to tame one." Odessa chuckled, the shadow of a cruel smirk twisting her lips; Flowridia's skin bristled at the sight. "All right—you kiss her pretty lips and whisper in her ear, and both of us live happily ever after. Tell me what you need from me. How may I help you? Do you have a plan to revive her?"

"I spoke to Izthuni," she said, pride filling her at Odessa's shocked expression. She returned to the workroom and unlocked the lid of the coffin. "She needs to be bathed in the blood of the moon. Neoma's power is the key."

"Interesting," Odessa replied, and she watched with interest as Flowridia swung open the lid. Ayla's gruesome countenance, twisted and shriveled, stared up from eyeless sockets. "The Lurker isn't known for exchanging pleasantries with mortals."

"He said it was because of my importance to her." A hint of sadness bled into her tone. "Is the cauldron clean?"

"A year of dust, but not much else."

Flowridia nodded and stood, taking a spare rag and wiping out the inside of the enormous instrument.

Odessa watched her with interest. "And how did you coerce the Scourge of the Sun Elves to fall in love with you?"

"Obliviousness," Flowridia said instinctively, and then a forlorn smile came to her lips. "In truth, by her own admittance, it was because I made her feel safe."

A mischievous grin spread across Odessa's face, a wicked chuckle at her lips. "Once we've brought back your lover, we'll have a discussion on sexual ritual. You might be surprised to learn what sort of spellcrafting a pair can create." Her words stopped abruptly, and Flowridia looked up to see Odessa pursing her lips, deep in thought. "I've never tried any of it with a woman before. Much less, an undead woman." That mischief turned wicked, and Odessa watched Flowridia with interest. "Oh, the potential."

"I really would appreciate stopping this conversation now," Flowridia mumbled, a faint blush coloring her cheeks.

"Oh, don't be embarrassed," Odessa said. "I've heard women are marvelous lovers—I'm almost jealous of your affection for them. Oh well. Men are so pitifully endearing when you've got their cock in your-"

"Please stop."

"I was going to say mouth."

Flowridia grimaced as she dropped the rag. "That's not better."

"Oh, you Daughters of Neoma have no sense of humor," Odessa said, swatting her on the back, though of course her hand went straight through. A sting of ice caused Flowridia to stiffen. When she turned to glare, she saw that Odessa's expression had softened. "But it truly was love?"

"Yes," she replied. No hesitation.

"You darling thing. I'm happy for you."

Flowridia's soul craved the affirmation, she was startled to realize. As she looked to Odessa's countenance, she saw all the kindness she had yearned for as a child.

She wished to badly to believe it. Her soul longed to be soothed by lies. Instead, bitterness steeled her heart; she returned to cleaning, hand trembling from subdued anger.

She finished wiping the cauldron and set the rag aside. With the tenderness one might lift an injured dove, she took Ayla's body into her arms and placed her into the center of the cauldron. Then, from her bodice, she withdrew the ear, a rush of cold burning her torso as she tried to place it atop the body. She brought it to her lips and whispered, "All that I do, I do for you, my love."

The coldness clung to her, and Flowridia lingered, longing to return the desperate embrace. Softer still, she whispered, "I love you, Ayla. I swear to never leave you." The sensation waned. She placed the ear down. "When I kill Lara, I'm going to hang her over the cauldron and let her blood drain out." Rusted hooks hung from the ceiling, perhaps there for a similar purpose long ago. Flowridia didn't wish to ask. "And that's it."

"Who's Lara?"

"Empress Alauriel Solviraes," Flowridia whispered.

Odessa placed her hand over her ethereal mouth. "And how do you plan to accomplish that exactly?"

Flowridia stared down into the cauldron, at the shriveled corpse screaming in eternal agony. "Lara is a friend." She shut her eyes and rested her forehead on the rim of the cauldron, fist clenching as she gripped the edge. "If I can bring her here, I can distract her long enough to–" Kill her? The words choked in her throat.

"You clearly underestimate the Solviraes." Odessa's voice floated smoothly in the stale air. "Assume you can't use any magic. Do you have a plan?"

Flowridia felt her limbs numb as she nodded, details of a plan she hadn't dared to think through filling her with dread. "The beginnings of one."

Odessa quirked an eyebrow. "You did say she was a friend. Does she trust you?"

A pit formed in her stomach at the thought. When offered the bouquet, Lara's visage had conveyed joy, and her eyes had lost that lonely haze, replaced by a fondness threatening to shatter the foundation of Flowridia's fragile resolve.

"I think so," Flowridia finally said, and as she spoke, Ayla's terrorized visage gazed up at her. She did not shy from the morbid image but clung to it, desperate for any reminder of Ayla's living form. Already, the memories were fading, but when she shut her eyes, fangs peeked out from behind a predatory grin. Vulnerable words drifted through her mind: *"I love you, Flowridia. Please, never leave me."*

When Flowridia finally tore her gaze away, she realized tears welled in her eyes.

An incorporeal hand touched her face, causing a faint, cold tingle to brush her skin where the forms met. Odessa's soft expression held wide eyes. "I wish that I could twist the knife for you. I will do all in my power to aid you, sweetheart, but slitting her throat must be your own doing. If your hand falters, think of your beloved. Would she hesitate to do the same for you?"

It had been Flowridia's murderous wish that led to Ayla's death in the first place. Ayla would have leveled kingdoms for her. Flowridia shook her head, forcibly holding back her threatened tears.

"My sweet Flower Child," Odessa mused, leaning her face in close, "the years we spent together are memories I cherish. All the world's potential rested in your shy countenance, and with me at your side, you made such progress."

The sincerity in Odessa's words welled dread into Flowridia's soul. Her fists clenched as her mind fought the truth in her words.

"You're a gem in my lineage," Odessa cooed, cruel delight twisting the kindness in her countenance. "Imagine all I can teach you, once we're truly reunited. I only wish I'd known back then that you'd have a penchant for necromancy."

"I didn't know," Flowridia whispered, fighting the bitterness threatening to stain her words—Odessa didn't deserve the satisfaction of her anger. "Not until my time with Casvir."

Odessa finally pulled her hand back, a bit of scrutiny in her gaze. "Imperator Casvir of Nox'Kartha?"

Grateful for the segue, Flowridia nodded. "He's a friend."

"A powerful friend," Odessa replied, smiling with some mischief. "Perhaps introduce him to me once we're done—I might find a castle for myself after all, or at least a throne to sit on."

Flowridia hadn't the heart to tell her Casvir's true opinion of her; besides, she was much too appalled at her words. "I really would prefer to not discuss your interest in Casvir's throne."

"You do know I mean his–"

"Stop."

She was saved when Ana bounded into the room, her little nails clicking on the ancient wood floor. Flowridia knelt to pet her skull, listening as Odessa said, "Most undead minions aren't infused with as much personality as your little fox."

"Casvir told me it was impressive she retained any personality at all," Flowridia said, reaching over to pet Ana on her skull. "She obeys commands perfectly, but I'm content to mostly let her be."

"Did you wield this power over your vampire as well?"

Flowridia frowned, but with some humor. "Certainly not."

"A few choice herbs and magic words, and we could change that," Odessa said, looking at the cauldron with intrigue. "You'd have a vampire at your beck and call."

Flowridia shook her head. "Ayla isn't one to be controlled."

"But who better to control her than you, the one who loves her most?" Kindness shone in Odessa's gaze. "The legacy of Ayla Darkleaf is met with terror to those who remember her. You could prevent history from repeating itself."

A bit of coldness seeped into Flowridia's blood at those words. Ayla, even under Casvir's thumb, had returned to her old game of torture and experimentation, but if

Odessa spoke true, wouldn't this prevent Flowridia's darkest fears from manifesting?

Yet, the thought unsettled her. "Love isn't about control. I'm saying no."

"You have a gentle heart, sweet Flower Child. But consider the greater good."

The greater good said she ought to not bring Ayla back at all.

"You do not have to decide now," Odessa continued. "Consider it, once Lara is slain. It would be trivial to slip an herb or two into your ritual. Then, when your vampire seeks to murder, it would be for you and only you."

And Flowridia, despite her years living in fear of the woman who birthed her, despite her bitter longing for acceptance, felt her blood suddenly boil. "Look at me," she said, eyes steeled as Odessa did so, bafflement on her lovely features, "because I will only say this one more time—*no*. If I were stupid enough to listen to that gods-awful plan, it would ruin *everything* I'd worked for. I wouldn't have a lover to hold; I'd have a slave who resented me, and if you don't understand how truly monstrous that is, I don't know that I have anything more to say to you."

The tension lingered. Odessa held her stare, a flicker of her true, wicked character showing in the slight twitch of her eye. "Night will be here soon," Odessa said, forcibly polite. "Have you eaten at all?"

Flowridia shook her head. "Not since coming to the swamp." She left through the front door again, ignoring the ghosts and their reminders of hell. This time, she returned with Casvir's trunk of food. Demitri would be starving as well.

"If I could make you a hot meal, I would," Odessa said with a sigh. "But there're still dried ingredients in the pantry you might find a use for."

Standing at those words proved to be a mistake; Flowridia felt faint. She leaned against the wall and managed to shake her head. "No, I have food."

"If you're certain," Odessa replied, pouting slightly. "Oh, once I'm returned to a body I promise to care for you again. You know I pride myself on cooking."

Flowridia left the room without a reply, stepping past Demitri who had been watching from the doorway. He followed her as she set the trunk beside the small table in the kitchen. *You're looking awfully pale.*

"I'm just hungry," Flowridia said softly, withdrawing an apple from within. Demitri stuck his face in and withdrew an enormous piece of meat. It dropped on the ground with a sickening squish, and Flowridia shut her eyes. Revulsion brewed within her, brought to a peak at what memories the noise incited. She set down the apple and placed her hands in her lap.

"Flower Child, won't you help me clean this up? Human blood is so difficult to remove, once dried."

When she didn't hear the brutal ripping of raw meat, she opened her eyes. Demitri stared at her, ignoring his dinner. *You have some bad memories here.*

Flowridia simply shrugged, aware that Odessa lurked somewhere nearby.

This place is toxic to you. That, or it's just her. I don't trust her. I don't like that you're making deals with her. It's not too late to leave.

Lips pursed, Flowridia glanced toward the walls and doorframe before whispering, "This is the only place Ayla's body will be safe. My wards are good, but mother's are unbreakable."

You don't need her.

"What other choice do we have, Demitri?"

You'll accept her help but not Casvir's?

"I couldn't accept his deal."

But you'll accept hers?

"Is something wrong?" Odessa's voice rang from the doorway.

"All is well, mother. Demitri is simply nervous about leaving Ayla's body."

That fit the tone of her words, right?

"Well, reassure Demitri that my home is a safe haven to you and yours. That includes Ayla, and it includes him, too." She floated over to a cupboard. "Flower Child, would you open this? I would like to give a peace offering to your familiar."

Flowridia stood, confused until the deep cupboard swung open and she saw an array of hanging, dried jerky.

"Perfectly preserved and full of potential," Odessa mused. "I think you helped me prepare a few of these. They'll give him strength."

The cupboard slammed shut. Heart racing, Flowridia managed to smile at Odessa. "Dried meat upsets Demitri's stomach."

Blatantly false. She prayed Odessa accepted that.

"That's unfortunate," Odessa said, frowning. "Once I'm restored to life, I'll make him something fresh. Oh, but take some for you, Flower Child. And take some on your journey."

The cupboard swung open slowly this time. Flowridia reached inside, flinching when her fingers brushed against the jerky. To offend Odessa now could have consequences, but memories of years spent being reprimanded for her so-called 'picky palate' no longer filled her with panic, she realized; only a simmering anger. "With all due respect," she said curtly, withdrawing her hand, "I no longer eat meat. Of any species."

Odessa's pleasantries were suddenly painted onto her ethereal face, her smile showing her teeth. "I see."

"I think I'll go to bed now," Flowridia said quickly, ignoring Demitri as he chewed on the raw mess on the floor.

"My room is as you left it. Hope you remembered to make the bed," she said, winking.

Flowridia marched past without a word, first into the workroom to grab her bag, and then into the dark bedroom. She clicked the lock shut, alone with only Ana.

She stripped from her dirty travel clothes and put on a nightgown, feeling exposed in the loose fabric. Scratching at the door stole her attention, and when Flowridia opened the door, Demitri tried to push past her, his bulky frame too much for the door.

"Demitri, you'll hurt yourself."

I refuse to leave you alone with her.

Flowridia reached out to stroke his soft face. "Then I'll come out and sleep in the main room. You're more comfortable than a bed."

With some struggle, Demitri managed to wrench himself backwards from the doorframe, scattering slivers of wood onto the ground. The warming crystal cast comforting shadows across the room, and even with the eerie garden graveyard, Flowridia thought she might be able to muster at least a nap.

Demitri curled by the fireplace. Flowridia rested against his side, humming contentedly when he squeezed around her. There was no sign of Odessa, but her presence certainly lingered.

Demitri spoke. *I would rather she not hear this. Just listen.*

Flowridia nodded slightly, enough to acknowledge.

I don't know much about her; I just knew you got quiet anytime she came up. But I think I've seen enough in the last hour to know she's bad for you.

Flowridia couldn't argue with any of that.

We shouldn't be here. She needs your help so I don't think she'll betray you, but . . . Mom?

His words faded when the first of her tears fell. Flowridia quickly wiped her eyes, lest Odessa come to offer comfort. Her heart wouldn't be able to take that.

"I know," she whispered, hardly audible. "But I . . ." She clenched her fists, knowing Odessa could likely hear all she said. "I know. Just let me sleep."

Flowridia shut her eyes. Demitri said no more.

Etolié went to the library and saw a pile of collected, glittering glass beside her scarves. "Zoldar . . ?" she said, but it wasn't his form she saw.

Silver wisps of light from the waning moon cast gentle beams through the broken skylight. Khastra sat in relative shadow beyond the scarves, seated at Etolié's desk. A bright, white light illuminated her grand physique, though her slumped posture revealed no magnificence.

Within the very box Khastra had built to protect and shield the orbs lay one in pure shades of white. Khastra's eyes met Etolié's, and she shut the box with no aplomb, the click of wood and metal loud in the taut silence.

Darkness shrouded Khastra's visage, the faint light of her eyes and the shadows cast from the moon all that revealed her presence.

"Khastra," Etolié whispered, daring to come forward. "What is that?"

The bitter truth settled in her soul like a sickness, slowly poisoning her with every loud beat of her heart. Khastra said nothing, and somehow that spoke a truth more damning than words.

Etolié swallowed and grit her teeth. "What did you do?"

"Let no one know you have it," Khastra said simply.

"What did you do?!" Etolié's cry echoed across the skylight and the walls, lingering like a poisoned cloud in the library.

Khastra looked away, eyes shut.

Etolié stepped toward this stranger of a De'Sindai, barely able to see her features in the faint light. "Khastra—" Etolié's voice choked, the accusation unbearably heavy.

In the silence, Khastra shifted, the barest hints of light casting her cheeks in stone. She was beautiful, Etolié saw, in the way of legendary statues acolytes built to gods, even though she sat as a supplicant. Khastra opened her eyes and said, "I did what I had to."

Soliel hadn't spoken, hadn't wielded all the weapons Etolié knew him to have. He had slain his quarry with brutality, the collateral damage heartbreaking and damning, yet when Etolié had stood in his path, he had done little more than push her away.

"How did you do it?" Etolié asked, more a plea than diplomatic words to the general of a foreign and dangerous ally. "Not alone, surely. You can't create illusions."

Khastra said nothing.

"I don't understand. This isn't you."

Khastra kept her stare to the wooden table, the moonlight casting shadows onto the built musculature of her arms but little else, her eyes the only indicator of her face. Etolié could not guess her expression, merely fail to decipher her words. "I no longer work for Solvira, Etolié."

"Are you suggesting that Casvir told you to *assassinate* the Archbishop of the Theocracy?!"

Again, the words rang across the ceiling, Khastra's silence louder than Etolié's cries.

"There were others," Etolié continued, resisting the urge to scream. "You killed his entourage, you killed guards—innocent people are dead, and you have the audacity to deliver the gods-forsaken orb as a *fucking penance!"*

Khastra stood up with enough force to topple her chair. Etolié saw the shadows highlighting her scars, the metal protruding from her chest, the fury in her glowing eyes as she strode forward. Etolié backed away, Khastra's great height and bulk capable of crushing her skull in her hands—

She'd seen it herself. Etolié wanted to weep.

But Khastra stopped, her fists clenching. "In the roulette of rulers," she whispered, her voice seething, "I chose to save you."

Etolié whimpered, "What does that mean–"

"Etolié!"

In over twenty years, Khastra had never raised her voice. Not to Etolié.

"Fools die in politics! *You know what I mean!*"

The cry echoed across the walls, lingering evidence of Khastra's rage. But then, Etolié watched the half-demon's fists relax, watched her take a stumbling step back into the shadow, watched her stand without her magnificent aura—instead as a flagellant awaiting the whip.

Etolié's jaw trembled as she warded away her threatened tears. "It was him or me," she whispered. "You did this to save me."

"It was not a choice, Etolié. I would have slit my own throat before I hurt you. But it was not my life that would have saved yours." Bitterness stained her words, each one filled with unspeakable pain. "Tell no one you have that orb. If you speak to anyone of what you have seen or what you know, it will damn all my efforts today. No one will strike against you; that is the promise I was given. I would rather have you alive and hate me than have you dead."

For the first time in over twenty years of knowing the other, Khastra turned her back on Etolié and left.

Stunned by the gesture, the admittance, and the drowning sensation in her soul, Etolié stumbled forward. "Khastra, wait," she pled, and when the half-demon stopped, Etolié hugged her from behind, face pressed against her back, hands touching the etched lines of her abdomen through her shirt. "I don't want to not trust you."

The statement welled tears in Etolié's eyes, tears she couldn't fully fathom the meaning of—only that she *hurt* down to her very core. "You were everything to me," she continued, swallowing her rising emotion. "And you are. You still are–" Her voice caught; Etolié fought to not choke on her suppressed sob. "I hate that things are different. I miss you every day. When I thought you were dead, I always waited for your laughter in the hallways, or for you to bring me food and threaten to stuff it down my throat. And when you were alive again, the feeling didn't fade." Her embrace tightened, though Khastra's core didn't budge. "And I'm sorry I've been so awful to you. I don't hate you at all—I *love* you. I don't know that there's anything you could do to make me not love you. Let's forget this. Let's pretend . . ."

She inhaled a shaking breath, addled by pain and suppressed sobs. "Let's pretend all is well," she whispered, and from her eyes, tears fell. "I love you more than political bullshit."

A pause; a realization. "I love you more than anything."

Hands, impossibly stronger than hers, clutched her arms and pulled them away. Panic rose in Etolié's stomach. "Khastra, please don't leave–"

But instead of leaving, instead of abandoning Etolié to her tears, Khastra turned around and lifted her up to embrace her. With one arm around her body and the other supporting her bottom, Khastra clung to Etolié like a gravitational force, the moon to the stars, and when she shuddered, Etolié realized there were tears in her eyes as well.

When her surprise settled, Etolié wrapped her arms around Khastra's neck and rested her head beneath her chin. Khastra's voice, when she spoke, reverberated against her core. "You are my home, Etolié. I could never leave forever."

Somehow, a more intimate phrase had never been uttered, and Etolié realized she felt the same.

When Khastra put her down, Etolié instinctively reached forward and grabbed her hand. Every modicum of self-preservation screamed at Etolié to yield, to *stop*, to walk away and let all of this be a blip on an otherwise pristine record of friendship, but Etolié's insatiably curious mind spoke louder.

The scientific method involved experimentation from every angle and of course included a control, the single factor set aside and given a different task, one that ran contrary to everything else. So, after over twenty years of friendship, with all that time spent enjoying little more than innocent affection with the half-demon, Etolié did what any proper scientist would do.

She tugged on her arm, surprised at how amiable Khastra was as she bent down, and, with thoughts of the scientific method and of how those blue cheeks seemed to blush, Etolié kissed her.

It felt like flying.

It was hardly a butterfly's touch, but then Khastra's lips stole hers again, and this time Etolié sighed at the contact, letting her lips part in tandem with her demonic companion. Khastra kissed with purpose, conveying an offer with her mouth Etolié longed to accept.

It was so easy to succumb to her. No fear, no hesitation—simply falling beneath the skylight into the nest of scarves. Like some spell had overtaken her, and in her trance Etolié pled for Khastra's touch. "Khastra, please," she whispered, her tears having never staunched.

Khastra removed her clothing, the shadows revealing her magnificent build, the wall of muscle that was her abdomen, the curves of her breasts, the metal protrusion of her heart. She was beautiful, and Etolié wondered how she'd never noticed before, wondered when her feelings of friendship had slipped into amorous territory, or if it had always been there, silently waiting for trust to build.

When the illusion of Etolié's clothing disappeared, Khastra touched her like some fragile, precious thing, savoring Etolié's skin with her lips and her hands and whispering words too sacred to repeat: *"Oh Etolié, you are so beautiful . . ."*

Every kiss on her breasts filled Etolié with light, until she swore she'd ignite, the feelings evoked within her body unlike any sensation she'd felt before. Wherever her hands settled, light sparked, Khastra's tattoos illuminating their passionate embrace.

Her focus shattered. Her wings appeared, and the pair of them shone like celestial lights.

"Let me make love to you," her demon said, and Etolié begged for it, sobbed when Khastra moved within her, pained and complete. Khastra kissed her below like she kissed her lips, every motion something sacred.

In the quiet of evocative, passionate gasps, Etolié felt the chasm between them fade away.

It took only minutes. Etolié's body screamed for pleasure, the great tremors of her orgasm held safely in Khastra's hands. The spell faded, leaving only tangled limbs and gasping breaths.

Etolié savored the safety of Khastra's embrace, her earthy scent mingled with sex and sweat. In the ethereal light, she might have thought it a dream.

And perhaps it was, for fate decreed she could not keep this sacred thing.

Khastra kissed like the world might end, the motions marred by the great finality of it all. Etolié tucked locks of her hair behind her pointed ear, memorizing every tactile sensation beneath her fingers.

They did not say goodbye, merely shared a final glance in the faint moonlight, Khastra's glowing eyes more beautiful than the stars above.

Khastra dressed, and Etolié caught glimpses of her in the trickling light, a flash of her skin, of her horns, her hair. Etolié thought to touch her one last time, to steal her hand, but regret stilled her actions, frozen by the crippling realization that their time had ended before it could begin.

Cloven footsteps disappeared behind the bookshelves. The door shut.

Etolié curled into her blankets, naked and raw, her body still pulsing from Khastra's pleasured touch.

Making love, she had called it.

Etolié wept, and not for reasons her mind could quite comprehend—only that she knew how it felt to be truly lonely now.

And what it meant to be cherished.

Sunrise peeked through the window when Flowridia awoke. When she pulled herself from Demitri's embrace, the giant wolf let her go. She looked to his face and realized his eyes were already open. "How long have you been awake?"

I never slept.

Flowridia frowned. "I'm sorry you couldn't sleep, dearest Demitri."

I refuse to let my guard down around that woman. She watched you while you slept. Watched you like meat.

"I think you might be exaggerating."

Ayla watched you like meat, too. But at least she was honest about her intentions.

"We'll discuss this later." Flowridia left him to his paranoia, instead going to the unused bedroom and brushing her tangled hair. Once she'd changed clothes, she stepped into the workroom, stopping when she saw Odessa staring down into the cauldron.

Flowridia joined her, peering down at Ayla's body, sadness filling her soul. Her next words spilled out in a rush. "Swear to me that Ayla will be kept safe here."

"Were an intruder to enter," Odessa said gently, "the best I could do is cast them out." She placed an ethereal arm on Flowridia's back, that odd tingling sensation once again radiating where incorporeal met flesh. "But that is enough, I think. And no one will come here. No one has tried since my passing."

Flowridia nodded slowly.

"Keep a piece of your lover with you," Odessa continued. "There are spells to find the rest of her body should the worst happen—spells I can teach you."

"That's very wise."

"I did not rise to power with a feeble mind," Odessa said with a smirk.

From within, she gently lifted the severed, shriveled ear—still pierced and chained—and set it around her neck. A smile pulled at her lips, the familiar weight a comfort, even as cold enveloped her body, shards of ice piercing her skin.

"So what is your plan to get your Lara here?"

Flowridia's skin crawled when Odessa's face appeared only inches from hers. "Lara tasked my kingdom with finding a series of magical artifacts. If I tell her that I've located one here in the swamp, I could ask for her help to retrieve it."

"And the empress will accompany you personally? How do you know she won't try and send an envoy?"

Flowridia hoped the shame she felt didn't blossom onto her face, though her cheeks burned. "I have a plan." She was remiss to explain it, given it involved destroying Odessa's wards. "That, and Lara and I . . . She has some affection towards me. She'll believe anything I say."

The smile on Odessa's face held vicious intent. "Wonderful," she said, intrigue lacing the word. "And you'll use that, of course."

"I don't want to break her heart." Flowridia said softly.

"So you'll stab her heart, but you wouldn't dare to break it? Your standards are an odd thing." Before Flowridia could retort, Odessa pulled back, standing straight as she stared. "Why break her heart at all? Warm her heart. Cherish it. Kiss her as you slit her pretty throat." Odessa chuckled darkly. "You'll hardly need precautions. She'll never even see it coming."

Flowridia swallowed her revulsion. Murishani had said the same thing.

"And if you cannot do it," Odessa added, *"pity.* Become whatever it takes to succeed."

She looked away, staring again into the cauldron as she nodded.

Odessa flew again into her line of sight. "So, when you say 'your kingdom . . ?'"

"Staelash."

"And what position do you hold in Staelash, Flower Child? Clearly something of importance."

"I'm a diplomat." Flowridia paused, and with a sigh, clarified, "Lady Flowridia, Grand Diplomat of Staelash."

"In one year you crawled from peasant to Grand Diplomat and endeared yourself to Imperator Casvir of Nox'Kartha *and* stole the heart of a thousand-year-old vampire? Perhaps I'll also demand a story from you as additional payment for my services."

"When you say it like that, it sounds impressive."

"I have never birthed an unimpressive daughter."

The statement brought no pride, merely an unnerving reminder—that there had been others, and those others had been murdered by Odessa's hands.

With her supplies gathered, Flowridia placed Ana into her bag and settled it at her hip. She left the precious spear, deeming it safer here than on the road, and the last of her supplies—the warming crystal—she held in her hand as she approached the door. "Mother, I'm leaving."

Odessa appeared. "Become whatever it takes to succeed, Flower Child," she echoed. "I'll be waiting."

Further pleasantries seemed unnecessary. Flowridia led Demitri out the door.

Outside, the barest hints of light peeked above the horizon, yet the swamp still held a muggy, dark aura. "Leave the wagon. We won't need it anymore. Now, shut your eyes. I'll tell you when to open them again." She led Demitri past the ghosts, her heart hurting at their ghastly stares.

They crossed the clearing before the cottage, and only then did she bid him to open his eyes. "We have a long journey ahead of us."

But you still want to come back?

"It's the best way."

Demitri gave no argument, for which she was grateful. She pulled the orb from her bag and held it close, letting the soft blue light be of some comfort in the dank atmosphere.

Ice steadied their path. Demitri spoke. *Will we be napping soon, at least?*

"You're the one," Flowridia said with some exasperation, "who chose to not sleep."

I'm not arguing. I'm just tired and hungry.

She saw exhaustion in his golden gaze, and her heart softened. He meant well; Demitri always did. "I know." She stared at the path to the cottage, though it had vanished behind ancient wards. "And I don't think I thank you enough for accompanying me on my insane endeavors."

What would I be doing besides following you?

"Eating like a king and watching over Etolié's library," Flowridia said, giggling at the thought. "But I'd be lost without you."

They continued forward.

Etolié awoke as empty as she had ever felt.

She pulled herself from her nest of blankets and scarves, the morning light filtering from the skylight above. Birds sang, grating on her senses. She summoned her flask and drank and drank . . .

A ghostly touch lingered, the dream she'd had too strange and beautiful to be real. Yet the signs persisted, evidence she couldn't contemplate but had to—the slight ache between her legs, the faint scent of sex staining her bed, even her own nakedness.

The last was simple to fix. As she stood up, she summoned the illusion of clothing and nearly stumbled into Zoldar.

"Listen, whatever you saw last night . . ."

But her words trailed off when Zoldar clicked in reprimand; he offered a handkerchief instead. She stared, confused, until he came closer and gently dabbed the dampness beneath her eyes. He placed it into her hand, and Etolié simply stared, even when he skittered away.

She went to the washroom, scrubbing the lingering traces of Khastra's scent from her skin, slowly feeling her soul settle back into her body. She washed her hair; she brushed it and willed the star-lit locks to dry quickly. When she caught sight of herself in the full-length mirror, she saw a thin and sickly woman, gaunt and pale, the outline of her ribs and hipbones apparent. Not so thin as to drop dead—she could thank booze for that—but far from pretty.

Khastra though . . . Khastra thought she was.

And . . . perhaps she was all right with that.

The hollow in her stomach could be filled. Etolié ended up in the kitchen, a very plain and boring slab of toast in front of her, as well as a full glass of wine. For the first time in months, the compulsion to eat actually seemed worth listening to.

Thalmus sat in the corner, ignoring her as he read whatever documents Etolié had neglected and instead mulled over himself.

Etolié took tiny bites, drinking in between, her stomach growing hungrier each time she swallowed. In the burn marks of her toast, she was fairly confident she saw Sol Kareena's countenance, and she wondered if this were a sign to eat or to definitely not eat her aunt's face.

She didn't notice when Sora entered, an unholy amount of bacon stacked on her steaming plate—not until the half-elf sat across from her, her dark-ringed eyes sunken and confused. "You all right?"

Etolié turned the plate around. "Does this look holy to you?"

"If I were starving, it might."

Etolié lifted the toast and took a bite out of Sol Kareena's blessed ear.

"Are you all right?"

Etolié shrugged, unable to summon the energy to face her, but now asked herself the same question—*what the fuck even were her emotions?*

Rather than answer, Etolié took another drink.

"Starshine!"

Etolié spat out her gulp of wine, splattering Sora but sparing the bacon—Sora whipped it aside just in time.

Her wine rippled, then the deep red liquid began swirling unbidden, a small whirlpool that rose and formed a humanoid figure standing no more than six inches high.

Eionei's powers were odd, and manifesting in her wineglass was one of the oddest.

"Starshine," her tiny grandfather said. His eyes, though maroon and monochrome, were bright. *"First of all, breathe. You're turning blue."*

Etolié obeyed.

"Sol Kareena's heartbroken over the tragedy yesterday, but she wanted me to send her thanks to you for–" Tiny grandpa suddenly stopped, liquid-y eyes widening. *"Are you eating?"*

Etolié held up her half-eaten toast, ignoring the slack-jawed Sora before her and the forcibly stoic Thalmus at the other end of the table.

"Your empress has been worried. She's told your mother all about it in her prayers."

"Lara fucking what–"

"Keep it up." He stopped again, this time his gaze narrowing. *"What is that?"*

"What's what?"

"On your neck. What in Onias' Hell is that?"

Etolié touched her neck, feeling nothing, but across from her, Sora's shock managed to grow. She whipped her mirror out of the air, the one generally used to contact Flowers, oft forgotten to be a perfectly functional mirror.

There, on the center left side of her otherwise rather smooth and pale neck, was a mark the same shade as Eionei's earthly manifestation.

"Starshine–"

Etolié panicked and chugged the wine. Bitter liquid burned her throat as alcohol and nothing more.

Thalmus continued pretending he wasn't listening. Sora audibly gulped. "Did you swallow Eionei?"

Etolié nodded.

"Why do you have a hickey?"

"I don't have a hickey." Etolié had, of course, illusioned it away.

"You'd lie to a priestess?"

"Don't you have bigger problems right now?"

Contrite, Sora returned to her bacon. "We've been officially invited to the funeral of Archbishop Xoran," she said between bites. "It's in a week. I'm going to go. It would probably be a gesture of goodwill for you to accompany me."

"I agree." Etolié poked her toast, resting her chin on her fist. The horrors of yesterday felt . . . muted. All of Etolié felt muted, her mind instead replaying the scene of last night, the flashes of Khastra in the dark.

"Are you sure you're all right? Yesterday was awful. The courtyard still smells like blood. I was going to lead a worship at the temple today to help comfort the masses, if you wanted to . . ." Sora stopped when Etolié shook her head.

"If I wanted to talk to Auntie Kareena, I would."

Were it Meira—Meira, who had recently been declared a saint by the masses—harassing her about church attendance, Etolié might've snapped. As it was, Sora accepted both her refusal and the pet name, instead returning to her bacon. She had her priorities straight, Etolié decided.

Etolié took another nibble of toast.

Khastra was gone.

Etolié swallowed, the crusty bread scratching her throat.

She and Khastra . . . *what had happened?*

Thalmus periodically glanced up from his paperwork, perhaps confused by Etolié's silence. Sora munched on her bacon, looking anywhere but at her.

What did it mean? They'd kissed, but . . . They'd *touched.*

Khastra had touched her as deep as her soul, and Etolié had felt nothing like it before.

Etolié stiffened as she wrapped her arm around herself. It terrified her to be seen as anything, and Khastra had whispered words that were a nightmare from anyone else, but not from her because she was different; she was *Khastra,* and Etolié didn't know what that meant.

Khastra had touched her. The release had been overwhelming, but not as overwhelming as Khastra calling her beautiful.

"Etolié?"

Etolié glanced up, realizing tears had splattered onto her toast. It took her a moment longer to realize they were her own.

It wasn't Sora who had spoken, but Thalmus. The half-elf watched, concern etched into her countenance, but Thalmus had said her name.

"Yesterday was difficult on us all," he said, but he didn't know fucking half of it. "Perhaps you should take a day to recover."

It was the kindest thing he'd ever said to her. Etolié quickly nodded and left her wet toast behind.

What did it mean?

Her feet took her down a different path—to the outside, where fresh snowfall blanketed the world. Etolié was unhindered by cold, though she did illusion a lovely winter coat to dissuade passersby from worrying.

Etolié went to Flowers' garden. The world was quiet there—a perfect place to cry.

She did. But it felt like a release instead of a horrible choking thing. It hurt, but she breathed, like coughing up stardust from her lungs. Pain meant she lived.

Wasn't this the way of the world? People met and fucked and fell in love?

Etolié had never felt the magnetic draw that most others did, the desire to touch and to be touched. But that didn't account for her fear of it. It didn't explain why she missed Khastra so dearly, longed for that closeness once more, that bonding.

Etolié laid upon the frost-bitten grass, immune to the biting cold. It *was* the way of the world, to crave love. Perhaps she simply hadn't known it for what it was until it was gone.

With her back to the snow, she stared up at the sky, framed by tree branches.

"I would have been content to perish with that as my final duty."

Tears leaked from her eyes, cold upon her face but never freezing. Had this been the truth all along? A truth she'd simply denied? All those mornings waking in Khastra's arms . . . Was it truly so odd to crave the touch of someone you merely saw as a friend?

Perhaps it was, given her aversion to touch as a rule. The world itched; people itched. But Khastra's strong arms and callused hands had always been a comfort.

She shut her eyes, another sob escaping her throat. What use was it now, when Khastra was gone?

"We can only be as friendly as our kingdoms, lest we fall into scandal."

If Solvira knew she'd fucked the person responsible for the archbishop's death, her crown would risk forfeit.

But Khastra's lips had felt like pure joy, and Etolié wept to remember it, surprised to realize she'd do it all again, that when Khastra had moved inside her, they'd finally felt close enough.

And she wondered most of all, as she cried in a clearing filled with frost, if Khastra wondered all these things as well, or if it had meant nothing at all.

The next morning, Etolié sat inside a carriage, face pressed against the glass window, watching the world roll by. Across from her, Sora was knitting, that little bird of hers perched on her shoulder. This was a habit Etolié hadn't known about but, well, it wasn't like she was exactly perceptive of the world around her. Or inside her.

Making love, Khastra had called it. Etolié spun the ring on her finger. "Sora?"

Etolié felt eyes. "Etolié?"

"So . . . I have a friend."

After a full five seconds of Etolié saying nothing to explain that admittedly odd phrase, Sora said, "You have a few of those."

"You don't know this one. But she has, um, another friend, and they've been friends for a really long time—like twenty years, long time. And they were best friends. Best buds, bosom buddies, whatever the fuck you want to call it—but speaking of bosoms . . ." Etolié grossly regretted that segue. "Let's say they had sex."

"Your friend and her friend?"

"Yes. What would, um . . ." Etolié finally looked away from the window, content to stare instead at the funny little doily Sora held between those weird needle things. "What would that mean?"

Sora, however, looked directly at her with the sort of disparage that suggested she wasn't a total moron. "It would mean they had sex, Etolié."

"But what would it mean . . . for their friendship."

"I think they'd need to have a talk to establish if they wanted to remain friends or be something more."

"And that's the thing," Etolié said, realizing her gaze was rapidly shifting between the doily and the window, the ceiling and the floor—could she not just sit still, dammit? "Let's say she doesn't know how she feels about that."

"Your friend or your friend's friend?"

Etolié threw her hands up. "You just asked the next big question, which is 'how does the friend friend feel?' Does she want to have more sex with her friend? How *long* has she wanted to have sex with her friend? And how the fuck are they supposed to talk about this when they're a thousand miles apart?"

"I lost track of who–"

"And what the hell does that mean, for her to just do the fuck thing and then leave with no explanation? How am I supposed to fucking cope with that?!"

"I don't know, Etolié. How are you going to cope with that?"

Etolié shut her mouth, words catching in her throat. "I mean, on behalf of my friend."

"Right. Of course. Do continue."

"My friend doesn't know when they'll see each other again and . . ." Etolié swallowed an uncomfortable rise of something that felt suspiciously like tears. "My friend doesn't know how to deal with that."

Sora continued knitting her doily. Etolié wondered if knitting were just a nervous tick old women had—as well as restless half-elves. "Has your friend considered writing a letter?"

Etolié slowly laid herself upon the bench, now staring at the ceiling. "She hasn't."

"It might help her sort out her own feelings. And if she decides to send it, it would let the friend's friend know how the friend felt and then the friend's friend could write back–" Sora stopped and stole a deep breath. "That's a mouthful. Anyway, friend friend could write back because the postal service between Staelash and Nox'Kartha is really quite spectacular, thanks to the embassy."

Etolié perked up. "Really?"

"Assuming that's where the friend friend is."

She settled back down, wondering how many drafts it would take to actually break through the weird blockage between her and her feelings.

"And for what it's worth," Sora said, "while I obviously don't know your friend–"

"You don't."

"—I'm sure if they've been best friends for twenty years, whatever happens, it'll have a happy ending."

Etolié smiled, faint and wistful. "I don't really know what a happy ending means, but I hope you're right."

"For her sake."

Etolié nodded. "For her sake."

Silence settled, the only sound the constant crunching of dirt and rocks beneath the carriage wheels.

"Sora?"

"Etolié?"

"Do you have any paper?"

Sora had plenty.

Sleeping beneath the stars, Flowridia's heart yearned at the memories of her time in Nox'Kartha.

For three days they had walked north, avoiding civilization and resting in copses of trees. Mostly forest and grassland, but Demitri's speed was impressive, even if he often had to stop and rest.

You try sprinting for hours at a time, mom. I dare you.

So when he rested, he rested hard.

Every night, she had drawn a perfect circle through the dirt and grass around Demitri, marking it with symbols of another world. A ward for safety, one for invisibility, another for deafness to anyone who sought them harm . . . impenetrable and iron-clad, her mother's specialty.

Demitri's deep breathing helped her own hold a steady, relaxed pace. But as she rested against her familiar's fur that night, breaking twigs from beyond brought the eerie awareness that they were not alone.

Frowning, she stood, careful to not jostle her sleeping familiar. "Stay, Ana," she muttered, and Ana halted in place.

Beyond the trees, nothing but darkness and the occasional twinkling of stars from above met her view. Animals screeched and chattered. The night was far from quiet.

Flowridia stared into the dark forest, the comfort of the wards enough to prevent her from panicking, but something was here.

It was enough to keep her awake all night. Before sunrise, when Demitri stirred, so did she, sitting up to rub her eyes of exhaustion.

From the gifted trunk, she withdrew enough raw meat to create a second Flowridia, which Demitri quickly devoured. "I feel something. I don't know how to describe it. But please be careful today."

If I can't fight it, I can outrun it.

Soon, he stood, and she sat in silence as she dispelled the wards. Exposure smacked her from every side. The muted sounds of the night screamed, from chattering crickets to howling wolves. Day would come soon, but night had yet to settle. "It's so eerie," she whispered, "coming back into the world."

Everyone needs a safe haven. We're lucky ours can be portable.

She nodded faintly as she stood. "I only wish I could do better."

The blinding sun shone suddenly through the trees, illuminating she and Demitri and Ana. Yet, she felt no warmth, and as she brought a hand to shield her eyes, she realized it was not the sun she loved—but the Sun she feared.

The God of Order had come.

Flowridia cried, "Demitri—!" but as her familiar knelt to carry her, the roots of the trees suddenly rose to entangle him. Demitri howled as his limbs were tied up in thick, gnarled bark. He struggled, failing to tear himself free. Flowridia felt a rise of nothingness engulf her, purple smoke seeping from her pores as she touched the errant roots and stole the life they held. But even as she infused them with death, it held but a candle to the power she had wielded with the black orb.

More roots came. Demitri soon lay caged. Flowridia dove to her bag, realizing she had one weapon yet to save her—the very weapon the villain sought.

Thunder rumbled above them, the early morning light blockaded by clouds. "Lady Flowridia of Staelash, I will not hesitate to slaughter your familiar, should you take another step." Soliel had come, standing not ten feet away. He held an orb of swirling green and purple, but she knew the other two were tucked away into his armor. Flowridia rose, the bag touching her feet. "I felt your orb, but I do not feel it now. Where did you hide it?"

Thank every god—the maldectine was working. "I don't know what you're talking about—" The roots around Demitri tightened. Her wolf howled in pain, and Flowridia felt it in every nerve of her body. "Stop!"

Soliel did so; the roots loosened. "Well?"

"It's somewhere you can't find it. Hidden behind layers of wards that would take even you a thousand years to sift through. You'll never find it if you hurt me."

Soliel shook his head. "I think, if I hold a knife to your familiar's throat, you will tell me. And if I present you tied and helpless to the court of Staelash, they will bend to whatever I ask—including the location of the orb they hold."

"Staelash doesn't have an—"

Demitri suddenly howled in pain. Flowridia felt a laceration in her gut and realized, when she looked back, that a tree root had impaled him through his stomach. "Demitri!" she screamed, but when she tried to kneel at his side, fire rose to stand between them, controlled but no less dangerous. "Stop!"

"He'll bleed out in minutes, unless you tell me the location of your orb."

Demitri shook, and she heard his pained voice in her head. *Spite him. Don't give it to him—*

"Demitri, I can't lose you. I *can't.*" Flowridia covered her face with her hands, the heat from the fire threatening to sear her skin. "The Abyssal Swamp, outside Ilunnes. My mother's home."

The fire fell. Flowridia ran to Demitri, caressed his fur but realized she could do nothing to heal him—though the skin begged to be reformed, the branch was still tearing at his insides.

You liar, you.

To her surprise, Soliel knelt beside her. The root shriveled and shrunk, though Demitri howled at the touch. It pained Flowridia to watch him, but then Soliel's entire body glowed.

Like Flowridia's own dark power, but he shone from within in golden light. He removed his armored glove and touched Demitri through the branches. Flowridia gasped as the wound instantly sealed shut, leaving not a trace or scar.

And no pain for her dear familiar. Legends spoke of the God of Order as a benevolent deity who had walked among mortals, gracing them with wisdom and healing, hardly ruling; more a friend.

Somewhere, beneath his corrupted spirit, that same man lingered.

Soliel stood and brought his hand to his lips, then whistled loud enough to frighten the morning away. "You'll both be coming with me."

"I told you the truth—"

"Assuming you did, you said yourself that I would need you to break through the wards."

From the trees, Flowridia saw a strange creature emerge. Horse-like, yes, with its hooves and shape, but it was the sickliest horse she had ever seen—assuming that was what it was. Its snout was swollen, and it bore an enormous hump on its back, supported by impossibly thin legs.

It was also gargantuan, sized to perfectly seat the God of Order. Soliel approached the creature and stole a glowing, golden rope from a saddle bag. He brought it to Demitri and tied a loop around the wolf's neck, ignoring his furious growling.

The tree roots released Demitri. When the wolf struggled to bite his bond, it held—and sparked when he bit down. Demitri yelped; Flowridia's bleeding heart ached. "Stop hurting him."

"He's hurting himself, at this point." He spoke to Demitri directly now. "You'll be treated gently, if you behave. But while I would hesitate to slit the throat of your mistress, I have no such qualms about you." Soliel looked to Flowridia. "Understood?"

She nodded, and when he gestured for her to offer her arms, he tied her wrists with the same rope. "With your consent, you'll ride with me."

"I beg your pardon?"

"It's a long ride to Ilunnes." He offered a hand, and Flowridia realized he was entirely serious in his odd chivalry.

Nervous, she nodded, uneasy when he placed his hands around her and lifted her gently onto the saddle of the odd, monstrous creature. It reminded her of time past, when Casvir had helped her to ride her horse, but instead of cold claws, she felt a warm human hand and one armored.

She watched him place his glove back on before moving to settle behind her. "I think your horse is sick," she said, though when she touched it, she felt nothing amiss.

"Not a horse. In Moratham, they breed camels large enough to accommodate half-giants. You've never seen one?"

Flowridia shook her head. This did explain why he had come so far south, but while the camel might be perfectly nice looking for its species, she couldn't rid the image of it being the ugliest horse she'd ever seen.

His arms were a cage as he took the reins. With her back pressed against his chest, she felt his warmth, lit from within like a furnace.

Or, perhaps, a dying star. His supernova would destroy the worlds as they knew it.

The camel began a steady pace. Back into the thick gathering of trees, and Flowridia was utterly mute from fear. She felt Ana squirm in her bag and silently pled for her to still. Below, Demitri followed, and when she caught his eye, she felt courage enough to ask, "Are you all right?"

To be honest, better than I've ever felt. Even if I intend to rip his limbs off once you're safe.

But she forgot that Soliel sat beside her. "I don't believe I understand the question."

"I was talking to Demitri," she replied, surprised at the gentleness in his wicked voice. "But I suppose everyone needs someone to ask that sometimes." Empowered, though still near frozen from fear, Flowridia looked back at the glowing God. "Are you all right?"

The camel still moved, but Soliel stared down, his eyes adopting the softness of their color—a gentle brown, flecked with green. An amused chuckle escaped his chest, reverberating against her body. "I spent ten thousand years trapped in a ghostly shell beneath the earth waiting for the world to remember me. I cannot lie and say the last six months have been any more pleasant."

"With due respect, you don't have to be doing this."

She said it with as much sincerity as she could muster; still, he laughed. "It is my duty to balance the world after her wrongdoing. There is no other purpose for me. Once it is fulfilled, you may swing the sword yourself if you are alive to see the new world."

The reminder of her own mortality chilled her blood, numbing her limbs. She recalled his previous words—*"I know your death"*—and dared to ask, "What does it mean?"

"It means that I truly have no purpose once—"

"No," she interrupted, recalling the memory haunting her sleep, of the screaming dragon who had burned alive to save her. "I apologize. You told me once that you knew my death. What does that mean?"

The clouds had dissipated. Sunlight speckled down through the leaves, casting her dire situation into an almost cheery atmosphere. "You know I was born and raised in this era. I knew your name, and I knew your legacy. I know how you die."

"You called me Flowridia Darkleaf."

"Forgive me. It was who you were."

It was foolish—so terribly foolish—to let those words be of comfort, but it assured something dangerous and true—that at least in that timeline, Flowridia had found the life she desperately craved.

"Did you know me?"

This time, Soliel shook his head.

Morning birds sang. Flowridia felt uneasy, even with their comfort. "Valeuron deemed me worthy of the orb," she whispered. "Do you know why?"

"I do not know what Valeuron saw in your future to precisely decide you were worth granting it to. But to know your future would mean to take it away—do not ask me more of this."

Valeuron had been a son to him—she recalled the image Valeuron had shown, of Soliel standing with kindness in his visage; she remembered the comfort she'd felt in the arms of a woman she suspected was his counterpart.

"Did you create him?"

"She and I both, yes. Formed from clay and granted life. She had always wanted children but could not conceive them; she loved them with all her heart."

Yet, Soliel had slain one in cold blood.

No accounts she'd read had written of love between them, yet Flowridia suspected—she had seen it in the wistful works of art, in Valeuron's daring to use Chaos' legacy against Soliel. If he and the Goddess of Chaos had given life to something new, Flowridia struggled to imagine a truer expression of love. "She must have been dear to you."

"Yes."

"Did you love her?"

Something wistful settled onto his handsome face. "I loved her the moment I saw her. She was beautiful and vibrant, but in the way lightning foretells a thunderstorm. Dangerous. Intelligent. Unpredictable. The embodiment of chaos in every real way."

The words he spoke left gashes in her mind, memories welling from the wounds of a tempestuous woman too wicked for this world who held Flowridia's heart frozen in an icy stare. "I understand that love is complicated."

"The price of love is always high, Flowridia. I loved her for an eternity, and at times, she loved me too. But I think we were always meant to tear the other apart." Then, quite suddenly, his jaw grit. "Forgive me—I have said too much."

"I don't mind—"

"I dare not say more."

They lapsed into silence. Flowridia clutched her bag to her chest, knowing her fate would be sealed if he knew what she hid within it.

"Read this, won't you?"

Etolié handed Sora draft twenty-four of her letter to Khastra.

The half-elf snatched it away with much more force than Etolié's unnervingly sober mind could handle. She pulled her flask from the air and drank, not stopping until she heard a voice say, "You want me to read the whole thing again? Why not just recite what's new?"

Etolié sensed a bit of exasperation. "Look, I have to make sure it feels complete."

"I don't need to read a seventh time about how her 'sucking on my nipples evoked a tenderness I'd never felt before.'" Sora dropped the letter on the bench. "Sorry—the 'pink and sensitive buds of my breasts.' This is nauseating. And much more information than I needed to know."

Etolié curled up on her side, the bench cushioning her exhausted form—both from lack of sleep and too much thinking. Fortunately, embarrassment wasn't a word in her vocabulary.

"How is that pertinent, anyway? You emphasize how dark it was. You wouldn't notice your nipples when Khastra's tattoos are apparently 'glowing with the same vibrancy as the moon.'"

Etolié finally looked up and saw how thin a line Sora's lips had become.

"Besides, this is action-oriented. You don't actually talk about your feelings."

"Remember the part about breasts and tenderness—"

Sora ripped the parchment down the center. "Start over."

"I need that."

Sora opened the carriage door just enough to toss the papers onto the dirt outside. "Khastra knows what happened. She was there. Tell her something she doesn't know."

She offered a fresh sheet of parchment. Etolié accepted it, quill quivering in her hand. "You're oddly supportive for being a bitch."

Khastra,

But, try as she might, though she scrawled a few useless words, her emotions were locked behind a door she'd sealed years ago.

After an hour, she set the paper down and laid upon the bench once more. "Sora, may I be honest?"

"You've been disgustingly honest for the past three days, and you're asking permission now?"

"Do you want me to stop?"

Sora, nosey gossip that she was, begrudgingly shook her head.

Etolié set the paper aside. She thought of Khastra, of the night they'd shared, of those rough hands on her and in her and then their embrace—Khastra's kisses on her hair and lips as she held Etolié in her arms and coaxed her soul back into her body.

The world had never been so quiet or so peaceful. She longed, so dearly, to feel that again.

"I don't exactly have a brilliant track record when it comes to sex," Etolié continued softly. "It's a weapon; men are never more vulnerable than when they're grunting inside you, so I used it even though I hated it. I never saw it as love, probably because my momma—"

"Camdral, please, leave her alone," Staella pled, shielding Etolié with her own frail body. "She didn't mean any harm—"

Etolié watched as he ripped them apart and bent Staella over the table.

"Close your eyes, Starshine—"

In the carriage, Etolié simply stared at the ceiling, feeling nothing at all. ". . . it's manipulation. It's control. Sometimes it's a way to protect yourself." Etolié shut her eyes, a wash of dread stealing her resolve. "Perhaps it was monumental for Khastra to touch me and for me to trust her enough to want it."

She felt lightheaded, having hacked up enough weight to unbalance her for years.

"Tell her that."

Etolié turned to look at Sora.

"That's the most authentic thing you've said in days."

The words highlighted a precious and inalienable truth—that Khastra knew and carried secrets for her when Etolié hadn't been able to move another shaking step.

With some trepidation, Etolié sat up and picked up the paper again. She shut her eyes, recalling countless embraces, countless perfect nights drinking and laughing and craved them with all her heart and soul.

Khastra,
I need to say a few things . . .

Sunset cast an ominous shadow. They reached a clearing, a floral-dotted meadow Flowridia longed to nap in. She felt her eyes begin drooping, finally having accepted that, perhaps, Soliel could be trusted with her physical form, before realizing she wasn't the only one struggling. Soliel and his steed had no trouble, but Demitri had been running for days.

As she suspected, Demitri stumbled, stubborn but exhausted. She dared to look up. "Soliel, we have to stop. Demitri needs to rest."

"Then he is dragged behind. Or left. I need you, not him."

Anger surged at the statement. Flowridia glanced down at Demitri, watching the way his muscles quivered beneath his fur. She looked to Soliel himself, whose stance had softened in the hours they had traveled. With his focus set to the forest, he gave no reaction when she suddenly tipped over.

Flowridia fell from the camel.

Her back hit the forest floor with a *thud*. Flowridia groaned at the impact. Demitri immediately raced to her side. With her hands still tied, she sat up, just as Soliel's feet crunched upon the pinecones and leaves beside her. "You foolish–"

"Soliel, do you wish for me to be a thorn in your side? *Because I will*." When he didn't immediately strike her for the insolence, Flowridia dared continue. She stared up, matching his pointed glare. "I can't defeat you. I can't run away. But you won't kill me, and I swear on whatever gods dare to listen that I will make your life hell until we arrive."

Soliel stood tall. "I could also chop the head off your familiar and let you be dragged behind my horse."

"You could."

She held his gaze, willing her courage to hold. Soliel looked over at the enormous wolf standing beside her and matched his gaze. "We will stop for a time," he said, and he tied the rope attached to Demitri's neck to a thick tree trunk.

Demitri lay beside Flowridia, his voice heard only in her mind. *Pretty stupid.*

Flowridia kissed his nose.

She watched Soliel stand before his horse—camel, she corrected herself—and remove his glove before he ran his bare hand over the creature's nose. There was a heart in there somewhere, and it made her wonder more concerning Valeuron.

Had it bled at all to slay him?

She slipped her hand inside her bag, daring to touch the orb, to feel that it remained. Her hand brushed against that and more, including a mirror.

Surreptitiously, she slipped her hand out. She willed her heart to steady, then stood up as she said, "Soliel, I need to take care of a personal affair. A . . . *womanly* affair."

With the words came an impromptu stare-down as Soliel visibly contemplated her request. Flowridia knew her request was entirely reasonable. She also suspected that Soliel, with his unexpected chivalry, would never in a thousand years insist on supervising her. So she held his gaze, innocence in her fluttering lashes. Finally, his said, "You have two minutes before I hunt you down. Your familiar stays."

She ignored Demitri when he spoke. *What's your plan?*

Instead, she skipped through the trees, the fading sunlight still more than enough to illuminate her path. When she couldn't see him, she withdrew the mirror, quickly tapping the magic device.

It glowed; with her tied wrists, she faced it away from the temporary camp. When the Celestial's face appeared, Flowridia nearly cried from relief. "Etolié–"

"This'd better be about that fucking orb you stole, Flowers!"

The words sounded like shrill thunder in the quiet evening. She hadn't accounted for Etolié's temper. "No, listen–"

"I swear upon Morathma's Whore Mother if you think this is a fucking joke I'll–"

She shushed the irate Celestial, but to no avail. "Etolié, Soliel is–"

". . . just because you got the fucking artifact in the first place doesn't mean I won't wring your neck if you don't return it this . . ."

"Etolié—!"

A sudden earthquake stole her footing—Flowridia fell into a crevice in the ground, the mirror flying from her grip. Buried in earth from her waist down, thoroughly trapped, when she looked to the camp, she saw Soliel approaching, an unimpressed frown on his face as he held a green and purple orb in his hand.

Flowridia frantically clawed at the mirror, face down and just out of reach. Apparently losing sight hadn't detoured Etolié's tirade—she spewed obscenities until Soliel lifted it, keeping it facedown until his finger tapped the glowing glass. The Celestial's words disappeared.

"I was expecting something like that," he said, and then he crushed the magical device in his gloved hand. Shattered glass fell to the forest floor. He brushed it against his armor then offered his hand to Flowridia, but she hesitated to grab it. Despite her tied wrists, she tried to lift herself from the crevice with her elbows, but the earth inexplicably drew tighter around her. With a glare to Soliel, she accepted his aid; he helped her as the earth parted for her escape.

Nothing in his stance suggested anger. She held her bag tight to her body, feeling the shape of the orb through the thick material and followed as he led her back to their camp. "I didn't realize I had a reputation for being a nuisance."

Soliel shook his head. "No, but my mistake with you in the past was expecting you to ever be predictable."

"So now I'm predictably unpredictable?"

To her surprise, he chuckled. Discomfort welled in her stomach—forming a human connection with the worlds' impending doom hadn't been how she wanted to spend the evening, yet . . .

He had once been a man, and she was a fool to forget that. He was once a little boy born in Celestière. A lesson she was remiss to recall, despite its value, looped in her head: *"Sex, money, and power . . ."*

"Though I suppose you have experience dealing with unpredictable," Flowridia continued. She saw Demitri, yet resisted the urge to run to him. Instead she continued calmly at Soliel's side—a man who sought power, though only as the means to an end, and to whom money meant nothing. Yet, what was love but the greatest weakness of all? "What was her name, anyway?"

Soliel held a weakness, illustrated by the hesitation on his tongue. "Her true name is not for your ears."

"My apologies. I hold no disrespect toward the Goddess of Chaos. Merely curiosity. You seemed reflective earlier." When he said nothing, she sat beside Demitri and ran her hand along Demitri's fur. The wolf tensed, likely fighting the urge to sleep. "You were reborn with your birth. Will Chaos come the same way?"

Soliel sat apart from them, near his camel. "Perhaps." He frowned, painful reminiscence on his features. "But I hope to have this business done with before then."

"And then present her with a destroyed world?" Flowridia studied his contrite visage. "I don't know if she was known for wisdom, but perhaps she knew something we didn't. You could ask her yourself, once she's reborn–"

"Do not speak of what you cannot understand," he said, the rumbling of distant thunder in his voice.

But Flowridia had no more fear of storms. "She was unpredictable, yes, but she wasn't evil. We cannot know her mind, but–"

"Do not speak of her!"

Flowridia's words withered in her throat; Soliel looked nearly prepared to tear her head from her body, so vicious was his glare.

He said nothing else, merely slowly turned aside. Silence settled onto the clearing, the purple sky nearly dark.

Flowridia cursed her errant tongue, realizing she had acted too soon. She settled into silence and listened to the first hints of night creatures among the trees. Beside her, Demitri stirred, perhaps prepared to tear Soliel's face off—as he would phrase it.

"I never did ask where you were going."

Soliel's words startled her. Flowridia matched his gaze. "I don't see why I'd possibly answer that."

"You were heading north—to Neolan, perhaps? Or farther on, to Staelash?"

Flowridia shook her head, content to glare.

"I simply wonder why you left the orb behind, when you alone claim to have the capacity to reach it."

The sun set. Darkness settled upon them. Flowridia said nothing, lest she speak and condemn herself.

His face had never changed; it held the weight of his wicked quest. "Perhaps I'll know for myself, once we arrive."

She remained silent, the darkness stifling but the sound of night creatures soothing. In the distance she heard a howling wolf; Demitri perked up. *Mom.*

Flowridia looked to her familiar.

Something's out there.

She glanced about the clearing, watching as mist rose to match the growing dark. Something ominous settled in the atmosphere.

She looked to Soliel, noticing that he, too, appeared suddenly alert.

Reflected in the shadows of trees were hundreds of glowing, golden eyes. Flowridia stood up, the hairs on her arms raising when she heard the sound of countless predators snarling.

Wolves emerged. Starved and vicious, they stared hungrily upon Flowridia's party. But it was no alpha who led them—or, rather, it was an alpha of a very different creed.

A shadow emerged from the trees, walking past the pack of wolves with pure, ethereal grace. Paler than the silver moon, her long blonde hair lay braided across her shoulder, and she wielded two curved blades. Confidence radiated from her proud stance, fearless as she smiled. "So you're the ancient Sun God," she said, staring directly at Soliel. Flowridia saw pure white teeth glint in the bright light.

Soliel stepped forward. The wolves rushed. They bombarded him, even as fire engulfed his form. Thunder rumbled. But against a hundred wolves, even he staggered.

The earth rose to defend him. Pained howls met Flowridia's ears, but more wolves appeared where any fell.

In the chaos, the woman flew to her side, her swords already tucked behind her back. She smelled of leather and ice. "Come on, sweetie," she said, facing Flowridia. With a dagger that radiated an ominous aura, she cut her bonds with ease—and then Demitri's. "I'll carry you. Hopefully, your wolf can keep up."

A quick nod, and Flowridia stooped down to pick up her bag before the taller woman cradled her in her lithe, strong arms. Wind whipped across her face as she ran, and Flowridia tucked her head into the woman's chest.

They ran until the howling wolves were far behind.

The woman never faltered. When Flowridia looked up again, all she saw was fog and trees. Darkness engulfed them; she realized they had entered a cave. Winding tunnels met her obscured view. The terrain grew colder.

When they finally stopped, the black cave utterly consuming, the woman set her down with ease; Flowridia couldn't help but wonder what sort of unnatural strength flowed through her physique.

Flame illuminated; the woman held a lit match. Vibrant shades of orange cast color across her alabaster face, reflecting hellfire in her eyes. She brought the match toward what Flowridia saw was a candle, then took the lit candle and touched it to another, then another . . .

The light revealed a small campsite, comfortable but clearly temporary. A pack sat abandoned by the wall, and a scattering of potions littered the corner. Candles had been tucked into the natural rock shelves within the cave walls.

When the woman had completed her task, she stood before Demitri, inspecting him as she ran her hands through his thick fur. "You're in good health," the woman said to the wolf, and Flowridia took note of her sharply pointed ears. "It appears you only need rest." The woman looked to Flowridia directly, her stare utterly enrapturing. "And you?"

Flowridia shook her head. "I'm not hurt."

That woman . . . Flowridia immediately turned back to Demitri. *She smells awfully good.*

Demitri had only said that about one other person.

Flowridia stiffened as she stared at the tall woman watching from across the cave room. "Thank you."

"Here's hoping your friend has no experience tracking," the woman said, her voice as soothing and rich as warm honey. She paced, her idle steps deliberate and precise. "We left a clumsy trail."

Flowridia nodded, watching her graceful movements carefully. "Do you have a solution, or are you waiting for me to act?"

Intrigued, the woman stopped and turned with a coy grin. "What did you have in mind?"

"Wards," Flowridia said simply. "The magic is strong enough to keep us hidden, but not so strong as to draw his attention. I don't know if you need rest, but it would keep us safe indefinitely."

"Clever girl. Show me."

Flowridia, with a glance toward Demitri, grabbed a candle from the wall and walked toward the mouth of the cave, noting how the woman never came close, simply stalked behind.

When light appeared, though stifled by the darkness of night, Flowridia saw a murky forest shrouding them, full of fog and thick, green foliage. It embraced her, the fresh air damp and moist, and Flowridia saw the woman peering out from within the dark cave, watching, waiting.

Flowridia placed her hand on the outer wall, upon a patch of thick, wet moss. So simple a life form, and so easy to manipulate. With a steadying breath, she poured life into the collection of plants and forced it to grow, to rapidly increase, to follow her finger as she traced it along the stony wall.

And soon, written in moss, was an ancient Demoni symbol: *Beware.*

Then, she sat on the floor, daring to let her back face the suspected predator behind her. She shut her eyes, feeling the earth and the magic all around, touching the energy already permeating the area and circling it around she and her companions. A shield of invisibility, of silence, and of healing.

Content with her work, Flowridia stood and turned, noting the look of approval on her mysterious companion's face. "What sort of magic is this?"

"The moss will be more enduring than mere spoken words. Anything coming close will be revolted. The wards themselves will make us invisible, impossible to hear, and prevent undead from entering or exiting."

The woman raised an eyebrow. "Is your glowing friend undead?"

"No," Flowridia replied, and she began walking back into the cave. "But you're an elf; it's a safe assumption that you have little or no talent for magic no matter how old you are."

"And I'd be trapped here if I tried anything. Clever girl." The confirmed vampire followed but stayed several feet behind, her steps silent on the rough, stone floor. "I'm sure you have plenty of questions," she continued. "And I have a few for you. You can go first."

"What's your name?"

The woman smiled pleasantly, always five steps behind. "Mereen."

"And you're a vampire," Flowridia continued, and Mereen's grin spoke volumes. "Demitri, my wolf, told me so."

Mereen's smile broadened, her lips full and enticing. She was gorgeous, breathtakingly so, like all vampires. Perfect for luring in mortal prey. "You're a witch."

Flowridia nodded slowly.

"You're also awfully at ease when facing down a predator," she said, chuckling.

"You're not the first vampire I've met," Flowridia admitted.

"No? Well, sweetie, aren't you something. You kill vampires?"

Flowridia shook her head. "I'm a diplomat. Lady Flowridia, Grand Diplomat of Staelash."

Back in the cave, Demitri slept. Flowridia's bag rustled; she knelt beside it and withdrew her beloved, albeit twitchy, fox. Ana took careful steps, some of the crevices deep enough for her to fall into.

Charming laughter laced Mereen's words. "Well, isn't she darling."

Flowridia smiled, keeping her gaze on Ana as the little thing stumbled about.

"So you negotiate with vampires?"

"You jest, but I have dealt with one diplomat who was a vampire. She was from Nox'Kartha."

"Nox'Kartha is the only kingdom foolish enough to employ the undead in such high callings. We vampires are known for our charm and for our unfortunate habit of eating our guests." She waited, perhaps hoping for Flowridia to react. But Flowridia kept her same expression, and Mereen began laughing anew. "Gods, you are at ease."

"The Nox'Karthan diplomat and I . . ." She merely shrugged, shy to discuss her relationship with a stranger. The candlelight flickered, illuminate across Mereen's pale face. "We were close."

Mereen studied her, her beautiful countenance unmarred by the look of scrutiny crossing her features. "Are you always this spacey talking about your lover?"

Flowridia blushed. "Oh, probably."

"You remind me of my sister," she said, her wink as teasing as it was alluring. "Come now—I've been asking all the questions, and I still have a few good ones. Go on. Ask me anything."

"You *were* the who summoned the wolves, right?"

"I was. Most animals don't trust me. I've been sure to foster a close relationships with the few who will." Across the cave, Mereen lounged against the wall. "Animals are considerably easier for me to spend time with."

"You talk to animals, and you live in a cave? I thought most vampires were–"

"Insufferable assholes? Certainly, but you lose your entitlement complex once you've lived a millennium or so. No, no, Lady Flowridia, I am an oddity, and I know it. I set up temporary homes as needed to fulfill my sworn oath."

"What oath?"

"I slay vampires." She placed a dramatic hand on her chest. "From this day, back to my undead birth, I have never tasted unwilling mortal blood."

Flowridia raised an eyebrow. "But how is that possible?"

"Lots of dead rabbits, sweetie, and depthless spite."

Mereen hadn't come within five feet her her—not since reaching the cave. Watching Mereen's forced serenity suddenly made some sense—the woman was starving. The woman had survived on gruel and hardtack while a feast forever waited within arm's reach. Even now, she resisted the urge to sink her teeth into Flowridia's neck. "That's noble of you. But, why?"

"Now, that's a story," Mereen replied. "A good one. Hold on to that question, sweetie. It's my turn to ask something first." She tilted her head, eyes narrowing. "Where are you going?"

"I was going to Neolan, but the God of Order captured me first." Flowridia frowned. "You knew him."

"There've been many rumors flying around of returned gods and stolen orbs. Staelash is right in the middle of it, yes?"

Flowridia nodded, cold seeping through her core and to her limbs. Mereen knew an awful lot.

"Well, be careful if you end up heading south again. I spotted a slave caravan not three days ago, in the area." The elf smiled, teeth flashing in the flickering light. "It's not often I get to speak with such pleasant company. I suppose I should thank your vampire lover for softening your heart toward the cursed dead. Between that and your penchant for necromancy–" She gestured toward Ana. ". . . I'd propose a partnership if you didn't smell so decadently divine. I'm amazed your love didn't eat you right up."

Flowridia blushed. "Well . . ."

Mereen held out a hand. "What you and your love did consensually behind closed doors is none of my business. Now hush. You asked about my oath." And for the first time, Flowridia saw the age behind Mereen's ancient eyes. She had joked about millennia . . . Was she truly a thousand years old? "My entire village was burned in a night; I was merely the first to fall. When I awoke as a vampire, my living son was thrown at my feet by the bitch who turned me. He was three years old." Mereen's eyes shut, and she released a pained sigh. "In a thousand years and more, nothing has ever smelled sweeter than my baby boy's blood. And that was when I, newly risen, starving for life, had to make a decision. To be the killer I was apparently destined to be . . . or save an innocent life."

"And you spared him?" Flowridia offered, and Mereen's expression softened.

"I took him, and I ran. I couldn't raise him—the temptation was too much—but I watched him from afar." Her gaze hardened, rigid lines marring her perfect features. "And if I can spare the one whose blood was sweetest to me, what excuse do these monsters have for killing just for fancy? I know what I am, and I know it is evil." Her expression suddenly brightened again. "Your friend, the God of Order, isn't a vampire, so I ultimately consider him not my problem."

"I still appreciate you saving me," Flowridia said sincerely.

"You're a little girl lost in the woods. Now that I know a thing or two about you, you don't seem quite so little, but my point stands." She smiled as she stepped gracefully back to the tunnel. Every gesture of Mereen's was coy and teasing, alluring in ways as natural as the sunset each night. "I would happily talk all night, but I understand if you need to sleep."

"I think I'm too nervous to sleep," Flowridia said, but quickly added, "not because of you, though. From everything. My heart is still racing."

"Allow me to be more plain with you: you smell delightful, and I haven't eaten in several days." Mereen smiled curtly, revealing her teeth, the barest hint of a point appearing where her fangs would grow. Her hands twitched. "I need a moment to clear you from my senses."

"I apologize. Ayla shared the same opinion, but she didn't have the same honor code as . . ."

She realized her error, the risk of wielding Ayla's name so freely. But Mereen's expression remained the same, her countenance pleasant and sincere. "I'm an oddity of the vampire world," Mereen said lightly. "I shall go sit at the mouth of the cave and not touch the burning wards. We'll move on once you've taken time to rest."

Mereen winked and disappeared into the darkness. Amidst the flickering candlelight, Flowridia sat beside Demitri, unnerved for reasons she couldn't quite name. "Demitri," she whispered, "why do I feel like . . ."

The truth hit her like a blow to her stomach.

Remember Tazer?

"Tazel," she corrected instinctively. He had locked himself in a library to hide from the woman—*Mereen Fireborn.*

Remember his grandma he may or may not be having sex with?

She did, though she wouldn't have said it quite so crassly. "There's no way she knows . . ."

That was a terribly stupid thing to assume. Flowridia laid her head against Demitri, figuring if she hadn't been murdered yet, she wouldn't be while she slept.

"You really won't let me read it?"

Etolié shook her head, mulling over the written words she held in her hand. She'd only cried a little, and Sora had been kind enough to pretend to not notice.

Sora stared out the window, watching the sunrise. "What the hell do we do now, with Soliel having four orbs?"

"Pray a lot," Etolié said, because she didn't dare correct her.

"Lunestra will be proclaimed archbishop by the time we've arrive—she didn't want any spectacle, lest it overshadow the tragedy of her brother's death. The Theocracy will move forward, but people died, and she didn't want to detract from that. I think she's a good woman. I've always admired her."

Etolié remembered Khastra's defeated stance, her joyless confession. She was a fool to forget what Khastra was—an undead slave to a wicked, dangerous man.

"Have you spoken to Lara at all about what happened?"

Etolié shook her head. "I'm certain she knows, though. I'm surprised she hasn't tried to contact me."

"So are she and Flowridia . . ?"

"I don't actually know how it went. But she hasn't popped up next to me crying, *so* I'm assuming the best."

Oh, but that Flowers . .

"I think Lara would be a good influence on her," Sora said. "I'm happy for them."

"I don't disagree." Perhaps that's where the stolen orb was—in Solvira with Flowers and Lara, and maybe there was some perfectly reasonable explanation that everyone had just forgotten to tell Etolié.

Sora withdrew her knitting supplies, and Etolié glanced up as she resumed working on what looked increasingly less like a doily and more like a sock. Etolié plucked the mirror from her pocket dimension, glowering as she tapped the small artifact.

It glowed. The longer it glowed, the deeper she frowned. She stared a good minute, and when she was certain the lines from her frown would be permanent, she tucked the mirror away. Etolié swallowed her anger, choosing to assume that Flowers had a *very good reason* to have *stolen* a *world-ending* artifact, even though the coward had also had the audacity to ignore her before—and now Flowers was hiding from her, *she guessed*. "Flowers needs all the help she can get," Etolié said simply, and she returned to her letter.

With her quill, she signed her name at the bottom.

She stared at it, added a 'heart,' felt ridiculous and scribbled it out, then realized it looked much worse with a large ink splatter and redrew the heart but filled it in.

Now it was a black heart—nice and ominous. Oh well.

She gently blew on the heart-like blot of ink on the parchment, willing it to dry. A sense of finality filled her as she folded it in three and tucked it away, into the same inter-dimensional space she kept her mirror and flask.

She smiled unbidden, a fluttering sense of joy filling her stomach. Uncomfortable and light, it both nauseated her and excited her from her head to her limbs.

Etolié looked out the window, hoping the next few days would fly by quickly. As soon as she returned from the Theocracy, she'd send her letter and perhaps . . .

She wrapped her arms around herself, brought her knees up, and leaned against the wall of the carriage, secure on the bench. When she shut her eyes, she saw Khastra's face lit by the faint moonlight, her heartbroken smile as she pressed their lips together that final time.

And despite the fear she harbored in her heart . . . Etolié felt hope.

"I never did ask why you're headed to the capital."

Hours had passed, and Flowridia had managed a nap. Night held an oppressive weight, the stars hidden behind a thick layer of leaves high above. "To meet a friend," Flowridia replied honestly, and then she sat and shut her eyes, expanding her focus. She gripped the wards, all but the ones grown into the moss, and commanded them to dissipate, letting them vanish into the void.

She felt Mereen's eyes. "What sort of a friend?"

When Flowridia stood, she realized Demitri had awoken and loomed behind her. Ana teetered as she wove around his feet.

"As good a friend as Ayla?"

The name set Flowridia's nerves alight, and she wondered what Mereen thought she knew. "I suppose, yes, in a way," Flowridia admitted, hoping it might set Mereen's interest to rest. "I've accidentally caught the attention of the empress, and I'm hoping she might help me move on."

Mereen stepped out of the cave, the rest of her belongings slung across her back. "Let me escort you part of the way, assuming you have no objections to travelling strictly by night. I worry your friend will find you, now that your protections are gone. If he's been looking, he won't have gone far."

Flowridia gave a nod, though anxiety gripped her chest at the implications. "That's kind of you."

"What's the use of rescuing you if I leave you for the wolves? So to speak," she added with a wink.

Demitri gave a quick kiss to Flowridia's cheek, startling her. *Best friends with Mereen now?*

She ignored him.

In the woods, the fog thickened, and Flowridia wondered if it were possible to drown above land. The damp forest floor sloshed with every step. Creatures buzzed. "Mereen, how did you summon the wolves?"

"I tracked down the pack and dethroned their alpha. Wolves instinctively trust vampires; couldn't tell you why. A pity, their sacrifice, but all for the greater good."

No regret; simply acceptance. Perhaps becoming a vampire purged one's conscience. "I'm considered the greater good?" Flowridia asked, genuinely curious to hear Mereen's explanation.

"Intelligent creatures are more valuable than mere beasts; even humans."

Flowridia expected a wink, or some other sign of jest. Nothing. "As a vampire, do you still associate with elves?"

"When necessary, yes. My existence is known. But if I'm going to visit, I visit my family."

Flowridia placed a hand into her bag, reassuring herself of Ana's squirming presence. "Your family?" she asked, praying her feigned innocence would save her. Curse her loose tongue—why had she said the name Ayla?

"My son survived and bore two children," Mereen said, her steps graceful through the precarious, moist terrain. "I've maintained ties with all of my progeny, even trained some in helping my cause."

"To kill vampires?"

"To kill vampires," she affirmed. Mereen suddenly stiffened, her eyes refracting the minimal light as she stared into the darkness.

Flowridia followed Mereen's gaze, realizing that a noxious, purple cloud mingled with the fog, slowly emanating out. From the dense trees, Soliel emerged, centered in the cloud. The orb in his hand glowed a brilliant green in the darkness, cutting through the cloud and casting sharp, eerie lines onto his features. Despite the wolves' attack, his form was unmarred, no injuries as far as Flowridia could see.

A flaming blade appeared in his hand. Mereen kept her stare fixed solely on Soliel, unquestionable menace in her grin. Not so predatory as Ayla, but calculating, almost charming.

"There is a river three miles to the south," Mereen whispered. "Climb on Demitri and run. It'll lead you to Neolan."

"I can't leave you. Not after–"

"Don't worry for me, sweetie. I won't die today." Mereen said, and her teeth glinted in the faint light. "You'll see me again." She withdrew one curved blade, the siren call of metal on leather a whisper on the breeze.

And from her hip, she withdrew an elven weapon Flowridia had never personally seen, only depictions of in art. Polished wood and metal glinted in the faint light as Mereen took her aim. "On my count, you run. Three."

Flowridia climbed aboard Demitri. "Thank you for everything."

"Two."

Soliel rushed forward, the earth wilting as the toxic gas touched greenery.

"One." *Boom.*

An earth-shattering crash erupted. Soliel cried out, the breastplate of his armor pierced as the bullet embedded within. Flowridia nearly screamed for fear, watching Mereen rush to meet the God of Order, her swords ringing against the blade of flame he summoned.

Flowridia stared a moment, transfixed by the scene. Mereen's swords met flesh. Her body was as much a weapon as her swords, displaying uncanny acrobatics, even managing to flip over him when the earth erupted in flame. The gas engulfed her, nothing to choke for she needn't breathe.

Demitri began sprinting, but Flowridia watched the display of fire and poison and clanging metal. When a cry met her ears—feminine and pained—Flowridia felt her heart clench.

But Mereen's sacrifice, final or not, would not be in vain. With the orb safely packed in her bag, Flowridia ducked her head as Demitri ran through the thick trees.

They managed to find the river within the hour.

Stars glittered overhead, and Flowridia slid off her familiar's back, senses on high alert. But Soliel seemed nowhere near.

The full moon glistened along the river. Flowridia withdrew Casvir's gifted map, realizing Mereen had spoken true. North of Ilunnes was a river leading straight to the capital, Neolan.

Studying Demitri's powerful build, she recalled the beast below the ocean and how she'd maintained perfect control of herself beneath the waves. From her satchel, she withdrew the orb and the maldectine both.

Did she dare tempt the God of Order? What was more important—speed or stealth?

Flowridia hadn't gotten this far without taking a few risks. "Demitri, I want to try something." She stared at the orb, still muted beside the bracelet. "I think we can use this at the same time."

We?

"Get into the river."

Still atop his back, she tucked the map inside her bag, making sure to grip Ana with her free hand. Her familiar obeyed, though he hesitated once he'd dunked his feet. *This river is deep enough that even I'll get swept away.*

Flowridia braced herself and slipped the maldectine back into the bag. Immediately, she felt the orb's power radiate. The touch of nature infused her being, her awareness of the condensation in the air and the water beneath them as natural as her skin.

She pressed it against Demitri. "How do you feel?"

Wet.

She focused, grasping onto the energy inherent in the orb and then to Demitri. With the finesse of threading a needle, she wove their energies together, until—

Huh. Neat.

Demitri stepped farther into the river with no hesitation and swam. They both breathed beneath the rapids, bursting through the water at extraordinary speed. Flowridia clung tight.

Can you talk?

"I can."

I assume we need to travel faster than shiny boy?

"I would say yes, Demitri."

With the orb at their disposal, it might not be weeks of travel at all.

Demitri swam all night, until the first hints of sunlight glittered against the surface of the water. When they emerged, Flowridia dried them off, the orb's power more than capable of drying a water-soaked giant wolf and their supplies.

The scenery had changed, and it was a marvel to behold. No more forest, but a lush meadow, though it bespoke little shelter should an enemy come. They had covered significant ground—perhaps only a day or two more by river.

She told this to Demitri, who lounged in the sunlight. *Wolves weren't meant to be aquatic creatures. I'd rather be running.*

"You'll get your chance," Flowridia said.

She collapsed against him, exhaustion from travel and the eventful night settling into her bones. And so she drew her wards in the dirt, protection from anything that might seek them. They were far enough away from the forest that she hoped simple distance would cover their trail, but why take a risk?

Once the wards were drawn, she rested her head against his side and let Ana curl around her legs. She tucked the orb beside the bracelet.

Soon, they would reach Lara. The thought scared her more than Soliel.

Chapter 9

After two days, they emerged from a massive lake. Even in the fading light, the spiral towers on the horizon reflected the sun like a celestial beacon. The moon rose, and the city became a serene spectacle, the star-studded monument an homage to its late goddess. The rounded wall guarding it held intricate designs, entirely translucent, yet the faintest, glittering aura of magic could be seen between the swirling metal bars.

Fresh flowers wove blissful scents into her hair as she rode Demitri toward the enormous gates surrounding the city. The guard on duty studied the pair with curiosity. "State your name and business," he said, though not unkindly.

"I am Lady Flowridia, Grand Diplomat of Staelash. This is my familiar, Demitri. I am here to request an audience with Empress Alauriel Solviraes."

They let her through.

Solvira held a grandeur to match Nox'Kartha, with well-paved streets and a bustling market even in the evening. Flowridia kept her hold tight on Demitri, the stares upon her not fearful, no, but more intrigued than she would have liked. Solvira was a kingdom of magic, most of its citizens Celestial, and the sight of a witch and her wolf in the capital city would hardly frighten them, merely cause them to ask too many questions.

But the castle was unmistakable—the legendary Glass Palace. It reflected the moon's light, casting its shined walls in silver, not unlike the family it had housed for thousands of years.

In the center of the city, she saw a statue that gave her pause—a trio of women, though one lay shattered, only her feet and evidence of what might've been a dress remaining.

Another drew Flowridia's eyes with her gentle stance and her adoring stare upon a taller one, though her countenance had been ruined by the passage of time. When Flowridia looked at the plaque, she saw a name: *The Triage of Goddesses: Neoma, Staella, and Ilune.*

Flowridia continued to the palace gates, stopped by guards who scoffed at her intentions. "At this hour, an immediate audience with her majesty is unlikely." The guard grimaced as he stared into Demitri's large eyes. "Though given your status, I would say your chances are good of at least seeing her before the end of the tomorrow."

"Give her my name," Flowridia said, flashing a charming smile. "She'll be seeing me tonight, I'm sure."

"Shall we fetch someone to escort your mount to the stables?"

"I'm a witch. He's my familiar. We will be staying together."

They shared a glance, but the gates opened.

The castle rose before her, its glistening towers reminiscent of a pearlescent seashell. Flowridia stopped to admire it, thought it beautiful beyond compare, when the enormous doors before her suddenly burst open.

Flowridia looked up, and escorted by a pair of guards came Empress Alauriel, her eyes wide, movements harried. Yet her appearance remained immaculate, hair done up, her red dress bearing all the finery of her status. "Flowridia?" Lara appeared by her side, disbelief as apparent as the innocent joy radiating from her face. She offered a hand, and Flowridia accepted as she slid down Demitri.

"Lara," Flowridia said, offering as sweet a smile as she could muster. "I apologize for intruding so late at night."

"It's no trouble. Did you travel all day?" Lara looked between she and Demitri with concern.

Technically yes, but though they surely looked like messes, she chose to avoid mentioning the orb. Instead of trying to explain, she replied with, "Yes." Her hand settled on Demitri's back and scratched him affectionately. "I apologize, also, for our disheveled appearances."

"Please, no need for apologies," Lara said, blushing slightly. "I'm happy to see you, however you look. Come inside, please. I'll have a room prepared. I presume you would rather keep Demitri close?"

The distance between them seemed to magnetically shrink, and their hands brushed lightly as Flowridia followed. "I would. Though I'm not sure if he'll fit in a bath."

Lara stopped in the entryway, looking thoughtful. "If it isn't too demeaning," she said slowly, "we do have groomers in the stables who would be able to accommodate him."

Flowridia turned to Demitri. "What do you think?"

What I think is she'd kill herself to make you happy, hopefully literally.

She managed to keep a straight face as she stared at him expectantly.

But a bath sounds pleasant.

"Demitri would love a bath," Flowridia said, smiling at Lara. "As would I, if that wasn't implied. We've been travelling for long enough."

"And I would love to hear all about it once you're settled. I'd be absolutely honored if you would join me for breakfast." A pause, and then she quickly added, "And Demitri, too, of course."

"That sounds perfect."

A passing servant was given instructions to escort Demitri to the stables—a rather unfortunate maid who looked aggrieved to be faced with an enormous dire wolf—and Lara herself walked Flowridia to a pad beside the entry hall. The circular insignia glowed at Lara's approach, and once they had both stepped on, it shot straight up. Flowridia felt no discomfort, save a mild lurch in her stomach, and watched in wonder as glass windows revealed how high they ascended up the castle floors.

"My castle can be confusing," Lara said quietly. "Never hesitate to ask anyone for directions or an escort. You're my guest, and an honored one at that."

"Honored?" Flowridia smiled with her teeth. "Well, I certainly feel it."

"I meant because of your titles, but . . ." Lara's smile became shy, her blush returning. "I'll admit, I'm happy to see you." The lift stopped, and Lara stepped off. Ambient light illuminated the stone hallway, though it bore no discernible source, while paintings and statues decorated every bit of space. Lara motioned for Flowridia to follow.

"I do have a purpose," Flowridia began, studying the fine art and architecture, "but I should add that no one actually knows I'm here. I'd prefer it stay that way."

Lara nodded slowly. "Of course. This is an unofficial visit. Off the public record."

She stopped outside a door, demure as she twisted the handle. "This will be your room," she said, gesturing. "We can expand the doorframe so Demitri can join you, but it is the biggest we can provide."

She hadn't exaggerated. An enormous bed sat in the corner, bordered by draping, sheer sheets. Large windows granted a gorgeous view of the night sky and the lake beyond the city, and an open door revealed a washroom. With a desk and seating area, it was larger than Mother's entire cottage.

Flowridia stepped inside, admiring the comforts. "This is beautiful, Lara," she mused, smiling sincerely at the woman. "Thank you."

"I'll have Demitri brought here once he's done with the groomers," Lara said, lingering in the doorway. "Will you need a change of clothes?"

Flowridia shook her head and lifted the bag at her hip. "I have nightclothes. I think I'll bathe before I go to bed, though."

Lara gave a polite nod. "I'll leave you alone."

As the empress stepped back, Odessa's parting words rang through her head: *Become whatever it takes to succeed.*

Flirtation could be considered standard diplomacy. Anything further led to dangerous roads.

"Lara–" Flowridia stopped, hand reaching out, her throat choking at the thought of what she was about to offer. Could she follow through?

Lara stood poised at the doorframe, waiting for her to speak. Beautiful and regal, small and soft, Flowridia let the memory of her delicate lips fill her head.

"Lara," she repeated, this time with quiet resolve, "you don't have to leave me alone." Her arm remained outstretched, her hand an invitation.

Lara stared, eyes growing wide and vulnerable as she stepped forward. Her own small fingers intertwined with Flowridia's, and a gentle smile graced her lips. "Flowridia–"

Flowridia pulled her in for a slow, serene kiss. Lara tasted of warmth and comfort, her soft lips a pleasure despite Flowridia's torn heart. Her tongue slipped inside, Lara's moan as sweet as the taste.

Heat filled Flowridia's abdomen, the first hints of arousal pulsing through her blood. Perhaps Lara did not hold her heart, but the empress seemed capable of at least entertaining what lay between her legs.

Oh, gods—guilt filled her at the idea. But when Flowridia pulled back, she forced a smile and let her hands settle at Lara's waist. "Join me?"

Lara nodded, utterly enthralled, and let herself be led.

In the bathroom, Flowridia barely noticed the bright tile or the ornately carved porcelain tub. No supports rested beneath it; it simply floated an inch off the ground. With a wave of Lara's hand, water began pouring from a series of holes in the ceiling.

From behind her, Flowridia's hands slid around Lara's waist and up to cup her clothed breasts. The woman gasped, her own hands gripping Flowridia's as she massaged. "W-Wait," Lara said, and Flowridia pulled back, concerned by the empress' small stance. "I should tell you. I've never been with another woman before. I'm . . . nervous."

Flowridia knew the embarrassment of that particular reveal. "Don't worry," she said. "I'd be happy to lead."

Lara pressed their lips together, smiling against Flowridia's. With her hands skimming Lara's dress, Flowridia moved from her mouth to her neck, planting successive kisses along the smooth curve, Lara's moans gentle and foreign. She brought her hands up to cup Lara's breasts, rather enamored with the feel, if she were honest, their buoyant weight so different than what she'd known. "Take off your dress," she whispered, unprepared for the inarticulate whine she heard in response.

Flowridia pulled back, watching as Lara blushed a deeper red than her gown. "This is embarrassing, but . . ." The image of her dress suddenly flickered away, revealing a simple, silk nightgown. Her hair flowed free, gently spilling down her back. "My talent for illusion holds nothing to Etolié, but we do share a few abilities, given she's my aunt, give or take ninety generations or so. It's a useful trick, for unexpected guests in the night–"

Flowridia shut her up with a kiss. "I don't care what you're wearing. I only want it off."

Though Lara blushed, she wasn't shy, her smile twisting into something coy as she held Flowridia's gaze and slipped from her nightgown, revealing the soft curves of her breasts. They bounced as she giggled, the rest of the gown falling at her feet. "Oh, please—do keep staring."

Flowridia's eyes darted to meet Lara's, heat filling her cheeks. Upon Ayla's death, Flowridia had known she'd never love again . . . but it seemed she might be capable of lusting. It had been six months, and by every god—she felt guilt unparalleled to admit it, but she craved the feeling of skin against skin. "Sorry."

"Don't be," Lara teased, and when she bent over to pick up the gown, she made a point to stick her full buttocks out, revealing a hint of the lips of her vulva. She tossed the gown in the corner, her confident smirk starkly juxtaposed with the fierce blush blooming beneath her cheeks. "I love your stare. I think I'll love your hands much more, though."

Heat welled between Flowridia's legs as she slipped her own shirt over her head. But the gasp she heard didn't hold enamor, and while the idea that Lara was perhaps not so keen on breasts did occur to her, when Flowridia pulled the article off and tossed it aside, she followed Lara's gaze to her chest and—

The ear. The shriveled, chained ear of Ayla Darkleaf, despite resting between her bare breasts, still stole the show.

She grinned apologetically at Lara, who still stared, visibly wary. "Not exactly the most alluring of accessories." When she removed it from around her neck, something cold caressed her back—and Flowridia swore it clung, even as she held the ear away.

Oh, Ayla.

Lara offered a hand, but Flowridia's grip on it tightened protectively. "What is that?" Lara asked.

"It's, uh, a Nox'Karthan artifact."

Lara watched warily "Flowridia, that's ancient. Dark."

"I know. That's why I'm protecting it until I can get it taken care of," Flowridia said, forcing a bright smile. She placed the ear onto the sink and began stepping out of her skirt, forgetting all notions of putting on a show.

Then, Lara went to grab it. Flowridia's hand shot out to grab her wrist.

Lara's tender gaze matched Flowridia's obvious panic. "The magic in this radiates," she said slowly, each word carefully chosen. "I fear what influence it might have upon its wearer."

"I . . ." The words caught her off guard, far closer to the truth than she would have preferred. "I'll put it away. We can discuss this after." She winked and hoped it was lurid— seduction was hardly her talent.

To her amusement, Lara bit her lip, cheeks blossoming in brilliant red. "I'm sorry. The ear was startling, but it doesn't mean . . ." The enamor returned to her visage, her eyes flickering across Flowridia's breasts, then back to her face. "You are unendingly beautiful."

The words lingered, repeating in Flowridia's head as she returned to her room, half-dressed, and stuffed the ear inside her bag with as little ceremony as her speed could grant, ignoring Ana, docile as instructed.

Yet, she lingered. She paused. Ayla's spirit held awareness, however faint.

She withdrew it and held it to her bare chest, trembling as she contemplated what must be done. Was it a betrayal to her love if she did this for her? Or was the betrayal her own body's excitement at the prospect?

Flowridia stole a shaking breath and whispered, softer than night, "All that I do, I do for you, my love."

She placed it back inside, then swallowed her sorrow.

When she returned, Flowridia quickly escaped her skirt, amused at Lara's stare. She slid her arms around the empress' waist, pausing only to admire her soft smile, and pulled their nude forms together. Lara held her gaze, her pupils widening at the bare contact.

Their lips touched, and Flowridia's hands slid up Lara's back, marveling at how warm the empress felt against her body, how soft her skin was beneath her palms. Flowridia's mouth left Lara's lips and planted small kisses to her ear, where she whispered. "Come join me in the bath?"

Lara shuddered as she nodded, and Flowridia slid their bodies apart, keeping her hand along her arm so their hands could meet. The water had stopped, and Flowridia slipped into the large bathtub before pulling Lara into the water on top of her. The warm water sealed their bodies together, and Flowridia silenced all notions of guilt, content to kiss those lips instead.

Lara never initiated; she only reacted, and though she certainly reacted well, Flowridia found that strange. She rolled them over, pressing Lara against the porcelain wall and grabbing her breasts. Lara gasped, sighing as Flowridia twisted the sensitive nubs between her fingers. She couldn't hear Ayla in the sound; instead, she only heard herself.

Did that make her the dominant one? What would Ayla have done?

The memory brought warmth to her cheeks. With a small nip to Lara's bottom lip, Flowridia flashed a dangerous grin and let her hand slide beneath the water.

She forced Lara's thighs apart and immediately stroked a slow line from her entrance to her clit, her other hand returning to Lara's breast. She felt Lara quiver and shake, and soon hands gripped Flowridia's thick hair, encouraging her movements.

Flowridia kissed the empress' neck, finding she enjoyed the soft cries of pleasure. She sucked against the curve of flesh, touched Lara's breast, slid inside her—all in painful, leisurely motions, feeling Lara's abdominal wall steadily tense.

But not so tense as Ayla's. The skin of her core had been so thin, a millennia of dancing and acrobatics causing the muscles to be stone against her fingers. Lara was small and soft, a scholar and a sorceress.

Was that how Ayla had seen her? Small and soft, her scholarly pursuits leaving no time for physical aptitude?

Flowridia pushed inside her, distracted by the feeling of her soft flesh, and let her other hand drift down to join it, gently touching the bud atop her vulva. Lara gasped and whined, placing gentle kisses along Flowridia's hairline. "Keep going," she whispered, breathless at Flowridia's touch.

It took only a few minutes more; Lara's body rocked beneath her. Flowridia held on, maintaining her pace, until a particularly violent shudder signified that Lara had finished.

Flowridia met her gaze, charmed to hear Lara giggling between gasping breaths. Immediately, Lara's hands flew forward and pulled Flowridia into a passionate, elated embrace. "That was . . . *wonderful,*" she whispered, her laughter not quite ceasing. "I never know what to say afterward, sorry."

What had she and Ayla spoken of? Oh, the thought brought guilt, as well as memories of luxurious nights basking in the woman's touch. Ayla's vulnerable confessions had been bittersweet. "Feelings, typically. At least in my experience."

When Flowridia sat back, Lara's smiling face radiated joy. "Is this what sex with women is always like, or are you just exceptionally talented?"

"I'm not sure," Flowridia mused, cupping Lara's face. "I've never slept with a man."

"And I may never again." Lara turned her face to kiss Flowridia's palm. "Flowridia . . ." Her smile turned shy as her hand moved up to cover Flowridia's. "After the wedding, I wasn't entirely sure what to think—about you, about this. But . . ." She shut her eyes, releasing a sigh. "I'm glad you came."

"Technically speaking . . ." Even in the warm water, Flowridia felt thick wetness between her legs. She winked and said, "I haven't actually come yet."

Lara chuckled and leaned forward to plant a gentle kiss on Flowridia's lips. "May I wash your hair?" she whispered, her pale eyes conveying warmth.

An intimate gesture, and Flowridia simply nodded, surprised at the offer. She watched, expression blank, as Lara poured some sweet smelling substance into her hands and massaged Flowridia's scalp, bringing their faces closer and planting butterfly kisses along her cheeks and nose.

Intimate, innocent, and so unlike anything Flowridia could say she had experienced. Making love to Ayla had been riding a hurricane, tumultuous and wild, but the eye of the swirling storm brought peace from the chaos, precious moments to which Flowridia had clung and still never let go.

Lara's sweet kisses stirred affection within her, but with it came the guilt of insincerity. Ayla's bleeding heart had been stolen, desperately patched by Flowridia's tender care, while Lara's open heart came freely offered and with no strings.

Water rinsed the soap from Flowridia's hair, the bubbles pooling around their slick bodies. Lips brushed her temple. A soft voice whispered into her ear. "Let me take you to bed."

Flowridia nodded as Lara left the bathtub and stole a fluffy towel from a shelf. She beckoned for her to follow, wrapping Flowridia in one before taking another towel for herself. "If I may admit to something embarrassing," Lara continued, sopping water from her soft skin, "since returning from the wedding, I've been researching how to make love to women, as a woman . . ."

She trailed off at Flowridia's laughter—amusing, to think of the most powerful woman in the world as insecure. "You had intentions for me, then?" Flowridia said, yet uneasiness brewed within her, the rush of touching Lara's body fading, despite her own simmering arousal.

"My point," Lara replied, her happiness radiant, but not enough to break through the clouds surrounding Flowridia's heart, "is that I'm curious to try what I've learned. I've made love to men before, but they tend to take charge and do most of the work."

Flowridia bit back her next words—the natural and honest reply that she'd been fortunate enough to have a good teacher—but they burned to swallow, and when she blinked, she felt tears. Though she quickly pressed her face into her towel, she heard Lara say, "Are you all right?"

She steeled her breath, willing her emotions to settle, and forced a grin as she brought the towel to her hair instead. "Yes. Would you think less of me if I said I was impatient?"

Lara giggled as she came to kiss Flowridia's lips, easily able to level their faces if she stood on her toes. "Come to bed," she whispered, her hand settling at Flowridia's waist.

Flowridia dropped her towel, following as Lara escorted them to the moon-lit room, the parted curtains casting a silver sheen onto the bed.

Like a dream, it beckoned, the ambience romantic beyond anything she had ever known. Lara led her to bed; Flowridia's hair dripping onto the plush carpet, and rich fabric enveloped her as she sat at the edge of the mattress. Lara's lips brushed her jaw, her cheek, and finally her lips. Curiously, her warm hands touched Flowridia's skin, sliding from her slim waist to the gentle curves of her breasts, hesitant as they lingered at the sides. "May I?" Lara whispered, anticipation in her voice.

Say yes, say yes, her wicked mind said, and it sounded like Mother, who loved nothing more than to fuck men to kill them. Flowridia had touched Lara, had moved within her minutes ago, but there was little vulnerability in domination.

"Flowridia?"

Flowridia opened her eyes, realized Lara's lips ghosted inches away from hers, but instead of silver, those eyes refracted the blue of the blankets. For an impossible, crippling moment, the face she saw was not beautiful, but fierce.

Yet the touch was warm, the gaze was soft, and before her was Lara—beautiful Lara who bore every fine trait of her angelic blood—and Flowridia fell apart.

She did not quite break, no, but instead she made a careful withdrawal, taking her hands back before covering her face. Tears welled in her eyes. Trembling, her breathing grew ragged; her hands slid up to grip her hair.

The labyrinth of Flowridia's mind hid brutal betrayal behind every twist and turn. Lara's heart lie waiting to be staked, yet her own already felt shredded into ribbons.

The empress wrapped both arms around her in a tight embrace. "Lara–" Flowridia choked trying to hold back a sob, but succeeded, forcing a smile as she met Lara's gaze. "I'm sorry. I was–"

"Shh . . ." Kindness shone in Lara's pale eyes. Gentle fingers stroked at Flowridia's hair. She kissed a falling tear, as tender a gesture as Flowridia had ever known.

Something shattered. Her tears fell fast; quiet sobs shook her. Flowridia buried her face into her hands.

Lara held her close, tenderly stroking her hair. "Did I hurt you? Was I too much?"

The guilt in her voice at least gave Flowridia the resolve to shake her head. A kiss against her temple, and finally she managed to suck in a breath. In, out, in, out . . .

"Her name was Ayla, wasn't it?"

The question startled her, a slight gasp escaping her throat. Flowridia turned to face Lara, staring a moment before finding her voice, rough as it was. "Yes."

"I didn't want to accuse you, Flowridia. But is that her ear you're still carrying with you?"

"Yes," Flowridia whispered, heat rising in her cheeks. "I didn't know you knew about it."

The hand stroking her hair soothed down to touch her cheek. "Etolié tells me many things."

Flowridia sniffed, blinking heavily as she nodded. "I know I should be past this, but–"

"Stop," Lara gently implored. "Flowridia, it's been months since my father's death, and I still cry myself to sleep sometimes. The difference is, while I may be alone, no one would besmirch me the right to mourn him. But here you are, hiding your broken heart from the world."

A slow nod became her reply. Anything else she might say could be damning or break her shaken resolve.

"I've heard terribly unkind things about the woman you loved, but there must have been something wonderful about her, if she stole your heart. Will you tell me about her?"

Flowridia's eyes widened, a question in the gaze.

"If I am to know your heart, Flowridia, I would hear about the woman who holds it," Lara said, and her tone held only sincerity.

What to even say? Ayla was a creature of darkness yet held all the magnitude of the sun, and Flowridia would have followed her blindly to the end, content to burn in her great light. And Ayla had tried—by every god, Ayla had wanted nothing more than to ruin her—but instead she had fallen in love, their stars orbiting in tandem.

Ayla's star had burst, a supernova and then darkness, yet Flowridia still circled, waiting to be consumed by a black hole.

So what did one say about Ayla? Flowridia supposed she could only speak the truth. "I think I loved her the moment I saw her," she began with some uncertainty. "She stole every eye in the room, though I think mostly from fear. But I watched her dance, and I thought she was magnificent. And she truly was—she was magnificent and prideful and terrifying." Flowridia recalled The Endless Night, the bloodstained night wherein the Skalmites had fallen. Ayla had held no remorse; for nearly two thousand years, she had held no remorse for any act, save one. "But beneath her airs, there was something beautiful."

"I love you, Flowridia. Please, never leave me."

"She didn't mean to fall in love with me," Flowridia admitted, the words coming more easily. "And that hurts to say out loud, but it's the truth. Her love . . ." She sniffed, wiping a tear before Lara could. "It was so pure. She was a monster, unquestionably—after her death, I learned what sort of creature she truly was. And it hurt. Oh, it still hurts, Lara, but . . ." She shut her eyes, tears falling fast now. "But she loved so tentatively, so beautifully. Casvir told me I had tamed a monster, that Ayla's love for me was the only redeeming quality he ever knew in her. If I were sane, that might be enough to push me to move on."

When Flowridia opened her eyes again, she faced a mirror. Lara's gaze spelled trust and love, so blindly, freely given. That innocence reminded her of a time past, when she herself could love so fiercely.

Did that mean Flowridia had become the monster?

"Flowridia," Lara whispered, her tone as fragile as a drop of dew dangling from grass, "you must understand, since my father's death, I have been so alone." The statement rang a moment in silence, poignant and loud in Flowridia's mind. "I'd never considered a future with a woman, but then I saw you in the garden and it was as though we were fated to meet. And when you kissed me at the wedding . . ." A sad smile graced her lips, her own eyes brimming with tears. "Flowridia, it made my heart sing. I'm absolutely smitten by you."

She watched carefully as Lara lowered her hand away from Flowridia's face and let it wrap around the other side of her torso, completing the embrace.

"You aren't ready," Lara whispered. "You don't have to tell me that. You carry a heavy burden, that token of hers. You haven't let her go."

Flowridia couldn't bear to disagree. She simply nodded.

"Let me help you." Lara rested her head on Flowridia's shoulder. "The world won't let you mourn, but if I can ease the weight, please let me. When you're ready—if you even ever are ready—I'll be here, but in the meantime, you needn't be alone in your loneliness. I think you need a friend."

That bleeding heart, so freely offered, no strings beyond the ones Flowridia attached to make Lara dance at her command. A shadow passed over her resolve, one with the damning name of *doubt*.

Her eyes squeezed shut, fresh tears falling, and a sob tore from her throat. Lara held her tight as she cried, and Flowridia clung back.

Forever discontent. Odessa would mock her. Izthuni might smite her. Even Casvir would berate her indecision. She'd murdered for this—and yet here she stood, stopped at the finish line.

Lara's voice soothed her troubled mind. "I know it's an intimate gesture," she said softly, "but would you like me to sleep by you tonight?"

Flowridia managed a nod.

They dressed in their nightgowns. Flowridia lingered at her bag, clutching the ear a moment in her hand, uncertainty in the gesture. Lara had called it a burden. It was, though one Flowridia had freely accepted, one she carried on her own accord.

And like a dagger to her chest, the thought lingered that she could let it go.

Soon, buried in the sheets, she rested her head against Lara's chest, desperate for the offered affection.

Her beating heart met Flowridia's ears. She memorized the sound, knowing how precious a thing it was, so fleeting. Each beat counted down to the moment where Flowridia would draw the knife and stab it.

In the morning, Flowridia awoke facing closed curtains and an empty bed. She rolled over, surprised to see Demitri curled up on the floor, fast asleep.

What time was it? Flowridia sat up, set on opening the windows, when she noticed a note placed on the empty pillow. She grabbed it, eyes quickly roaming the meticulous script:

> *I'm sorry to leave you alone, but I know how much you needed sleep. Breakfast is past, and I have meetings through the morning, but meet me for lunch. Your company would be a perfect distraction from the monotony of my day.*
> *-Lara*

Simply 'Lara.' No titles or damning surnames; only 'Lara,' stripped of finery, laid bare like the body Flowridia had touched.

She stood and approached the window, peeking through the blackened fabric only to be met with bright daylight. The sun sat high, nearing noon, and Flowridia knew lunch would be soon.

Rather than disturb Demitri, she returned to the bathroom. Lara's clothing lay missing from the mess of her own—Flowridia's shirt crumpled in the corner, her skirt and belt pooled by the tub.

When she returned to the room, she knelt before her bag. She first withdrew sweet Ana, who came to life at her touch. "You're free to explore, but don't bother Demitri. Stay in this room." She released the little creature, smiling at how she investigated her world.

With Ana taken care of, Flowridia lifted the ear lovingly into her hands. She placed the chain around her neck, wondering when her chest would finally cave from the familiar weight.

Kneeling, she pulled the bag fully open and peered inside, immediately struck by the muted light of the orb. What would Lara think, to know she'd stolen it to get here?

She recalled Etolié's reaction through the now-shattered mirror. Perhaps Lara already knew, but Flowridia decided to keep the news to herself, for now.

She'd brought little clothing, having left most of it in the swamp. She donned one of Ayla's gifted gowns—one of her favorites, deep blue and embroidered in silver stars. Lacking flowers, she simply tamed her hair and pinned it away from her face.

Flowridia knelt before Demitri, knowing the wolf needed rest. Instead of waking him, she placed a kiss on his nose.

Once in the hallway, she realized she was unquestionably lost. She chose a direction and walked, hoping to find a servant or guard to guide her.

She did not have to wait long. A servant woman, holding laundry, pointed her toward the lift. *The throne room is only a floor up. I would look for her majesty there.*

Still not entirely sure of where Lara might be, Flowridia rode the lift, which came to life in her presence. With an idle thought to find the throne room, it obeyed, and she watched the kingdom beyond the window as she ascended. She came upon a foyer with two enormous doors looming at the end of an expansive hallway, guards standing on either side.

Flowridia would bet a considerable amount of Casvir's money that the throne room lay that direction.

As she approached, the doors opened on their own. Lara, her hair styled and her dress impeccable, stepped out. Surrounded by regally dressed individuals—her own royal council; Flowridia swore she recognized a few from Marielle's wedding—she spoke rapidly until her gaze fell to Flowridia. Certainly everyone, Flowridia included, could see how her eyes brightened, how her smile beamed.

"If you'll excuse me," Lara said, "I am having a personal guest for lunch." She stepped forward, as quickly as could be considered proper, and took Flowridia's hands in her own, oblivious or uncaring at how they watched her. "I know you wanted your visit to be kept secret. I've told no one of your name, only that you're my guest. And if they recognize you from the wedding, what harm can they do? The visit is on no records." She squeezed Flowridia's hands before gently releasing them. "Are you hungry? Lunch awaits if you want it."

"I'm starved, to be honest."

Lara placed a hand on Flowridia's back as she led her to the lift. "There's a balcony a few floors down, and I think you'll love the view. Lunch will be delivered there."

Down they went. Once stopped, Lara escorted them quickly down the winding, windowless hall, until a door to the side opened at their approach.

They faced the outdoors. Flowridia saw the city but also the majestic lake beyond. A slight breeze cooled the air, and a table and two chairs were already set up.

"It's beautiful," Flowridia said, as Lara pulled out her chair, oddly charmed to be doted upon. "Your entire kingdom is stunning."

Lara beamed at the sentiment. "I'll give you a tour, if you'd like. Before I was crowned empress, I would often take trips into the city and visit my subjects." Her expression fell slightly, and she stared out into the horizon. "I've isolated myself somewhat, in mourning my father's death."

Lara's hand rested on the table. With slight movements, Flowridia set her own on top.

"Warm her heart. Cherish it. Kiss her as you slit her pretty throat."

Lara's smile returned. "Do you recall the Skalmites? And the crystal you found?"

Flowridia nodded.

"My castle has been housing it. We've designated an entire underground sector as a haven for the displaced Skalmites. With study, we've learned to control the radius—it's not a perfect solution, but they're safe until we can find a better one."

"That's wonderful–"

On the table, glittering sheen radiated, and then two platters appeared. Startled, Flowridia withdrew her hand, but Lara simply chuckled. "You have a lot to get used to. These were sent from the kitchen."

She lifted the cover from her plate, revealing an array of fresh vegetables and some sort of decadently roasted meat. Flowridia lifted her own and saw the same. With the accompanied silverware, she pushed the meat to the side, preventing it from touching the greenery.

She wiped her fork on her napkin and happily picked at the vegetables, ignoring Lara's curious stare. Flowridia chewed slowly, despite the ravenous hunger growing in her stomach.

"Forgive me for ignoring pleasantries," Lara said, "but I know you're here for a purpose other than to see me."

Right. Flowridia had nearly forgotten. "I found an orb, but I need your help." Lara's surprise was made apparent in the slight 'o' of her mouth, and Flowridia admittedly found it charming. "I attempted to go after it myself, but the swamp it lies in is heavily warded, too much for only me to break through. But with your talents, you could absorb them. Taking the orb would be trivial."

Lara frowned, barely picking at her food. Flowridia took the opportunity to shovel vegetables into her mouth. "Who warded the area?"

Flowridia finally swallowed and spoke. "I grew up in Ilunnes, the village beside the swamp, and heard stories of an evil witch who once resided there. No one has heard from her in years, but her wards were legendary. No one ever found her; not if she didn't want to be found. She's dead, but her wards live on without her."

"If no one's heard from her, how do we know she's dead?" Lara's palpable concern grew with every question. "If she's there and we're unprepared, she could still be wielding the orb. We'll have to prepare for a fight."

On one hand, Lara had readily agreed to the task of retrieving the fictional orb. But more people marching into the swamp meant more people to stop Flowridia from completing her grisly task. "Lara, she's dead. The witch is dead. I'd rather this stay quiet, otherwise Soliel could be alerted to our intentions."

"How do you know she's dead?"

This was not a question she had ever thought to be asked. She had an answer—a truthful one—but could she speak of it? No lies spun in her head . . . Flowridia braced herself, and then whispered, "Because I'm the one who killed her."

Lara set down her fork, eyes narrowing, but not from anger. "Forgive me, but I feel there's more to this story. Will you continue?"

The gnawing hunger shrunk, and Flowridia turned away, letting the view of the expansive fields and the city distract her from the images passing through her head. "Four years ago," she said softly, "I was . . . taken in by the witch in the swamp. Scarcely a year ago, I killed her. I'd rather not say much more–"

"Magic often runs in family lines. Even witchcraft."

Flowridia turned, surprised when Lara leaned in and stared.

"The witch was your mother," she whispered—no judgement, but awe.

Dread filled her. Flowridia leaned back, arms folding across her torso protectively. "Why would you think that?"

Lara gently stole her hand and held it in her own. "Flowridia . . ." She ran her soft thumb along Flowridia's callused palm. "You told me once that you were forced to run away from Ilunnes at fifteen, and that's when you found your mother. Approximately four years ago, yes? Please, don't feel like you have to hide your history from me."

Flowridia forced a joyless smile. "Her name was Odessa." Realization appeared in Lara's expression. "Yes, she was my mother. I only lived in the swamp for three years, but she . . . she taught me many things. Most of them, quite terrible."

"And you had to kill her?" Lara's eyes grew wide at her own words, glistening as they rimmed with red. "Oh, Flowridia . . ." She clutched Flowridia's hand, still writing those soothing lines. "Flowridia, that must have been awful."

Flowridia simply nodded, surprised at her relief at Lara's unexpected acceptance. "But that's how I know she's dead. I threw a knife at her throat when–" The words struck her deep, even though she didn't say them. She stiffened, and she released a steadying sight before finishing. ". . . when I called on my familiar to come and rescue me. Odessa defended herself, and I . . . had to bury both of them." And others, she mused, but those were words she'd rather never speak.

"Not Demitri, then?"

Flowridia shook her head. "No, my first familiar, Aura." Aura who had all but raised her. Aura who had loved her and taught her every good thing she knew. "But, my point stands," she continued, shoving aside her rising emotion. To tell this to Lara, to let her in, be so emotionally close . . . Too much. Too dangerous. "The orb is in the swamp. There is no witch to defend it, but there are wards."

"Did you ever see your mother with it?"

Flowridia nodded, and the lie fell seamlessly from her tongue. "I didn't know what it was when I saw it. It wasn't until I was journeying with Casvir that I realized what it must be."

Lara nodded, calculating as she stood and stared beyond the balcony. "If you couldn't reach it, neither can Soliel. But he may still know where it is, given he has four orbs of his own—we must travel quickly and covertly."

"Four orbs?"

"Staella's Grace, you haven't heard..." Lara returned her focus, steel in those silver eyes. "After my party left, I presume you left shortly thereafter?" When Flowridia nodded, she added, "Soliel came to the wedding that afternoon. He murdered Archbishop Xoran, stole the white orb, and disappeared. We don't know how, but we have countless eyewitnesses—including Etolié."

Flowridia feigned aghast, recalling Casvir's story. "Oh, how awful." She wondered, perhaps, if the imperator now laid secret claim to the white orb as well.

"And so Staelash has the blue orb hidden away," Lara replied, "and the final waits in a swamp your mother once owned. The situation has become dire, but your heroics may have saved us." She looked back to the balcony, gazed upon the beautiful kingdom she was charged to rule. Calculation hardened her soft features, signs of her quick wit and intelligent mind. "You say there are wards? Certainly not in the village. I'll assemble a team to accompany us. We could be there and back in a day with a proper portal."

Taken aback, Flowridia frowned. "A team?"

"I'm a monarch. As lovely as a vacation with only you sounds, I can't travel alone." Lara returned her attention to her food, thoughtful as she stole a small bite. Flowridia joined her, feeling Lara's gaze as she picked at the offered food. Lara finally set down her fork. "I don't mean to stare. But is the meat unacceptable? I can have something different sent up."

Flowridia swallowed her bite, self-conscious as she considered what to say. "I don't typically eat meat," she admitted softly.

"I am so sorry," Lara said, visibly flustered. Immediately, the plate disappeared—the vegetables with it—and she forced an embarrassed smile. "Flowridia, I did not realize. I can send mine back too, if it offends you."

"Lara, no. It's perfectly fine." Flowridia stared apologetically. "I don't want to be a bother."

"You are not a bother." Before her, a new plate appeared, this one covered with an array of fruits, vegetables, and bread. "It's all they had with so short notice. Dinner will be better."

Hunger growled in Flowridia's stomach. Her will was set on not immediately devouring the plate. She forcibly remembered her manners, taking a slow bite before saying, "This is perfect."

Lara resumed eating as well, taking a few bites before asking, "I am curious, though—why don't you eat meat?"

The bit of bread broken in her hands was set back onto her plate at the question. Flowridia placed her hands in her lap, contemplating what to say. "Not to be too graphic at lunch," she said slowly, bracing herself for the truth, "but Odessa had a reputation for eating her children and guests."

Apparently this wasn't news; Lara watched, as though waiting for the rest, but then a slow horror descended upon her countenance. "Oh."

"Eating any sort of meat puts me into a panic. I can't eat mushrooms either."

"I swear I'm not judging you," Lara said, an apologetic smile spreading across her face, "but my stomach cannot continue this conversation while we're eating."

Flowridia laughed nervously, relieved when Lara joined her. To speak of shame . . . did help it feel a little lighter. She resumed her eating, quickly stuffing her mouth full of fruit.

"What I'll do, then," Lara finally said, "is discuss this with my council after lunch. With any luck, we'll be ready to leave in the morning." The food on her plate had disappeared, and Lara set down her fork. "If you think you'll be rested by then. I don't know how long you've been travelling."

"I'm used to travelling for days on end, at this point," Flowridia admitted. "During my time in Nox'Kartha, Casvir kept a quick pace, and we would travel for weeks at a time."

A slight grimace marred Lara's lips. "Forgive me, but there were rumors at the wedding–"

"Entirely unfounded," Flowridia interrupted, suppressing the urge to roll her eyes. Gods, this was her life now—constantly dissuading the rumors of she and Casvir's apparent dalliance. "He sees me as a child, and I spent the majority of our travelling mourning Ayla's death."

Lara's countenance softened, her slight laughter endearing. "You've said those words many times."

Flowridia elected simply to nod as she finished shoving the last bit of food into her mouth. Her body craved more—she realized she hadn't eaten well since the wedding—but she set that aside, for now.

The plates disappeared. Lara stood and offered Flowridia a hand. "My day will be spent preparing for the journey," she said, helping Flowridia to stand. She did not let go, instead holding her hand tight. "But if there is anything you need, seek me out. Nothing I'm doing is more important than tending to a guest in my home."

"That's kind of you," Flowridia whispered, smiling faintly.

"And make yourself at home, please," Lara implored. "I hope it isn't presumptuous to think you might spend time here, even after we return with the orb."

The sincere hope radiating from her silver eyes threatened to destroy what resolve Flowridia clung to. She nodded, internally wincing at the smile spreading across Lara's face.

As Etolié watched the great statue of Sol Kareena approach, she scoffed as she always did. The Goddess' arms were held to welcome the masses, to offer a kindness balanced with justice, though selective mercy and looking the other way was something Etolié had personally witnessed. But great accolades weren't her style; she suspected Auntie Kareena was likely embarrassed at the display.

Not a lot of fun, but she was a good lady. Etolié knew Sol Kareena personally, a fact she loved to remind uppity priestesses of.

Seated in the carriage, she said, "Did I ever tell you about the time I threw up in Sol Kareena's hair?"

Sora slowly turned her stare away from the admittedly very lovely outside world, visibly skeptical.

"I don't actually remember it. I was two, but Eionei loves telling the story."

They passed beneath the Goddess' shadow, the glory of the city unfolding as they entered between the gate. The funeral would be held the following day, but the city moved on as though a great tragedy had not struck. Mortals were resilient—this sort of death would have kept Celestière in mourning for weeks. Years.

That said, it was rare that a death struck the Angelic Realm. Angels so rarely died; gods, never so. Save one.

"Eionei had taken me to Vanir Sol to stay with he and Alystra for a few days after mom had a nervous breakdown–"

"Staella, what?"

"—and Auntie Kareena had been bouncing tiny toddler me on her knee, forgetting that Celestial children eat and sometimes have to burp. I puked all over her gown and hair. Just a fucking mess."

To Etolié's delight, Sora chuckled.

"You know," she continued, unable to help her smile, "with due respect to her name, you're much more relaxed than Meira. She had a conniption when I told her that story—a quiet one, but she berated my casual blasphemy."

"Personally, I find it fascinating to hear anecdotal accounts of my Goddess," Sora replied, leaning casually against the wall of the carriage. "You're a bridge between worlds, Etolié. You ought to speak more of her and the rest. It might incite greater worship."

"You're assuming I have any responsibility or care to do so." Etolié withdrew her flask, taking a sip before adding, "Besides, it might kill the magic."

"What do you mean?"

"People assume the gods are experts on humanity and life—but I can't say that's true for the angelic ones. Demon gods seem to actually have their shit together, but angels are just as shitty as any of us." She stole another drink, noticing Sora's interest. "All right, here's a good one: I could say that Morathma is a misogynistic bastard, but that isn't a secret to anyone outside of Moratham. The secret is that he's a withdrawn hermit who apparently regrets a decent amount of his shitty life choices. You know how the Snake God got his scales, right?"

Sora shook her head, her visible intrigue suggesting she didn't even realize that 'Snake God' was technically a blaspheme.

"He was mutilated by Silver Fire. This wasn't long after the Convergence. Pissed off the wrong Moon Goddess. My momma said it was horrendous to witness."

"But why?"

"Well, once upon a time, they said the Moon stole the Stars from the Desert Sands, because in that once upon a time era, any story that made Neoma look like a bitch was all the rage, but they never tell the first half of that tale—which is that the Desert Sands had beaten the Stars into a bloodied dick-sheath."

Sora looked properly horrified—nosey bastard that she was—but Etolié changed subjects. "Alystra is a tempestuous bitch."

Sora stared like absolute blasphemy had been spoken, and Etolié was living for it. "She hates me," she continued, but a chuckle escaped with her words. "At least, she did when I was a kid because she hates kids, but I'm also the one woman she'll let Eionei be alone with."

She couldn't suppress her grin when Sora said, "What? Why?"

"Because, while I love good ol' grandpa to death, he's a fucking floozy. Most Celestials are his progeny. Alystra trusts his dick to actually stay put with me."

Sora blinked for a bit before finally managing a few words. "Oh. Well. Good for him, I suppose."

"And Sol Kareena, because she'd have him castrated if he ever tried anything. And Momma, even though Alystra hates her too." Etolié smiled, though it hardly hid her scoff. "Between you and me, Alystra can smell the competition, even if my momma never chose to play."

Sora narrowed her eyes, the gears in her head visibly turning. "Are you suggesting that Eionei–"

"Whatever you're about to say, the answer is 'yes,' but that's an executive level secret."

It welled an old insecurity she couldn't quite bring herself to say—that Eionei had loads of progeny, and he gave zero shits about any of them. Except her, his granddaughter. Etolié, in her heart of hearts, knew he wished she were his daughter instead.

"I could go on," Etolié continued, the introspection more than her heart wanted today, "but I think you get my point. The gods aren't any better than us, but people need something to believe in. I won't go disillusioning anyone of that."

Sora looked to the window, her voice subdued as she said, "I never thought about it like that."

"That's why you don't meet your heroes."

"If you don't mind me saying," Sora replied, visibly hesitant, "you're always defensive whenever Sol Kareena gets brought up."

Etolié turned her attention to beyond the carriage, watching the bustling motions of people, the preparations underway for tomorrow's solemn event. But she saw nothing of it. Etolié thought of home.

"I'm not all-knowing, Etolié," Sol Kareena said, holding Etolié's tear-stained face to her chest. "I cannot say what your future would be, should you leave Celestière. I fear you would only find further heartbreak in the mortal realm, but I have made mistakes before." She spared a glance for the great mural upon the wall, the depiction of Sol Kareena herself and a woman bearing her face and the pendant of the moon. "I know you're guilty of your so-called crime. I cannot break my own laws, but I can offer you a comfortable life, should you confess before the people. If you go, you will be a fugitive of Celestière forevermore, but I will look the other way."

"That's because every self-righteous priest or priestess to her name gets uppity when I say how I really feel." Etolié looked to Sora, studied her curious demeanor, and stole a deep breath before continuing. "I've never seen her as some magnificent deity," she said, pulling out the words like molasses. "She's Auntie Kareena, and I wouldn't say we were ever close, but she saved me when the rest of my life fell apart. She's strict, but she's good and understands that justice can't be truly perfect, despite what people say." Etolié looked to Sora, bitterness released as she continued. "I resented her when she saved you and not Khastra, and I'm sorry for that. But I couldn't stay angry; it's because of her that I have a life at all. Plus I'm realizing I do kinda like you."

Sora smiled lightly, and Etolié hoped the half-elf accepted that this would be the closest she ever got to a declaration of affection.

"But I've seen what people have done to her teachings," she continued. "Anti-De'Sindai sentiment is high here in the Theocracy because Nox'Kartha embraces necromancy, but even before that it was still a crock of shit. With Casvir, they finally have an excuse other than 'oh, no demons—dark and scary.'" Etolié bit her lip, remembering when even a little human girl had nearly been turned away from the cathedral just for the crime of having a wolf for a familiar.

Etolié recalled Flowers' innocent offering, even now surprised at how vehemently it had been accepted. She watched the flock of people beyond, studied their finery. "Meira was annoying as shit, but at least she wasn't a hypocrite," she whispered. "There are good people in the Theocracy. Archbishop Xoran was one of them. Lunestra reeks of politics, but she's done wonders for the orphans in her care. So many people are awful, though. Sol Kareena is one of the few genuine beings in the realms, but most De'Sindai fear her because of what her followers have done. I never sent freed slaves here because I'd seen how people have turned her teachings of justice and mercy into a mantra of 'convert or die'—unless you're demon-descended and then it's often just 'die.'"

Silence settled in the carriage as Sora visibly contemplated Etolié's words.

Preparations for the funeral were underway. Etolié watched as a path was set, various streets slowly cleared and closed for the procession the next day.

She thought of Lunestra, a woman who had lost her brother, and wondered how she fared.

They reached an inn, wherein a room had been designated for the Staelashian Royalty. Marielle enjoyed her honeymoon; Etolié wasn't even certain she *knew* about the tragedy, to be honest. She hadn't heard anything of her, Murishani's insistence on post-wedding secrecy aggravating and frankly a violation of basic safety procedure.

Marielle placed an alarming amount of trust in him, and Etolié realized she resented her for it. She should be here. Her wedding was over; her luxury did not outweigh the importance of this. Thalmus had been left alone to survey the affairs of home—a task he'd begrudgingly accepted, understanding the importance of it.

The room was expansive, meant for far more than two people. Etolié settled in her own private suite, content to be alone after a week spent sharing a carriage with Sora.

She bathed. She ate, and the hole in her stomach slowly filled, even if she picked at the food with the enthusiasm of a bloated bird.

Khastra thought she was beautiful. Etolié still contemplated that.

Introspection hurt, manifesting in tears as she reread her letter, signed with an ominous black heart and bearing words foreign to her own mind.

"There is no heavier burden than a secret, Etolié. To speak of it will set you free."

And Etolié, for the first time in years, let herself think authentically of a crime plaguing her guilty conscience. Khastra knew everything. Khastra alone carried the burdens of Etolié's heart.

A new truth fell into place among the jagged pieces of her life—that, perhaps, to love Khastra as an equal, she had to free her of that.

Steeling herself, she set the letter aside and left her private room. She knocked on Sora's door, heard an affirming, "Come in," from within, and opened the door.

The half-elf wore clean clothes, her hair slightly damp. She sat on her bed, smiling expectantly. "Etolié?"

Etolié lingered in the doorway. "You love nosey stories about the gods of Celestière. Want one more?"

"You know I won't say no."

Etolié was a storyteller by nature, years of entertaining masses of people coming as naturally to her as breathing; on a smaller scale, a little Celestial princess named Lara had loved her talent for illustrating tales of grandeur with glitter and illusionary figures.

Etolié braced herself and summoned an image she was shy to gaze upon—her own momma, wings and all, though stylized like a galaxy, the domain she once ruled. "Once upon a time, there was a Goddess of Stars in the world of angels, and her life was ruined. Her wife and daughter were stolen from her, leaving her with nothing. The world moved on, thinking she'd died. I guess she had, in a way."

The figure silently wept upon the floor—Sora watched it as Etolié continued her words. "One day, a man came to her and said he could take away her pain." A second figure appeared, one bearing no wings as he stood above the sobbing supplicant. "He was Camdral, Son of Eionei, and he had unparalleled knowledge of plants and their properties; with magic, he could dilute and strengthen them to his will. They could soothe panic, heal sorrow ... even create false realities in the user's mind. The Goddess of Stars had nothing, and so she said yes."

The figures faded into formless masses, sparkling as they disappeared. "He didn't want money," Etolié whispered.

"He only wanted her. She was addicted to what he gave and couldn't leave. Even when he beat her. Even when he raped her."

The silence lingered; Etolié's lip trembled as a new set of figures appeared—the Goddess of Stars holding an infant with wings as magnificent as her momma's. "The inevitable happened. The Goddess of Stars bore his child. She was a difficult little thing—wouldn't talk for years, would scream if you touched her. All she wanted to do was sit in the corner and summon illusionary glitter and watch it sparkle. But her momma did her best."

The image changed. The child had grown—six years old, Etolié knew, and daring to stand between the Goddess of Stars and the beast she called *father*. She screamed in silence, until the Goddess clung to her instead, shielding her from the monster. "She was a courageous little shit who tried to defend the undefendable. She spent her entire childhood in the shadow of a monster she couldn't fight."

The Goddess disappeared. The child grew—fourteen now, and Etolié realized her own eyes had misted. "The man largely ignored her, but it didn't matter. There's only so much shit a girl can see before she loses her mind." The girl composed of stardust held a knife behind her back as she approached the man. He drank from a glittering flask.

She kissed him.

Etolié took artistic liberties to skip the rest; her body still numbed to think of it. Instead, the illusionary girl stabbed the man—he exploded into a sea of stars.

The girl simply . . . faded away.

"She confessed her crime to the Goddess of Light, who had no choice but to condemn her. The girl was guilty. Sol Kareena offered to let her run away. She would be a fugitive of Celestière forevermore, but she would be free."

Etolié sought judgement in Sora's face, but instead saw the same sorrow in the half-elf's countenance that she'd seen on Khastra's. Nearly sixteen years ago, in the first few years of Staelash, Khastra had found out her darkest truth and loved her just the same.

"I just don't understand how you can't see me as disgusting. What kind of sick fuck seduces her drunk father–"

"You were a child, Etolié. He raped you, but I do not think you see that." Khastra's eyes seemed larger when filled with tears, the first of which trailed the elegant lines of her face. "You were

powerless, because he stole that power. You used the only weapon you thought you had–"

Khastra's voice broke. The great half-demon wept as she clung to Etolié's form. "You are not disgusting," Khastra whispered. "You are not ruined. You survived."

Every secret shame Etolié clung to, Khastra had gently pulled away and replaced with devotion and love.

"She never saw her momma again," Etolié whispered, the image of the Goddess of Stars reforming before them. "The Goddess of Stars is finally healing, but needs to do so on her own. That's what . . ." Etolié sighed. The image vanished. "That's what Eionei said. To me. I'm the–"

"I know. You made that clear." Etolié forced a smile as Sora approached. "So anytime you've mentioned your mother–"

"I've been lying about having a relationship with my momma for thirty-four years, yes," Etolié said, vomiting the words like a riotous night gone wrong. Time flowed differently in Celestière, and so she'd had far longer to heal than Staella, as well as the mortal resilience to accept the need to do so, but . . .

Though she barely noticed the pain in her chest anymore, sometimes little things would twist the knife.

Sora approached, a kind smile on her full lips. "You hate hugs, but could I squeeze your hand or something?"

Etolié's countenance softened as she offered her hand, touched when Sora lightly squeezed.

"Thank you for sharing."

"You're thanking me for discussing child rape?"

"No. But it does explain a lot about you."

Etolié frowned at that. "I give off the aura of 'rape victim?'"

Sora quickly shook her head. "No, but you're the defender of the undefendable, like you said. You spent your childhood protecting your mother, and then you spent years freeing slaves. The shit that happened helped make you the hero you are today."

That was . . . really kind, actually. "Thanks," was all Etolié could muster, her soul oddly light despite the weighted words. "So . . . do you want to get drunk?"

Sora nodded.

They spent hours giggling like madmen in the public area of the suite, jesting of Staelash, of the wedding, and

Etolié felt, for the first time in too long, a feeling of comradery.

A wonderful thing, to have a friend.

Flowridia returned to her room to find Demitri stretched lazily across the floor. Ana bounded up; Flowridia took the affectionate little fox into her arms. "Where did you sleep last night?"

In the hallway. Lara let me in when she left this morning.

Realization struck her, and just a bit of guilt with it. "Did no one let you in before that?"

I wouldn't let them. The floor is the floor wherever you sleep. I don't care. But I do care about intruding on naked time with your good friend Lara.

"Dearest Demitri, I will smack you if you ever use that phrase again."

Were Demitri capable of laughter, Flowridia knew this would be the time. He stretched and yawned instead. *What I do need is some breakfast.*

He plucked her food trunk from the floor and stuck his nose in, withdrawing raw meat. She grimaced when it touched the fine carpet. "Demitri, that's disgusting."

Someone's paid to clean up, and it isn't me.

Flowridia curled her lip in disgust as he ate. "Well, when you're done being a pig, come and explore with me. I need to keep myself busy."

Instead of thinking about Lara?

"I'd rather not talk about Lara, Demitri."

For once, he listened.

Soon, Flowridia and Demitri, with Ana bouncing behind like an excitable puppy, left their generous quarters, and she asked for directions to a library, unprepared for the gargantuan collection of books she stumbled upon.

Nox'Kartha's library had been an ever-expanding collection of knowledge, limitless and unraveling as you walked; the Solviran library displayed all its magnificence at the door, with walls a hundred feet high stocked with books, and small magical lifts to help one navigate. It extended below, the middle hollow and surrounded by an ornately carved barrier, the bottom depthless to Flowridia's eyes. She stared down from the wide balcony, her mouth agape.

It smelled of ancient history, lit by enormous, narrow windows lining the walls from floor to ceiling and globes of light that danced about and followed the patrons—odd, but unquestionably useful when night would fall.

But this place was more than a collection of books—it harbored priceless history, with doors branching out into rooms and staircases filled with relics. Within one, she found an entire dragon skeleton, strung up anatomically from the ceiling, and upon the floor, displayed on pedestals, were pieces of a second.

It was beautiful and alarming both, for Flowridia remembered Valeuron's vision where she saw two behemoths fall to silver flame.

New goal.

Surprised at the words, Flowridia gazed oddly at Demitri. "I beg your pardon?"

That's how big I'll be.

"Follow your dreams, my darling Demitri."

Evening fell by the time she entered a room filled with ancient art.

She recognized the depictions of gods, knowing one small statue as Sol Kareena, and another as a magnificent painting of Eionei, with his coy smirk and rapier, facing a fearsome man, disfigured from brutal scars—perhaps he had been burned? The plaque named him as *Morathma, Jewel of the Desert.*

But the grandest of all stood at the far wall. Within the great hall, Flowridia stopped before the splendid mural, marveling at the spectacular image.

Three gargantuan figures, painted nearly from the floor to the ceiling, stood upon pedestals, each with their own unique pose and features. Standing tallest of the trio, a woman with onyx hair and a gaze as withering as disease surveyed the scene. Silver fire rose at her feet, gently caressing her skin, and power radiated from her stance and poise. She was an angel, with wings as silver as the moon's light and a crown to match.

So this was Neoma. Flowridia knew it in her heart.

Beside her, her hands clutching one of the Moon Goddess', a woman with a gentler stance gazed up in adoration. Her hair was as radiant and silver as the stars, and

Flowridia knew her—knew her translucent wings and darling, upturned nose. This was Staella, the Goddess of Stars and Etolié's mother.

Staella still lived, though she had shut herself away.

But the final looked away from the pair, pride in the sneer of her full lips. She was beautiful in the way of storms and volcanoes and other great calamities—glorious to behold, yet to come too close would mean an assured death. She wielded fire—silver at her feet, and purple smoke in her hand—while her other held a staff topped by what Flowridia swore must have been a De'Sindai skull.

Ilune, the Great Necromancer. The God of Death.

This was Solvira's legacy.

"Magnificent, isn't it?"

Flowridia's breath caught at the words, loud in the stark silence. Lara approached, and Flowridia watched her regal stance, for though she was gentle, she walked with power.

There stood a distant resemblance between she and the goddesses depicted. Lara's bloodline remained potent, dangerously so. But she had inherited Staella's gentle stance and eyes, instead of her more tyrannical counterparts.

"It's stunning," Flowridia replied as she looked back to the mural. "I'm surprised this is here. Your people no longer worship the Triage."

"My people thought the Triage were all dead for a thousand years. It's only because of Etolié's appearance in our realm that anyone knew Staella was still alive. Did she tell you that?"

Flowridia shook her head, gazing upon the supplicant goddess. How beautiful she was, with her tender countenance, her eyes shining with light.

"There's been a small movement in recent years, a resurgence in her worship. Though most have moved on to Sol Kareena, my people still remember their founding goddesses. The Triage was known for balance—they say Neoma stood at the head while the others would whisper in her ears to sway her. Neoma was Justice, pure and callused. Ilune was Power, chaotic in her mastery of death. Staella was Mercy, and so became the patron deity for children and the downtrodden. And while I don't believe Solvira will quickly move beyond its reputation for tyranny, Staella's worship has increased. I'm shy to admit it, but I may have started it."

"You're pledged to Staella?" Flowridia asked, surprised at the words.

Lara nodded. "It's Etolié's fault. She's the Daughter of Stars. As a little princess, I practically worshipped her, so when I learned who her mother was, I studied all I could. During my adolescent years , I helmed the restoration of an ancient temple in her name. I go once a week, at least, to try and commune. The goddesses used to manifest in the temples—I would love so dearly to renew that tradition." A shy smile appeared on Lara's lip, reminiscence in her gaze. "As a little girl, I would dream of her. Some say Staella would commune with her followers through dreams; I don't know if it were that or merely my imagination, but they are memories I cherish, even now."

Lara beckoned, and Flowridia followed as she escorted her to the next of the many pieces of art. "'Staella's Mercy,'" she read aloud, and the painting depicted the gentle goddess embracing a weeping supplicant .

"Are the angels humanoid, then?" Flowridia asked, realizing she truly didn't know. "Or is it a mortal interpretation?"

"Yes, and no. They're beings of light, but they still hold substance, and some say they resemble humans with wings."

Lara brought her to the next painting, a depiction of embracing lovers—Neoma and Staella. "Staella was the only temperance Neoma had, or so they say. The Moon Goddess was known to be brutish, cruel at times, and she was largely at odds with the other gods—including her sister, Sol Kareena. But she loved and adored Staella with all her heart. Staella made her . . . softer."

"I think that's wonderful," Flowridia said, wistful at the thought. For she knew a brutish, cruel woman, loved her with all her soul, and knew what it meant to be cherished by someone as tempestuous as the sea.

Guilt rose in her heart to think of Ayla here and now. Instead of dwelling, Flowridia looked back to the trio of goddesses. Lara said, "Most depictions of the God of Death were destroyed after the Civil War. This mural is one of the last."

"Why does Ilune hold a masculine title?"

To her surprise, Lara laughed. "Forgive me—it's technically slander, but reclaimed slander, by Ilune herself. Legend says Morathma sought to defame Ilune at every turn, deeming her conception unnatural and so despised all she was. Ilune was rather infamously involved with men and women both, like most angels, but he referred to her as the 'God of Death' as a means to insult her and her relationships with women of every species. Many details of Ilune's life are lost with time, but apparently she laughed in his face and wore the insult like a badge of honor, deemed herself the God of Death, and dared the world to call her anything else."

Flowridia grinned at the story, finding that level of spite rather inspirational. "So it is true, then? Neoma created Ilune with the Silver Fire?"

Lara nodded, visibly wistful at the words. "The Silver Fire created her, with Staella's womb to carry her. All the books say it, and if you ask Khastra, she'll confirm it as well. She's more valuable than ancient texts."

Flowridia gazed up at the embracing lovers, wondering if, perhaps, Staella might be a goddess she could pledge to as well.

Lara said, "I'm sorry I left you alone. Have you spent all day in here?"

"Yes, but we've had a wonderful time."

Lara pointed at the skeletal creature smacking her tail against the stone floor. "I didn't see her last night."

"I keep her in my bag when I ride Demitri," Flowridia replied, kneeling beside Ana. "When I tell her to sit, she stays, but I felt too guilty to leave her behind." She kissed the skull and beamed, giggling when Ana rolled over on her back. Her fingers stroked against her ribcage.

"She has so much life in her, Flowridia."

When Flowridia looked up, the warmth in Lara's eyes conveyed something maternal. The thought burned her, even more when Lara moved to kneel beside them.

"May I touch her?"

Flowridia nodded, and Lara brought her hand down to caress Ana's face. Ana nipped at the offered finger with affection, and Flowridia removed her own hand, watching Lara as she laughed at Ana's antics. "She's a marvel. If all undead creatures were as charming as she, I think they'd make fine pets."

"Most don't have this much personality," Flowridia said, watching as Lara lifted Ana into her arms. "Not my intention, when I raised her. I impressed Casvir, though."

"The spellwork holding her together is so intricate." Ana lay cradled in Lara's arms, and she cooed over her like an infant. "I'm impressed, too. To be able to hit with precision is better than to hit with power."

"If you're trying to downplay your own talents, that's ridiculous. You're a legend."

"Born to be a legend, yes. But I think you've already earned the skill to sit among the greats."

Confusion struck her at the words. "Is everyone in your kingdom so accepting of necromancy?"

"Likely not. But closed minds hinder growth." Lara looked forlornly to Flowridia. "You've been rejected before."

Flowridia settled for a simple nod, unwilling to entertain the shame that came at the reminder. If to lose all those she loved was the price of greatness . . . could she stand to pay it?

"Flowridia." Lara's gentle voice pulled her from her downward spiral. She glanced up as Lara scooted herself closer and placed Ana into her arms. Flowridia cradled Ana close, wondering for the thousandth time if the creature was capable of feeling love. Hands wrapped around her waist, and Lara smiled as she gazed at Ana. "Did you kill the fox so you could raise her?"

Flowridia shook her head, shocked at the notion. "I raised her because I couldn't save her."

"Your intentions matter. I don't think anything evil went into the creation of your little one."

Intentions matter . . . Oh, that stung. "If I had raised a human corpse instead of a fox, would you feel the same way?"

Lara hesitated. That was enough. Flowridia stared down, unwilling to face her, and flinched when she heard her speak. "Intentions matter," Lara repeated. "I believe the dead should remain dead, but we aren't our bodies; we're our souls. To restore a soul to a dead vessel seems like a hellish fate, especially since their mind would belong to the necromancer. But if it's merely a body, and their soul has gone on, I don't see why it would necessarily be evil." Her expression softened. "I don't know how I would feel to have a host of undead servants at my beck and call, but if I were to give that power to anyone, I would trust you to wield it responsibly."

The embrace tightened a moment as Lara squeezed her affectionately, and then she let her arms slip away. "I came here to invite you and Demitri to dinner with my council. Ana, of course, is welcome to join, though I will request she remembers her manners." A teasing smirk twisted her lip as she offered Flowridia her hand.

"I don't know, to be honest," Flowridia said, accepting the gesture. Ana remained in her arms. "Have you told your council who I am?"

"No, though I suspect many of them know, since they saw you this afternoon. If you'd prefer, I'll happily take dinner with you in your room instead. You'll have to meet some of them in the morning, though. I've assembled a small team to accompany us to the Abyssal Swamp."

Flowridia fought to hide her fear at the words—her resolve threatened to shatter simply from the sincere kindness in Lara's visage, much less the realization that there would now be witnesses, and thus more deaths. "I think I'd rather take dinner in my room tonight. It's been a long couple of days."

Lara nodded kindly. Flowridia set Ana onto the floor. "Stay close," she commanded, then Lara intertwined their fingers. Flowridia stared at their hands, but tightened the grip when Lara tried to pull away. "No," she whispered. "This is nice."

It truly was. Not quite romantic, but comforting, familial. Her growing affection for Lara threatened to rip a hole in her heart.

Lara's smile lit the room, but that only added to Flowridia's gloomy shadow. She led her forward, opening the door and stepping aside so Ana and Demitri could walk through.

Fingers intertwined, Lara led her down the hallway. Demitri's voice caught her off guard. *You two are awfully touchy.*

Quietly, she turned around and shot him a glare.

If your goal was to get Lara to slip the noose around her neck herself, I'd say you're doing a great job. I can smell it; she's smitten.

The words slipped from her mouth unbidden, a manifestation of her grief. "Shut up."

"Pardon?" Lara stopped, brow furrowed in confusion.

"Sorry. That wasn't for you," Flowridia said, now openly glaring at Demitri. "Demitri has a habit of pointing out the obvious."

But not of casting judgement.

"Just because you're not judging doesn't mean you have to say it."

I think you're projecting because you feel guilty.

"You don't know my feelings."

I know all your feelings, stupid.

Lara placed a hand on Flowridia's shoulder when she tried to step forward. "May I ask?"

"It's nothing," she said, petulant at her own defensive tone. "It's unimportant. Something about you being smitten. You and I already discussed this."

"Do you mind if I speak to him?" Flowridia shook her head, following as Lara looked to the large wolf. "Demitri? I am smitten. And I don't know how much you know, but Flowridia and I did speak about this last night. I know about Ayla, and I've offered her all the time she needs to mourn. She and I have agreed to be friends, and I hope you and I might be too."

"He would like that," Flowridia whispered.

"You're a considerate friend, Demitri. I'm trying to be considerate too."

Tell her she's too good for this world.

"Demitri thinks you're a good person."

Don't misquote me.

Lara chuckled, extending her free hand. Demitri rubbed his head against it. "Oh, you're sweet." Her eyes suddenly widened, and she withdrew her hand. "Is that patronizing?"

No. I'm sugar sweet. The sweetest ever.

Flowridia's sigh was nothing less than long-suffering. "As long as Demitri is the *most* sweet, he's happy to be sweet."

"Good to know," Lara said, petting his head again. "I haven't met many witches, so if I ever over-step my bounds with your familiar, please tell me."

"My permission isn't what you need to worry about. As long as you have his, you can touch him all you want. I think he'd appreciate the attention."

I'm starting to like her. I see why you're conflicted about killing her.

"And I'll *gladly* interpret anything he has to say," Flowridia added, her smile only slightly forced. "But he understands you."

"Demitri, you are wonderful," Lara said, pulling her hand back. "And I've made sure there's a plethora of different meats for you for dinner." She turned to Flowridia and whispered, "He does eat meat, right?"

Flowridia nodded, and Lara squeezed her hand and resumed leading them through the library.

Dinner was a relaxed affair—simply she and Lara giggling at Ana's antics, Flowridia occasionally interpreting Demitri's attempts at humor. It warmed her heart, to simply sit with a friend and speak of idle things, and for a few precious moments, Flowridia forgot her quest, forgot her own inevitable betrayal.

But once the food had gone, when the sun was a forgotten memory, time moved forward. "We leave tomorrow after breakfast," Lara said, when the night had concluded.

"I can be packed at a moment's notice. Most everything I own is in my bag."

Lara nodded. "I'll leave you to sleep, then. Get some rest."

Flowridia hesitated, placing her hand at Lara's hip. "You don't have to go," she muttered.

"I wouldn't be sad to stay," Lara said slowly, "but I don't want to encroach on you. You need time."

But Flowridia's grip tightened. "Stay," she pled, realizing how desperately she meant it. Was it her guilt? Some deep-seated affection? "Nothing has to happen. But sleep beside me?"

Lara slowly nodded.

They did not embrace as they slept, but to hear someone breathe beside her held comfort, even if it was a comfort she hadn't known since the days she'd lived in an orphanage.

Ayla, after all, had never needed to breathe. And Lara's breaths, as fleeting as they were, seemed a precious thing.

The next morning, Flowridia waited outside the stables, listening to Lara discuss the best location for a portal with a man as ancient and eccentric as she'd ever seen. From his umber skin to the stark white of his hair, everything about him cast a presence, the flamboyancy of his robes suggesting either insanity or a high prowess for sorcery—or both. She recognized him from the wedding—Magister Reginal.

"I have no intention of drawing any attention from the populace of Ilunnes," Lara said. "Perhaps a few miles out?"

The smell of manure was oddly soothing—familiar among the bureaucratic finery. But anxiety brewed in Flowridia's stomach, to consider the newfound impossibility of her quest. She stood near a young Celestial priest—Coal? Coal . . . *something*, was his name. He would be joining she and Lara on their journey to the swamp, and Flowridia felt much more comfortable standing beside him than the other two members of their small party.

Two paladins of Sol Kareena busied themselves saddling their horses. Flowridia spared a glance for Ana at her feet, bidding the little fox to stay close.

Coal looked at her, hesitant as he caught her eye. "I think I've seen you before. Were you at Queen Marielle's wedding in Staelash?"

She saw nothing but earnest sincerity in his gaze. "I was. I spent most of my time standing next to Imperator Casvir, trying to be invisible."

She said it in jest, amused at the nervous glance she received from the younger paladin. He'd been introduced as Ser Luftlight, and she wasn't quite certain if 'Luftlight' was his last name or first, or if 'Ser' was a title or a name, but she'd felt much too awkward to ask.

He seemed relatively harmless for a paladin—his eyes were wide and unseasoned, perhaps having never seen bloodshed. He knew how to hold himself in armor, but she couldn't say much more for his prowess.

"You're friends with the imperator?" Coal said. "Can I ask something?"

She braced herself for the predictable line of questions, prepared to deny all flirtation.

"I heard once that Imperator Casvir can only come out at night. Is that true?"

Flowridia shook her head, smiling for relief. "No, certainly not."

"I also heard he summons packs of wolves to fight for him."

"Oh, no. Living creatures instinctively distrust Casvir," she replied. "Including Demitri, and he's a rather intelligent one."

"Perhaps more intelligent for it," Luftlight muttered, though he could barely be heard.

"Oh, perhaps," Flowridia said, staring at him directly. "But Casvir never would hurt anything needlessly."

Luftlight's slight blush was readily apparent in the morning light. "Is it true Imperator Casvir drinks only the blood of virgin Celestials?"

Taken aback, Flowridia actually laughed at the accusation. "I only saw him eat a handful of times; if he drinks virgin blood, it's for fun, not necessity." The horror on their faces only made her laugh more. "He keeps some in his service who will drink virgin blood, but I sincerely doubt that he partakes. Though I've never met a vampire who discriminated based on sexual habits."

Luftlight looked a bit faint at the remark, but Coal's intrigued bordered on enamor, his eyes wide and bright. She wrote the priest off as naïve. "You met a vampire?"

The question brought mixed emotions—Flowridia recalled Ayla, yes, and Mereen, but also Palace and her screams. "Several—"

Suddenly, her stomach lurched, vertigo striking as the world spun. A massive portal, far larger than any summoned by Casvir, expanded before them. "There we go," Lara said, a subtle dullness to her aura.

Flowridia distracted her addled mind with the darling creature provided for her. She offered a hand to a lovely grey mare, her rump speckled in white. *"You beautiful creature,"* she said, her words laced with power. *"I promise to treat you well."*

"You charm the living the way you charm the undead?"

A shadow cast itself across her. The second paladin had been introduced as General Irons of Solvira, trained and handpicked by Khastra as a replacement when she'd been sent to Staelash. His graying beard covered a weathered face—and any glance he gave to Ana was pure disgust. Imposing upon his decorated steed, General Irons stared with a set jaw and narrowed eyes.

"Is 'charm' really the word for casting influence upon the undead?" Flowridia asked, offering pleasantries to his palpable disdain.

"It's as polite a word as I can summon in front of her majesty."

Flowridia simply smiled. "General," she said curtly, "you and I clearly have our disagreements, but I'm willing to set that all aside and be friendly acquaintances if you are."

His gaze narrowed, and Flowridia was acutely aware of the sword at his hip. "That will depend on your intentions for Empress Alauriel."

Flowridia recognized his implied intent. "Only the future can say."

Irons gave a curt nod of acknowledgement. Flowridia was quite confident he could stick his sword through her stomach with no hesitation. He held himself with power and assurance running deep, no false airs or pettiness. This man held the conviction to slay her.

And she was only marginally certain she held the conviction to slay him first.

What a pleasant man.

Flowridia looked to Demitri, who Irons had thankfully ignored. "I beg your pardon?"

See? I'm a good liar too.

Flowridia rolled her eyes and gave a quick pat to her familiar's head. "Never change."

She mounted her horse, resolving to write a 'thank you' letter to Casvir for teaching her to ride. They all stepped through the portal in a line—

An odd sensation, to fly through the worlds upon a horse.

She gripped the reins when they landed, nearly falling off her mount into the lush field of grass.

A few hours' journey from the swamp? Flowridia surveyed the area, realizing they stood a far distance from a forest.

The Forest of Wisps, bordering Ilunnes. This was her home.

A cool breeze ruffled Flowridia's hair, bringing with it memories of Casvir. When their entire party had passed through the portal, they set off with Irons in the lead.

The sun shone bright, and Demitri stood taller than the horses. Even Lara's, blonde and speckled with white, could not quite match his massive height and bulk.

They travelled largely in silence, but Flowridia appreciated how the sunlight warmed her skin through her embroidered dress. Lara's clothing remained rich, but more practical, her regal skirts exchanged for leggings and a split, but fanciful skirt, feminine and easy to move and ride in.

At midday, they reached the edge of the forest, Lara by her side. Off in the surrounding meadow, bunches of purple daisies littered the scene, and Flowridia longed to stop her mount and pick a few for her hair.

So, when Ser Luftlight announced his intention to relieve himself, Flowridia took the moment to do so. General Irons proposed they take time to stretch; Flowridia had a few minutes yet.

Lara followed beside her, apparently bemused by her actions. Flowridia stepped into the field, grass clinging to her skirts and tickling her bare legs. She knelt beside a particularly vibrant patch and plucked a few, expertly weaving them into her thick locks as Lara watched.

"I'm impressed you can do that without a mirror."

Flowridia laughed lightly. "Years of practice. I know it's a bit juvenile, but I feel naked without them."

"Not juvenile," Lara said, sitting beside her in the dry grass. "I think it's cute."

Lara's hair held a practical bun, so Flowridia took a particularly large daisy and stepped toward her, balanced on her knees. She threaded the purple flower to the side, weaving it so the stem remained unseen. "Fit for an empress," Flowridia said warmly.

Lara's blush radiated more heat than the warm air. "I will warn you—if I'm seen wearing this by the populace, it will be the style of every woman for the next year. Becoming a fashion icon unfortunately comes with my title."

Flowridia laughed, Lara's charm infectious, yet . . .

The thought twisted her gut, that she would soon slay this lovely, kind woman. Her laughter faded. Flowridia resumed placing daisies in her hair, imagining lithe cold fingers caressing the strands instead of her own.

"Are you all right?"

She'd lapsed into silence, she realized. Lara waited beside her, watching as Flowridia continued weaving flowers into her hair. "It's been a long few months, I will be honest," she said, hoping to distract from her true anxieties. "And I don't think General Irons likes me much."

"Did he say something to you?"

"Nothing *rude*, exactly, but he didn't have to be."

Lara glanced back to their party, eyes narrowing when they landed on Irons. "I'll speak with him."

"Lara—"

"Flowridia, my own feelings for you aside, he has no business insulting a foreign dignitary. Once we've returned, he'll be reprimanded."

Venom had seeped into Lara's voice. The woman she had shared a bed with begged for domination, but Alauriel Solviraes was born to be an empress, and no matter how sweet her demeanor might be, Flowridia suddenly understood how she could control a room. "I think it's your feelings for me that he's worried about."

"I see—*Ah!*" Lara suddenly yelped, stumbling to her feet as she frantically brushed her skirts and hands. Silver flame rose as she stomped on the ground, and beneath the faint scorch marks, Flowridia saw the remains of an impressively large spider. "No. Bad. Very bad."

Flowridia bit her lip, actively fighting laughter as the most powerful woman in the world squirmed in the face of a harmless arachnid. She swallowed her amusement, instead offering a few forcibly calm words. "Not a fan of the outdoors?"

"I love the outdoors, but . . ." She grimaced, true fear flashing across her eyes. She lifted her skirts, checking the folds of the fabric. *"Things* live outside."

A smile tugged at Flowridia's lip. "I have a few spells to never cast in front of you, then."

"Oh, please no," Lara said, squirming. "I know enough about traditional witch spells to know I'd really rather not see spiders crawling out of your mouth."

"I can't do that, but I can summon the ones already around me." Lara grimaced and shuddered; Flowridia giggled. "Casvir taught me that one."

"Here's me swearing to never find myself in a duel with Casvir, then."

"I doubt he would do that," Flowridia said, a conspiratorial grin twisting her lip. "More than likely he'd cause horrendous boils to burst from your skin—" Lara squeaked, and Flowridia laughed as she continued, ". . . and slowly eat at you. He's awfully proud of that one. Used it to ward off a rather famous half-demon."

"He should be proud."

"I'm sure you have a few nasty spells up your sleeve as well."

"Of course I do," Lara said in mock offense. "But my nasty spells aren't literally nasty. They'll make you do perfectly normal things, like spontaneously combust."

Flowridia laughed. "Perfectly normal, yes. Most of mine are actually normal. Healing is my best talent."

"And necromancy?"

Flowridia hesitated, pursing her lip as she decided how to answer. "It's not something I truly understood until recently."

Lara knelt, apparently over her panic. Her hand moved to cover Flowridia's. "As I said before, if I were to trust anyone with those talents, it's you." Those silver eyes suddenly seemed distant, unfocused. "Our magics aren't so different. The Silver Fire and necromancy aren't opposites but two sides of the same coin—one dealing in life and the other in death. Just as you can create a false semblance of life, I can create a permanent, irrevocable death."

Flowridia spared a glance for their companions, busied with tending to the horses, paying no mind to the two women sharing a moment of peace. "Tell me more," she said, curiosity and genuine concern filling her at Lara's change in tone.

"As you know, it's an inborn trait in my lineage," Lara said, shrugging slightly, "to absorb pure energy and to release it again, to control the Silver Fire. We're each taught as children how to slowly expand the pool of magic we can safely hold—by pushing our bodies more and more, beyond capacity. My father explained that it's like a well; it slowly grows deeper, wider, but then it takes more and more to fill it. It's why magical addiction is a fear of mine."

Flowridia recalled Casvir's warning, that necromancers often fell prey to addiction, and saw how she and Lara's powers ran parallel.

"But that's simply fact and history," Lara continued. "It doesn't give gravity to what unhinged, uncontrolled power can do. And it doesn't explain the consequences of long-term drainage. Life is magic—the Silver Fire can destroy a person's soul." A slight rim of red surrounded Lara's bright eyes, but no tears fell. "You told me of your mother; may I tell you of mine?"

Flowridia gave her a slow nod, patient as she waited for Lara to continue.

"Her name was Ralaena, and she was a noblewoman who hailed from the outskirts of Solvira. It's a simple, but beautiful story; my parents fell in love, and they were married. My father was the second child, never expected to take the throne, and so was free to marry whomever he chose—but when his brother died and he was crowned emperor, he and my mother had to bear a child."

Lara stared at Flowridia's hand as it rested on hers, her posture slipping. Her opposite arm moved to cover her chest. "I never met my mother," she whispered. "I killed her. Solviraes pregnancies can be dangerous for the mother, unless she is a Solviraes herself. Our talents are inborn, and they are powerful. The fetus can drain energy, and my mother had little energy to drain."

Flowridia's hand tightened around Lara's. "Lara—"

"I know, I know—it isn't my fault," she said, still avoiding eye contact. "My father never blamed me either, instead vowing to love me twice as much, for both she and he." The hand underneath Flowridia's tightened into a fist. "But I've never forgotten, and I've always lived in fear of what my power can do."

Flowridia lifted Lara's fist and took it in both hands, gently stroking it, coaxing it to relax. "And yet you do not fear necromancy?"

Lara finally looked up at her, vulnerability in her stare. "I do fear it. I also respect it. I've vowed to use my powers for good, though so many of my ancestors were known for madness. Our destinies are our own."

Flowridia slowly leaned forward and pulled Lara into an embrace. The slight woman in her arms felt so warm, so small. Ayla had been small, but her cold form never could be held for long. Always twitching, always calculating—to have a moment alone, serene and still, had been so precious a thing.

Lara seemed content to melt into her and settle in her skin and bones. Flowridia breathed deep, smelling the floral scents woven into Lara's hair, memorizing how it mingled with her natural aura. Ayla had smelled clean like the rich soaps she used, or the earth and blood if she were dirty, or even slightly floral if her skin had lingered against Flowridia's for long.

When Lara pulled away, no tears had spilled, and she smiled faintly in the brilliant sunlight. "It's not a story I tell often," Lara admitted, taking Flowridia's hands in her own. "Thank you for listening."

Flowridia looked down at their hands and whispered, "Thank you for trusting me enough to tell me."

Their fingers interlaced. Any joy in it was marred by guilt.

The next day, a somber mood settled in the Theocracy of Sol Kareena.

Clouds had gathered, as was both fitting and not. Of course Sol Kareena could be metaphorically present without the actual sun shining upon them, but the omen was not a good one, and Etolié saw a crowd of citizens looking dismayed.

She itched; the world was too loud, too grating on her senses. The large procession walked through the crowded streets, a clear path marked for the pallbearers to take. A closed casket passed Etolié and Sora by, decorated in flowers, but all Etolié could think about was Xoran's gruesome end.

Khastra's hands had shattered and crushed his skull, the same hands that had touched Etolié like she was an idol for worship.

The memories of the apparent God of Order's appearance and the archbishop's subsequent murder had paled to the events of that night, but now, faced with a procession carrying a good, innocent man, Etolié's gut clenched. She recalled his horrid scream, the blood seeping from cracked bone, the taste and smell, the warm spray as it coated her naked body—

"Breathe, Etolié . . . Breathe with me."

Etolié shut her eyes and released a pained breath, methodically rubbing her hands. Then, she took out her flask and drank.

Etolié saw her majestic friend's defeated stance behind her eyelids, the regret in every silent gesture. Khastra had done this; Khastra had done this for her.

"I would have been content to perish with that as my final duty."

A ghost touched Etolié's back. It sent a jolt up her spine, and for a brief and beautiful moment, it was Khastra, here to hide her and soothe her sensitive nerves.

"Etolié?" Sora said, and Etolié opened her eyes. "A line is forming, if you want to pay your final respects."

They wouldn't be showing the body itself. The corpse had met a gruesome end.

"No," Etolié said, watching as the crowd steadily approached the cathedral. "I saw him die. It's . . . It's too much. I do wish to give Lunestra my condolences after, though. Xoran is dead, but the rest of us have to keep living."

Sora nodded, understanding in her gaze. Etolié watched her go, then walked opposite the crowd.

The sky held all the gloom of evening, despite being midday. Shadows blocked the sun, and Etolié feared it would rain. As she wound her way through the crowded streets, her soul felt as weighted as the clouds, pregnant in their mourning.

At her finger, she spun her puzzle ring. Damn Khastra and her charming engineering skills. In a week's time, she'd yet to solve its mystery.

Tears filled her eyes, the weight of the day too much.

Etolié's wandering feet had taken her to a secluded district of the city. Typically, the marketplace would be bustling, but today the doors and windows were shut, closed for business in light of the terrible tragedy. She heard nothing, except some idle scratching from the alley—when she peered inside the darkened space, she saw rats munching on garbage.

Alone, Etolié revealed her impressive wings, allowing them to stretch in the vacant space. She flew up, the ethereal appendages carrying her to the rooftops, and higher still—she set her course for a watchtower beyond, presumably abandoned for the mournful event.

The circular tower ended in a flat roof, and Etolié settled atop the cold stone, wrapping her wings around herself in an illuminate blanket. Something was different—rather, something *different* was different, but she was less remiss to actually hold a mirror to herself now, because although introspection was scary, she had at least a taste of the depth of it and what it meant even if a thousand questions remained unanswered, and even if Etolié wanted to puke from nerves at any given moment, at least she could *breathe* because something in that night had pulled out the stopper for a thousand different feelings that Etolié still struggled to understand.

She recalled the boundless passion when Khastra had returned Etolié's tentative butterfly kiss, saw the unquestionable adoration in her glowing gaze, her tears as she held Etolié after their tender affair.

It was sacred.

It was beautiful.

It was . . . *goodbye.*

Loneliness welled tears in her eyes, but when Etolié might've succumbed to sobs upon the watchtower, she noticed an oddity on the horizon.

Something flickered upon the landscape, and were she not a master of her own illusionary talents, she would have dismissed it as a trick of the light or a mirage displaced from its desert home. But Etolié frowned, knowing that illusions were only as real as she believed them to be.

The lush green of the fields and the flowing river flickered in her vision, revealing monsters in the sky, silhouetted against the clouds. A sea of undead rapidly approached, spreading a field of blight wherever they stepped.

Shock stilled her limbs. How no one had seen this, she could not say. Perhaps portals. Perhaps some secret of necromancy. But rapidly approaching the City of Light was an army of death, led by two enormous *dragons.*

Etolié spread her wings and dove from the tower, shooting toward the cathedral.

Buildings rushed past. Etolié's heart pounded in her ears. In the air, she quickly reached her destination, ignoring the mourners who stared at her presence—as one of the only known Celestials with wings, she made for a sight.

As she soared down, she tucked her wings to her back, shooting through the ajar doors of the cathedral. People gasped as she dove above their heads, but the expansive cathedral easily accommodated her need for space.

She spread her wings as she came toward the archbishop's casket, causing a rush of air to billow against Lunestra and the other citizens politely paying their respects. The new archbishop, to her credit, looked appalled but didn't immediately snap at her.

Etolié's feet touched the ground. "Archbishop Lunestra, you have to clear the city!"

She ignored the gasps around her. Lunestra frowned and said, "Magister Etolié, what are you talking about—"

"Nox'Kartha is here. They've brought an army."

Audible panic rippled through the citizens at the front of the cathedral. Lunestra's frown melted into fear. "What?"

"They're on the horizon—"

Etolié felt a great *boom* rupture not her ears but her soul. She looked to the window and saw that all daylight had vanished. Screams from beyond met her ears.

Eionei, tell Sol Kareena—

She was merely thinking to herself. She felt nothing— no connection to Celestière. When she glanced to Lunestra, she saw the archbishop look in horror at her familiar on her shoulder—as though the little bird were nothing, as though she felt nothing too. Lunestra stared at her hands, and Etolié saw other priests and priestesses do the same.

Those with a godly connection had felt it sever. But how?

Lunestra cried, "Guards! Sound the alarm. Every citizen must go underground immediately!"

"What can I do to help?" Etolié said, but Lunestra shook her head.

"You owe us nothing—"

Etolié snapped her fingers, and an illusionary flock of birds burst from her hand, flying up to the rafters of the building. "I can't speak to Eionei, but I'm not crippled. Let me help."

A set of guards approached Lunestra as she nodded. The panic in the room rose as people ran away. "Archbishop, we must get you to safety—"

Another great *boom,* but this one reverberated against Etolié's entire body. A great roar echoed from beyond.

Dragons.

"Your duty is to protect my people," Lunestra said to the guards. "Get everyone underground."

Etolié felt Sora's presence as the half-elf suddenly appeared beside them. "They're crawling over the walls—the dead!"

How they had come so quickly, Etolié feared to guess. "Your people need their archbishop," she said. "Let your guards protect your own, but let me protect you. I say this not as a foreign magister, but as a citizen of Celestière, as the Chosen of Eionei, and as one of godly lineage—I swear you will leave this alive."

Lunestra accepted her outstretched hand, and Etolié prayed she had not condemned a woman to die. "My city holds catacombs, specially warded to protect from undeath," Lunestra said. "During the Civil War, Sol Kareena feared the violence would bleed into her borders and so created them specifically for detouring the God of Death's forces—and thus the forces of the dead."

The great bells of the cathedral rang, rousing the city from its lethargy and into action. "And they'll save us?"

"They will." Lunestra beckoned for her and Sora to follow and led them to the doors behind the great statue of Sol Kareena. "During the war, it was a race to collect allies—Ilune against Neoma, and each of them frantically grabbed those who would join their respective causes." Through the back hallways, she led, not running, no, but hurried. "When Ilune enlisted the demon god Onias, so too did Neoma and Sol Kareena plead for Demoni intercession—Ku'Shya joined in Neoma's cause. I say this because it was Ku'Shya who aided in creating the underground caverns, offered wards written in Demoni tongue, for Ilune could not speak it and deactivate them. They are impenetrable to undeath."

Lunestra knocked upon a door and peeked her head inside. "Children, take nothing. Come with me now."

Etolié peered past her and saw a bunkhouse full of children—eight in all, each wearing the robes of Sol Kareena. Her gut clenched as some sought to grab blankets or toys despite the archbishop's reprimand. Etolié saw the stakes before her, the lives of these children now held in her unworthy hands.

Sora, too, visibly steeled her courage, but her gaze had hardened, cold calculation in her words. "Where do we go?"

"There are five catacomb entrances scattered throughout the city, all of which lead to a central cavern. We must direct as many citizens as possible as we run—the undead cannot pass the threshold, so once they're underground, they're safe. The nearest is north of the cathedral, in the artisan's district."

Sora stepped forward, beckoning to the children. "Everyone, find a friend and hold their hands with all your might, all right? Don't let go for anything. We're going to see some scary things, but I promise if you stay with us, Sol Kareena will protect you."

One little girl said, "Are you the priestess Sol Kareena brought back to life?"

"I am. So you know my promises mean something."

Another child, a little boy of no more than five, looked to Etolié and her wings. "Are you an angel?"

Etolié shook her head. "Almost, but not quite. My mother is Staella, Goddess of Stars."

All the children flocked to inspect her wings, and though Etolié flinched at their grabbing hands, her heart ached. She had little understanding of children, but nearly cried when the same boy said, "You'll protect us?"

By Morathma's Whore Mother, she was leading children to the slaughter—

Etolié smacked that thought from her head. Let this be her great work. "Absolutely, but we'd better get moving."

Lunestra and Sora each carried one of the smaller ones, but Etolié elected to merely hold their tiny hands. "Remember what the half-elf said—hand holding."

They obeyed. Lunestra led them out. Not to the front, no, but to a door at the far back, one that showed the outside world.

Etolié's grip on the tiny hands tightened when she heard pained screams from beyond. The sky had darkened, black clouds blotting out the sun. People ran. She saw no dead—not yet.

But in the dank, heavy air, Etolié saw a great skeletal dragon hovering above the city, clutching a gigantic box pulsing with dark energy, lightning in hues of purple and black radiating in erratic waves. Etolié's head revolted at the feeling, the power unparalleled, the box serving to magnify whatever dark artifact lay within.

She, who had once wielded an orb of fire, realized she knew its kin.

"Etolié, let's go!"

Sora's voice pulled Etolié from her horror, and the Celestial ran to keep up, dragging the three children clutching her arms along. More than once she nearly lost Lunestra in the crowd, the open area and stone streets surrounding the cathedral soon narrowing into organized, grid-like alleyways.

A great *thud* shook the earth behind them. Etolié dared to look back and gasped. The second of the dragons had landed, not a hundred feet away, uncaring of the people it squashed beneath its now bloodied limbs. It roared; the children screamed, but Etolié ran and pulled them along.

When she looked back once more, she saw the dead beneath the dragon's feet rise. Screams erupted. From the dragon's back stood a figure that chilled her blood, one wearing blackened armor she knew, a helm she did not, and weapons crackling with dark matter.

Imperator Casvir leapt from his dragon and barraged into the crowd, merciless as his weapon tore through citizens and soldiers alike. They rose in undeath before they could even fall, joining the ranks of the Tyrant of Nox'Kartha.

Etolié dragged the children through the alley, disappearing around the stone corner only a few steps behind Sora and Lunestra.

The carnage quieted as they ran through an untouched street. "This way!" Etolié cried to a panicked family, and they ran behind a larger group of citizens, directed by a single guard.

Etolié heard a foreign *skittering* sound and knew in her blood it meant death. "Run!" she cried when she saw a monster claw over the roof—rotted flesh met her nostril as a figment of death landed before her. It bore no features, merely a cadaver's face, stripped of flesh, but its claws had grown, the clothing it bore in tatters.

Etolié shoved the children away, ignoring them as one toppled. From the air, she withdrew a sword, created from her own imagination. When she released it, it attacked on its own accord, driving back the monster of dead flesh. She pulled the children along, running to escape the monster.

More appeared from the rooftops. Etolié heard screaming from behind but knew there was naught she could do without sacrificing her wards.

She had one vow—to save Lunestra—and in turn had adopted Lunestra's—to save the children in her charge.

Before them, she heard the distant shouting of, *"Go, go, go!"* Etolié followed Sora and Lunestra and came upon a large archway, perhaps ten feet tall. Ancient stone stairs led down. Flocks of people fought to enter, directed by guards who shoved the stragglers through. Behind, Etolié saw a group of the dead approaching and knew her quarry would fall.

Etolié brought the children to Lunestra. "Stay here," she instructed, then turned to Sora. "I trust you with a sword. Want to fight back a small legion of the dead?"

Sora looked to the street, then grabbed the little bird from her shoulder and shoved the poor thing down her shirt. "You're one of the few people I'd die beside."

Etolié offered her a sword, then pulled another from the air. She and Sora ran toward the oncoming death.

Sunlight managed to cut through the thick leaves, but the ground grew moist and the creatures singing were of a different sort, dark and eerie. During quiet moments, Flowridia shut her eyes and practically felt Aura's presence—they had spent many years together here, learning all the wonders of the world.

Damp leaves shuffled beneath hooves and paws. The trunks of trees forced their group to deviate from each other, but never for long. They managed to maintain a circle of sorts, with Lara and Flowridia in the lead and their companions at the rear.

A question from behind startled them all. "Lady Flowridia?"

She recognized Coal's voice and smiled as she faced him.

"Is it true you've been to Nox'Kartha?" Coal stared at her, hesitant as she nodded. "Is Nox'Kartha full of coffins and crypts like everyone says?"

"Not at all. It's a beautiful city, full of gleaming buildings and paved roads and fountains. The castle itself is a little imposing, but that's Murishani's doing. I suspect he had more say in the architecture than Casvir."

"So you've met the viceroy, too?"

She chuckled at his interest. "I have met Murishani, yes," she replied. "He's . . ." A charming, lecherous monster? "He's an interesting man. I like Casvir much more."

"I've heard," Coal said, visibly excited, "that Viceroy Murishani once wrote up a contract between himself and Morathma."

Flowridia shrugged. "That could be true."

"I also heard," he continued, blushing fiercely, "that he bedded a hundred virgin women at once."

"Also, probably true. Though I'd be amazed if at least half of them weren't men. Murishani gets who he wants." She turned to Lara, though continued loud enough for Coal and the others to hear. "Apparently, Ayla told him that if he so much as looked at me, she'd rip his head off. Casvir has reinforced this as still true."

Demitri suddenly perked up, stopping his footsteps as Lara said, "Was there any threat of him trying to sleep with you?"

"He made his intentions known, more than once," Flowridia admitted, praying her grimace properly conveyed her disgust. "Khastra was kind enough to deter him the first time." She slowed her horse. "Demitri?"

I hear something.

Thoughts of Soliel bombarded her memory. "What sort of something?"

No warning. Just a whirring and a thump as an arrow struck Lara's back.

She gasped. Their entire party froze. Flowridia slid down from her horse and caught her as she fell.

Another arrow whizzed by her ear, missing her but striking Demitri. He howled, snarling in rage, and ran to join General Irons as he leapt from his horse. "Ambush!" the paladin cried, and Luftlight and he both drew their weapons and shields.

Amidst the chaos, Flowridia helped Lara fall gently to the ground, noticing the faint green aura emanating from the wound. "The head is deep," she said, praying Lara could hear, "but this is maldectine. I have to pluck it out to heal—"

A weight smacked her in the throat, the momentum pulling her down. Gasping, she couldn't breathe, realizing a chain had wrapped around her neck, weighted on both ends by small, iron balls. She tried in vain to unravel it, but she only managed to loosen it enough to cough a pained breath. "Lara—"

Clanging metal pulled their attention. Flowridia looked up just in time to see Demitri rip the arm from a masked attacker. The muted browns of his costume were unfamiliar; Flowridia knew not what this meant, only that from all sides, masked attackers appeared, swords readied. Irons already held two in combat.

Ropes flew, ensnaring Demitri as he roared. He crushed the head of one attacker, only to be met by three more, all lassoing him. He toppled, his back legs tied together, but still he fought those who dared approach.

She could hardly breathe, but by every god—she would fight. Flowridia shut her eyes, even as rough hands grabbed her. The men screamed as black lightning suddenly danced across her skin.

The earth rumbled. Flowridia grasped at every dead thing she felt, all the rodents and predators buried beneath the earth. When she opened her eyes, black spots danced in her vision, but she saw her quarry swarm the attackers—

Pain radiated through her arm. Still her undead attacked, but an arrow penetrated deep into the muscle. She tried to shriek—but oh, her breath was faint.

Demitri's pained howl stole her attention. He fell to the ground with a sickening rumble, tied in every way with ropes. Metal clicked as they attached a chained collar to his throat.

An envoy of men stole the limp Lara. By every god, what if she were dead? Flowridia tried to stand, but her vision swam. She fell to her knees.

Ser Luftlight cried out as his weapon was ripped from his grip. They slit his throat; the spray of blood splattered Irons. Battered, beaten, his attackers pushed him to the ground and stole his sword. He stared up, ever belligerent.

A man—bearded and graying, his skin reminiscent of Thalmus'—strode in atop an armored horse. He slid down, smiling viciously at Irons. "It isn't often a Solviraes travels in such light company."

Irons scoffed. "You would dare–"

"I would." The man shrugged. "Now, General Irons of Solvira, for the sake of your dying empress, do you yield?"

Flowridia watched the fight steadily drain from the general's eyes as he looked over to Lara, deathly still in her capturers' arms. He looked back up. "I yield," he spat, and a collar immediately clicked around his throat, along with chains at his wrists and ankles.

The man continued his rounds, staring at Demitri with interest. "A remarkable creature," he mused. Demitri's growl echoed with menace, but the man simply smiled. "Dangerous. He'll fetch a high price. Keep this one looking pretty, boys. He's meant for display."

Two men shoved Coal forward, and the man narrowed his eyes. "Tie him up. I hear he works for the High Priestess," he said, and then he approached the men supporting Lara. "Amazing. The most powerful sorceress in the realms—but all it takes is a little arrow to cut through her like paper." Lara stirred, eyes rolling back in her head before she went fully limp.

The man caressed Lara's hair, revealing her neck. Revulsion rose in Flowridia's stomach. He withdrew a collar from around his belt—a collar embedded with a single shard of maldectine. It clicked as it sealed around her neck.

He reached over and grabbed the arrow nestled in her back. The snap of wood sickened Flowridia; he left the head embedded. "Without your blood powers, you're nothing more than a scared girl." He glanced up to his men. "Tie her up."

They did, the powerful empress held thrall with ropes. Her eyes rolled back in her head, unconsciousness stealing her.

Around Flowridia was a void of men, but their leader approached with no fear. She forced herself to stay awake, spiteful as she managed to steal another gasping breath. "You're a nuisance," he said, and he spared a glance for the distant man still beating off undead rodents from his legs. "Lady Flowridia of Staelash, yes? Someone has a very weighty grudge against you. They've offered a hefty bounty."

Her voice sounded of gravel, but she spat the words all the same. "Who are you—?" She coughed, the man's image quickly turning to liquid.

"You may call me Shem." He knelt beside her, then motioned to the men around them. Flowridia tried in vain to steady her breath, but no cloud of death seeped from her skin. Instead, the men snapped a collar around her neck—

All her magic, her connection to Demitri, vanished.

Though she spat at his feet, he stole the bag from her shoulder—helpless, she watched. "What do you mean?"

He ignored her, instead withdrawing tiny Ana, held by her spine and ribs, her tail wagging obliviously. Flowridia's heart pounded in her ears at his intrigue. "Interesting little monster. Not worth a dime, considering it belongs only to you, though."

"Who sent you?" Flowridia cried, though it was hardly a croak in her throat.

He dropped Ana, letting her clatter to the ground—she ran to join Flowridia, her little feet clawing at her dress as Shem withdrew the blue orb and the maldectine bracelet. "Fascinating."

"Don't." Flowridia gasped, her breath only half inhaling. Spots appeared in her vision. "You don't know who you'll summon."

"This is some sort of summoning sphere? We'll let the buyers decide what it's worth, then." With a knowing grin to the maldectine, he shoved the duo in the pouch at his hip.

Flowridia coughed, and perhaps Ana sensed her distress. She stepped back and sat on her haunches, her front paws in the air as she mouthed a *yip*. Instead, her jaw snapped shut, bone against bone. Shem glanced at her and said, "Creepy little monster, that."

Flowridia gasped for breath, actively fighting the blackness filtering into her eyes. It happened slowly, each blink feeling like molasses, but Shem brought his boot down onto sweet Ana—

And stomped down, her snapping bones louder than the cacophony of the forest.

In her last moments of consciousness, Flowridia recalled screaming as men grabbed her arms. She tried in vain to gather the crushed remains of her dearest pet, the sight of a tiny, shattered skull as sharp as a stab to her heart. Her hand skimmed the bones as the men wrenched her to her feet.

She managed to pocket a single shard. The world went black.

Etolié wouldn't say she was good with a sword, but she was pretty fucking good at summoning a dragon of equal or lesser value to the ones Casvir had brought along.

He was a little guy, though still taller than Etolié, created from images of dragons she'd seen in books in Solvira. With glittering, white scales and eyes as golden as a halo, her dragon valiantly distracted the undead, occasionally breathing fire the ghouls slaughtered their peers to avoid.

They couldn't die of fear, but they were smart enough to know certain death—even if it was less than assured, given the fire was fake.

The dead only increased in number—whenever she and Sora beat back a small group, another would approach, the waves ever growing. When the numbers grew too dense, the ground split before them, deep crevices etching into the earth. The ghouls stumbled, but when they didn't fall in, that particular illusion failed.

Sora did not tire, however. The half-elf had been born to this, it seemed, decapitating ghouls with the fluid motions of a seasoned soldier, precise and graceful. Etolié could only spare the occasional glance to admire her, however, given her own attention to directing her illusionary dragon. She looked back and saw that the crowd had shrunk. Lunestra gathered the children to her side.

Then, an actual dragon crawled over the rooftop. Within its skeletal mouth, Etolié saw dark matter form. Its glowing, purple eyes settled onto them. She screamed, *"Sora, run!"*

The dragon spat its black, cloud-like flame upon Etolié's dragon—who kept fighting, of course, much to the real dragon's apparent frustration. Etolié, with her limited strength, grabbed Sora and yanked her into the air, pure adrenaline fueling her as they clumsily darted forward, her wings aloft.

They nearly tackled Lunestra, but Etolié managed to gather the children with her wings and lead them through the tunnel just as the street swarmed with death.

For space, Etolié tucked her wings against her back, their light fading as she illusioned them away. Torches lit the underground staircase, as well as runes glowing in vibrant orange upon the ceiling. Etolié looked back and saw the undead swarm the entrance and beat upon it like a stone wall—and when the dragon blew its terrible, necrotic flame, it dissipated harmlessly against the invisible barriers.

Finding their path blockaded, the undead disappeared from the door. Etolié could hear her own pulse.

"Etolié–"

Etolié whirled around, realizing Sora and her charges had waited a few steps down. "I just survived the undead. Don't murder me with a heart attack now."

Sora merely grinned and handed her a crying child to carry. "Lunestra and the rest are waiting at the bottom of the stairs."

Etolié clung to the sobbing girl, the innate need to comfort the poor thing overshadowing all else. She pressed the child's tear-streaked face against her shoulder. The little girl's sweaty arms clutched her tight, and Etolié whispered, "The worst is over."

She took careful steps down. Upon the ceiling, ancient runes pulsed with faint light.

Etolié read and wrote angelic words, had learned them in her youngest years from Eionei, even understood wards and their use, though certainly not as intricately as Flowers. But as Lunestra had said, these were not Celestial writings—they were Demoni, written by Ku'Shya because the God of Death couldn't understand them.

But she knew the symbols. She herself had traced them upon Khastra's forearm scarcely a week ago and many times before. *"Wards against undeath, Etolié,"* Khastra had explained years ago, *"so I may tear them apart."*

Dread pulsed cold through Etolié's limbs. "Sora, we aren't safe here," she whispered, lest she panic the masses with her echo.

The cavern branched off into a maze-like pattern, perfect to blockade for a siege should the need be foreseen. As it was, the surviving populace slowly filled the enormous center, or so Lunestra had explained, lambs for the slaughter when the undead breached them nonetheless.

Sora stopped. "Archbishop, wait a moment." Lunestra joined them, confusion marring her elderly features.

Children clutched her arms as she patiently waited for Sora to continue.

"Etolié," Sora said, frowning as audible tension filled her words, "explain."

"This cavern was created in the war against Ilune. Ku'Shya set them to protect Sol Kareena's citizens–"

"I do not happily admit that I knew Ilune," Khastra said, grimacing as she sipped her ale. "But I worked for Solvira during the Civil War and well before. At the final stand, I stood between Ilune's forces and the City of Light and helped defend the city when the dead were breaching the walls–"

"Nox'Kartha's general knows the catacomb's weakness," she said, hardly audible, scarcely breathed.

Sora's face lost color, and Lunestra said, "You mean–"

"We have to collapse the entrances–"

A wicked tongue echoed throughout the cavern, speaking the Demoni words. Etolié knew it, had granted it a healthy respect in the past, but never had it chilled her so, the Bringer of War's unmistakable cadence. No discernible source; it simply echoed across the cavern. She would be here; of course she would be here.

It was the very damning truth Khastra had hinted at all along.

Shadows rose around them, the torches' lights struggling to breach the rising darkness. The runes on the walls grew blinding—then extinguished.

Etolié let her wings expand to fill the large hallway of the cavern, radiating a light the shadows could not consume. From behind, up the stairs, she heard the first signs of chittering, bony limbs, and already Sora had begun running, dragging three children behind. Etolié clung to the girl in her arms, tenderness filling her when the girl grabbed her silver hair—not tugging, no, but stroking it for comfort. Once upon a time, as a small girl, Etolié had done the same to her momma's star-lit locks.

Lunestra said, "I can lead us to the center–"

"No." Etolié knew the time for tact had long ago passed. Tears filled her eyes unbidden. "We need to find an alcove. I can't protect us out in the open, but I think I can save us that way. Trust me."

"Etolié, you cannot be suggesting that everyone else will die."

The universe answered Lunestra's damning challenge—beyond, Etolié heard the first screams echo across the cavern. "The undead have breached the tunnels," she managed to say, voice quivering. "Please, trust me."

Lunestra ran, and Etolié couldn't see her expression. But she saw Sora, heard the half-elf mumble a prayer as they followed.

The dead-end tunnel should have been a death sentence. Etolié caught a glance of cruel undeath rapidly approaching. Ghouls howled, but Etolié stood at the turn and held up a hand, the other still wrapped around the small girl clinging to her body. "Don't even breathe," Etolié whispered to the girl. She cast her spell. Though to Etolié the wall maintained some translucence, to the rest she knew they'd see nothing—merely brick.

The ghoul who had followed slowed before them, sniffing around the walls before releasing a guttural cry. Etolié stared at the wall she had summoned, willing it to hold—she trusted it would, but one distraction, one flicker of doubt, and the ghoul would come to slaughter them.

And even if Sora chopped off its head—which she would, Etolié held no doubt—the attention it would attract would damn them all, and the precious cargo in Etolié's arms might be lost.

The ghoul moved on.

Etolié dropped her hand; the wall stayed. When she tried to place the child down, the girl released a desperate sob. "Shh," Etolié cooed, and beyond she heard the screams of thousands. "What's your name?"

The small girl, surely no older than four, stole a gasping breath. "C-Ceile."

"Ceile, do you sing?"

The girl nodded.

Etolié turned to Sora and said, "I've blocked sound and sight." She looked to the children weeping at their feet, though some were too panicked to even do that. "But while I'm pretty fu—*freaking* good at sight, sounds can slip through. I can only block my own with any certainty, or people I know well." Etolié soothed the girl in her arms, then looked to Lunestra, who visibly fought to keep composure.

"When I was young," she said softly to Ceile, a part of her mind always on the wall beside her, "I would make up silly songs to cheer up my momma." Etolié heard scratching—when she glanced toward it, a small group of ghouls ran past, paying them no mind. She sat on the ground and beckoned the children to join her. "My grandfather,

Eionei, also knows lots of songs—he's a god of secrets, and there are no better secrets than those found hidden in the songs of travelling bards."

The children gathered around, their tear-stained faces old beyond their years. All of them had lost parents and families—only orphans took residence in the cathedral. "I know a few about Sol Kareena. Eionei made certain I had a wide repertoire."

Etolié dared to smile as she softly sang:

Sol Kareena, She of Light,
Let my sword be filled with might
All my trust shall be in thee
Your banner waves;
my enemies flee

Before her, the children listened, their cries soothed. Etolié's voice was something she kept as a hidden weapon of sorts—Eionei was a fantastic tenor, and Etolié held talents as a soprano she was quietly rather proud of.

Few beyond Staelash knew. She had concocted a few ditties for Khastra in the past.

Etolié's slurring words echoed across the high library ceiling. "Your tattoos glow as bright as your eyes, but they ain't as slammin' as your thighs!"

"Etolié, you are embarrassing yourself."

The children listened; Etolié continued, singing hymns to praise the Goddess these children loved, almost lost in the words until a horrid scraping of stone and rough dirt caused the children to cringe and cover their ears. Etolié kept her song, faltering only when a figure slowed beyond the wall, unseen to all but she.

With a battalion of the dead came the transformed Bringer of War, covered in gore, her armor splattered in blood. The horrid sound was her hammer dragging upon the ancient stone floor, casting a faint purple glow upon the walls beyond. Her entire body had stretched to impossible capacity, growing in every dimension—the true power of her demonic blood. She glowed, her tattoos illuminating the cavern around her, the skin beneath them taut enough to tear. Her horns nearly scraped the ceiling. Khastra's lips bore no smile, but Etolié saw sharp fangs and a bestial visage.

Etolié's lip trembled as she sang:

Courage, come and set me free
My Goddess, I ask to shelter me

Etolié knew that gaze; it had torn straight through her time and time again, seeing past her layers, illusionary and not. Khastra knew her better than anyone, better than she knew herself. They matched eyes, though Etolié's welled tears.

Grant me mercy; grant me life
May my days be free of strife

Demoni words echoed across the halls—everyone within her cavern cowered; the children sobbed. Only Etolié saw the great half-demon, however. Only Etolié pled at her feet.

I'll pledge my soul to glory thy name
Until my final, dying day.
And when I pass, give my soul flight
I love thee, Goddess, She of Light

The dead swarmed past the Bringer of War, and when one ghoul faltered, peered a moment at the wall, the great demon tore its head from its shoulders. The undead fell to the ground in two meaty pieces, slumping against the stone floor. *"Etolié."*

Etolié's voice faltered; everyone froze. "Step back," Etolié whispered, and the children scrambled to obey, them and Sora and Lunestra backing against the far wall. Etolié stood tall, her ward in her arms as she looked up to Khastra through the false wall.

The monstrous visage looked a moment to the ceiling. She released her beloved weapon and instead tore her claws through the stone above. The entire cavern shook.

With a great heave, the Bringer of War yanked the wall down. Etolié screamed, turning to protect the child from falling rocks and debris.

She heard fading, clopping footsteps, but now was hardly the time for jokes about goat hooves. When the dust settled, Etolié saw that the ceiling had collapsed before them—creating a physical barrier where Etolié's had been illusionary.

Horrendous screams echoed beyond, sickening sounds of carnage and pain. Etolié and her party were trapped.

But they were safe.

Flowridia awoke to the setting sun and the sounds of misery. She sat up, neck throbbing, and as her vision settled instead of swam, she realized she lay in a small cage.

Within a clearing in the woods, she saw more cages and tents. A temporary camp from the looks of it, with a caravan of empty carts surrounding them, but in the center were cages of captured humanoids, helpless as they peered from their bonds.

She saw Demitri, still chained and helpless in a cart, much too far away to speak to. An odd barrier surrounded him—like lightning, cast between four great poles around the cart. Perhaps not impossible to penetrate, but Flowridia knew it as a branch of magic she held no talent in.

She saw General Irons and Coal still shackled but stripped of their bloodied armor and clothing. Clad in their underclothes, lest they be hiding any weapons, Irons still kept his calculating gaze, visibly contemplating escape.

In a cage beside her own was Empress Alauriel, collapsed in the corner. Blood stained her back, the fabric soaked in deep, vicious red. Flowridia saw hints of her neck, of the collar suppressing her powers—then touched her own.

She bit back a curse as she tugged on the maldectine collar, fury rising in tandem with her tears. She willed her breath to steady as she placed a hand upon the small, rough stone, focusing on the inherent power within it, trying to grasp it and—

Splitting pain shot through her head. She gasped and drew back; the pain immediately dissipated. There was something more here, and Flowridia fought the urge to scream.

Something sharp pierced her thigh. Flowridia peered into the pocket of her skirt and saw the sliver of bone she'd manage to drop inside.

She remembered Ana. By every god, she recalled her darling Ana with her prancing feet and enormous eye sockets—destroyed beneath Shem's boot.

Tears welled in her eyes, along with the pulsing heat of rage. When she looked up, Shem approached. She swallowed her tears, refusing to show weakness. Behind him burned a fire at the center of camp, perhaps meant to warm the chill of the oncoming night. "Glad to see you awake," he said, his grin wide and leering. "You aren't worth anything dead."

Flowridia forced her own smile. Using the bars, she pulled herself into standing. A stark chill washed over her skin—but unnatural, not from within. At her sternum, the ear burned from cold. "Shem, you do realize you're inciting the wrath of three kingdoms in this useless gamble of yours?"

"Am I?" He kept his grin. "I've pissed off royals before."

"If I'm not returned, Imperator Casvir won't stop hunting you. I assure you that."

"You're Nox'Kartha's pet? Perhaps they'll match the money I was offered for you. If they pay double, perhaps you'll be sent back untouched." He kept coming forward, and Flowridia's blood boiled at the slight lick of his lip. "I almost hope they don't, with a face like that."

Of course it scared her. Every hair on her body stood on end at the threat, but Flowridia grit her jaw and glared, even as ice as sharp as daggers suddenly suffocated her. "You don't know who you're instigating."

"It's true you fancy women, yes? Will I be the first man who's ever fucked you?"

"You would be." She kept his eye, wondering if her lips were blue from chill. "You'd be my first, and I'd be your last."

His chuckle held no ire; merely amusement. "I like a girl with fire."

"Tell me who sent you," she replied, fury rising with her fear.

He chuckled as he said, "I'd be a piss-poor businessman if I told you that."

"Tell me!"

But shook his head, amusement twisting his lip. When he stepped away, Flowridia dared to reach into her blouse and touch the ear, knowing full well it remained.

Ayla held awareness, slight as it was. Were she restored, nothing, not even Flowridia's pleading, would protect Shem from her wrath. Not that Flowridia would besmirch her the pleasure.

In the cage beside her, Lara hadn't stirred. Flowridia reached through the bars, not quite able to touch the empress. "Lara?" she whispered, as loud as she dared. "Lara?"

Whatever they'd done, Lara held no awareness—and truly, what safer way was there to transport a Solviraes? Flowridia feared it might be a poison and tried again, her shoulder aching as she failed to touch the prone woman. "Lara, please," she said, but her arm fell slack, hope seeping away.

She pulled back, instead slumping against the bars. With the ear grasped in her hand, she wondered to what god she could pray, wondered if Sol Kareena cared or noticed, if Izthuni would think her a fool for failing.

For Ayla to have once written Izthuni's sigil in Flowridia's blood did not mean she belonged to him—a demon could take no one without their will behind it, with a few exceptions. And to ask his help, to use her blood to summon him herself, would be all but a pledge to his name . . . as well as a death sentence to her mortal body.

She could ask the Shadow God for help, but even if he answered, no one could say the consequences.

She shut her eyes, meditating upon her fear. She wondered who would have the cruel audacity to do this.

Soliel came to mind, but this spat in the face of all she knew of him. Perhaps Murishani—rid the world of her without getting his hands dirty. Perhaps that was all his help was—a farce. Fury seeped into her breathing, spiking her heart.

Within the hour, the sun set.

"Flowridia?"

Flowridia gasped. Not Lara's voice. Instead, when she turned, she saw an eerily familiar figure. "Mereen?"

Mereen wore a hood and sat with her back to Flowridia's cage and the camp, staring into the woods, perfectly still. How she had gotten there undetected was for the gods to say, but when Flowridia sat at the opposite side of her, she felt the vampire shift. "Quite the conundrum you've gotten yourself into."

Suspicion rose, her blood running cold. "I think it'd be redundant to say I need help."

Mereen turned ever so slightly towards her, her alabaster skin practically glowing in the dark, the white-blonde of her hair hardly a shade off. "Sweetie, before you ask, I fight vampires, not slavers. I do, however, occasionally steal keys."

A gloved hand touched hers. Mereen slipped a small key into her hand. "For your shackles. There's also a horse waiting in the woods—animals don't exactly love me, so it was a testament of my liking to you to steal it."

Flowridia wasted no time in poking the key into the hole in her collar, keeping her gaze on the slavers around the bonfire all the while. Barrels of ale had been provided for the men, reminding her of the dwarves and Etolié a lifetime ago.

The latch clicked. She pulled the collar away, cringing as it tore strands of hair with it. But when she tossed it away, the world returned to her fingertips. Energy coursed through her veins, and for the first time, she *breathed.*

"Brace yourself, sweetie."

Flowridia stood up and away from the cage. Mereen, with the strength of the damned, snapped the metallic bar at the top and then the bottom, leaving just wide enough of a space for Flowridia to slip through. "Why are you here?"

"Quite the story. Perhaps once we've gotten you and your empress out of here, we'll share, yes?" Mereen crept toward the opposite cage, easily snapping the top of the bar.

"What the–"

Flowridia saw men approaching from the bonfire. "Mereen–"

When she turned back, Mereen had vanished.

Flowridia stood with her back to the broken cage, blocking it from their view in the dark. Her hair hid her neck, and with a slight motion of her feet, the maldectine collar hid beneath her skirts. "Gentlemen?"

Five men approached, Shem among them. "Thought I heard something," he said, his words slightly slurred.

"Perhaps you're simply drunker than you think you are."

His laughter chilled her blood. "I like your spirit, Lady Flowridia of Staelash." He placed his hand on the door of her cage, leaning slightly against it. "You'll be a fun one to break."

He reached for the keys at his hip, beside which Flowridia recalled there was an orb. Not quite paralyzed, but not quite aware, she gripped the bars beside her as the door swung open, her body hiding the gap.

It wasn't Shem who entered, but the four other men, each smelling heavily of ale. The cage door shut. One grabbed her arm, his intentions clear by his leering eyes and grin. She stole a breath as he tugged her forward.

Necromancy, they said, came from setting aside pain, but Flowridia forgot every lesson, every word and warning Casvir had taught she threw aside because by every god—she so *loved* to be angry.

She grabbed his forearm; the man screamed as her body suddenly crackled with illuminate energy, purple and black, like lightning across her skin. She felt his life escape in droves and breathed a heavy sigh, gaseous magic escaping with her breath. In the thrall of euphoria, she felt him fade; she heard the chorus of dying men.

When she opened her eyes, four corpses lay around her, and Shem stared with wide, baleful eyes. "Foolish of you," she spat, "to lock them in here with me."

"Witch!" he cried, with all the hate of a time long past. "Men! Grab this woman!"

His attention stolen for the moment, Flowridia ran through the opening in her cage and stared into the woods.

"Flowridia!" came a loud whisper.

In the darkness, Flowridia saw a flash of white skin—Mereen beckoned, and in her arms lay Lara.

Her body itched to run. Magic pulsed through her veins, bringing energy and awareness.

She looked back to the camp, watched Shem and his men congregate to chase her, saw droves of people—but among them lay half her heart.

Demitri matched her gaze.

"Flowridia?"

Flowridia's very skin seemed to tear as she moved toward them both—for Lara, safe enough in Mereen's embrace, and to Demitri, whose golden eyes spelled fear.

An arrow shot past her head. She hardly heard it. Instead, she stared at Shem as he and a small envoy ran to her.

Within her, there was no void, no absence of feeling—instead her rage spiked. She recalled the forest of months' ago, her anguish manifesting in destruction and death. Here, the ground around her withered and dried, the very life sucked from the roots, bombarding her with radiant, sickening energy.

By every god—the power was bliss. She relished the sensation, held to the energy until one man aimed his crossbow.

She released. With a scream, the dead earth infused with life, the ground churning as the dead creatures within rose from below, as grassroots strengthened and grew, grasping at the men's legs. In their shock, Flowridia had a moment to breathe and calculate.

Pain suddenly tore at her shoulder. Fueled by adrenaline, she tore out the crossbow bolt, managing to duck as another might have ripped into her face. She saw the man from afar and commanded the dead grass beneath his feet to consume him.

Focused on one, Flowridia guided the grass to climb around him, then inside him, relishing in his cries as the plants grew into his pores and ravaged him from within. Unlike their animal counterparts, the plants required more focus, more guidance, but as the man collapsed, grass sprouting from lacerations in his skin, the results were no less powerful—merely more precise.

More approached. She ran around the outskirts of camp, toward where Demitri waited, leading the envoy away from the empress and Mereen. A cloud of death emanated from her figure, though it would do nothing if they shot at her again.

But they wanted her alive. Dead, she was worth nothing.

She passed cages of frightened people, commanding the earth to upturn, the cages unsettled by the roots shifting beneath them. Perhaps they might escape; perhaps not. She didn't stay to watch, merely ran for Demitri.

Behind the wall of energy, Flowridia watched her familiar rise in his chains. *I don't think you can touch that.*

Shem himself approached, his sword aloft. "We need her alive," he said, his sneer cruel. "She's tiring—look at her."

"Demitri, I won't leave you."

She locked eyes with her wolf, her beloved Demitri, his golden gaze mesmerizing. *Mom—*

Hands grabbed her. Flowridia's skin seeped a haze of purple, but even as the man who touched her screamed, she felt the truth of Shem's words—she was faltering.

Mom, go. I'll be fine. There was fear in his precious voice—oh, she longed to comfort him. *You and I both know who can save me.*

Tears filled Flowridia's eyes. "I love you."

She ran into the woods.

Past crossbow bolts and screaming men flailing with sentient plants, panic guided her steps. Not toward Mereen—simply into the thicket, only the night air to witness her tears.

Darkness fell upon her. She heard footsteps following and knew it wasn't Mereen. Mereen would never be so clumsy.

By every god—what of Demitri? She would leave him behind to die? For this?

A hand grabbed her shoulder. A fist slammed her face; Flowridia crumbled, then cried as a kick rammed her ribs—

A great *boom* shattered the peace of the night.

The man fell backward, lifeless as he hit the ground. Flowridia looked up and saw Mereen, saw her holding her fearsome weapon with Lara tucked against her chest. The metallic curves reflected the moon's light, and Mereen brought the barrel to her lips to blow away the smoke. "Your nobility will be a death sentence, but I do admire your spite. Follow me."

Flowridia pulled herself up, the wounds and bruising healing with each step. She ran to follow; Mereen led her to a horse tied to a tree, who shifted nervously in the presence of the predator. "Keep on running, sweetie. There's a town a few miles north."

Flowridia mounted the horse; Mereen helped balance the listless Lara into her arms. "M-My familiar–"

"I'll see what I can do about the rest. But you should go." From her pocket, Mereen withdrew a priceless object—the blue orb. "I believe this is yours."

"How?"

"I have experience picking powerful men's pockets."

Flowridia accepted it, realizing with the orb's power she could save the rest—perhaps even Demitri.

But it was she and Lara alone. All she wanted—yet the prospect of victory was still unsure.

Mereen waited expectantly, a single eyebrow raised. Flowridia looked instead to the camp she'd left behind, listened to the continued cries from the destruction she'd wrought.

I'm sorry, Demitri, she thought silently, tears welling in her eyes. She looked to Mereen, seeing only sincerity in her eyes. Still, discomfort welled in her stomach, a suspicion too wicked to voice. "Thank you."

"Best of luck."

Mereen backed away into the shadows. Flowridia swallowed her sorrow and rode off into the night.

Chapter 11

Flowridia returned to Ilunnes. She knew the path well.
At the outskirts, at the cusp of the swamp, she finally slowed her horse. Gazing upon the flourishing town, watching the lanterns flicker in the dark, she wondered if they would know her, if they remembered at all.

Lara barely stirred, but she lived, and Flowridia feared that whatever she'd been shot with had been more than simply maldectine.

"Who the hell are you?"

So focused she'd been that she hadn't realized the small collection of people approaching, a few of whom held lanterns. "I'm no one–"

"By Sol Kareena's light," one whispered, recognition in his shadowed features. "She's the Swamp Witch reborn."

"N-No," Flowridia stammered, cursing her own visage. "I'm not Odessa–"

"Flowridia?"

Among the throng was an older woman Flowridia had known for years in that lifetime before. "Matron Willa," she said pleasantly, for this was the orphan matron who had all but raised her—though not quite in love. "Delightful to see–"

"Flowridia, the witch?" a man said, and the throng drew their weapons. "She bears Odessa's face, the monster reincarnated."

"Please, I swear to you I'm not–"

When the first one held up a bow, Flowridia flinched. Fear shone in the man's hateful gaze. She clutched the reins, but held Lara tighter. "Please," she pled, "let me save this woman; she'll speak for me."

"What wickedness are you concocting?"

She looked to Matron Willa, seeking recognition, any semblance of affection. "I don't want to hurt anyone–"

It happened quickly—the flying arrow, the sudden, searing pain in her throat—and Flowridia fell from the horse, her own body cushioning the empress' descent.

Blood pulsed in her ear, pain with every throb. Warm liquid gushed against her hand as she clutched her throat. The villagers approached with their torches and hateful glares.

In her arms, Lara groaned, and Flowridia's fury spiked.

One breath. The people came close.

Two breaths—all was clouded in necromantic magic.

Three—

An audible *thump* shook the earth as life suddenly infused her body. She tore the arrow from her throat, the cries of insects and birds as loud as the people. By every god, the euphoria was grand, life singing through her veins, but when she opened her eyes, she saw the truth of her carnage.

She thought of the forest of months' ago, and now here, at the edge of a village she'd once loved and a swamp that brought nightmares, Flowridia stood within a sea of blight. The grass prickled at her feet, blackened and grey, and siphoned corpses—the villagers and horse both—lay in a heap beside her.

The few who lived, standing at the outskirts, ran.

She stared at her hands, horrified. Only a moment of lost control, yet here was her legacy, one of darkness and death. Tears welled in her eyes, the loss of life weighing down her soul.

But Lara lay pristine, barely breathing but alive. The collar at her neck had saved her. In unsteady, muted motions, she lifted the empress into her arms, the limp woman a heavy weight.

She felt nothing, heard nothing, as she carried her quarry into the secluded shade of trees, the barest beginnings of marshy terrain slogging her footsteps.

A slight groan escaped the precious weight in her arms. "Lara?" she whispered, nearly sobbing for joy when she felt the woman stir. She fell to her knees, shaded from watchful eyes by nightfall and haunted trees. In the moment of peace, she pulled the key from her pocket and unlatched the collar at Lara's throat, carefully pulling it aside without tearing her disheveled hair.

But why? Lara was helpless; she was alone. Flowridia could take her to Odessa's home and be done with it all. She could practically taste victory, taste Ayla's sweet lips, yet here at the final stretch, she hesitated.

She would heal her first. That was all. Flowridia turned Lara over on her stomach to inspect the arrowhead. Oh, it was deep. She cringed at the task at hand, but she knew it well, knew anatomy from her days with Mother.

With no knife to wield, Flowridia's own fingers touched the wound, her tears falling fast as she jostled the broken shaft, braced herself as she gripped the weapon, felt Lara's blood and muscle and bone and sobbed as she wrenched it out—

Lara immediately screamed. She screamed and sobbed as Flowridia set the arrowhead aside. "You're safe," she soothed, stroking her bloodied hands in Lara's hair. "I'll heal you now; you're safe."

Life pulsed through her blood, made manifest as it left her fingertips. Flowridia felt Lara gasp as the magic coursed through her body. Flowridia coaxed the wound to heal, the skin to grow and stretch and leave no scar. She felt sinew reattach, felt the muscles repair, and when she finally withdrew her power, Lara sat up on her own accord.

The Solviran Empress looked about frantically, visibly confused. "W-Where are we? Where's everyone?"

"They're back at the slave camp. I had to leave them behind." Flowridia's lip trembled as she reached up to cup Lara's face.

Lara settled into Flowridia's lap. "I'm so sorry."

A damned fool Flowridia was, but she pulled Lara into a tight embrace, struggling to stay composed. She thought of her Demitri, left far behind, the screams of the villagers—by every god, why did death have to follow wherever she went?

As she contemplated this bitter truth, she grabbed the arrowhead of maldectine and turned her focus upon it. Though it fought her influence, Flowridia pushed as she had learned to long ago . . . and felt its influence fade.

Very little could defeat a Solviraes—save a small shard of maldectine.

"Where are we?" the empress whispered.

She pocketed the arrowhead. "The outskirts of Ilunnes, at the edge of Abyssal Swamp."

Flowridia could fix this. She could still save the encampment. Odessa's house stood so close now, and once

Ayla returned, Demitri could be saved. Ana could be mourned.

She held Lara to the crook of her neck, content to warm her heart, cherish her . . .

And then kill her?

Flowridia pulled away, grateful when Lara released her. She offered a hand to help her rise as she stared beyond the line of trees.

"You grew up here."

A palm cupped her cheek. Fingers stroked her cheek, but Flowridia couldn't face her tender companion. She merely nodded, a cold claw crushing her chest.

"Flowridia, look at me," Lara said, placing her other hand on Flowridia's cheek. Their gazes met; Lara smiled, though it held sadness unparalleled. "We're so close. All we have to do is destroy the wards and grab the orb. We'll return to my kingdom and have a rescue party sent before morning."

"Lara . . ." She shut her eyes and placed her hand atop Lara's. With all the gentleness she possessed, lest she reveal the turmoil in her thoughts, she pulled it away, instead coaxing Lara's face to hide in her chest. Her breath caught as she spoke, yet the words escaped nonetheless. "Let's take you home."

She felt Lara shake her head. "We have time enough for this. The greater good says–"

"Lara, you've been through too much already." Flowridia's hold tightened. Lara felt so soft, so alive.

"Flowridia–"

"Lara, no, we're leaving," Flowridia snapped, harsher than she felt. But desperation led to panic, and her heart began racing.

Lara tried to pull from the embrace, but her grip only tightened. Flowridia met Lara's eyes, the small empress frowning at her insistence.

Lara's quiet strength would be her downfall. "Lara–" Flowridia stopped, eyes rimming red as she swallowed. "Lara, there is no orb."

Lara's gaze narrowed. "What do you mean?"

"Just go home; I lied!" Flowridia exclaimed, this time pulling her arms away. She stepped back from Lara, horrified at her own words as she turned around, unwilling to face her. Angry tears welled in her eyes. She had come so far, but for what? Oh, Izthuni would berate her. Her mother would mock her, call her a fool for lacking the conviction to murder so angelic a being.

Anger pulsed at the thought of Ayla; anger towards the woman she loved for haunting her dreams, driving her to this moment—such was the price of loving.

And Lara, sweet Lara, how she raged at Lara. Alauriel Solviraes with her patience and kindness, the way she loved so sincerely. How could she kill her now, after she'd given so much to save her?

In another life, they were friends. In another still, they were lovers, perhaps not soulmates, but dear to each other, standing together to create their own beautiful world.

In this life, the best gift she could give was the truth.

She sniffed, fighting tears as Lara's voice, darker than she'd ever heard, met her ears. "What do you mean, 'you lied?'"

"There is no orb," Flowridia repeated, voice soft in her reveal. "Lara, there is no orb. Not here."

"Why?" When Flowridia didn't reply, she continued, bewilderment lacing each word. "Why did you lie?"

"I needed you," Flowridia said, each word pure pain as they left her tongue. "I can't tell you why–"

"Flowridia!" Lara cried, and Flowridia turned, jumping at the sound. "Why did you need me?"

Lara's struggle to stay composed became increasingly apparent, and Flowridia couldn't say whether or not she would cry or boil over with rage. Perhaps Lara wasn't sure either. "I was told that to bring Ayla back I would need to perform a blood ritual. But only the blood of the moon would–"

"... restore her to life," Lara whispered, jaw dropping as the truth settled. Her hand flew up to cover her mouth, silver eyes rimmed with red as they watered.

"But I can't, Lara," Flowridia finally admitted. "You are the kindest person I have ever met. This world is so much better for having you in it." Her words choked, eyes squeezing shut. "I can't do it."

It felt like such a weakness. Yet to say it, her soul felt lighter.

Silence held strong a moment, until Lara's words cut through her clouded thoughts. "I love you."

Flowridia's eyes snapped open, a morass of guilt steadily rising in her chest.

Tears fell freely down Lara's face. "Flowridia, I love you. Was that your plot? To have me fall in love with you, to kiss me while you stabbed me in the heart?"

Yes, and somehow that sentiment was the cruelest of all. But she said nothing, remiss to say it aloud.

"You succeeded," Lara continued, crying softly as she sucked in a pained breath. "My heart feels thoroughly broken. Will that bring your love back?"

To claim her own heart was as brutalized as Lara's felt unfair; still, hers bled and tore with each earned reprimand. "I've come to care about you so much, Lara–"

"But only because you came with the intent to kill me." Lara's lip trembled, tears still falling.

Flowridia shut her eyes, slowly nodding.

Silence settled. She wondered if the empress had simply vanished into the void. But when she finally looked, Lara stood there, defeat in her stance. "I'll help you get back Demitri," she said softly. "But then I will politely request you leave my kingdom."

Flowridia quickly shook her head. "I won't ask you to do that–"

"Flowridia, they have my general, and they have an innocent priest. They're daring enough to try and sell a Solviraes as a toy. They need to be stopped, and Demitri is simply another victim." She paused, her anger visibly slipping away as she shut her eyes. Her tears continued falling.

Flowridia longed to hold her, to pull Lara into her arms and give what comfort she could. But she had caused this. To hold her now, to soothe her with sweet words, to lie . . .

Once upon a time, she had been berated for her inability to lie. Now it seemed it was all she could do.

"I'm sorry," Flowridia whispered, as lost as she'd ever felt. "I'm so sorry."

Slowly, Lara nodded, her face crumbling. "I know you mean that."

Footsteps drew Flowridia's attention. From behind Lara, a silhouette stepped out of the trees, distant but unmistakable. At her panicked gasp, Lara followed her gaze.

Soliel walked towards them, his pace steady and calm. "I wondered how long it would be," he said, voice soft yet booming. His armored form shone in the eerie moonlight.

Lara stood tall, and Flowridia instinctively stepped closer, placing an arm in front of her. But Lara stopped her, instead guarding Flowridia with her small frame.

"I feel your orb," he said to Flowridia. "Give it to me, and I'll let you both live."

Lara stood tall, her station apparent in her stance. "You'll have to best me first," she said, any fragility drifting into the void. Her face held tears, but her tone betrayed none of that.

"Did Flowridia tell you what I did to the imperator? Do you think you'll fare better?"

"You showed no mercy, as you did when you slew the dragon you once called your son," Lara replied. "But you'll find a different sort of challenge with me."

He withdrew two orbs from his armor—lightning and fire. When he idly tossed them up, they slowly orbited his form, caught in his gravity.

Flowridia waited for the third, yet never saw it. Instead, fire erupted in a fissure before them, growing ever higher—

Lara stepped forward, arms parted as she let the light strike her. Not even a flinch; she simply began to glow. Light emanated from her form as the fire dissipated at her touch, only to burst from her hands in a radiant silver.

At every side, the flame whirled about, shooting toward Soliel. Instead of a concentrated dose, they hit in rapid succession, bombarding him. Flowridia heard him cry out—then, the fire burst, his own sword of flame cutting through the silver.

Lara took the moment to speak. "Flowridia, step back."

Flowridia obeyed, watching as the ground before Lara cracked, spreading like a shattered egg, and from the fissures came fire.

Not true flame—blinding light of silver and white. Flowridia's head reeled at the massive energy, yet mesmerized she watched as the cracks surrounded Soliel, preventing escape.

A slight rumble of thunder, then—

Flowridia's stomach reeled as Lara pushed her—

The scenery changed; Flowridia suddenly watched the fight from a distance, watched as a blast of lightning struck the ground Lara stood—and where Flowridia had once been.

Yet the silhouette of Lara within the blast of light never seemed to disappear, and when the torrential burst faded, she stood as a pillar of pure flame, her skin erupting in power.

Soliel blasted fire; Lara blasted her own. The energy met in the center, and Flowridia swore she felt the very fabric of the world bend. She clung to a tree, knowing she should run, yet fear froze her form as she watched this calamitous clash of magic.

Red and silver blended into an unholy culmination, the trees catching fire around them. Lara stood as a small figure to the ancient god, yet suddenly silver flame overtook the red—

Soliel couldn't even scream, hardly a shadow within the mass of silver. When it faded, he knelt, hardly moving, yet Flowridia saw him shine from within.

Lara suddenly appeared beside Flowridia in a blink of glitter and twisting power. Sallow and grey, she immediately fell into Flowridia's outstretched arms. "I have to . . ." Her heavy breaths overtook her words. "Have to touch him. I can absorb his soul; this might all be over. Or I could . . . I could banish him."

"How can I help?"

"Stay out of sight. He'll kill you in an instant; he won't be so lucky with me."

When Lara tried to stand, Flowridia steadied her, sparing a glance for the god who righted himself. "Forgive me, but you look–"

"I'll be fine. There's something odd here. I simply have to grasp it."

Flowridia had felt it too. "It's the wards. There are layers and layers of my mother's work the deeper we go into the swamp."

"So you were telling the truth about that?"

The words shouldn't have cut quite so deep, but Flowridia felt guilt well at the reminder. "I didn't lie about my mother," she admitted. But then a thought struck her. "Lara, her wards are powerful. Absorb them–"

"To fuel me. Oh, you are wise."

From her bag, Flowridia withdrew the blue orb. The glow illuminated Lara's grey aura. "And this."

"So you do have an orb. I'd berate you for stealing, but you might've just saved our lives."

Lara took the orb. An immediate glow filled her countenance—her body shone as the orb dimmed, the absorption of power enough to lift her, it seemed. She touched Flowridia—

Again came that sickening lurch in her stomach. Flowridia realized they had teleported once again, but not so far away—deeper into the swamp. "Lara–"

"The wards are as strong as you say; this is as far as I can take you. Stay hidden. Don't engage him. I know you want to help, but I can't be worrying about you."

"Lara–"

"Flowridia, I have to–"

The world quieted when Flowridia touched Lara's cheek. "Why? I meant to kill you."

Lara's lip trembled, her smile sincere and soft. "You didn't. And so you must know why."

In a gesture welling from a place beyond reason, beyond thought and order, Flowridia leaned forward and gently placed a tender kiss upon her lips.

And it felt beautiful.

Beyond came a glow of rapidly approaching light. Flowridia and Lara parted, the smile they shared more precious than gold.

Then, Lara ran. At the perimeter of the first ward, she reached her hand out and physically gripped it. Flowridia watched, her view perfect, and marveled at Lara's control. She herself could pluck out a small string of magic and hold it with acute precision, but Lara gripped a heavy chain, bending it with her tremendous power and glowing as she absorbed the ancient protection.

From one hand blasted a small bit of flame. The approaching titan easily brushed aside. But Flowridia watched her other hand as it tore a line in space.

She blasted flame through the portal—it shot down as a vortex directly above Soliel's head.

Flowridia could not even hear him scream, so great and magnificent was the display. She watched as Lara reached out again, gripping whatever warded bits of energy she could to fuel her magic.

It wasn't until she dulled, both in color and in aura, that the flame relented. Flowridia saw a sizzling supplicant sway as he rose to his feet. The burns upon his body were not charred but colorful, like oil and metal, coating the raw, flayed skin of his face. His armor was not ruined, no, but strips fell to the ground.

Then, he glowed once more from divine light.

Lara glanced to Flowridia; she felt it from afar. Hair disheveled, clothing ruined, the small sorceress ran, silver flame at her feet, as she lured Soliel away.

Flashes of light continuously lit up the swamp, illuminating the dark night for miles. But more than sight, Flowridia felt unease as that sixth sense—her talent of plucking on the strings of magic—rang like a deafening bell in her ears. Her head swam at the concentration of energy. Lara and Soliel fought, and the very fabric of the world bent as they harnessed unfathomable amounts of energy.

Flowridia could only see the lights. Fear led to panic as she realized what she had suggested to Lara—harnessing the wards would lead them closer to Odessa's house.

Unprotected, what of Ayla's body? All might be lost.

Flowridia pulled the maldectine arrowhead from the bag. She frowned, intrigued by how it radiated. If non-sentient objects could have emotion, the crystal seemed enraged.

But she concentrated her energy and allowed the crystal's aura to expand and surround her. Protected by that invisible barrier, Flowridia ran forward, careful to keep a close watch for Soliel and Lara.

Flashes of light and her own intuition told her the correct path. But no magic protected it. Where once there had been wards of fear and nausea, there was only an empty path.

Closer she ran, darting behind trees whenever she feared she had come too close. The crystal protected her, but she could visibly see the leaves of the trees vibrate, the water in the marshes sloshing as though some ancient being disturbed it from beneath.

She wondered what Ayla would have done, shadow dancing from tree to tree, fully hidden by the darkness. Flowridia, instead, darted back and forth, catching her breath and praying she wasn't spotted.

As she neared, she realized she might be the farthest thing from their minds. She stopped at a low-hanging branch and climbed, pulling with all her strength to bring herself higher and higher into the tree.

Not a moment too soon. A blast of silver light decimated the area she had just stood. Flowridia cowered closer to the trunk of the tree, watching two silhouetted figures conduct a magical dance through the swampy grove. Red and silver fire blended with moonlight to backdrop the duet, their disjointed steps resulting in a beautiful calamity.

Flowridia watched as Soliel held his hand to the sky, only to bring it down in tandem with a lightning bolt. Lara already glowed to a dangerous, blinding degree. It bombarded her, and Flowridia feared she had witnessed the killing blow. First she absorbed it, then it swallowed past her, her body engulfed in the orb's power.

When the light faded, Lara lay on the ground. Soliel approached; Lara barely breathed. Flowridia's heart clenched as he turned his attention away, eyes darting through the trees. She sat far away, yet he stared directly at her. "You're a clever girl," he said, his deep voice carrying all through the swamp. "Using your crystal to hide the orb. I understand now."

Flowridia slid down the tree, eyes darting back to Soliel every few moments as he walked toward Lara and the orb lying beside her.

She twitched. Flowridia's heart soared when she saw Lara stumble into standing, orb in hand, the marshy ground rippling with every motion. Soliel faced her—both were flagging. Silence reigned.

The orb glowed. Lara vanished.

Soliel looked to Flowridia, the orbs at his back casting his sneer in shadow.

A figure appeared in the distance, brighter than a star.

Beneath him, the ground glowed. A perfect sphere steadily expanded. Across the winds came a voice: *"Flowridia, run!"*

She obeyed, though she saw a portal to hell.

She ran, yet some force dragged her back, all of gravity in flux as the light became the center of the world, pulling all into its clutch. Soliel yelled in pain as he slowly sunk into the void, his movements labored. Trees ripped from their roots; animals shrieked—the portal sucked the very air, leaving a void of nothing. It glowed, yet Lara shone brighter.

Flowridia lost her footing, slipping in the dirt as the portal dragged her back. Squeezing tight, she concentrated on the maldectine, willing its aura to expand even wider—

She stopped, perfectly safe in her bubble.

She saw Soliel flailing, the orbs glowing wildly at his back. The sky rumbled; lightning struck the portal, upon Soliel directly, the very power of the sky absorbed into the void's light. The portal glowed—the orb faded—Lara ignited—

The sky exploded in a flash of silver light. The entire world stripped raw as layers upon layers of magical energy twisted and snapped. Lara's body shone like a newborn star, radiating light until it imploded, ricocheting back into her body and bursting out, engulfing the swamp and sky in blinding, silver light. Flowridia cowered behind her crystal shield, bracing herself as the explosion expanded to entrap her, too.

She watched the whole world disappear in silver. Behind her shield, she alone lay spared.

When the light faded, the world had become quiet. No portal or void, merely a black pit of glass where it had once swirled.

A sickening splash and crunch broke the taut string of silence. Lara lay face down in the water. Flowridia dashed forward, fear driving her. Her crystal's aura faded.

But she stopped when a decrepit figure emerged from the pit of black glass.

Soliel's armor had nigh incinerated, ruined and charred and hanging in sheets, but divine light shone from within, the lacerations and burns upon his skin steadily fading. When Flowridia tried to run past him, he grabbed her collar and shoved her to the ground.

On her hands and knees, she watched Soliel approach the fallen monarch. Flowridia stood as he lifted Lara by her hair, revealing gaping holes in her velvet, glittering dress. Her entire chest had blown open from within. Grated and gashed, holes had been torn from her center to the outside.

The faintest of moans escaped her throat. Her eyes fluttered open, visibly pained. By every god—she still lived.

Flowridia stepped slowly, unsure of this God and his wicked intentions.

He withdrew a knife.

Flowridia screamed as she ran forward—

Soliel stabbed the knife into the side of Lara's throat, then tore it forward, nearly beheading her. Her gasping cut off. The light faded from her silver eyes.

Flowridia fell to her knees, losing her strength as Soliel dropped Lara's body back into the murky water. Shock stilled her tongue; she could not even weep.

"You'd best hurry," he said, yet she could not face him, "lest her blood be wasted." She didn't move when he stooped down and stole the orb from the murky ground, the cyan blue illuminating his face.

Flowridia's hands shook as they covered her mouth; she could not tear her gaze away from the corpse.

"This is what you wanted. Face it. But soothe yourself by saying it was not your fault—that the blood of the moon is not on your hands."

No matter how desperately she wanted to block out his hateful words, they were all that rang in her head.

Soliel lingered as he waited for an answer. Flowridia merely stared, shock stilling her tongue. "This is my aid to you, but I will not do the rest. Get up. Move forward."

She heard his footsteps fade.

As though a ghost possessed her form, Flowridia shuffled into standing, watching her own body perform though her will stayed behind. She knelt before the disfigured corpse, the empty vessel of a woman too kind for the world. Soaking wet, she was a heavy weight, but Flowridia cradled Lara all the same.

She gently shut those beautiful eyes, dull in death. Her tears fell like rain.

Flowridia leaned down and placed a lingering kiss upon Lara's forehead, pausing a breath away as her hold tightened. With Lara's head against her breast, an old prayer fell from her lips, one she'd once heard Etolié hum.

> *Mother Staella, carry me*
> *Into your arms where I may be*
> *Safe and sleep upon your breast*
> *and take my final rest*

She knew not the rest of the words. They drifted off into the silent night, leaving Flowridia alone to weep.

Countless hours' worth of screams. Etolié sang to distract from the weighted mood, her attention free to cast glowing illusions to entertain the children. Not one of them was older than eight, and she learned their names, told them tales of gods and dragons, illustrating them all with glowing, ethereal pictures.

The distractions were enough to tear her own attention away from the continuous screams. Even Ceile smiled in her arms, the endearing nugget having to be shushed to tamper her enthusiasm—Etolié could dampen sound, but she daren't risk too much.

Hours passed. Etolié told the tale of the Bringer of War and her aid in destroying slave camps, reveling in their giggles as the illusionary slavers exploded into glitter, when cloven footsteps stole her voice. She shushed her wards, looking to Sora who grabbed the knife at her hilt. Lunestra stood up, her pristine clothes now marred with dust and dirt.

Etolié tried to set Ceile down, but the kid had a grip like a snake. Instead, she shielded the girl with her body, even as she stood between the fallen wall and the children.

The wall shook. Dust rose. A vicious claw burst through the stone and pulled debris from the cavern. Etolié met the Bringer of War's glowing eye and nearly sobbed— but for relief or fear, she couldn't yet say.

When a path had been carved, Etolié saw the monstrous woman glance beyond the cavern, then beckon with her clawed hand. The single word she uttered sounded pained and forced—Etolié had only ever heard the Bringer of War cry Demoni phrases.

The monster said, *"Quickly."* Guttural and clumsy, but unmistakable.

Etolié gathered her quarry, the children who followed like ducklings to their mother, and watched as the Bringer of War changed, shrinking before their very eyes, her armor shifting in mechanical deviations to accommodate her smaller size.

Not a monster; merely Khastra, her blue skin and armor coated in ash and gore, her hair matted and caked in blood. "Come," came her dearest demon's voice, exhausted and faint. Despite their dire circumstances, the horror they had survived, Khastra's voice settled Etolié's agitated soul. "I will sneak you out. Be silent."

No one said a word or questioned their savior. Etolié led behind Khastra, and Sora and Lunestra rounded the back, watching the row of children.

The path was clear, but the scent was enough to sicken Etolié's stomach. Not a single corpse, she realized, but evidence of blood stained the walls and the staircase, emulsified meat too destroyed to be deemed useful by the imperator. She covered Ceile's eyes, wishing she could do as much for the rest, and heard Lunestra whispering words of comfort.

Night had fallen. Khastra's hammer waited at the entrance. Her glowing eyes studied the abandoned street, and Etolié's soul lurched at the bloodbath spraying the road before them. It stained the walls and streets, bits of shattered bones shifting beneath her boots as she stepped onto the path.

An entire city—annihilated. Slaughtered. Thousands of screams suddenly silenced in a night.

Shock prevented her tears. When Khastra beckoned, she followed, grasping the hand of the child behind her as she did.

Even now, Etolié would hear a distant scream, only for it to be cut off. Another soldier for the army. When they passed an envoy of ghouls, they growled—only for Khastra to step forward and growl much louder.

The freshly dead stumbled back, their hungry gazes as pitiful as dogs denied meat. Khastra beckoned and they followed, though she kept her watchful eye on the undead, baring her teeth when they stumbled forward.

Through the backstreets, they crept. Khastra was hardly silent in her armor, but she scarcely made a dent in the night; the eerie quiet was punctuated too often by screams and howling cries.

"Once we reach the canals," Khastra said softly, her gaze constantly shifting across the scene and Etolié's companions, "there is a boat waiting, large enough for you and yours. You will escape down the river. There are no undead beyond the walls, and Imperator Casvir has no plans to march forward yet. You have time to set sail to Staelash."

Breathless, Etolié nodded, glancing back to the rest to see if they had heard. "Isn't this treason?"

"He does not know you are here. Cannot be treason if the imperator did not command against it."

Nothing humorous in the phrase; were Etolié not holding one child and grasping the hand of another, she would have stolen Khastra's, desperate to comfort the half-demon. "Khastra–"

She cut herself off, too enthralled when the half-demon finally turned her glistening gaze to Etolié. "Do not worry for me, Etolié."

There was so much more to say, for Khastra's eyes shone in the full moon's light and Etolié's very soul rejoiced to be near her again. But the canals approached, and this was hardly the goodbye she craved.

Instead, as they approached the distant, single boat, Etolié whispered, "I didn't think I'd see you again so soon, ya big lug."

"I cannot say I am happy for the circumstances."

"Agreed." Etolié watched Sora run forward to where the boat was docked. The half-elf gathered the rope, pulling it to shore. Etolié released the little boy who walked beside her, letting him join Sora. "Guess you can't help but see me, though. That wall was rock-solid."

"Not solid and certainly not enough to shield your scent. The Bringer of War knows you well, Etolié." There was no teasing or happiness in the words; merely truth.

"Khastra, tell me honestly—what do you want me to say to Solvira? I know you had no choice in this. If you'd resisted, the imperator would have broken your mind. If you hadn't told him everything . . ."

Her voice trailed off at Khastra's smile, soft and joyless, but it was one Etolié knew.

"You'll be condemned, unless I tell them the truth."

Khastra shook her head. "Should word reach the imperator that I helped Archbishop Lunestra escape, my life would be pain beyond what I have ever known. I beg of you—say nothing. And have them swear to say nothing as well."

From her pocket dimension, Etolié withdrew her letter. She offered it to the half-demon she adored, who risked martyrdom to save a woman she had led an army to destroy.

Sora had the boat and began positioning children within its confines, balancing their weight with care. Khastra tucked the letter into her armor, safe from blood and by discovery from her superiors. "I–" Etolié cut herself off, the words fluttering in her stomach and rising in her throat.

They burned, but they longed to be free, and Etolié, in the midst of a carnage-stained canal, clasping a child on the verge of falling asleep, covered in sweat and blood and her own tears, whispered the words, "I love you."

Khastra said nothing, merely bent over and touched their lips together, gentle until Etolié deepened it with her tongue. All the pain and sorrow and hope of the past few days sealed them together, and for a beautiful, breathless moment, Etolié kissed the woman she loved, cupped her cheek and tangled her hand in her matted braid.

Against her lips, Khastra whispered, "I have loved you for so long."

Etolié pulled back, fresh tears brimming in her eyes. A great divide sat before them, carved by politics and regret and cruel, evil men, but their hearts were one, and for a brief, exhilarating moment, Etolié felt hope.

Lunestra lived, and with her the heart of the Theocracy. The tragedy would never be forgotten, thousands of souls awaited vengeance, but a flickering candle shone through the darkness.

"Etolié, we have to go."

Etolié placed a final kiss upon Khastra's lips, lingering in her presence a moment before turning to Sora, who beckoned for her to come. Seven children sat in the boat, with Lunestra and Sora waiting on the shore.

Etolié squeezed Khastra's hand and released. She walked toward the boat.

She was stopped by a slow clap and a chuckle that chilled her heart.

From the shadows emerged Murishani, flanked by a small battalion of skeletons. "Such a beautiful reunion! General Khastra, you and your love truly are a story for the ages—two lovers, divided by fate but stealing kisses upon the battlefield. It warms my heart, truly." His smile was infectious, yet it filled Etolié with dread. "Sora, dear, you won't get far." He snapped, and the skeletons lifted bows, aimed at the boat full of children. "Do not fear. Imperator Casvir wants the story to be told, for the tale to spread of his victory here today. What use is there if there are no survivors?" He looked to Etolié, mischief spreading into his grin. "Now, kindly come with me. The imperator surely has words for you. Valiant of you, to come this far."

Sora drew her dagger. The skeletons drew their bowstrings. "My friends aren't particularly intelligent,"

Murishani said, gesturing to the undead around him, "but endlessly loyal and absolute perfection at their one task. Now, Sora, you wouldn't wish to be responsible for more deaths than necessary, would you?"

Sora slipped her dagger back into her sheath. The skeletons lowered their bows. "Come with me," he said. "All of you."

They were escorted through the streets: Etolié, Lunestra, Sora, and the eight children in their charge. Etolié stayed as near to Khastra as she dared, busy shushing the trembling girl in her arms. "Ceile, it'll be all right, I swear," she whispered. "They said they'll let us go." The girl tucked her face in Etolié's shoulder, hiding from the carnage.

What remained of the cathedral were ruins, shattered by the dragon who sat in what was once the chapel. Entire walls lay stripped away, revealing the statue still standing, the benevolent Goddess cursed to gaze upon her ruined city. A battalion of death filled the entire square and beyond—the sea seemed endless, filled with nightmares sure to haunt Etolié all her life.

She prayed she lived long enough to fear them.

Standing triumphant at the footsteps of what was once the cathedral, Casvir was as still as a statue, stone until Murishani waved for his attention. "Casvir, won't you take a look at the marvelous gift General Khastra brought for you? She found them attempting to sneak out through the canals."

Casvir removed his helm, revealing his glowing, red eyes, his severe face pulling into a frown as they approached. "Magister Etolié," he said, nodding in acknowledgement, and then to Sora, no name, but a slight nod. Then, he looked to Lunestra, and Etolié's very soul recoiled at the slow spread of his smile. "Viceroy Murishani, separate them."

It happened quickly—Khastra grabbed Etolié's shoulder and yanked her back, her grip iron. Sora stood between Lunestra and Murishani, wielding a dagger in her off-hand. The woman would die to defend the Goddess' speaker, Etolié knew, but neither expected Casvir himself to approach.

"In deference to our kingdoms' alliance, you live this once." The imperator backhanded Sora across the face, sending her dagger clattering to the stone steps and her stumbling into Murishani's grip. When she struggled, the viceroy's eyes suddenly flashed silver, and Sora gasped, frozen as a faint glow surrounded her body.

"Be still," Murishani whispered in her ear. "A soul would be a terrible thing to lose."

Casvir gazed upon Lunestra and the cowering children, the ancient archbishop standing tall as he surveyed her. He glanced to Etolié. "And that one."

He meant Ceile, and for what purpose, Etolié feared to truly contemplate. But she knew—fucking hell, she knew. Trembling, Etolié struggled to place the now-shrieking child upon the ground. "No, Etolié, no—don't let them take me!"

"It'll just be a moment. Close your eyes. It'll–"

"Close your eyes, Starshine–"

Etolié's stomach lurched, lip quivering as she clutched the sobbing girl to her chest, her cries so familiar, reminiscent of a little Celestial girl cowering from a monster. Beyond, the ghouls watched the group of children like fresh meat. She looked to Casvir, his stare nothing less than relentless, piercing through to her very soul. And though it took every ounce of courage she still held, she stepped forward.

She felt so very small, but though he was Imperator, godly blood flowed through her veins. Steeling her resolve, she recalled the truth she should not know—that her life had been paid for.

Imperator Casvir could not kill her.

"Imperator, these children mean nothing to you," she said, strength and fury rising in tandem with each chosen word. "If you slaughter them here, before Sol Kareena's statue, you'll be known as a monster."

"Then I shall slaughter them behind her back, if that would preserve your sensitivities." The barest glimmer of annoyance threatened to break through his forced stoicism— Etolié saw the faint twitch of his lip, the narrowing of his red eyes. "My forces slew thousands of children this day, and you would bargain for these eight?"

At the word 'bargain,' Etolié's blood pounded loud in her ears. She pressed Ceile's face to her shoulder, hiding her lest Casvir chose to kill her nonetheless. "I suppose I would."

Subtle intrigue shone in Casvir's gaze. "They mean nothing to me, but everything to you. What will you offer?"

In the tense moments of silence, Etolié dared not look to Khastra, nor to Sora, still held in Murishani's grasp. She thought a thousand different things, of money and trinkets and all manner of useless tripe Casvir wouldn't care for, but the loudest thought of all was Ceile's gentle gasping, her cries quieting as she clung to Etolié's hair.

Anxiety stilled her tongue. Casvir waited. She merely stared, her racing thoughts stilling, settling on nothing.

"Well?"

"I-I . . ." Etolié glanced back to the children and Lunestra, wondering how many she could carry if she tried to run, and how quickly the dragon would drag her down. "What do you want?"

"I want every last citizen of this city dead. Offer me something better."

Etolié stepped back—and perhaps that was her mistake, for Casvir came forward, and in his hand he summoned his weapon of dark matter. There was murder in his stone visage. "Set the child down," he said, "or make me an offer. I grow impatient."

In a moment either too brave or too *stupid* to fathom, Etolié spread her wings aloft and shot into the air, Ceile in her arms—

Only for a large, clawed hand to grab her foot and tear her down. Pain radiated from her ankle, until the ground came to cushion her. She heard herself cry out, heard Sora's scream of *"no,"* saw blood drip from her head onto the stone floor, and when she looked up, it was Casvir's fearsome silhouette, illuminated by silver moonlight leering above her. She pushed Ceile away; if she were to die this day, she would not sacrifice a child to go with her. Instead, she alone stared into the shadowy visage of the man who would be god—

A great hammer came down. Thunder sounded upon the steps, along with a caustic wash of black ichor splattering across Etolié's body. Children screamed; beside her Ceile was covered in that same viscous substance. Between them was a massive shard of metal—any closer and it would have impaled her.

And there beneath the purple, glowing gem, nearly as long as Etolié was tall, she saw the remains of mutilated flesh and broken bones, crushed armor and a twitching, clawed hand. Beside Etolié was a second one—all around, the imperator's remains lay strewn.

"Oh, my," came a breathless, tenor voice, and though Etolié struggled to sit up, she did with Ceile's coaxing. Murishani released Sora, who collapsed into a heap. Never had Etolié seen him look so pale.

Khastra stared blankly upon her carnage, the quiet rage in her glowing eyes steadily falling into something pained. When she released the hammer, it remained a stone statue upon the ground, sealed in black ichor upon the cathedral steps.

Etolié finally breathed, realizing she'd lost feeling in her limbs. She watched Murishani's gaze drift slowly from Casvir's remains to Khastra, who took an idle step backward, and then another. The half-demon's exhausted gaze never left her fallen imperator.

The world shook.

The dead shrieked. Khastra's stance faltered. The children screamed, and Etolié looked out to see Lunestra stumble and Murishani look to the sky in wonder. Etolié's stomach lurched, and had she been standing, she surely would have fallen to her knees. As it was, she vomited on the ground, her head reeling at the sudden influx of magic.

The entire sky illuminated in *silver*.

As though the moon itself had exploded, silver light radiated across the sky, its origin far away, yet the entire fabric of the world lurched in response, threatened to tear at the seams.

When the light faded, it left the lingering question of *why*.

Etolié stood up, grime and gore coating her body, and stepped away from circle of children. Her gaze shifted between the sky and the carnage before her, the remains of blood and skin and armor forever cursing the steps of this once holy place.

In the residual silence, the whole world held its breath.

The door creaked open, and an irate voice immediately cried, "What have you done to my home?! My wards are all but–" Odessa's voice faded at the sight of Flowridia in the doorway, shaking from the weight she cradled in her arms.

Flowridia's lip trembled, and she brushed past Odessa's ghostly form, ignoring the floating phantasmal as she stepped toward the back room.

The cauldron waited, Ayla's body still dried and withered inside. With all the tenderness her exhausted muscles could muster, Flowridia laid Lara's body onto the floor, cringing at the blood splattered along her arms and clothing. But there was no time for revulsion and no time to grieve; instead, Flowridia pulled up a chair and stood upon it, arranging the chains and hooks above the cauldron.

Odessa's voice startled her. "And this is your dearest Lara?"

Flowridia nearly shattered at the thought but nodded nonetheless.

"Flower Child, what happened? Even I could feel the energy swirling in my swamp." When Flowridia didn't immediately respond, Odessa flew directly into her face. "I would like to clarify that I'm *dead*. I don't feel things."

"The God of Order was here," Flowridia whispered, stepping down from her chair. "Lara sacrificed her life to save me."

Trembling, she stole a knife from the wall and cut a careful line down the center of her ruined dress. She removed the gown and set it aside, along with the rest of Lara's clothing. With all the care her limited strength could give, she scooped Lara's mutilated, nude form into her arms and cradled her close.

"Good of him, to slit her throat for you." Odessa grinned; Flowridia's blood turned to ice.

Flowridia said nothing, merely heard his hateful words and wondered how in the hells he had known. He knew her future, always stood a step ahead of her own fate, and now he'd slaughtered someone she held dear and it came with the dreadful question of *why*.

He'd thrown Lara at her feet. Paved the way to victory. Someday she would hold a knife to his throat and demand the truths he veiled.

But for now, there was no rest. Get up. Move forward. Yet she trembled as fresh sobs shook her form.

With her arms clutching Lara's corpse, she mourned a friend—dear and true and perhaps something more—who had given her life to save her.

For a terrible moment, she contemplated the dangerous notion of restoring Lara's life. Her hands stroked tender lines upon the empress' face, the radiant potential of undeath waiting at her finger tips, asking only for a host.

But wouldn't that be the cruelest act of all? Lara herself had called it a hellish fate. Undead foxes were one thing; what would Lara's life be besides stagnation and grief?

No matter her actions now, the Moon's blood died with Empress Alauriel, and with it the Silver Fire. All she could do was let Lara rest.

"Flower Child!" A frantic voice interrupted her wallowing. "Come here!"

Though pained beyond measure, Flowridia gently laid the body onto the floor. She stood, frowning at the desperation in Odessa's voice. Out in the dark main room, the ghost flickered faintly by the window, staring outside. Flowridia joined her. Lights in the distance met her view, flickering faintly.

"Do you know what that means?" Odessa said darkly, and Flowridia shook her head. "You've been followed."

"Followed?"

"Your friends caused quite a bit of commotion here. It seems you attracted attention."

Realization struck her, and Flowridia gripped the windowsill tight. She, the witch, had returned to the village, had killed to save herself, and then an earth-shaking catastrophe had ensued in the swamp.

"Over the years, countless mobs came to try and find me," Odessa mused. "But my wards deterred them. Now, we're an open wound. There's nothing to stop them from finding you." She stopped, and Flowridia cowered when she felt her gaze. "Do you know what they do to witches, Sweet Flower Child?"

Flowridia shut her eyes, but still the distant lights danced behind her eyelids.

"They burn them."

Run, her mind whispered. She could take the body and live. But all else would burn. Lara's sacrifice would be nothing, forgotten. Demitri's fate would be sealed. All that work, all she'd done—

"NO!" she screamed. Something shattered in her mind, a glass barrier, translucent and confining. She shrieked as she punched the wall, uncaring at the pain in her knuckles.

In the ensuing silence, her cry echoed from the walls. She steadied her breathing, fury rising with each exhale. Her failures had damned Demitri, damned Lara and Ana, but she could still save Ayla.

"Damn yourself, and have no regrets."

Flowridia returned to the cauldron, her mind static as she lifted Lara's corpse into her arms.

Odessa's light filled the room. "Did you hear anything I said?"

Flowridia ignored her, struggling to balance the small woman well enough to grasp one of the hooks.

"Gods, Flower Child, you were always prone to daydreaming. Fine. I'll help."

Around the chains, a ghostly hue suddenly illuminated. Flowridia nearly stumbled from the chair, clutching Lara's body protectively as they moved on their own accord. One wrenched through one of the holes in Lara's back, the sickening squish of flesh sure to haunt Flowridia until her dying day.

Fresh tears clouded her vision, but Flowridia forced herself to watch the ghastly chains do their bitter work. "All but powerless, are you?" she said, and beside her, Odessa chuckled.

The limp body swung slightly as the chains ceased their sentience, Lara's arms dangling down. The blood from her throat slowly dripped down her chin and face.

"Now," Odessa said, her panic thinly veiled, "this could take hours. Or minutes. There's truly no telling, though I might recommend slitting her wrists to help the blood flow faster."

Flowridia stepped down from the stool, mind muted to all but the task ahead as she took back the knife.

"That said," Odessa continued, her voice resuming its normal pleasantries, "I do know a few tricks for speeding this sort of ritual along." Already, she moved to her wall of jars, her eyes studying the ingredients. "Just a sprinkle or two of a few herbs and we'll–"

She stopped when Flowridia pointed the knife at Odessa's throat. It would do nothing, Flowridia knew, but by every god—Mother's words made her sick. "Don't you dare."

Sanguine innocence pouted Odessa's lip. "Flower Child–"

"'A few choice herbs and she'll be mine to command,' yes? If you even so much as look at that body, I'll leave your house to burn, you bitch."

For a beautiful moment, Flowridia forgot her sorrow and regret; for there in Odessa's visage was a flicker of true fear.

She turned away, breaking their stare, and stepped up onto the stool again.

Skin sliced. Blood dripped from the fresh wounds on Lara's wrists. Where it touched, Ayla's body seemed to absorb it, patches of skin growing flush with life before fading again. Lara's eyelids opened into an eerie slit, revealing only white. Flowridia withdrew the ear from around her neck, removed the chain, and stared a moment at the desiccated piece.

There was no resistance, no cold chill clinging to her. She trembled as she tossed it inside.

But still the world encroached. Flowridia turned around, teeth clenched as she approached the door. Odessa followed. "Where are you going?"

"I've come too far to lose," Flowridia seethed, and she swung the door wide open.

"Can you defeat them all, Flower Child? Who can say how big the mob is?"

Flowridia shook her head, pausing at the door. "I don't have to defeat them. I just have to give Ayla time."

The door slammed behind her, and Flowridia ran out into the night. Her feet splashed against the murky terrain, and as she ran, she heard faint voices from afar.

Time was scarce. She followed a path she had not travelled in years. It lay sealed in her memories, though, each step trudged back and forth between mother's home and her destination long ago.

A mass of graves met her view, marked only with a stone for each. Men and young girls, Odessa's lovers and daughters, rejected and left to hellish fates.

Aura was not among them. She had dragged her familiar farther away.

Flowridia had thought the best kindness she could do was give Odessa's victims a final resting place. She hadn't been wrong. What she did now was the vilest act of all.

She stopped before the nearest mound and knelt. Flowridia's hand touched the cold dirt. Underneath the earth, she felt all the potential buried beneath, not only of the corpse under her hand, but all of them, each of them begging for her influence and touch.

A distinct purple glow shone from within her being. A *thump* as her power hit the earth, and then silence. Flowridia stood, breathing heavy as she waited, intimately aware of the magic happening below her feet.

Damned to hell she would be.

A hand shot through the dirt. It bent, gripping the ground as another burst through to join it.

All around, skeletal hands appeared in a mass of swirling purple and flying dirt, clawing their way out, desperate to escape their final prison. Flowridia watched, eyes darting from corpse to corpse. The one nearest her twitched as it stood, free from its grave. The stench of earth and rotting flesh met her nose, and when it stared at her with empty sockets, she saw the maggots feeding on the decayed flesh. Skin hung in tatters from its bones, but its nails seemed sharper, as did its teeth, practically begging to sink into warm, living flesh.

All of them swayed as they stood, various stages of rotted corpses shuffling quickly towards her. One struggled to free itself, its tiny hands clutching more at air than dirt.

The mere sight of those hands, minutes old upon the victim's death, sickened Flowridia's stomach. She couldn't face it; she withdrew her power from the baby boy's corpse.

She looked to the rest, tightening her jaw as she spoke, voice strong. "Come with me. All of you."

There were twenty-three in all that followed her back to Odessa's home. She remembered each and every one and had offered prayers to Sol Kareena for their souls scarcely a year prior.

She wondered what Sol Kareena thought now. She wondered if Sol Kareena thought of her at all.

Odessa watched from the window. All around the house, Flowridia stationed them, her undead servants spreading wide as they twitched and released hollow moans. Two she set on the porch, on either side of herself, and when she finally opened the door, Odessa's said, "This might be madness, Flower Child, but I won't say I'm unimpressed."

"If anyone tries to enter the house," Flowridia said, grabbing her beloved spear from beside the fireplace, "cast them out."

She shut the door, staring out at the approaching lights.

The torches were close enough that she could make out individual shapes and silhouettes between the trees.

Flowridia released a breath, purple smoke escaping her mouth, then realized something was missing.

She looked to the windows, realizing no ghostly interlopers watched. She prayed it meant that with the dissolution of the wards, they had been released into the beyond.

Time passed in anxious, precious moments. Her warm, amber skin turned nearly white as she gripped her spear. Her heart thumped in her ears. She stepped down the porch to the murky, dank mud. The lights had expanded, illuminating the swamp in eerie hues. Still, Flowridia moved forward, stopping near the outskirts of her defenses.

"Stop!" she cried. Perhaps startled by the force of her word, the shuffling feet did stop, for a moment. "I am not Odessa. I'm not the witch who terrorized your village."

Silence, and then a single set of footsteps met her ears. One man emerged from the trees, holding a torch. His armor reflected the light as he glared. "We aren't here to negotiate, witch."

"Then why speak to me?" Flowridia matched his gaze, wondering what a sight she must be, covered in blood and dirt, her body emanating an eerie purple.

"To plead for you to avoid needless bloodshed and surrender."

Flowridia glanced at his sword. He stood only a few feet away; one swing, and her head would fly. "You're afraid of me. That's very wise. Walk away now, and you'll live. You have my word. But if you stay, I won't be able to stop what's coming."

Behind her, her undead gathered. The man's grip on his sword tightened, his eyes glancing from creature to creature, and finally to the cottage behind her. "What madness are you brewing, witch?"

"I'm *not* Odessa," she repeated, power lacing each word—by every god, she had never felt bolder. "Merely a woman with nothing left to lose. Perhaps that's something far worse." She took a step back, vision narrowing. "Your decision. Stay or go."

He took a step back and disappeared into the darkness.

Fearless among the raised dead, Flowridia returned to the porch of the cottage. As her sight adjusted, she saw that the sea of torches was hardly limitless—a mass of fifty at most. Still more than double her own forces.

She might've prayed for them to run, but she knew not what god to pray to anymore. Flanked on either side by her horrid minions, Flowridia surveyed the trees, watching for any sign of movement.

An array of voices echoed through the swamp. Angry shouts spurred them forward; the mob rushed.

Flowridia braced herself. A purple cloud seeped from her pores, rising in tandem with her controlled rage.

Her undead ran to meet them.

Sword met bone, and screams filled her ears as her undead ripped and tore through the mob. Flowridia, meanwhile, shut her eyes, and pulled to her all the life in the clearing. Human life resisted, but the rest fell to her—the mushrooms clinging to the cottage, even the trees at the outskirts. All of them relinquished their life and power to her.

She thrust it back. Opening her eyes, she watched the charred earth suddenly imbue with life, brilliant and vibrant in the dank atmosphere. Flowridia stumbled back against the door, the release unlike anything she'd ever felt. Her head swam, but she pulled herself up, throwing her consciousness into the fray.

The moss upon the ground clung to the legs of the villagers; vines tangled, seeking to strangle them. Trees whipped their branches about, lacerating and grabbing those who passed, cries of pain and terror erupting across the battlefield as men and women were tossed and crushed by the undead plants.

With them, all manner of dead creatures dug themselves up from the damp earth. Bits of rodents, reptiles with jaws the size of a man's leg—they, too joined the fray, gnawing at the furious mob.

But none did so much damage as her humanoid dead.

The battle stood illuminated by torches, and Flowridia could see with perfect clarity what destruction her undead wrought. Limbs were torn. Blood sprayed. One ghoul gnawed on a fallen man, oblivious to his screams as it consumed the entrails seeping through his torn stomach. Another ran to his aid, lopping the creature's head off in a single, swift motion—still, it moved. A final strike, and the monster lay severed at the torso.

Another ripped at a woman's face, her body still convulsing as her conscious form held too long to life. Arrows embedded into the monster's back, but they did nothing to detour it. Someone threw a torch. When its tattered clothing caught fire, the creature continued, but steadily its skin melted. By the time it stopped moving, the woman was long dead.

Flowridia stared forward, realizing she was being approached. Two men with clubs rushed her, but when they swung, the creatures flanking her leapt forward. One managed to tackle the attacker to the ground, gnawing at his throat as he released a gurgled scream. But the second fell as the man swung his club. Its skull shattered; it wandered aimlessly without it.

Flowridia realized she'd meet a similar fate and instinctively thrust her spear, stance strong as Casvir always taught. Her stomach lurched when it ran straight through the man's gut. He fell. The weapon fell with him as he cried out in pain, off the porch and into the murky terrain.

The mass of trees and vines brought destruction, slamming into the ground and tossing her enemies left and right. In the fray, she could see her undead troops dwindling, horrendous in their strength and sheer terror, but overpowered by the mob's numbers.

Her favorite trick, then. From her very skin seeped a noxious purple gas, the cloud expanding and choking those who dared approach. The mass engulfed one man entirely, desiccating his skin in seconds, leaving a fallen husk on the ground.

Still, the mob closed in. Flowridia refused to show concern. Her strength steadily depleted—unlike the animals and humans, the plants required some focus, and it was becoming increasingly difficult to breathe. Her ranks dwindled, but still they fought on, unhindered by fear like the living.

But piercing pain suddenly punctured her shoulder. She gasped, her hand instinctively grasping the arrow. With a cry, she ripped it out, stumbling into the wall of the cottage. Flowridia shut her eyes, letting a flow of healing energy stitch the wound back together, the pain decreasing with each breath she took.

She opened her eyes just as a lasso ensnared around her neck. With a yelp, her hands gripped the rope as she was pulled across the porch and down the stairs. Murky water engulfed her as she fell.

She forced her eyes open, struggling against the rope. She called out to her undead; soon what forces remained rushed at the man holding her bonds. Burly and barely armored, the man screamed as monsters tore at his flesh with their teeth. Flowridia managed to stand, struggling to remove the rope tightening around her neck.

Another arrow lacerated her side. She gasped, just as another rope lassoed around her hand. A swift tug, and Flowridia fell face-first onto the ground.

Dizzy from the impact, Flowridia struggled against the hands seeking to tie her up. She managed to let purple lightning crackle against her skin, burning those who touched her, but necromancy did nothing against rope. She was dragged along by her wrist and neck, breath cut off.

Water choked her; mud blinded her eyes. Shock stole her focus, and she felt the influence she had cast upon nature dwindle and stagnate. Her face finally managed to lift up from the dirt and grimy water, only to be scraped against the trunk of a willow tree. She winced, bark stinging her cheek. A hand gripped the rope at her neck. She gasped as she was forced to stand, head swimming as the rope tightened.

Odessa's cottage stood a ways away. The mob of people had their sights set on her, the last of her minions falling lifeless into the swamp. Furious cries bombarded her ears. More ropes tightened around her limbs, her body twisting as she was forced against the tree.

The bark dug into her back, but any movement forward only tightened her noose. Angry tears stung her eyes as two men pulled a rope around her stomach, letting it sink into her flesh before tying it off at the other side of the tree.

An armored man, the same she had spoken to before, approached, his face torn and bleeding, and through her misted vision she realized one eye was missing from its socket. He limped, spitting blood at her feet. But no words crossed his lips; instead, he dropped his torch at her feet, letting the flames lick at the roots of the tree.

The damp wood would mean a slow, smokey burn, but the noxious fumes from the swamp guaranteed it would. Flowridia's feet, tied to the tree, could do nothing to kick it away. To watch her burn, to watch their literal nightmare turn to ashes would make for a bittersweet victory.

Flowridia, however, stared beyond them to the cottage. Something shifted through the window. Curious, calm, she watched as the door slowly swung open. A small figure stood shadowed in the doorframe, casting its gaze upon the swamp. No features could be seen—the darkness saw to that—yet Flowridia swore she could feel that familiar, predatory grin.

It vanished.

A scream erupted from the back of the mob, drawing the attention of all. The people turned, and Flowridia watched a man fall to the ground, gore splattering as a small arm withdrew from his torso. Vibrant blood stood in stark contrast to pale skin as Ayla Darkleaf, fully nude and flush with life, studied the crowd.

She charged. The villagers screamed as she sunk her teeth into her second victim; the woman cried out as she was drained of blood. Ayla flung her withered body against another, the sheer force snapping bones in half.

An axe swung at her, but the vampiric woman was no longer there. Instead, her nails raked at his neck, severing his head in one motion.

Mesmerized, Flowridia's focus was stolen when searing pain struck her leg. She looked down, gasping when she realized her dress had caught fire. "A-Ayla!" she cried, and when the vampire met her gaze, never had she seen such fury in that icy blue stare.

Ayla emerged from a shadow beside her and ripped the ropes in twain. Flowridia fell forward, landing on her hands and knees. Murky water cushioned her fall; she smothered her burning skirts. When her eyes darted up, she realized Ayla no longer stood beside her. Screams met her ears. Ayla had returned to the fray.

Prayers to Sol Kareena sang through the battlefield. But how much righteous conviction would it take to stop a thousand year old monster? Ripping, slashing, Ayla tore heads from their necks and spines from their bodies. She feasted as she fought, draining one victim as she ripped the arms from another. She needed no knives, no weapons—her claws wracked through flesh with ease, and her teeth glinted against the torches as she leered at her victims. Entrails and bones littered the swamp, and within mere minutes, there remained only Ayla, engulfed in moonlight, victorious as she stared with her back to Flowridia.

Flowridia stood as Ayla turned. Silence loomed. Ayla's gaze met hers, intense blue eyes reflecting the silver light. She was all Flowridia remembered—standing with such power, such confidence, her lithe musculature melding with faint, feminine curves. The shadows of her cheekbones cast a gaunt shadow, her thin lips nearly white. A perfect picture from Flowridia's memory, nothing out of place except for her vulnerable, fragile stare.

Ayla rushed her. Flowridia gasped, fear forcing her heart to start.

But the small woman collapsed at her feet. Fingers tugged at her skirts, and Flowridia realized Ayla sobbed. "Oh, Flowra, Sweet Flowra." Blood and tears streaked Ayla's face, her hands gripping her skirt like a young child to her mother. Flowridia fell to her knees, pulling Ayla into a tight embrace, the feel of that petite frame so familiar and wonderful.

"Flowra–" A kiss cut off her words as Flowridia crushed their lips together. Ayla didn't fight it; Flowridia felt her melt into the touch.

"Ayla," she whispered, and with each touch of their lips, her embrace tightened. Desperation rose, and her hands roamed the taut body, determined to study each blood-slicked curve. "Ayla, I love you." Her voice grew soft, reverent as she pulled her head back. To face her love, to match Ayla's eyes—oh, it overwhelmed her so. "I will never leave you."

Her fingers met ice as she cupped that sharp cheekbone. Her hand slid into Ayla's black hair, sleek with blood, and nearly drew back from shock.

She brought her other hand up, slowly parting Ayla's hair to reveal two pointed ears. Flowridia laughed, but before Ayla's curious eyes could ask, their lips touched again, blood staining both their faces. Flowridia let the kiss deepen, Ayla's head cradled in her hand. Her other hand slid down to caress Ayla's waist as lithe fingers slid up her back, their gentle touch forming an ache within her. It wasn't enough. Nothing would ever be enough.

Flowridia's grip tightened, and with a surge of desperation, she pushed against Ayla's chest. By every god— she needed to hold her, to own her. Ayla was back, and Ayla was hers. "I need you," she pled, though it was far more a prayer. She pulled back enough to face her love. "I need to know you're real."

Close now, Flowridia saw flecks of silver surrounding Ayla's pupils, fading into that penetrating, icy blue. Had that always been there? Vulnerable and wide, those enthralling eyes held her gaze as Ayla nodded.

No words were spoken; Flowridia crushed their lips together, desperate to close the distance between them. She pulled back, nearly ripping her dress as she tore it and all her clothing from her body. The chill night whipped at her exposed form, but the frost radiating from Ayla proved a stronger force. Cold held comfort, and no comfort had ever been stronger than when she pressed their naked forms together. Blood mixed with mud and tears. Ayla's back touched the ground, frantic kisses passing between them.

Flowridia's hands roamed the thin skin, each sharp valley of Ayla's body something to explore, to rediscover. The slight hill of her breasts fit perfectly in Flowridia's hands, and when she squeezed, Ayla's gasp filled every crevice of her mind. Her dreams had been but a crude sketch; reality seemed a vibrant painting, each color brilliant and bright.

Still, they kissed. Flowridia heard Ayla's soft moans of pleasure hum against her lips.

Her hand trailed down, meeting jutting ribs and the sharp contours of Ayla's toned stomach, slick with blood. Like a sleek cliff-face, Flowridia scaled downward, her hand settling in the valley resting between her thighs.

Ayla gasped when Flowridia's finger stroked against the wetness in between, her hands tangling into her thick hair, gripping with menace. When Flowridia's fingers slipped inside, relief laced Ayla's shallow breaths. Flowridia felt tears spot against her face.

To feel Ayla move, to be buried inside her—Flowridia wondered if she had ever felt so complete. All the months of sorrow and loneliness lay forgotten, the atrocities and tragedies so muted. Ayla's pleasured cries echoed in every corner of her mind, stifled until she finally pulled her mouth away. Ayla's eyes opened, silver and blue and glistening with tears.

From those thin lips came desperate words. "You brought me back," Ayla whispered. And again, this time louder, managed between cries of pleasure. "You brought me back."

"Ayla, I love you." Powerful words, and Flowridia let them gently flutter from her tongue. Let there be no question. When she was tried for her crimes, let that single statement stand as her defense. Hell itself might swallow her whole, but the pathway would be paved by devotion.

Let no one forget that simple truth. No one. Especially not Ayla.

The hand in her hair pulled her down, and Flowridia's lips met Ayla's once more. Their bodies touched; still she moved within Ayla. Teeth scraped her lip. She wondered if the blood she tasted was her own or one of Ayla's victims.

Ayla's body tensed beneath her, her cries a higher pitch. Balanced on her knees, Flowridia let her other hand slide down, stroking gently while the other increased in pace.

Ayla shuddered, squeezing around her fingers. Gasping breaths blew against her lips. Flowridia planted a tender kiss at the corner of her mouth, letting Ayla ride out the wave of her orgasm.

She stilled. Tears streamed down Ayla's face in silence; she had no need to breathe. Moonlight cast deep shadows, and Flowridia carefully pulled her fingers out.

"I love you, Flowra," Ayla whispered. Her eyes remained shut as she pulled Flowridia into her arms, turning them both over onto their sides. Flowridia held her, relishing the feeling of that cold form curling into her arms. Her face lay muffled between Flowridia's small breasts. Ayla trembled; Flowridia realized she still sobbed.

Gentle fingers wove themselves into Ayla's hair. Flowridia embraced the naked, raw figure, arms wrapping tight around the taut skin and muscles of Ayla's back.

Amidst the carnage, Flowridia clung to tentative peace.

Epilogue

"It was a damn foolish tip you gave us."

Behind the worm named Shem, Mereen saw evidence of chaos, of a envoy of men repairing cages and cleaning up bodies. Their camp was nearly ruined, perhaps half their prisoners having escaped in the confusion, and she studied every piece of damage with her keen eyes.

That human girl had quite the spine. Mereen smiled to know her victory had come about—even if she had needed a little help.

"Shem, I told you the truth—the Empress of Solvira would be accompanied by an impressive envoy, *including* Staelash's little necromancer. Not my fault you didn't properly prepare."

At the far side of camp, Mereen saw the girl's familiar curled up asleep.

"Either way, you aren't getting your necromancer."

Mereen idly nodded. "Fair enough."

Shem sputtered like a man denied a fight. The fool had been all too easy to coerce. "T-Then perhaps you should still be paying that bounty. I've lost thousands worth of gold—*more,* from the empress. But if you helped us get her back-"

His words stopped for the knife at his throat. No witnesses—they met in a collection of trees, his men still detained searching for escaped slaves in the woods. "It would be a mercy to kill you now," she whispered, "but you disgust me. You aren't even fit for worms to eat, but I'll grant you one boon—*run.*"

A single droplet of blood streaked down the blade. Mereen stiffened, refusing to give consideration to that intoxicating bit of blood. She saw the shift in his stare, smelled fear course through his veins.

"Something is coming. Something more terrifying than even your black heart can fathom." Mereen removed the knife, the siren call of his blood forcing her breath the still. "She'll come for you first, and once she's satisfied herself with your blood, the whole world will tremble at her freedom. Only one person holds the monster's leash—and you threatened to rape her and return her to her homeland in chains."

"What daft fairytale are you spouting, woman?"

"I'm a woman who's seen nightmares." She stepped back, knowing she could vanish in an instant—but oh, she reveled in this man's fear. "I'm a woman who's *fought* nightmares, but never quite succeeded in slaying the most feared of them all. Now, I have a chance. I thank you for the role you played."

Ayla's return would damn the world, but not for much longer. A sacrifice for the greater good.

Mereen slipped off into the night, leaving the flea-bitten swine behind. She stared into the distance, recalling her quarry.

Only a few miles to Ilunnes and the swamp. An innocent woman's body had been used for a ritual as wicked as Mereen's own kind. What a damning sort of accident it would be, if someone were to discover it.

From the pouch at her hip, she withdrew a green, luminous orb, one they said held the power of all the earth. Mereen felt nothing more than mild heat, but the nuances of magic were a mystery even to her. She couldn't wield this.

But she needn't. Someone else would. The God of Order sought this, and so she slipped it back into her pouch, beside a stolen bracelet of maldectine.

The world turned, and Mereen reveled in imminent victory.

General Khastra of the Deathless Army tucked a letter of infinite worth back into her armor, careful to stain only the edges in blood and dirt.

Khastra,

I need to say a few things.
I hope, after everything that's happened between us both last week and these past twenty-something years, that it isn't too much for me to say thank you.

"I love you," the gifter had said, and Khastra had kissed her, though she no longer deserved her. Once, in a time she desperately missed, she had died by Etolié's side and embraced a glorious end.

Now, hell had come to claim her.

My life was pretty fucked up, you know? And I could've been just as fucked up, but you saved me. If you take nothing else from this letter, know that much. You were the first person who told me I was worth something, that maybe I had hope to be whole someday. You held my hand while I healed, and sometimes you carried me when I couldn't go on.
It's a debt I can never repay. But you never expected anything back; you just liked me for some reason.

Khastra stood as the victor upon a kingdom of ruin.

She had left Murishani alone to scavenge the remains of the imperator. The threat of death needn't be said, should he harm those who still lived. Her brain remained addled from the Bringer of War's manic influence, her blood pulsing, stomach screaming for sustenance—but she did not have the blessed release of sleep. Not anymore.

Training in the castle of Nox'Kartha held little consequence. Here, for the first time in nearly ten thousand years of life, Khastra was lucid for the aftermath of her own carnage.

I also wanted to say that I'm sorry.
I'm realizing that I used you as a crutch, sometimes. So when you were suddenly gone and I lost that . . . It turns out I hadn't taken root like I should've. I mourned you, and then I resented you when you turned up in Nox'Kartha— but it was selfish. You weren't there for me. Me, me, me . . .

It took me too long to think about how you must be feeling. New life, new boss, new heart—it'd be a lot for anyone to take.

I resented you and it wasn't your fault. I'm sorry.

Undead parted for her passing. Their soulless eyes watched her with hunger; others feasted on dismembered corpses too ruined to join the Deathless Army. Khastra stepped into a narrow alley, baring her teeth to a ghoul who stared at her a moment too long.

Undead only knew the fear of their masters. Khastra was no necromancer, but she had been granted the boon of their obedience, all the same. With Casvir gone, the Deathless Army was hers to wield as she would.

For now.

You said it yourself, that you aren't around to take care of me anymore. I have to be a big girl and move forward on my own.

But I think that's how it should be. When I think about it, we weren't a relationship of equals. To have what I think I want, I have to grow.

Upon the wall was smeared the remains of a small girl, a mass of emulsified flesh within a bloodied, torn dress. Pieces of her remained splattered against a broken wall bearing the perfect symmetry of a hammer as ancient as the New Gods.

There was glory in besieging a city that had stood for thousands of years. There was glory in victory, to have toppled a kingdom in a single, bloodstained night.

There was no glory in the cost. Khastra dipped her finger in the girl's drying blood and wrote Sol Kareena's symbol upon the wall, trembling all the while.

What happened that night was fucking monumental. I trusted you. I trusted you enough to let you kiss me and touch me, and I felt safe for every moment of it. I loved it.

Khastra, I think I might love you.

Kneeling before the murdered child, Khastra contemplated the bitter truth—that she would be a pariah of the angelic gods forevermore.

Khastra stood, her limbs numbing with each step. Were it not for the faint ticking within her chest, she might've thought her heart had failed once more.

If she tore it out, would she be left to rest?

I don't know what feelings feel like. But based off research and perusing pornographic novels for study, I'd say what I'm feeling is something I'd never even thought to acknowledge or consider. My mother's life was ruined because of feelings. Why would I ever want to risk that?

I don't know when or how it started, if it happened that night or if it's always been there, waiting for trust to grow.

Sudden scuffling drew her focus. As she looked behind her, she matched eyes with a condemned soul, a woman whose fearful eyes bespoke visions of terror. She held hands with a man and a boy of perhaps ten.

She saw the woman's mouth open, then heard a whisper on the wind: *"Bringer of War."*

The man drew a sword as he looked to Khastra, who smelled his sweat and fear, saw the trembling in his arm. He did not even know how to wield it, and Khastra simply turned away and continued her path, listening as their footsteps disappeared.

Then, she heard screaming. A plea for mercy. Cries cut off in the night. Khastra swallowed regret and moved forward.

But our future is bright when I think about it—you said we could only be as close as our kingdoms, but Staelash and Nox'Kartha just unified in symbolic matrimony. There could be a future for us.

She emerged from the narrow alleyway, eyes studying the expansive scene of splendor and carnage. Khastra saw the city's main square as it had once been, gleaming and wondrous, blessed by the Goddess it worshipped. She saw shops and patrons, glorious statues to beloved gods and goddesses, as well as a magnificent cathedral with windows that glittered in the sun.

She blinked away all memories of peace. The world returned to carnage, save for a spot of light in the darkness— Etolié stood within a throng of children before the Goddess' statue, told to remain lest they perish in the night by ravenous ghouls.

I've never given any regard to finding anyone attractive, and to be honest, I still stand by that, but I would be the biggest liar in the realms if I said you weren't the most beautiful person I've ever seen. Touching itches—but it's welcomed from you.

Etolié captivated the children with words and sparkling displays, their tear-filled faces managing to smile. She radiated light despite the dried ichor on her body, and Khastra loved her so.

Khastra remained quiet as she passed the viceroy gathering pieces great and small of mutilated flesh, bone, and armor. His pile of carnage slowly grew, the collected pieces radiating an unmistakable energy. Shattered metal and gore and viscous black ichor lay scattered around her hammer, and peeking from beneath the gargantuan, glowing head, she saw a great hand, callused from centuries of battle.

It twitched.

Necromancers never died. Khastra knew this like she knew the sweet adrenaline of bloodlust and the boundless passion of endless nights. She knew it like the shame of betrayal and shattered pledges of loyalty. She knew it like the nightmares that rose from shadows.

Necromancers never died. Casvir would not forget. There would be hell to pay.

Khastra approached, watching as Sora glanced up from the stick she sharpened with her dagger and as Lunestra warily held one of the smaller, sleeping children. But she kept her focus on Etolié, though her mind was too loud to hear the tale she told.

At the statue's feet was what appeared to be a pile of ashes within a glass dome. She recalled, a lifetime ago, when Etolié had told the tale of the tiny one's offering to the Goddess, how her flower had been accepted and had taken root in the statue's base.

The offering, once deemed a miracle, had been rejected now. That, or the Goddess no longer held the strength to hold to anything.

But that aside, I have to consider your feelings too, even if I've been shit at it in the past. You were always what

I needed you to be, and so I worry you only fucked me because I basically asked you to.

But then I think about your smile and your kiss, and even if you don't love me, I know you at least care.

Khastra took tentative steps forward, feeling the gaze of a beloved angel whose touch remained a beautiful memory even in the midst of a bloodstained nightmare. Behind the statue, away from Sol Kareena's gaze, she took a seat, watching as Etolié beckoned for Lunestra to take watch of the children. Etolié came to stand before her, uncaring of the blood on her breastplate and cuirasses as she stood at the juncture between her legs.

In the moment they matched gazes, Khastra thought her a spot of light amidst darkness, an angel to ease her condemnation to hell.

Khastra, I think I might love you, and that's the scariest fucking feeling in all the realms. But I know if I were to trust my heart with anyone, I know you'd cherish it—because that's who you are.

"*I love you,*" she had said upon the bloodied battlefield—the bridge across the great divide between them; words that would have once brought an impossible, peaceful joy but now tethered their wrists together, though their kingdoms would seek to tear them apart.

So let me know, ya big lug. This is your chance to make a clean break. Because you're right—I have to take care of me. Maybe I'll even be able to take care of you. But I don't see why it means we can't be together, if you'll have me.

Etolié gently brought her hands to Khastra's head, stroking her hair and horns, and Khastra wrapped her arms around her body, gripped the dress she knew was false as her head fell upon Etolié's breast, splattered in ichor. The Celestial stood as a sentinel upon the watchtower, surveying the battlefield as Khastra clung desperately to her own humanity.

How much longer would it be before she became as soulless as the ghouls?

"Khastra," Etolié whispered, and the word meant everything.

Khastra wept.

Your dearest friend (by your own admission),
Etolié

"Tell me what you want. Anything at all."

Flowridia's body bristled against the night air, her senses piqued after the sweet pleasure of Ayla's mouth. She reached to cup the back of Ayla's head, shutting her eyes as she stroked her fine, black hair. She breathed deep, letting Ayla's presence settle against her skin. "All I've ever desired was you. And now I have that–"

"Not good enough," she interrupted, ice lacing her tone. "Tell me what you would have." Ayla pulled her face away, the intensity of her gaze sending a shiver down Flowridia's spine. "I owe you everything."

"You owe me nothing. I did this for love."

"I was shackled to Casvir for far less." Ayla's arms wrapped around her body, the chill of her form bringing comfort. Senses enraptured, Flowridia gripped Ayla's body, her presence surreal. "It's an odd irony, that in my new freedom, I would happily enslave myself to you."

The word brought pain and the memory of it. "Would you help with something, then?" she said, gently stroking her finger along the sharp edges of Ayla's cheeks.

"Anything."

Flowridia's heart had belonged to only one for so long. When she had fallen in love with Ayla, her heart had expanded, making room for two. Now, in his absence, she still ached. "Demitri was taken from me."

"What?" Ayla's demeanor switched from intrigue to rage. "By whom?"

"Slavers in Solvira. Only hours ago."

"And they will be dead before the night is through." She stood, palpably seething, then grabbed Flowridia's hand, yanking her up. "I remember . . ." She trailed off, suddenly quiet. "I was there. You were taken, too."

Flowridia stooped down to grab her muddy, ruined dress, the one embroidered in flowers and leaves. She managed to slip back into it, her body chilled by the night air and the proximity of her undead lover. "So you did have awareness?"

Ayla's arms wrapped around Flowridia's waist. "Somewhere, yes. But it's hazy—terribly hazy."

Flowridia embraced that tiny form. "Do you want clothing first? I–" She nearly laughed, recalling her own silly sentiment. "I have one of your dresses in my bag."

Ayla's eyes, silver paint flecked onto a blue palette, blinked thoughtfully. "I will accept a dress."

"Once we have Demitri, I'll help you remember. I'll tell you everything." She reached up to cup Ayla's jaw, still reveling in the feel of having her so close. A kiss met her palm, and heat blossomed against her cheeks. Ayla was here, Ayla was real . . . The subject of her nightmares had become a perfect reality. "It's been six months, Ayla. So much has happened."

Ayla nodded slowly, skin brushing against Flowridia's palm.

Flowridia left her, though it wounded her to do so. Ayla's disorientation was understandable, given she'd literally been reborn of blood less than half an hour ago.

Her bag waited by the door. When she peered into the cottage, she caught sight of an ethereal figure watching her expectantly. Odessa smiled, victory in her visage. Her bargain remained.

Beyond, Flowridia saw through the doorframe a bloodstained hand and arm idly hanging above the barest hint of a cauldron.

And her heart . . . ached.

She shoved the pain aside. When she returned with the gown, she saw Ayla staring at her hands.

She said nothing as she accepted the black fabric. Within seconds, Ayla's body filled the slim dress, the plunge of her neckline leaving little to the imagination, even with her minimal cleavage. The ribs of her chest cast deep shadows in the moonlight. Curiosity laced Ayla's words. "Solviraes blood?"

Flowridia thought of the corpse in her mother's home, maimed and gored by hooks and streaked with blood. Dead, silver eyes waited in every shadow. "Yes."

Intrigue radiated from the predatory smile pulling on Ayla's lip, fangs steadily growing from that ever-twisting grin. "I feel something," she whispered, eyes nearly black as her pupils expanded, reflecting the moon's light. "Something different. Something . . . *powerful.*"

She exhaled a forced breath, and Flowridia's heart stopped at the first flickering of light. A silver aura shone from her skin, luminous in the night. At her feet, silver flame sparked, expanding to rise from the pores of her flesh. Ayla burned but did not burn, the Silver Fire dancing from her skin and escaping her mouth when she laughed. "I feel so *alive.*"

Was it fear or lust gripping Flowridia's heart?

Author's Note

Thank you for reading!

You, my dear reader, are the reason I do this. Thank you so much for your support and love. Flowridia has a story, and I'm so grateful that you took the time to read it. We're only halfway done, and I appreciate you joining me this far on her journey.

If you enjoyed what you read, consider leaving a short review on Amazon and Goodreads. It's the greatest gift you can give an author (and the best incentive for the next book to come out even sooner!).

If you're impatient for more, check out my newsletter at sdsimper.com! I'm currently offering two free short stories—one about Flowridia and Aura in the time before Odessa and another about that one time Etolié got blackmailed into running a kingdom (and unknowingly ended up on a date with a certain half-demon).

If you want to reach out to me, Twitter is your best bet, but I also run a Facebook page and Instagram. I'd love to hear from you!

Keep on reading for a bonus short story about everyone's favorite drunk Celestial—my gift to you!

Much love,

♥ S D Simper

"Become the greater monster."

The God of Order marches on, approaching victory with every stride. Frustrated with the stagnation of politics, Etolié takes matters into her own hands, resolving to find the reborn God and defeat him herself—with the help of her favorite half-demon, of course. An unexpected ally finds them in the woods, claiming to know his whereabouts, and while Etolié knows better than to trust vampires, Mereen Fireborn seems honest enough.

Meanwhile, Flowridia basks in her impossible victory, even if the haunting memory of its cost lurks in every shadow. Joy comes with compromise, however, because the woman she loves will never die, and so neither must she. Immortality holds a soul-wrenching cost. Flowridia agrees to pay it with a single addendum—that they first be wed.

Gods rise, kingdoms fall, and a monster is unleashed in the fourth installment of FALLEN GODS.

Read a sneak peek of *Tear the World Apart* and more at
S D Simper's website—sdsimper.com

Etolié and the Horrible, Awful,
Messed-Up, Worst Kind of Day

By S D Simper

© 2019 Endless Night Publications

Etolié focused on the squabbling toddler playing with blocks on the floor, fucking relieved to have something to listen to other than her own blood pounding in her ears. Her side throbbed. The healers had patched her up and made her drink something nasty to accelerate the healing, but punctured kidneys weren't exactly a walk in the fucking park. It would be a few more hours of agony.

"Marielle, stop eating that!" Queen Lyra said, snatching a pointy, star-shaped block from the little girl's mouth. "Do you want syphilis?"

Marielle shook her head, and Etolié legitimately didn't know if Lyra was failing at humor or simply an idiot and decided not to comment.

From beyond, she heard footsteps, some heavy and some merely frantic. "General, I promise she's fine–"

The door slammed open, cracking the wall with the doorknob, but Khastra was known for only having so many fucks to give. The half-demon towered over them all, her aura as daunting as her visible ire. Etolié should have expected this; what she didn't expect was for Clarence to be trailing behind her, apparently trying to calm her.

Say what you would about that aggressively ginger-haired man—he was fearless in the face of eight-foot tall half-demons. "See, she's patched up. No longer bleeding. And the half-giants pummeled the attackers into meat, saving you the trouble."

But Khastra ignored him, instead kneeling before Etolié, her eyes furious yet glistening as she inspected her bandaged torso. "Etolié, you should not be sitting."

"I'm fine, Beefcake. My kidney's just a little skewered." Her joke fell flat, apparently, because Khastra's worry visibly escalated. She sat beside her, hunching to come closer to her face, her rough hands stroking aside her hair.

"Please, I cannot bear with jests," Khastra said softly, and from the corner of Etolié's eye, she saw Lyra give a silent wave as she took Marielle out. "What happened?"

"I was stabbed in the street by a couple of Celestials. Clarence was there. He screamed through the whole thing like a little girl–" Right. No jokes. "Well, he was understandably panicked, I mean."

Khastra's severe gaze turned to Clarence, who held his hands up defensively. "You should have taken the wound for her."

"I?" Clarence's incredulous jaw-drop pulled a giggle from Etolié, which she grossly regretted because it likely ripped something new open. "The *king?* The human and incredibly squishy king should have taken what would have been a fatal blow for the girl whose lineage says she'll likely live forever?"

"He didn't have time, Beefcake," Etolié said, hoping to draw Khastra's palpable fury away from her favorite ginger boy. "I barely matched eyes with the man before he stuck a knife in me, much less the rest of them."

At which point Etolié, beloved Magister of Staelash and Savior of Slaves, had found herself lying in the middle of the public street, moaning. Somehow, her populace hadn't been fine with that. The perpetrators—had there been eight? That felt right—had been, as Clarence intellectually put it, pummeled into meat by a legion of angry half-giants.

You know, the same half-giants Etolié had saved from captivity and given a new life. She was a popular girl around here.

"Do you know who did this?"

Clarence also watched her after that little damning question. Etolié forced a smile, having been confronted with faces she hadn't seen since she was a child. "It's possible."

Well, that wasn't a suspicious answer or anything. Gods-damn it.

"Who?" Khastra asked, any kindness in her gaze having vanished.

Etolié knew the severity wasn't meant for her. She knew it in her heart yet she withered, the disdain absolutely crippling. "Khastra, it doesn't matter. They're dead."

"But you do know?"

She nodded, even if she aggressively wanted to vomit.

"Will there be others?"

Words were becoming increasingly difficult. Etolié settled on a shrug, knowing full well that Khastra could likely hear her heartbeat. Literally.

"Etolié, if you want us to protect you, you have to tell us everything you know–"

"Not gonna happen, Beefy, because it's not a big deal and I don't want to talk about it."

Khastra's anger dissolved into confusion, which was a much easier emotion for Etolié to try and process. Behind her, Clarence took a step back. "I can let you two speak alone."

"No, stay. She'll have to pummel it out of me, so there might as well be a witness."

Oh shit, she regretted that. Etolié bit her lip at Khastra's visible hurt, her elegant face suddenly deep with lines. "Etolié–"

"I'm sorry. That's not what I meant." Etolié shut her eyes, but in the dark she saw hateful Celestial faces, among which mingled the most hated of all. "I think I need to be alone."

Khastra stood up, but her touch lingered, her hand trembling as she finally pulled it from Etolié's arm. Her gaze hardened as she gave a curt nod, and to Etolié's surprise, she left without another word.

It wouldn't be the last she heard of it, she knew.

Clarence hadn't budged. "Well, that was uncharacteristically rude of you."

"She asked too many questions."

"They're important questions. If your life is in danger, we have to act accordingly."

"Listen, Gingerbread. I'm not in danger. I suppose I don't know if anyone else might come to stab the shit out of me, but believe me when I say I'll be fucked whether we take precautions or not."

"Etolié, you're being stubborn."

Etolié bit back her standard 'go to hell' response, instead releasing a steadying breath. "Look. I have some things to think about. Will you please go interrogate someone else?"

Clarence offered a slow nod. "You can trust us, Etolié," he said, but she wasn't sure if that was true, even if he thought he meant it.

Etolié knew there were a few secrets she'd prefer to keep to herself.

After an alarmingly irate argument with the healers about the need to be supervised overnight, Etolié was given permission to sleep underground, and so she laid beneath the skylight, the clouded sky revealing no celestial bodies.

It was best. Best to not think of mom, which she definitely refused to do.

Perhaps she'd been a fool to think she could hide from the past. No matter how fast she ran, it seemed it had found her nonetheless.

Though, to be fair, she wasn't exactly hiding in recent years.

Etolié blinked, releasing a rather unlady-like, "Damn it," when her vision misted. Perhaps that was her problem. She wasn't hiding. Fugitives couldn't exactly be free to run in the sun.

Perhaps Staelash was a mistake.

The door beyond opened. Etolié quickly wiped away her tears, because signature clopping could only mean one person. "I'm not exactly keen on company, Beefcake," she said as the familiar half-demon peeked around the bookcase. Khastra came forward nonetheless, a plate of cookies in her hands. "Leave the pastries, though."

Khastra knelt beside the pile of scarves, the concern on her face hollowing Etolié's stomach. "Etolié," she said softly, placing the plate upon the ground, "I went to the Temple of Eionei."

The hollow was replaced with nausea. "Oh?"

"I spoke to Eionei."

Etolié grinned, even though she desperately wanted to spontaneously immolate. "I'm sure that went well."

"He is a bastard, but he loves you very much. I told him what happened."

Betrayer. Etolié kept her mouth shut, however, her blood suddenly loud in her ears.

"And he thinks he knows who is responsible. He told me something very strange."

Oh, fuck—there was that familiar dread. Etolié's smile faltered, her tears threatening to return.

"I did not know you were a fugitive of Celestière."

No, but all of Celestière did. Etolié's hands tensed around the bundles of scarves around her, still prone within her cave.

"But he would not say why."

And to Etolié's horror, a sob escaped her own throat. She pressed her hands to her eyes, praying she could pass it off as an unattractive cough, but every breath was pain, both in her stomach and with each heaving sob. The very air stifled her; she couldn't breathe; her skin went cold—

The blankets shifted. She cringed at the contact, at Khastra's mere presence, her body revolting when Khastra tried to remove her hands. "No!" she cried, immediately freed of the touch, and wished she'd been murdered in the street instead of spared to face her recompense.

Because nothing—*nothing* in all the worlds, she realized—would hurt like Khastra's rejection. Her breathing grew ragged, desperate, each influx of air pure pain as panic stole her senses.

"Etolié, please breathe."

Oh, the world grew small, smaller still when a shadow moved across her. Cornered, how she longed to flee. Etolié brought a bundled scarf to her face and *screamed,* hiding from her shame, crying louder still when something tried to tug it away.

She slapped away the touch, too panicked to consider any action but *running,* but impossibly strong hands grabbed her wrist, hard enough to bruise. The scarf was tossed away, and Khastra stole her other wrist and held them both by Etolié's head. Straddled by the great half-demon, she held no hope for escape.

Etolié's eyes seeped tears, breathing still ragged, but Khastra's gaze held kindness unparalleled and a maternal concern that would be Etolié's downfall. Her grip loosened, then fell away. With infinite gentleness, she whispered, "Breathe, Etolié . . . Breathe with me."

Callused hands cupped her face, catching her tears. Etolié managed shaky breaths, following the cadence of Khastra's own.

"There is no secret you hold that would ruin my love for you. Now, start from the beginning."

She took her touch away. Khastra sat back, removing herself from atop Etolié.

Etolié rolled over, using her shaky arms to lift herself up. All the while, Khastra's gaze seared her skin, her unspoken question threatening to pull Etolié back into a panic.

She carefully stood up, knowing perfectly well that Khastra would likely tackle her if she tried to run. "I haven't been to Celestière in eighteen years," she said, her forced nonchalance kinda losing its luster given her continued tears. She wiped them away, her smile unflappable, lest she be damned. "I committed a crime, I was found guilty, and Sol Kareena took pity on me and said I had a choice between eternal house-arrest or running away."

"Eighteen years ago, you were fourteen," Khastra said, as though Etolié couldn't do basic fucking math. "You were only a child."

"Yes, but they don't have many children in Celestière, so they don't exactly have laws for children who murder people, all right?" Etolié paced. She rambled and twitched. "So, yes. Now, you know. I killed a man. His name was Camdral, and the worlds are better without him. Happy?"

She couldn't meet Khastra's eye, the stare too familiar, too much of many things, and so she merely looked at the ceiling when the half-demon said, "Who was he?"

"He was the asshole who bent my momma approximately nine months before my birth. And a few times before that. Likely during. Certainly after. And that's the end of his contribution to anything of my benefit. They weren't in love. Momma was sad. Camdral had drugs to make her forget for a few fucking moments that she was sad. All he generally asked for in return was a few pumps on his crusty dick."

Whatever Khastra had expected, Etolié felt a cold suspicion that this wasn't exactly it, her subdued horror apparent as she watched her every motion.

"He ignored me, mostly. He was a beast to mom, but I was an irrelevant annoyance on his radar. The only time he touched me was when I initiated it."

Khastra's eyes followed her as she paced, concern coloring her features. "I beg your pardon?"

"Listen, sometimes you fuck your dad so you can kill him. He stabs you and you stab back. It's only fair--"

"Etolié, please stop joking."

The silence held a few moments, tension building between them as Etolié finally met Khastra's eye. She swallowed, the words forced and pained. ". . . I-I'm not."

Khastra slowly covered her mouth with her hand, something condemning in her gaze; Etolié saw it as clear as day. "It's kind of a conversation ender, I know," she continued, swallowing the fresh rise of panic. "But, good ol' Camdral came over drunk as fuck one night looking for someone to beat the shit out of, and I cracked because there's only so many times you can hear your momma cry. Got him alone. Got him naked. Stabbed him forty-seven times. If I have no other talents, it's illusioning knives to be invisible."

Oh, by Alystra's Smooth Ass, she was saying a lot of words. Khastra had said nothing.

"I mean, it was likely a bit much. He died on the twentieth stab, but I was having a bad day."

Khastra stared. Her glowing eyes held horror, and Etolié wished she'd never had the misfortune to be born.

"What?" she asked, arms spreading in challenge. "Nothing to say? You asked. You *fucking asked!*"

Khastra lowered her hand in tandem with her standing. "Etolié . . ." She stepped forward, but Etolié flinched and stumbled back. She barely whispered, "There is little to say."

She searched Khastra's face, seeing only condemnation, the same derision shared by all of her people. Her feet stumbled as she backed away. "Aw, see—that's judgement! I see you fucking judging me, but it's fine, though I might be seeing myself out of Staelash for the foreseeable forever."

She was stopped when Khastra looped her arm around Etolié's torso, stopping her in her tracks with her superior strength.

"Khastra, please just—"

But Khastra pulled her to her chest, her strong arms shielding her from the world. Lips brushed Etolié's hair, as well as tears. "I am merely heartbroken that you were ever put in that position."

Etolié shattered, collapsing into sobs.

Somewhere in her conscious mind, she felt Khastra lift her, cradling her as she was carried back to her nest. She felt familiar calluses soothe lines through her hair, smelled the grounding patchouli scent of her skin, and all the while wept as her mind expelled images she had not visited in over a decade. The tattoos of Khastra's chest glowed as her cheek pressed against the familiar lines peeking above the collar of Khastra's tunic, yet there was no temptation to trace them. Etolié sought only to vanish, and behind Khastra's arms, she did so well enough.

"I killed him," she said between sobs, her voice quivering and broken. "I hardly remember anything. My memory stops the moment I said his name, but I remember his smell; I remember feeling him but feeling nothing at all. I remember the knife and counting the stab wounds—" She brought her hands up to cover her face, already hidden behind Khastra's embrace. She swore the half-demon shook. "And then there I was, naked and soaked in blood. I didn't even cry until . . . until my momma . . ."

And there it was, in her memory—the final image of her momma, her gasping horror, her embrace as Etolié screamed in her arms.

"I don't regret it. I spent my entire life living in that monster's shadow," Etolié said, her voice shaking from sobs. "He destroyed my momma—she had nothing." She wept into her hands, which Khastra gently stole, her glowing eyes replacing the hateful sights in Etolié's head. "I only exist because her life was ruined."

"Did she tell you that?"

Startled at the words and Khastra's dark tone, Etolié stammered a shaky, "N-No. But sometimes you just know."

Sometimes, someone else tells you for her.

"You carry so much shame, Etolié." The darkness in Khastra's tone had receded, leaving only words as soft as the fingers in Etolié's hair. Her eyes glistened, yet her gaze never wavered. "I am so sorry you thought you must keep this a secret from me."

"I just don't understand how you can't see me as disgusting. What kind of sick fuck seduces her drunk father—"

"You were a child, Etolié. He raped you, but I do not think you see that." Khastra's eyes seemed larger when filled with tears, the first of which trailed the elegant lines of her face. "You were powerless, because he stole that power. You used the only weapon you thought you had—" Khastra's voice broke. The great half-demon wept as she clung to Etolié's form. "You are not disgusting," she whispered. "You are not ruined. You survived."

The words screamed in stark dissonance to Etolié's thoughts, yet they were spoken by the woman who never lied.

Etolié clung to Khastra's neck, hiding her face against the half-demon's chest as she sobbed. Yet, it felt like a release, the pain steadily ebbing with each tear trailing down her face.

Khastra loved her still. Etolié felt a great burden lift from her shoulders—perhaps taken on by the half-demon herself.

As the pain settled, so did her cries, and soon enough she laid as an exhausted heap against Khastra's chest, eyes surely swollen and red. When she sniffed and looked up to face her companion, she saw that Khastra's own tears had also abated, though evidence still remained in the glistening lines on her face. So strange, to see Khastra's tears. She realized she never had before.

"Look at you," Khastra whispered, depthless adoration in her smile. "Look at all you have done. You have saved countless lives and become the magister of a kingdom full of people willing to murder assassins on the street for you." Khastra smiled, though her lip quivered. "There is an elven children's tale that says we are all pottery in a kiln, fired by the hardships we face. Your father does not define you, but his influence does remain. I cannot fathom the hell you lived as a child, but I know it made you strong, nor can I comprehend the pain of having to hold your mother through her own, but it gave you a heart that weeps for the downtrodden. Look at you, Etolié—you emerged from the fire as something beautiful."

Etolié wept again, but not for shame.

"Celestière is wrong to condemn you. I would say that to Sol Kareena herself."

"None of them know the whole truth," Etolié said, her gasping breath more of a hiccup. "They know I murdered him. No one knows why or how, except Sol Kareena, my judge and jury. Eionei only knows I killed him—he walked in on Momma and I trying to clean it up. And I don't know what Momma thinks happened. That was the last time I saw her."

"You have not seen her since?"

Behind the shield of Khastra's arms, Etolié shook her head. "She needs to heal without me. That's what Eionei said."

There was pain behind the disbelief in Khastra's eyes. "As a mother, I cannot fathom telling my child to stay away."

Etolié said nothing to that.

"This does not change anything," Khastra whispered, her lips brushing Etolié's hair. "I love you, Etolié; as much as I did before. It hurts me to see you clinging so tight to your shame, and if I can ever help to ease your burden, let me.

Would you ever consider speaking to a priest or priestess? Many acolytes of Sol Kareena are trained to help ease emotional burdens, better than I could."

Etolié shook her head. "Someday, maybe. Not today. This is a lot, you know?"

"I understand," Khastra said, her fingers returning to Etolié's hair.

"To answer your next question," Etolié added, remiss to admit it, but it had to be said, "the men who tried to kill me were friends of Camdral. I recognized a few of them. So I don't know if I'm safe or if there're still more coming. If you told Eionei, I think he'll do what he can to fix it up there, though."

"As he should."

"He always thought Camdral was scum, so even though he never quite knew why I did it, I think he assumed I had a good reason." Her laugh was genuine, poignant after so many tears. "He never knew the extent of what was happening to mom—not until after. But whatever his faults, I'm grateful to him. He's my only link to home."

"Then I shall try to be more polite to him, next time he and I speak." Khastra's smile was endlessly soft, and Etolié's heart soared to know it was for her. "Do you need to speak more of this? I would like you to sleep, but I understand if the burden of the day is too much."

Etolié's head fell back against Khastra's chest. "I'd like to talk about other things. Then I'll have a fighting chance at sleep."

Khastra's tale of ancient Solvira captivated Etolié's manic mind, her voice soothing and assured. Every word she spoke slowly opened Etolié's sealed heart. She loved Etolié still.

And Khastra's opinion had always been the only one that mattered in the end.

About the author:

S D Simper has lived in both the hottest place on earth and the coldest, spans the employment spectrum from theatre teacher to professional editor, and plays more instruments than can be counted on one hand. She and her beloved wife share a home with their three cats and innumerable bookshelves.

Visit her website at sdsimper.com to see her other works, including *Carmilla and Laura,* a retelling of the classic vampire tale.